Stirring the Plot

"Readers will enjoy immersing themselves in a mystery that celebrates the quirkiness of the Halloween season as well as its magical allure."   —*Kings River Life Magazine*

"Delightful . . . Gerber manages to incorporate Halloween, food, an excitement about books, and a touch of romance. It's a fun, seasonal treat."   —*Lesa's Book Critiques*

"Gerber has written a very bewitching mystery . . . You really can't go wrong with a cozy by this author whether she is writing as Daryl Wood Gerber or Avery Aames. All her stories are completely captivating and very entertaining."   —*Escape with Dollycas into a Good Book*

"Each book is better than the last, and they have all been wonderful."   —*Open Book Society*

Inherit the Word

"A mystery featuring a cookbook bookstore is completely irresistible, especially when the author combines it with complex and very well-developed story lines."   —*Kings River Life Magazine*

continued . . .

"Readers will relish the extensive cookbook suggestions, the cooking primer, and the whole foodie phenomenon."

—*Library Journal*

"Kudos to the author for creating a welcoming store with such a strong cast of characters. There's more than one reason to return to the Cookbook Nook Mysteries."

—*Lesa's Book Critiques*

"Murder, betrayal, and a grilled cheese contest are found between the pages of this wonderfully prepared drama, and I can't wait to see what the future holds for the residents of Crystal Cove in this delectably appetizing series."

—*Dru's Book Musings*

Final Sentence

"Murder, revenge, secrets . . . and cookbooks! *Final Sentence* . . . is a delectable page-turner with a tasty mix of characters, crime, and cookbooks, blended beautifully in a witty, well-plotted whodunit that will leave you hungry for more."

—Kate Carlisle, *New York Times* bestselling author of the Bibliophile Mysteries

Berkley Prime Crime titles by Daryl Wood Gerber

FINAL SENTENCE
INHERIT THE WORD
STIRRING THE PLOT
FUDGING THE BOOKS

Fudging
the Books

DARYL WOOD GERBER

BERKLEY PRIME CRIME, NEW YORK

An imprint of Penguin Random House LLC
375 Hudson Street, New York, New York 10014

FUDGING THE BOOKS

A Berkley Prime Crime Book / published by arrangement with the author

ISBN: 978-0-425-27940-3

PUBLISHING HISTORY
Berkley Prime Crime mass-market edition / August 2015

PRINTED IN THE UNITED STATES OF AMERICA

10 9 8 7 6 5 4 3 2 1

Cover illustration by Teresa Fasolino.
Cover design by Jason Gill.
Interior text design by Kelly Lipovich.

Penguin
Random
House

To my husband. I adore you. I am so blessed!

Acknowledgments

Thank you to my family and friends for all your support.

Thank you particularly to my husband, my first reader. I love your insight and enthusiasm. *I am so blessed.*

Thank you to my talented author friends, Krista Davis, Janet Bolin, Kate Carlisle, and Hannah Dennison for your words of wisdom and calm. Thanks to my brainstormers at Plothatchers: Krista, Janet, Kaye, Marilyn, Peg, and yes, another Janet (we all have aliases, I think!). Thanks to my blog mates on Mystery Lovers Kitchen: Cleo, Krista, Leslie, Mary Jane/Victoria, Roberta/Lucy, and Sheila. Love you all!

Thanks to the team who has helped make the Cookbook Nook Mysteries a success: my fabulous editor, Kate Seaver, as well as Katherine Pelz, Danielle Dill, and my terrific copyeditor Marianne Grace. Thank you Teresa Fasolino for your brilliant artwork! John Talbot, thank you for believing in every aspect of my work. Sheridan Stancliff, you are an Internet and creative marvel. Kimberley Greene, I appreciate everything you do for me. You have no idea, or maybe you do.

Thank you librarians, teachers, and readers for sharing the delectable world of a culinary bookstore owner in a California seaside town with your friends.

And last but not least, thanks to my cookbook consultant, Christine Myskowski. May your new direction in life bring you years of fulfillment.

*He who asks a question will be a fool for five minutes.
He who does not ask a question will remain a fool
forever.*

—Chinese proverb

Chapter 1

CHOCOLATE. IS THERE anything not to like—excuse me, *love*—about chocolate? And it's February, so it's National Chocolate Month, which means I can focus The Cookbook Nook's theme on chocolate. Heaven. I plucked a homemade chocolate-cherry bonbon from a bowl sitting on the sales counter and popped it into my mouth, relishing the burst of flavor. *Yum!* Definitely not poison.

"Back to work, Jenna," I whispered.

I was alone in The Cookbook Nook. My aunt had yet to arrive, and Bailey, my best friend in the world and the main sales clerk at the shop, had called saying she was running late, too. I enjoyed mornings in the shop by myself. I could take time to scan the wares and appreciate what I'd been able to build in the past few months.

Back in August, I gave up my cushy job at a swank San Francisco advertising firm and returned home to help my aunt Vera open our culinary bookshop. I am so proud that, with my aunt's financial backing and my marketing expertise, we have created this must-visit haven for foodies and lovers of cookbooks. The floors are filled with movable bookshelves upon which sit hundreds of cookbooks with tasty titles. On the shelves along the walls are colorful arrays of cooking utensils, salt shakers, pepper mills, aprons, and more. We fashioned the rear corner as a young cooks area, where kids and their parents could sit and read or even do crafts. My aunt, who loves to tell fortunes, set up a vintage kitchen table near the front entrance where she offers occasional readings. She isn't a seer; she doesn't have extrasensory powers, but she believes her readings help her friends and clients cope. I'm not a believer, but I would never tell her sharing her passion is out of the question. Sometimes, her predictions come true.

"Work!" I reminded myself.

I moved to the display table, where I had arranged delicious cozy mysteries with some of my favorites by Krista Davis and Jenn McKinlay. I added a new cozy to the grouping, *Murder of a Chocolate-Covered Cherry* by Denise Swanson. I also added a couple of new books to our permanent supply of food-related fiction: *The Chocolate Lovers' Club* and *The Loveliest Chocolate Shop in Paris*.

"Perfect."

Next, I gathered a stack of chocolate-themed cookbooks from the sales counter and skirted around the centermost movable bookshelf, while gazing lustfully at the top book— one I intended to take home with me, written by the renowned chocolatier Michael Recchiuti: *Chocolate Obsession: Confections and Treats to Create and Savor*. Granted, it was not a book for beginners, like me. In fact, one woman who had reviewed the book on Amazon said to do exactly what Recchiuti said *or else*. Um, okay, perhaps she hadn't written that as a specific threat, but it was implied. Make sure to buy the higher butterfat butter was one of her suggestions. Also, use the expensive chocolate. Forget about baking with Hershey's. Now, I adore Hershey's Kisses and those adorable Hershey's Miniatures, but even I can tell the difference between an everyday chocolate and Scharffen Berger.

I placed the chocolate books on another display table, stood the Recchiuti book upright with its pages fanned open, and set a pile of books behind it. I laid out other titles, like

Crazy About Chocolate: More Than 200 Delicious Recipes to Enjoy and Share—the cover alone with a dozen mouthwatering mini chocolate éclairs would sell that book in a heartbeat—and *Absolutely Chocolate: Irresistible Excuses to Indulge*—its sinfully all-chocolate cover was great, as well. I had space for a few more titles and hurried back to the stockroom.

When I returned carrying a stack of books that reached my chin, a forty-something woman with sleek black hair, one of our regulars, rapped on the front door, which I'd propped open—I love crisp, fresh air. She wiggled her fingers. "Jenna, are you ready for a few customers?"

It was almost nine. "Sure."

"Can you help us?" She and two friends made a beeline for the paleo diet section of books. I followed. "Paleo," she said matter-of-factly. "Can you explain the regime to us?"

Although it wasn't my preferred way to eat—I savored carbs—I knew the basics. Paleo involved eating the way cavemen did, which meant consuming only things we could hunt, fish, or farm. Sugar-packed cereal and pasta made with white flour were out. P.S. I really like fettuccine Alfredo.

"We're confused, then," she said when I finished speaking. "How can this be right?" She held up *The Paleo Chocolate Lovers' Cookbook: 80 Gluten-Free Treats for Breakfast and Dessert*. The woman's forehead and eyes were pinched with concern. "I thought you said sweets were out."

I smiled, having wondered the same thing. With a little research, I'd made sense of the notion. "None of the recipes include gluten, grain, or dairy. The author, a popular cooking blogger, has created many of the recipes using coconut or ground nuts. With the help of the herbal sweetener stevia, she shows you how to keep the honey and coconut sugar—her preferred sugars—to a minimum."

"Ooh, I get it."

"By the way," I added, "I've heard the chocolate pie with raw graham cracker crust is to die for."

Bailey tore into the shop and skidded on her wedged heels, almost taking down our customers and me. "Sorry."

"Excuse me," I said to the ladies. Juggling my pile of books, I scooted Bailey around a stand of bookshelves and whispered, "What's gotten into you?"

"I did it."

"Did what?"

Bailey fluffed her fringed hair and batted her baby blues. "As head of the Chocolate Cookbook Club, I declared we are going to celebrate the entire month of February by purchasing a new chocolate-themed cookbook each week." The book club meets on the first Thursday of every month. "I've contacted all thirty members, and everybody is on board. Do the math. Ka-ching!" She mimed opening a cash register then grabbed me by the shoulders, her hands barely able to reach me because of the books I held. I forced myself not to laugh. She was, after all, at a disadvantage being shorter than I was by almost a foot. At five foot eight, I stood taller than most women I knew.

Bailey shimmied me. "C'mon, girlfriend, do a happy dance with me."

My hair bounced around my shoulders. My tower of books teetered. "Cut it out."

"Not until you dance."

I shuffled my feet. "Look, Ma. I'm dancing."

"You call that dancing?"

"Let me go."

Bailey giggled but obeyed. "Get this, I talked them into buying Coco's latest cookbook first. *Sweet Sensations: All Things Chocolate, from the Delicious to the Fantabulous.*"

Coco Chastain was one of Bailey's and my good friends. We had known her since high school, although at the time we didn't hang out. Bailey was in the popular girl group; I floated between the studious and theater group; Coco was part of the art crowd. Now, she was a local chocolatier who owned Sweet Sensations, a delectable candy store. I couldn't walk by the place without stopping to inhale. Coco, a lusty woman with a curvaceous figure, had been engaged once, but her fiancé left her for a younger, skinnier woman. *Boring*, as Coco would say. I glanced over my shoulder at my customers. They didn't seem to mind that Bailey was distracting me.

"Go on," I said.

"I asked Coco to speak to the group," Bailey said. "She jumped at the chance. She even offered to invite Alison."

Alison Foodie, a successful independent publisher in San Francisco who specialized in cookbooks and related nonfiction, was Coco's publisher. We carried a few of Foodie Publishing's titles on our shelves. Foodie was Alison's real surname, Scottish in origin, and not a fictitious name for her business. She originated from Crystal Cove, too. In fact, her family lineage, which was colorful to say the least, dated back to the first settlers. However, up until a couple of years ago, I had never met her. Neither had Coco. Alison was a few years older than we were. Bailey had brought us all together. Bailey and Alison met at a businesswomen's retreat. When they realized they came from the same town, they became fast friends. Small world.

I said, "Alison will deign to come down from San Francisco?"

"Stop it." Bailey swatted the air. "You know she's not a snob."

Actually, Alison had a wicked sense of humor. She was incredibly smart.

"She doesn't come back to town often because she's super busy," Bailey went on. "She does visit occasionally to check in on her mother."

"That's sweet," I said, though I had to wonder. Alison's younger brother lived with their mother. Didn't Alison trust him to tend to her?

"Coco said Alison will give the club the inside scoop on the publishing world. Isn't that cool?" Bailey clapped her hands.

"Super cool. Maybe she'll give me an insight to the next best thing in the cookbook world."

A swish of fur swiped my ankles. I sidestepped and peered at Tigger, my silly kitten. At least I think he was still considered a kitten. He'd wandered into the shop—and into my life—a few months ago. At the time, I'd pegged him at two months old. I had him neutered in November. *Ouch*, but necessary. As a result, he hadn't ever sprayed my cottage, and he had retained his kittenish playfulness.

I set the books on a nearby table, scooped him into my arms, and scruffed him under the chin. "What's up, Tig-Tig?" I'd dubbed him Tigger because, like the Disney character that pounced and trounced, Tigger had done twirls and other fun gyrations that first day to win my heart. "Did silly old Bailey and her loud voice wake you up from your nap?"

Invariably, when we arrived at the shop, Tigger moseyed into his spot beneath the children's table for a lengthy snooze.

Tigger meowed.

"I am not loud," Bailey said.

He yowled again, disagreeing with her.

"Are you hungry? Let me check your bowl." I signaled the three ladies by the paleo section. "I'll be right back, if you need me."

Bailey trailed me through the shop to the stockroom. She propped the drape open with a hip and continued her conversation while I refreshed Tigger's goodies. "I was thinking we should hold tomorrow's book club meeting in the Nook Café since we'll have special guests."

The eatery, an adjunct to The Cookbook Nook and connected by a breezeway, had become a wonderfully profitable side business, thanks to the budding reputation of our inspired chef, Katie Casey, another high school buddy of Bailey's and mine.

"Katie agreed to close the café," Bailey went on.

"You already cleared it with her?"

"Yep. She'll make a tasting from Coco's latest cookbook," Bailey went on. "Not just the sweets, but the savory things, too, like the chicken with the luscious chocolate *mole* sauce."

"Yum."

"Or the mixed salad with orange slices dipped in chocolate. And, of course, an assortment of desserts. C'mon. This'll be fun." Bailey rapped me on the arm. "Girls' night out. We'll help Katie with the cooking."

"We?" I gulped. "For thirty?"

"With Katie's supervision."

Remember, earlier, when I mentioned that Michael Recchiuti's *Chocolate Obsession* might be beyond my ability? That is because I'm not a cook. I'm trying to learn. I've graduated from making five-ingredient recipes to multiple-ingredient ones. I've even tried my hand at cooking entrées as well as desserts. The chocolate cherries on the sales counter? Mine. But creating an entire meal for what could be a possibly hypercritical crowd? My heart started to chug until I channeled Sophie Winston, the event planner from the Domestic Diva Mysteries. She made cooking sound so easy; she always had things prepared way in advance, much of it stored in the freezer. I could do this. I could. Yes, indeed, with a battalion of cooks and Katie's supervision, a soiree was going to be a snap.

Tigger butted my ankle with his head. He opened his eyes wide, as if offering reassurance.

"Please, pretty please," Bailey said.

"Okay. We'll do it."

"Yeah!"

I fastened a pearl button on my cardigan sweater and moved past Bailey into the shop. More customers had arrived. Many were ogling the aprons. A few were admiring the selection of chocolate-themed fiction. One, a darling older woman, had nestled at the vintage kitchen table to tackle the latest food-themed jigsaw puzzle. We always had one going. Customers loved to piece them together. I think it made them feel like family. I tucked in behind the sales counter.

Bailey joined me. "Do you have a favorite dessert recipe in Coco's latest?"

"The chocolate-cherry bonbons, which I've already made." I gestured to the batch on the counter. "Try one."

"Before lunch?"

"Chocolate is good at any time of the day."

Bailey bit into one. "You made these?"

"Yep." I polished my fingernails on my sweater.

"Girlfriend, I'm impressed."

"Thanks." I opened the cash register drawer and counted ones and fives. "Do me a favor and check again with Katie. Make sure she knew what you were asking." Sometimes Katie, distracted by the many duties of running a restaurant, would bob her head in answer to any question.

"Will do." Bailey whooped as she hurried to the café.

At the same time, a shaggy-haired pirate—kid you not, *pirate*—darted into the shop. He was wearing pantaloons and a red waistcoat. Sword drawn, he crept stealthily behind one of the bookcases at the center of the store.

The customers, including my paleo cookbook hunters, gasped.

Tigger poked his head through the split in the drapes from the stockroom. I waved at him to retreat. He didn't. He stared bug-eyed at the man.

Seconds after the red pirate hid, a pirate in a blue waistcoat and pantaloons entered, followed by a pair of robust women dressed in ecru blouses topped with lace-up vests and gathered skirts. All of the intruders wore boots; the men wore feathered tricorn hats.

The blue pirate yanked his sword from its scabbard and yelled, "Where are ye, ye whining, yellow-bellied landlubber?"

The red pirate bolted from his hiding spot, sword raised.

The blue pirate lunged. Metal clanged. The red pirate hopped backward onto one of the chairs by the vintage kitchen table. The blue pirate ducked, pivoted, and came up on the other side of his enemy. He thrust the tip of his sword at the red pirate's throat.

The red pirate dropped his sword and raised his hands.

Chapter 2

"**O**FF WITH YER head!" the blue pirate said. A tense moment followed. Then the blue pirate laughed and lowered his sword. He offered a hand to the red pirate. "Grab hold, mate." He helped the red pirate to the floor, and each clapped the other on the shoulder.

"Well done," the red pirate said.

I stomped toward the pair. "What the heck, you two? What's going on? You nearly gave me . . . us"—I indicated the crowd—"heart attacks."

The red pirate grinned. "Lass, have ye forgotten? It's Pirate Week."

Forehead smack. I had forgotten what my aunt told me only yesterday—at times I have a short memory span. For the last five years, during the first week of February, the people of Crystal Cove celebrated our pirate heritage. Pirates hadn't settled the town, but there were plenty of ships that had sailed along the coast of California, and tales were told of thievery and conquest. Heck, the California coast was rich with stories from Zorro to Russian fur-traders to Spanish missionaries. However, in honor of the pirate part of our sketchy heritage, our energetic mayor, always ready to capitalize on a tourism theme, had established Pirate Week, which ran from the first Wednesday in the month to the following Tuesday. Why Wednesday? Because during the winter months, Crystal Cove tourists primarily arrive on Wednesday or Thursday and stay for a week or long weekends.

I recalled asking my aunt why Pirate Week was such a big lure, because pirates were notoriously not nice people. She said the intent of Pirate Week wasn't for one minute to suggest that real, honest-to-goodness pirates were in any way, shape, or form worth emulating, but the image of swaggering *pirateness* was fun and exciting and, in her words, harmless. The *Pirates of the Caribbean* movies were a success because being a pirate looked like a blast.

The blue pirate swaggered toward me. "Milady, truth? Did ye take us seriously?"

"Aye," I said, kicking in with pirate speak. "I did. The whole lot of us did."

Some argued that, seeing as International Talk Like a Pirate Day—yes, there is such a day—was celebrated in September, shouldn't we have Pirate Week in that month? The mayor countered that September in Crystal Cove was already packed with activities. We needed a lure for tourists in February, when the temps were cooler. During Pirate Week, we were encouraged to converse in pirate speak whenever we encountered someone dressed as such. Aunt Vera had *not* told me that during Pirate Week, participants would show up in costumes and plunder the shop.

The blue pirate grinned and addressed the crowd. "Don't worry, folks. We were only joshing."

"However, if ye are interested in seeing more," one of the robust women said, "come one, come all, to *The Pirates of Penzance* at The Theater on The Pier."

For Pirate Week, the mayor had also arranged to have specialty plays, dinner cruises, duels, and more. At the end of the week of events, the mayor would hold a town meeting. She would draw a ticket, and some lucky person would win a pot of gold doubloons. People could pick up their free drawing tickets at any of the shops on the main strip of town or on The Pier.

"The musical," the blue pirate continued, "is a rollicking comic opera by Gilbert and Sullivan."

"Good fun with a one-drink minimum," the red pirate added. "A bargain at any price. And, remember, when we're not playing, we're singing." When a show isn't in progress, The Theater on The Pier serves as a piano bar.

If you haven't visited Crystal Cove, it's a seaside community consisting of three crescent-shaped bays. A range of modest mountains defines the eastern border and traps ocean moisture, blessing our sweet community with a temperate Mediterranean climate. The boulevard that runs parallel to the ocean is rife with shops and restaurants. On the southernmost end of town stands The Pier, which features shops, restaurants, a carousel, some carny games, and a rousing dance hall–style theater. At The Pier, people may also hire boats for sunset or sightseeing cruises and fishing expeditions.

"Farewell, fine maidens." The blue pirate doffed his hat and made a deep bow. The red pirate copied him. The ladies at the rear of the store giggled.

"Farewell, sweet furry critter," one of the wenches cried. She wiggled her bright red fingernails in Tigger's direction. He crept from behind the curtain and ducked behind my ankles.

"And we're off!" said the red pirate. He and his friend hooked arms with their female companions and headed to the next stop on their get-the-word-out journey.

As Bailey returned and offered a thumbs-up gesture— Katie was on board for tomorrow night—I realized we had to get cracking and put up our Pirate Week display. ASAP. So much to do. Always! Personally, I like being busy. Less time to let my mind dwell on sad memories.

Using poster board—we kept plenty on hand in the stockroom—Bailey and I created a pair of pirate silhouettes. We added cutouts of tricorn hats and eye patches to the silhouettes and set them in the window. In front, we placed a toy galleon that my aunt had purchased expressly for the display—about four feet long and metal, fitted with three masts, a pointed bowsprit, and spanking white sails—and then added a low cutout of blue waves. We dangled a seagull overhead and set out a variety of Caribbean cookbooks, including the tasty *Caribbean Potluck* written by a pair of sister chefs. And we added the pirate-themed children's books that my aunt had suggested. When we finished, I posted a banner: *Children's Pirate Day Saturday*. For that event, I would have Katie make sugar cookies iced with pirates, skeletons, or skull and crossbones. Perhaps some kind of chocolate-making demonstration with free giveaways of almond- or pistachio-laced chocolate would be a nice treat for the adults.

While Bailey toured the shop looking for a place to hide a rubber goldfish—the first lucky child who found the toy would win a free book—I put together a flyer to distribute to local shops encouraging children to come to the event dressed as pirates. Any child who wore a costume would receive a goodie bag filled with gold foil–wrapped candy. One family would win the grand prize: *Dessert for four at the Nook Café*.

The rest of the day went off without a hitch. People poured in. Children scoured the shelves, but none found the rubber goldfish. Bailey had hidden it well. Adults were fascinated with the choices of pirate-themed cookbooks. One of the most popular was *A Pirate Cookbook: Simple Recipes for Kids*, which featured fun recipes like Gangplank Dippers, Chocolate Gunpowder, and Parrot Punch. The author offered darling tips like reminding her readers to wash their hands because pirates were dirty. What parent could resist that?

THURSDAY MORNING ARRIVED as fast as a speeding bullet. Thursday night, even faster.

"It's time," Bailey yelled. "Get ready to be chocolatized!"

She nabbed me and led me to the Nook Café kitchen. The aroma was heavenly. My stomach grumbled dramatically.

Bailey slung on an apron and handed me one. "*Arrr*." She faced our chef Katie and snarled like a pirate. "What now, oh mighty captain?"

Katie Casey was a jolly soul with bright eyes and an easy laugh. She chortled so hard her toque nearly fell off her curly mop of hair. She righted it and glanced at the pocket watch she always wore pinned to her chef coat. "Jenna, fetch the oranges from the walk-in."

"Aye, aye, Captain."

"Not you, too." Katie frowned, which made her hangdog-shaped eyes turn even more downward, an intentionally comical look. "There'll be no pirate talk in my kitchen. I run a tight ship."

"Ho, ho," Bailey said. "Very funny."

"Don't ye mean yo ho?" Katie grinned then twirled a spatula in the air. Chocolate *mole* sauce ran down the length of the handle and splatted her apron. "Oops!" One of the two sous-chefs Katie had brought in for the event—she had also appointed two of the regular waitresses to help us out—rushed to her aid and offered a wet towel. Katie cleaned up and said, "Keller"—he was her boyfriend—"is totally into this week of pirate events. He's spending all his time on The Pier vending his ice cream just so he can be close to the action, and he's forever saying, 'C'mere, me beauty.'"

"Well, at least he thinks you're beautiful," I said.

Katie reddened and tucked a loose hair behind her ear. "Yeah, right. Bailey, what do you think of Jenna's idea to do chocolate-making demonstrations in the shop?"

Bailey giggled. "You have to ask? You know me and chocolate." She pressed two fingers together. "We're tight."

"As tight as you and Tito?" Katie teased.

Tito Martinez, a local newspaper reporter, was Bailey's newest boyfriend.

Bailey blushed. "We're not that tight."

"Yes, you are." I nodded. "I've seen you two gaze into each other's eyes." I hadn't always been a fan of Tito's. However, the more I'd gotten to know him over the past few months, the more he had grown on me. As for Bailey, he had won her heart with his sense of humor and his penchant for volunteering for good causes. The fact that he could also, magically, pull a quarter out of her ear at any given moment made her smile. She loved to be surprised.

"We're not as tight as you and Rhett," Bailey countered.

Rhett Jackson is my boyfriend, going on a couple of months. We haven't said *I love you* or anything like that yet, but whenever I'm with him, the world goes still, in a good way.

"Wipe that silly grin off your face," Bailey said.

"Why should I?" I would never forget my first glimpse of Rhett. Tousled dark hair, sparkling eyes, and jeans that fit just right. I would also never forget our first kiss. And our first dinner alone at his cabin. He'd farmed out his dog so there would be no intrusions. And our first—

Bailey fanned me with a pot holder. "Wowie! What are you thinking about, girlfriend? Hearts afire! Katie, look at Jenna's cheeks. They're red-hot with lust. Get the extinguisher."

I smirked. "Ha-ha."

"By the way," Bailey went on, "have you seen what Rhett has done outside Bait and Switch on The Pier?"

"No, what?"

Bait and Switch Fishing and Sport Supply Store is one of the largest buildings on The Pier. Rhett owns it. Previously he was the chef at The Grotto, a four-star restaurant that used to be located on the second floor of Fisherman's Village—just upstairs from where The Cookbook Nook and Nook Café are located. The restaurant burned down, but surprisingly no shops below or to the right or left of it were touched. Rumor was that Rhett had started the fire. Rhett swore he didn't, which turned out to be true. Only recently, our clever chief of police, at my urging, pulled together all the clues and found the previous owner hiding out in New Orleans. As Rhett had asserted all along, the woman had absconded with a horde of priceless art. Not only was she sent to jail, but she had to relinquish the hefty insurance settlement. Mystery solved. Hooray!

Bailey said, "Rhett constructed a rock climbing wall."

"Why?"

"He's gung ho about this pirate thing, too."

Katie grinned. "Keller's already climbed the wall five times. It seems pirates were adept at climbing up things."

"Like enemy ships," I quipped.

Bailey aimed a finger. "We should do it."

"We?" I said. "As in the three of us?"

Katie grinned. "I wish I could. Too much to do this week."

"I'll have to put on tennis shoes," I said. I preferred flip-flops to just about any other kind of shoe. Not stylish, I know, but comfy. "I'm pretty good at rock climbing."

"You are?" Katie looked astounded.

"Don't you remember how I used to go backpacking with my brother?" On a trip to Yosemite, he taught me how to rappel off the top of a mountain. I remember how cautious I was at first. Tiptoeing down the rock wall backward. Worrying that my brother was secretly trying to do me in. Was the belay device threaded right? Would the rope hold my weight? However, within minutes, I was pushing off and whooping with glee. It was a great bonding moment for the two of us.

"Hey, Jenna. Hey, Bailey." Coco Chastain poked her head into the kitchen. "We're here. Can I come in?" She didn't wait for an answer. She hustled in and struck a pose. The magenta dress she wore looked painted on. Forties-style curls framed her face. *Va-va-voom*, as a couple of non-PC male coworkers at Taylor & Squibb Advertising, where I used to work, would have said. "I want you to come out to the dining room and meet the others before the book club members arrive."

"Don't you mean *other*, singular?" Bailey asked.

"Didn't I tell you?" Coco moved closer, her stylish, ankle-laced heels clacking the floor. "In addition to Alison, the copyeditor, Ingrid—she's a newbie—wanted to come along for the experience, to see what it's like for an author to schmooze, and the photographer, Dash—he's such a talent." Coco laid a hand above her voluptuous chest. "He loves everything pirate, so he begged to tag along, too." She lowered her voice. "Wait until you see all his tattoos. *Arrr*, matey." She gripped Bailey's elbow. "C'mon. Katie, you, too."

Katie wagged her head. "Aye, there's the rub," she said. "I've got work to do."

"Please?" Coco said in a girlish way. "Tito is already out there taking photographs. I want you in them."

"Uh-uh," Katie said. "Way too many pots on the stove. You all go ahead. We"—she indicated the sous-chefs and waitresses—"need to keep this under control."

Two tables, set for sixteen diners each, stood by the windows with the ocean view. Alison Foodie, a largish woman with a strong jaw and thick black hair, sat at the head of one table. She paused what she was doing—tapping in a message on her cell phone—and glowered at the screen. She took a sip from a glass of water and started in again. Tap, tap, tap.

"Alison, look over here," Tito Martinez ordered. When I first met Tito, he reminded me of an insecure boxer, the four-legged kind: broad face, broad shoulders, short legs, and eager for a confrontation. Now, he was smoother, almost suave. "Look this way." Bailey had asked him to do a front-page spread about Alison and Coco's united rise to fame. The story had local roots. Tito was totally on board. "No more business, Alison. C'mon. Smile."

Alison dropped her cell phone into her purse and offered a big, toothy grin. Wearing a swatch of a red-patterned tartan—what many in America call a plaid—slung over the shoulders of her sweater, she reminded me of a Scottish warrior.

Spying Bailey, Alison set her glass aside and scrambled to her feet. She wasn't much taller than I was, but when she hugged pint-sized Bailey, she seemed to consume her. "Darling, how are you?" Five years ago, when Bailey broke up with fiancé number two—or was it number three?—she crashed on Alison's floor. Bailey could have stayed with me, of course, but she hadn't wanted to intrude upon my new, albeit short-lived, marriage. A brief thought about my deceased husband was all I could manage. *No more dwelling* had recently become my mantra. I pushed the memory aside and strode ahead.

"Alison," I said, extending a hand. "Welcome."

"What a gig you have," she said. "Well done, Jenna. Let me make the introductions." She gestured toward the two people sitting at her table. "Bailey and Jenna, please meet our photographer, Dash Hamada."

I bit back a laugh. I heard Bailey swallow a snort, too. Dash—an unusual name for a Japanese man—looked every bit the pirate. He wore a bandana over a head of long black-gray hair. He was wearing a rumpled white shirt, opened at the collar, its sleeves cut off. Multiple tattoos, as Coco had warned us, decorated his arms and the V of skin beneath his neckline. He was paying us no mind. He was aiming a high-end Nikon camera at Coco and then Alison, taking snapshot after snapshot. A photographer's vest, the kind with a horde of pockets, hung over the back of his chair. He pulled a swatch of silk out of a pocket and polished his lens, shoved it back in the pocket, and resumed shooting.

Bailey bumped me with an elbow and rasped under her breath, "You're gawking."

"I am not."

"Yes, you are."

"Dash. Avast, me hearty! Stop what you're doing," Alison chided. "Be polite and focus!"

Dash released the camera—it hung from a strap around his neck—and his mouth curled into a rakish, albeit bordering on menacing, smile. "I'm not Yakuza, ladies, if that's what you're worried about."

I understood his reference. I happen to know that Yakuza are members of an international organized crime syndicate, most predominantly located in Japan. A couple of years ago, I read *Tokyo Vice: An American Reporter on the Police Beat in Japan*, a riveting story by an American investigative journalist. My husband had loved true crime.

Dash added, "I do it for the appreciation of the art."

His tattoos were gorgeous and singular. The dragonfish

down his right arm was surprisingly intricate. The aging ninja warrior that wrapped around his left bicep was fierce. The word *love* blazed across his chest.

Alison said, "Dash—short for Dashiell, his father adored pulp fiction—takes photographs of tattoos, as a hobby."

"Not a hobby."

"Fine." She flicked a finger at him. "He's written a book about the art of tattooing, starting with woodblocks from the eighth century. He focuses on works by Horitaka, Shige, and more. You should see his website. It's very deep."

"Deep, as in lots of pages," Dash said.

"He's very Internet savvy." Alison smiled at him in a patronizing way. "By the way, he doesn't mind if you stare."

Dash grinned. "I wouldn't have gotten the tattoos if I didn't want you to check them out. They all mean something special. This one"—he used his ring-clad pinky to point out the dragon—"represents the fiery danger I had to go through early on in my life. I was an abused child. This one"—he rotated his forearm to reveal a tattoo of an ear floating on top of tight abs—"represents my former line of business. I used to do tattoos and piercing."

Alison said, "Some people think when others tat and impale themselves, beyond the norm—you know, a tiny rose tattoo on the ankle or pierced ears—that the person is weird. He or she must have issues. However, Dash sees piercing or tattooing as a personal expression."

Dash cocked his head. "It's a way of showing to the world what you've accomplished and experienced. A life story, if you will. You'd be surprised who gets tattoos these days. People from all walks of life. Schoolteachers, lawyers, nurses."

Though tattooing was in vogue, I had chosen not to add artwork to my body.

Dash spread the neckline of his shirt and revealed that there was more to the *love* tattoo. The word circled a globe. He smirked. "This one doesn't need an explanation, does it? But enough about me. Have you met Ingrid Lake?" He aimed a forefinger at the lean woman sitting beside him and then resumed taking photographs.

Ingrid was pretty in a put-together way. Chin-length, smooth blonde hair cupped her face. "Hello," she whispered. At least I think that's what she said. Her lips moved; her teeth didn't budge. Perhaps she had been a ventriloquist at one time in her life, I mused, but then revised the idea. Ventriloquists didn't move their lips. Maybe her teeth were wired together for dental purposes.

"C'mon, me lass." Dash nudged her, his pirate-like brogue thick and leaning toward a British accent. "Speak up."

Ingrid blushed through her pale makeup. "Don't speak pirate-ese to me, Dash." Even with prodding, her teeth didn't move. "It's infantile."

"Don't yerself," Dash shot back. "I'm here to have fun. And, if I recall, you asked to come along. Look lively."

Ingrid toyed with the top button of her frilly blouse.

"He's right, Ingrid," Alison said. "Lighten up. No lemons, only lemonade." She turned to Bailey and me. "Ingrid is the copyeditor at Foodie Publishing. Very detail oriented." Alison glanced over her shoulder, making sure she caught Ingrid's attention. "Perhaps too much so."

"I am not," Ingrid whispered.

"No T's uncrossed, no I's undotted," Alison said. "And heaven forbid if I or any of my authors use the words *I* or *me* improperly in a sentence."

"The way we speak exhibits the level of our education," Ingrid said.

"To quote your mother," Alison teased.

Ingrid sat straighter. "She was a genius."

"As are you."

Coco planted a hand on one hip. "Aha. So, Ingrid, you're the one who's been changing all my cooking directions. I like them to be written in what I call easy prose. Chatty. I don't want them spruced into perfect English."

Ingrid shook her head. "No, that's not me. I would never change your voice. However, Alison—"

Alison cleared her throat.

"I mean Miss Foodie—"

"No, Ingrid!" Alison cut her off. "I didn't mean for you to correct yourself. Just don't speak."

Coco's face clouded over. She rapped Alison's shoulder. "What is she trying to tell me?"

"Nothing."

"You're not messing with my voice, are you?"

Alison didn't respond.

"Are you?" Coco picked up a glass of water from the table.

Alison eyed it and smirked. "Don't tell me you intend to throw that at me."

"Promise me you're not changing anything I write"— Coco's mouth curled in a snarl—"or else."

"Or else what? You'll douse me?"

"It's in my contract that you can't edit without my approval."

"Can't? *Can't*?"

"It's proprietary."

"I'm your publisher. I can do anything I want. Read your contract."

"Why you—"

Tito raised his camera. I whipped my arm up to block his shot.

Chapter 3

"**S**TOP!" BAILEY SHOUTED.
Everyone in the café but Tito froze in place. He clicked his camera in succession. Multiple flashes went off.

"No, Tito, stop!" I said, as visions of front-page photos reeled in my mind. *The Nook Café: A perfect spot for a fight.* Or *Want to make a splash? Visit the Nook.* Argh! Not all publicity was good publicity.

"Oh, relax," Coco cried. "We're not really going at it." She set the water aside, and she and Alison erupted into giggles. "Gotcha." She addressed the crowd. "Every one of you, close your mouths. My, oh, my, the looks on your faces. You especially, Ingrid." She bumped knuckles with Alison. "We were good."

"Yes, we were." Alison grinned. "Practice makes perfect."

"Or makes fun," Ingrid grumbled under her breath. Her pale eyes glinted with malice. Apparently she didn't like to be an unwitting patsy.

Neither did I, truth be told. What on earth had Alison and Coco been thinking? Was I just being a fuddy-duddy?

Dash guffawed. "Way to go, me lasses. You had us all by the throat."

I leaned over to Bailey and whispered, "Were you in on this?"

"Nope. I didn't have a clue." Bailey eyed Alison and Coco, who were still high-fiving each other like pranking sorority sisters. "When did you two cook up this stunt?"

Coco chuckled. "Last night over one too many cocktails. And champagne. I'm such a lightweight when it comes to that."

"Ahem," Alison said. "Only you were drinking." She yawned and quickly covered her mouth with a hand. "I wasn't."

"That's because you're such a party animal," Coco teased.

"Hear me roar." Alison clawed the air and mouthed a *growl*.

Ingrid *tsk*ed. Her nose flared. She was clearly displeased.

"I was the designated driver," Alison said. "I had to get the two of us home in one piece."

"Alison is staying with Coco," Bailey explained.

"Why aren't you at your mother's, Alison?" I asked.

"I stayed there the night before last, but Ingrid needed a place to sleep. Coco suggested that my mother and Ingrid would get along well. Mom loves to gab because . . ." She cocked her head. "With Dad gone." Her father had passed away a few years ago. "Coco suggested I crash at her place. That would create a little more space at Mom's." Alison eyed Coco. "And I guess it provided us with extra time to cook up a little tomfoolery." She clapped her hands. "Okay, enough of this hoo-ha. Let's raise the sails and set to sea. Where's the grub?" She poked Dash. "Is that enough pirate-ese for you?"

"Not by a yardarm." Dash cut a glance to his right. "Hey, scat, cat!" He waved his hand. Tigger appeared on Dash's chair.

"Tigger!" I said.

The cat blinked to feign innocence. Had he been poking around in Dash's photographer's vest?

"No, kitty. Bad kitty." I nabbed him. "Sorry, Dash."

"No worries," Dash said. "I just don't want cat nose smudges on my contact prints."

Contact prints are strips of photographic images produced

from negatives. Back at Taylor & Squibb, the location scout would put together a spread of pictures, in the form of contact sheets, so we could peruse them to determine which location to use.

"What do you have contact prints of, you sneak?" Alison asked. "We've been in town less than five minutes, and Coco hasn't cooked a thing."

Dash's mouth quirked up on the right. "I'm allowed to take photos on my own, Al."

"Of course." Alison explained to the rest of us, "Dash won't go anywhere without his latest contact prints, like someone might swipe them from his room. Talk about paranoid."

A guarded look passed between them.

"So what were you shooting?" Alison said.

"The scenery. Crystal Cove is a vision. Did you see the coastline?" Dash spread his hands as he described the bay. "Deep blue with a fine tinge of green close to the shore. And the mountains? Breathtaking in their simplicity. Don't get me started about the lighthouse. You know how I love lighthouses."

Alison said, "In addition to tattooed bodies, Dash loves to photograph lighthouses as well as monkeys, of all things. The San Francisco Zoo has a fine set of the latter, I've been told."

"Yep." Dash nodded. "They're rascals."

Ingrid nudged Alison and whispered loudly enough for all to hear, "I spied him taking photos of pirates." She made it sound like that was a horrid offense.

"Yo ho, Dash." Alison winked. "Got a thing for the mates, do ye?"

"Yo ho, yourself." He grinned. "What do you think?"

Alison assessed him head to toe. She raised an eyebrow.

Dash blew her a raspberry. "Hardly. I'm photographing wenches, if ye will, the pretty kinds of pirates."

"We had a few pirates in full regalia dart into the shop yesterday," I said. "They broke into a sword fight."

Bailey gawped. "Where was I?"

"In the café kitchen, I think."

"And you didn't tell me?"

"Oops." I addressed the rest of the folks. "They scared the wits out of me, until I realized I'd forgotten what day it was."

"The beginning of Pirate Week," Bailey said. "So that's why we got cracking on the display window."

I aimed a finger. *Bingo.*

"Pirate Week is a draw," Dash said. "Quite colorful. I have a mind to do a story about it, maybe sell it to the local papers."

Tito, who had been hanging back taking more photographs, said, "Oh no you don't, you scallywag. Don't even dare."

Dash saluted. "Aye, mate. Just joshing. That's your arena. No worries."

Someone rapped on the café door.

Pepper Pritchett, a thick woman with a beaky nose, poked her head inside. "Hello. Are you ready for us?" Pepper owned Beaders of Paradise, a beading shop next door. She was one of the first members of the Chocolate Cookbook Club. Prior to a few months ago, she wouldn't have been caught dead in my presence—she had an ancient beef with my family—but we had mended fences. It hadn't hurt that I'd cajoled Katie into making some spicy chocolate to win Pepper over. Having Pepper as an ally made working in the same complex so much more enjoyable.

Gran, a gray-haired but bright-eyed grandmother who owned the finest collection of shawls I'd ever seen, followed Pepper. Bailey's mother, Lola Bird, who was like my second mother, trailed them.

"Hello, everyone!" Aunt Vera entered. She was a study in red—red turban, red caftan—red being her color of choice for the month of February.

Cinnamon Pritchett, Pepper's daughter and our chief of police, lagged behind the pack, her cell phone pressed to her ear. Cinnamon was a stark contrast to my aunt. Her brown hair was as dark as my aunt's red hair was bright. Aunt Vera looked like the sun had never kissed her skin; Cinnamon was a tanned, outdoorsy beauty. She, like me, wasn't much of a cook, but she was a chocolate hound, and like so many of us in the Chocolate Cookbook Club, she confessed that she adored looking at chocolate *porn*—photographs of cookies, cakes, and candy. Whipped cream in a picture was an added bonus. Of the group, Cinnamon owned the largest collection of chocolate-themed cookbooks. With one arm, she balanced a platter covered with a checkered cloth.

Ending her conversation, Cinnamon pocketed the cell phone and grinned. "I'm ready to taste everything. Where's Coco?" She lit a path to our guest of honor. After exchanging a few words, she whirled around and unwrapped the platter she was carrying. It held a selection of chocolate cookies and pastries. "Jenna, take a look at these. I made them myself."

"Liar."

"Truth." She crossed her heart. "I've been taking lessons."

"From whom?"

Cinnamon mimed sealing her lips.

"No fair," I said. "Blab."

"I've been told I'll suffer a rogue's death."

"Talk!" I knuckled her.

"Okay." Cinnamon chuckled. "It was Lola."

Lola, a tiny bundle of luscious energy, much like her daughter, fluffed her spiky silver hair and offered a hearty laugh. "I knew you couldn't keep a secret, Cinnamon."

"How could I hold back?" Cinnamon snickered. "You're such an inspiration. I feel like I've made leaps and bounds of progress in the past week. And possibly gained five pounds in the process." Cinnamon was lean, like me, and exercised regularly. She claimed she had to remain buff to maintain her prominence in a department full of men. I doubted she would ever put on weight. "It's a recipe out of Lola's latest cookbook," she added.

Lola, who owned The Pelican Brief Diner, had written two books. One focused on fish entrées; the other was dedicated to desserts. Foodie Publishing had put out both. Alison liked helping locals get ahead in their careers.

"You aren't trying to outdo me, are you, Lola?" Coco asked.

"As if I could."

"Try one, Jenna." Cinnamon thrust the platter in my direction.

I plucked a frothy-looking chocolate cookie from the

assortment and popped it into my mouth. "Mmm." I licked my fingertips. "Meringue?"

Cinnamon nodded. "With a hint of . . ." she said leadingly.

"Cinnamon."

"Ha! You've got a good palate."

I might not be an ace cook, but I've always appreciated delicious food. I recalled a campaign we did at Taylor & Squibb for Zazzle Spices—*Put a little spice in your life!*— where we hired celebrity chefs to do a taste test and reveal flavors they detected in each course. A few of the executives on the campaign were invited to taste the samples. Of the five execs, I was the only one who had named all the spices correctly. Later that same day, Zazzle tried to hire me away from my job. I passed.

Minutes later, the café filled with more women and a few men, all of whom I recognized; in total, twenty-four of the thirty members. Bailey directed them to sit at the preset tables while I alerted Katie that we were ready to chow down.

Chatter rose to a crescendo as the waitresses served the meal. We had stuck to Bailey's menu: chicken with chocolate *mole* sauce, a mixed salad with orange slices dipped in chocolate with a cocoa brioche crouton, and a savory chocolate baba ghanoush, an Eastern Mediterranean dish of mashed eggplant mixed with olive oil and seasonings. We didn't serve wine. Bailey thought most of our guests would want to enjoy the pure, unadulterated flavors of chocolate without complicating the sensations with alcohol. Coffee with dessert, however, was permitted.

During dinner, Alison regaled us with publishing business tales. While dessert was being dished out, Dash excused himself, claiming fatigue.

"A likely story," Alison teased. "You're off to join the pirates. Avast, me hearty, have at it!" Yawning, she waved for him to leave. "Go. Don't let us stop you. But you'll be sorry you missed the best part of the meal."

Dessert was a smash hit. Katie had prepared a silk chocolate pie using a recipe directly out of Coco's cookbook. After each guest was served, to our surprise Coco lifted a tray filled with assorted chocolate truffles. She had hidden the tray on one of the chairs.

Chow down didn't half cover what we all did. We pigged out. Some of our guests even chose to taste Cinnamon's home-made concoctions. No one was disappointed.

Tito skirted the group while taking photo after photo. Ingrid jotted notes on an iPad. And Bailey was grinning from ear to ear. After all, she was the glue that had brought about the union of candymaker and publisher, and she was also the inspiration for the creation of the Chocolate Cookbook Club.

"Coco, stand up," Bailey said. "Everyone, Coco has offered to tell us about the history of chocolate. You do not need to take notes." She zeroed in on Ingrid. "No tests will be given."

The crowd tittered.

Coco rose and smoothed her body-hugging dress, making sure the hem reached her knees, and then she launched into a spiel about chocolate. "The history of chocolate can be traced back to pre-Olmec people. The Aztecs treasured cacao beans, which they believed were gifts from the gods, and they used them for currency."

She continued, sharing much of what I already knew. I had pored over the histories offered in a number of the chocolate-themed cookbooks we had in the shop. Chocolate gave the person who drank it strength. Sugar was added to chocolate around the sixteenth century, and soon the candy became a favorite of the ruling classes.

I bit into my silk chocolate pie. Heaven.

When Coco finished her chat, Bailey said, "May we ask you a few questions?"

"Shoot."

Pepper raised her hand. "Tell us the real secret. Why do we crave chocolate?"

"Because it tastes good."

A ripple of laughter swept through the crowd.

"No, honestly," Coco continued. "It's true. Chocolate tastes good. It smells good. It feels good on our tongue. Why do these feelings occur? They happen because our brain is releasing chemicals as we experience chocolate."

"Don't get too academic on us," Bailey cautioned.

"I wouldn't think of it." Coco grinned. "But I have made a study of chocolate. The stuff releases neurotransmitters, mainly dopamine, to the frontal lobe, to the hippocampus located in the medial lobe, and to the hypothalamus." She used a finger to point out the various medical locations on her head. "Dopamine is released whenever you experience something that you love, like laughing or watching an exciting pirate movie. *Arrr.* Oh, I forgot. Dash isn't here."

Alison said, "*Arrr,*" in his stead.

"Dopamine is even released when you experience sex."

A few of the women club members fanned themselves. The men, to their credit, blushed.

"Chocolate is the perfect orosensory experience to seduce the palate," Coco went on.

"Orosensory," Alison teased. "Big word."

"I read it somewhere," Coco responded. "I couldn't spell it if you dared me. By the way, do you know there are people in the world who don't like chocolate?"

"Sacrilege!" Bailey shouted.

"But true. We're hardwired by genetics."

"Is all of this going to be in your new cookbook, Coco?" I asked.

"Hmm." She eyed her publisher. "I doubt I could do the material justice. Perhaps we'll get a certified scientist to explain it in laymen's terms. Next question?"

The door to the café flew open. Our mayor rushed in. "Chief Pritchett!" Though squat, the mayor was a bundle of energy. Her hair looked frizzier than I'd ever seen it. The moisture in the outside air couldn't be helping. "It's horrible." She wiggled her hands overhead as if summoning a rainstorm.

Cinnamon rushed to her. "What happened?"

"It's gone."

"What's gone?"

"The pot of gold doubloons. Someone stole it."

Chapter 4

CINNAMON HUSTLED OUTSIDE the café with the mayor. My aunt, one of the mayor's best friends, hurried after them. So did Tito. Although the theft of the pot of doubloons wasn't a national emergency, by any means, it was a local interest story.

A buzz of questions about what happened charged through the remaining cookbook club members.

I stood in the center of the café and clapped my hands. "Hey, everyone, don't stress too much. The doubloons aren't worth a bloody cent. They aren't real gold."

"It's a shame, though." Coco rose to her feet and joined me. "People buy tons of raffle tickets to win the pot. Why, I know a guy who sets his trophy on his mantel and brags about it, in appropriate pirate speak, of course."

The money from the raffle tickets benefited a home for orphans at the north end of town. The mayor, Zoey Zeller, or Z.Z. to her friends, was a big proponent of saving kids. She'd lost a two-year-old child to a tragic disease. Soon after, her husband succumbed to grief and left the state.

Coco sighed. "It sure puts a damper on the evening, doesn't

it?" She whispered, "*Pooh*, Jenna. I hate when people rob, steal, and plunder."

"Me, too." Who didn't? Except those that robbed, stole, and plundered. Those were people with no moral compass.

Coco addressed the crowd. "I guess that's it for tonight, folks. The party is over. Thank you all for coming."

Book club members rose and approached Coco with their purchases of her latest cookbook. She nestled into the seat she had vacated and withdrew a bright pink pen from her purse. As she signed the books, her fans lavished her with praise for her previous cookbooks and the unique recipes she made. She was, in many of the members' words, *without equal*, *imaginative*, *daring*, and *audacious*. Many of the club members offered Alison accolades, too, for the quality of Foodie Publishing cookbooks. The photography, a few said, was brilliant.

When the crowd left and before Coco pocketed her pen, I said, "Coco, would you sign the remaining books? I know we'll sell them. Our customers love personalized cookbooks."

"You bet." She finished quickly and hoisted her tote higher on her shoulder. "I guess that's it. Thank you so much for this opportunity. It was a true delight. I knew I had fans, but to meet so many in person was the highlight of my career."

"Our pleasure."

She patted Alison. "Let's get a move on."

I stopped her. "Can Bailey and I buy you two a glass of wine at Vines Wine Bistro upstairs?"

Coco grinned. "I love that place. That's where we went last night."

Alison begged off. "I'm beat. Coco, do you mind?"

"Work, work, work. C'mon. We'll only have one drink."

Alison shook her head and then yawned. "Not tonight." She addressed Ingrid. "Are you going with them?"

I hadn't invited the tight-toothed copyeditor, but I was too embarrassed to disinvite her.

"No, I'm exhausted, as well," Ingrid said. "Can you drive me back to your mother's, Alison?"

Alison agreed. They left, and I heard Alison, sotto voce, asking Ingrid whether she'd learned anything of significance. Ingrid tucked her iPad into her oversized tote and nodded profusely, looking slightly goggle-eyed, as if she had gleaned way too much to retain.

"Let's go," I said to Coco and Bailey. "I'll tell Katie where we'll be."

"I'll give you a lift later, Coco," Bailey added.

"Deal."

VINES WINE BISTRO, the wine bar on the second floor of Fisherman's Village, was the perfect place for those who wanted a nice glass of wine and quiet conversation. The handcrafted tables were set to seat four patrons or fewer. Only a few stools stood beneath the curved bar. Classical music played softly through a speaker system. Most often, strings of tiny white lights were the only decoration. Tonight, however, the place looked like a rustic beach palace. Nets stocked with colorful plastic fish swooped from chandelier to chandelier. Tiki torches poked from potted plants. Cutouts of pirate silhouettes adorned the walls.

Simon Butler, the owner of Vines, approached us. "Ladies, what a pleasure." He reminded me of a forty-year-old Simon from Alvin and the Chipmunks: big, round glasses, a thatch of spiky hair, and an educated, almost crafty-in-a-cute-way look. "We're one server short tonight, so"—he made a grand sweeping gesture—"I'll do the honors. This way." Simon walked ahead of us. "Table for four or five? I assume Katie and Alison will be joining you."

"I'm sorry to say neither will," I said. Before coming upstairs, I had scooted into the kitchen to invite Katie, but she begged off. "Do you know Alison, Simon?" I asked, then revised, "Of course you do. She was here last night with Coco."

"I know her professionally, too." Over his shoulder, he said, "I happen to have a book on her desk, thanks to Coco's introduction. A family history with recipes, if you will."

"It's wonderful," Coco said. "I've read the foreword and a number of the stories. Dash is slated to do the photography."

"We'll have to carry it in the shop," I said. "When will it come out?"

"I'm not sure." Simon shook his head. He looked to Coco for an answer. She had none. "Soon, I hope. It would make my mama proud. She's . . . ill." He winced. "Dying, in fact."

My heart wrenched. "I'm so sorry."

"Me, too." Coco reached out and touched his arm. "Why didn't you tell me before?" She swiveled to face Bailey and me. "Simon is one of my steadiest customers. He's always interested in how I do everything. He adores my milk chocolate nougat."

"And your chocolate-coffee dipped pretzels." He seated us at a table in the corner.

I sat beside Bailey and glanced around the bistro. "I like the pirate theme you've got going, Simon."

"Let's just say we're seriously into looting and pillaging." He chuckled then tilted his head in Coco's direction. "You look nice, all dressed up, your hair"—he indicated from his neck to his shoulder—"loose."

"Why, thank you, sir. No hairnets for me on a night out." Coco's typical uniform when working at Sweet Sensations was a hot pink dress, hot pink apron, and hot pink hairnet. Fashionable but practical.

"By the way, Coco"—Simon offered a quirky smile—"my wife thanks you for the extra special attention you gave to the cocoa-covered truffles for the baby shower."

"Your wife is pregnant?" Bailey squealed.

"No. My sister. My wife threw the shower."

Coco said, "His wife is a real exercise buff, a personal trainer. Haven't you met her?"

"Numerous times," I said. "She's bought a couple of cookbooks. Her latest was, let me see"—I tapped my lip—"*The Paleo Approach Cookbook: A Detailed Guide to Heal Your Body and Nourish Your Soul*."

"Gosh," Coco said. "I love how lengthy cookbook titles are."

"I know. Right?" I giggled. "The book just came out. I'd never heard of it until your wife mentioned it, Simon. It's written by a doctor who provides all sorts of tips about how to make the switch to paleo."

"Then you know by that title alone that chocolate never touches her lips or hips," Coco teased.

"That's not true," Simon countered. "She indulges occasionally."

"Whatever." Coco twirled her finger through a lock of hair. "You're welcome. It's a recipe handed down to me by my *bunica*, my grandmother."

"Is *bunica* Russian?" Bailey asked.

"Romanian. On my mother's side."

"I was lucky enough to taste one of those truffles." Simon kissed the tips of his fingertips. "Delicious." He beckoned a passing waiter. "Neil, bring some menus, will you?"

I said, "Say, isn't that Alison Foodie's—"

"Younger brother, Neil." Simon nodded then lowered his voice. "She asked me to do her a favor and give the kid a job. Anything for my publisher, right?"

Neil wasn't a kid. He had to be in his late twenties, and although he was as tall as his sister, unlike Alison, who had the build and fortitude of a Scottish warrior, Neil was on the pudgy side with a double chin, cherub cheeks, and a receding hairline.

Simon continued to whisper. "Be nice to him. The kid is learning, but he's got a long way to go. He's had a rough time of it since his father died. A handful of odd jobs. Nothing's sticking. And, let's face it, he can't compare to his sister. She excels in everything." Simon raised a palm. "I totally get that. Been there, done that." He cleared his throat. "Might I recommend the MacMurray Ranch pinot noir if you're in the mood for red tonight? It's our special pour." He grabbed a carafe of peanuts off another table, set it in the center of ours, and brushed his fingers off on his pant leg.

Neil appeared at the table. "Hiya, ladies." He handed each of us a menu. "I've got this, boss."

"Mr. Butler," Simon corrected.

"Mr. Butler. Sir." Neil's mouth curved upward, like he might break into a wicked grin.

"Wipe down the nut carafe, would you please?"

"Yeah, sure thing. There's a guy wearing an eye patch at the bar. He's asking for you. He's got lots of questions about The Prisoner Wine Company selection. I think it's called Blindfold." Neil paused then guffawed. "Blindfold. Ha! That's funny." He smacked his leg. "I hadn't made the connection. Eye patch. Blindfold."

Simon didn't see the humor. "It's a fine wine."

"I know," Neil said and put on a serious face. "Don't worry. I told him the wine was bold and intriguing."

"Good." Simon addressed us. "Ladies, enjoy the evening. Neil, take care of these women."

When Simon was out of earshot, Neil said, "Some people do buy wine because of the art on the bottle. It's pretty ridiculous, if you ask me, but—" He gaped at Coco. "Hey, you're one of my sister's authors, aren't you? Yeah, you're the candy lady. Coco . . . Coco . . ."

"Coco Chastain." She offered a hand.

Neil shook it enthusiastically. "You own Sweet Sensations."

"That's right."

"Sis is staying with you. Yeah, she loves your recipes. She's told Mother all about you. I would have recognized you anywhere. You look just like the photo on the book jacket."

"Haven't you visited her candy shop?" I asked.

"Nah. I can't do sweets. Borderline diabetic. No nuts, either. Major allergic." Using a pair of napkins, Neil deftly wiped down the nut carafe without touching any portion of the glass. "Lots of candies have nuts in them."

"I make sweets for diabetics. No sugar," Coco said. "And nutless candies, too."

"Aw, that's all right. No need to tempt myself." He patted his doughy stomach. "But I heard your stuff is great." Neil wrinkled his nose in an impish way. "You had people downstairs for a little soiree earlier, didn't you? Yeah, Simon—

Mr. Butler—told me about it. I think he was hoping to be invited. Did it go well? How could it not? My sister was involved. Everything she does is golden."

Did I detect a tinge of sibling rivalry? Simon had hinted at as much a few minutes ago.

"It was a great success," Coco said.

I added, "Until the mayor said the pot was stolen."

Bailey shook a finger. "Don't worry about that. If Z.Z. doesn't find the pot, she'll replace it."

Neil looked between us. "Oho. You're not talking about marijuana. You're talking about the missing doubloons, aren't you?"

"Yes," we answered as a trio.

"*Arrr*, lassies," Neil said with a thick brogue. "Shiver me timbers. Didn't you see?"

"See what?" I asked.

"The pot of doubloons. With the lion's claws feet. A picture of it went viral on the Internet."

"Why would a picture go viral?" Bailey asked.

"Because the pot is sitting on Mrs. McCartney's porch," Neil announced.

"Why there?" I asked. Mrs. McCartney lived in my father's neighborhood, way up in the hills. A real sourpuss, she wouldn't find the pot appearing on her porch funny in the least.

"*Arrr*. There were handcuffs around the feet, and there was a caption: *Rescue me*, all made of letters cut from magazines." Neil clapped his thigh. "That's hysterical, isn't it? *Rescue me*."

"For heaven's sake," Coco said. "I've never heard anything so ridiculous. Who would do such a thing?"

"Someone who wants attention, if you ask me . . . but you didn't. No one ever does." Neil pulled a pad and pencil from his apron pocket. "What do you want to drink? The wine the boss mentioned—" He hesitated. "I mean, the wine Mr. Butler suggested is good."

We ordered a bottle of the pinot and three glasses. We passed on food, too stuffed from our cookbook club feast.

Soon, a sprightly waitress with wavy hair that cascaded down her back returned with the wine. She uncorked it, handed me the cork, and poured three glasses.

"What happened to Neil?" I asked.

"Oh, him." The waitress hitched her chin to where Neil was standing, off to the side of the bar, texting someone with fast and furious fingers. "I think he has a secret life or imagines he does." She sniggered. "I think he filches singles from the communal tip jar, too. He's a sneaky devil, but far be it for me to tattle. I need this job, and the boss will believe him before he'll believe me. You know, men stick together." She set the wine bottle in the center of the table and hightailed it back to the bar to fetch another order.

"Do you think Alison knows her brother has an iffy reputation?" Coco asked.

"She's sharp," Bailey said. "I'll bet she does. I'm sorry she didn't join us, but here's to you." Bailey raised a toast to Coco. "To your continued success."

Coco tapped her glass to Bailey's and mine. "I couldn't have done it without you. You hooked me up with Alison."

"Speaking of hookups," I said, "is Alison into Dash?"

"Huh? Heavens, no!" Coco shook her head. "Dash is, well, at least I think he is into another type."

"No way," I said.

"I don't think so, either," Bailey said. "I saw the way he looked at her." She batted her eyelashes. "Dreamy eyed."

"Maybe you missed my innuendo." Coco tittered. "He's gay."

"Uh-uh," I said. "I know gay and he's not. Remember, we lived in San Francisco." I wagged a finger between Bailey and me.

"So does he," Coco teased.

"That doesn't make a guy gay," I said. "He's totally into Alison."

Bailey bobbed her head, agreeing with me.

"Ingrid hinted at the same thing I'm implying." Coco winked. "She said Dash was taking pictures of pirates."

"Yes," I said, "but Dash corrected her. Quite vehemently."

"Perhaps he doth protest too much." Coco took a sip of wine. "Maybe you didn't know, but Dash is staying with that jewelry store owner. The one who sells those gorgeous pearls." She shot a finger at me. "You know the guy I'm talking about. He wears tight jeans and T-shirts with the funky logos on them. Pierced earrings in his ears. And usually dozens of glitzy bracelets."

"That doesn't make *him* gay, either," I said. "That makes him an entrepreneur showing off his wares."

Coco laughed. "Either way, Alison isn't into Dash. She's not into anybody, as far as I know. I wish she had a boyfriend. She could use a little love, if you know what I mean. She has worked so hard to take her publishing company to the next level. But there's no one in her life. At the very least, she should go on a vacation."

I said, "Maybe she wouldn't enjoy such success if she slacked off."

"Is that why she hired Ingrid?" Bailey asked. "To ease the load?"

Coco leaned in and whispered, "Between you and me, I think Ingrid might add to the load. You heard Alison. Ingrid is a stickler for detail. That can slow down the editing process."

"You don't want a shoddy product out on the market, do you?" Bailey asked.

"No," Coco said. "You're right. I love the quality of books Alison puts out. Each one is individual and unique. You heard the fans tonight. They love the photographs, the paper, the high-gloss covers." She air-painted her vision with her fingers. "No, I want Alison to keep on doing what she does, as well as she does."

"To Alison."

We all toasted. Then the three of us yawned, and soon after, we called it a night.

EARLY FRIDAY MORNING, way before the sun was due to rise, the landline telephone next to my bed rang. It rarely did. I used my cell phone for practically every call. But Aunt Vera, who owned the cottage I lived in—her house was situated less than a hundred yards away—had installed the old-style telephone. She insisted I keep it in service. I didn't pay rent. How could I refuse?

I flopped onto my stomach and reached for the jangling disturbance. Tigger, who had nestled at my feet, roused. I told him to go back to sleep. He didn't; he roamed in a circle and pawed the comforter.

"Hello?" I rasped.

"Jenna." Bailey sounded stuffed up, like she had a raging cold. "I've been calling your cell phone. You weren't answering. I had to resort—" She sniffed. "Come to Coco's house. Please. Right now. I can't believe it. I can't—"

"What's wrong?"

"Alison . . . is dead."

Chapter 5

❦

COCO CHASTAIN LIVED in a darling house, not unlike my one-room cottage where the kitchen blended with the living room and bedroom, except her house was located in the swank part of Crystal Cove, near the top of the mountain, right around the corner from Nature's Retreat Hotel, which was a fabulous inn tucked into a grove of oaks. Most of the houses in the area were similar in size to Coco's. Many had been purchased by out-of-towners who wanted a simple but elegant vacation abode.

When I arrived at the house, Deputy Appleby, with whom I've had a verbal run-in or two in the past—he has been nicer ever since he started wooing my aunt—tried to block me from entering. He was big and burly. His moose-like face didn't flinch. "Uh-uh," was all he said.

"Bailey called me. Let me pass. Please."

"Deputy, it's okay." Cinnamon Pritchett, who was positioned directly inside the door, waved to allow me through. She didn't say a word to me as I crossed the threshold. She stood erect, shoulders rigid, jaw set. Her gaze moved deliberately around the expansive room, which was tastefully done in pink tones. The floor mats, towels, and kitchen pots and pans matched the décor.

Bailey and Coco huddled near the refrigerator, holding hands. Bailey looked scruffy, like something out of the movie *Flashdance*, in her leggings and sweatshirt with the collar cut off. Her eyes were puffy; her lips trembled. Coco, who was still wearing the formfitting magenta dress she had worn to the cookbook club soiree, looked torn up, too. Mascara streaked her face. Her foot drilled the hardwood floor.

Alison Foodie laid slumped forward onto the antique oak kitchen table, her back to the front door, her face buried in her folded arms. She, too, was dressed in the clothes she had worn to the book club event, although the red-toned tartan was slung over the back of another chair. A laptop computer stood open on the table about an arm's length from Alison's head, as if she had pushed it away to take a nap. A pair of intricate kitchen shears jutted from her back. There was a lot of blood. Some of it dried. She had to have been dead for hours.

On the kitchen counter to the right of the kitchen table stood a knife block, a toaster, a hot pink kitchen tool crock filled with pink-toned utensils, an opened recipe box, which was stuffed with recipe cards, a KitchenAid mixer, six or seven decorative floral canisters, a dusting of flour, a bag of cocoa pinched with a clip, and the remainder of a stick of butter. The scent of nutmeg hung in the air. A tray of bite-sized chocolate chip cookies sat cooling on a rack set on top of the stove. Had Alison baked them? Why? Hadn't our delicious meal satisfied her appetite? The sink held a number of bowls, measuring cups, and mixing blades.

On the table beside the computer rested a Sweet Sensations mug and a china plate. A decorative silver tea strainer as well as the remnants of a chocolate cookie sat on the plate. The window beyond the kitchen table was black with a faint hue of gray around the edges—dawn had not yet broken. I could see the reflection of Cinnamon, the deputy, and the rest of us.

Cinnamon looked like she was ruing the day she had accepted the position of chief of police now that we'd had four—no, *five*—murders since August, the month I returned to town. Thoughts about me being a bad luck charm for Crystal Cove whizzed through my head. I pushed them aside. My aunt assured me that my karma was no worse than anyone else's. My father said sometimes cities went through tragic cycles. He had seen it all too often in his previous line of work. He used to be an FBI agent; now he owned a hardware shop in town.

Finally, Cinnamon said, "Good morning, Jenna."

"Not so good. Not so morning."

"Right." She rolled her lower lip between her teeth.

"Did you just arrive?" I asked.

"Moments ago. Why are you here?"

"As I tried to tell Deputy Appleby, Bailey called me."

Cinnamon cut a look at Bailey and back at me. "How well did you know Ali—" She stopped herself from using Alison's familiar name. "Miss Foodie?"

"Well enough. Bailey introduced us. We were years apart at school. I think she was your age. Did you know her?"

"Yes." One word. Clipped off. No elaboration. "Miss Bird—" Cinnamon crooked a finger.

Bailey released Coco's hand and hurried over. "Please call me Bailey," she said to the chief. "I hate my last name. It's so . . . frivolous." Bailey often wished her mother, after she divorced Bailey's father, would have switched back to her maiden name, Hastings, but she didn't. How could Bailey? "You probably want the rundown."

Cinnamon nodded.

Bailey moistened her lips. "Coco found Alison when she came home. She was distraught."

"Naturally."

"She called me seconds later."

I cut in. "She came home as in, she was *out*? Where did she go?" We had called it a night around ten.

"Out."

"Out?" Cinnamon echoed.

Bailey worked her tongue around the inside of her mouth. "On a date."

I peeked at Coco. So that was why she hadn't changed clothes. "Who did she go out with?"

"She won't say."

"Won't?" Cinnamon shot a look at Coco.

I whispered to Bailey, "If she was getting it on, why did she come back before dawn?"

"She wanted to shower and switch into her uniform before going to work."

I gave my pal a knowing look. Coco very easily could have taken her uniform with her on the so-called *date*. I would bet she kept a uniform at the shop, too. There was another reason she would have come home early. "Is the guy married?" I asked.

Bailey scrunched up her mouth. "Probably, but who am I to throw stones?" Much to her dismay, Bailey had dallied with a married man in the past. He was out of her life now. She ditched him. But she still had emotional scars.

I glanced from Coco, who was studying the toe of her high heel and plucking at the seams of her dress, to Alison. Then I glanced past Alison, at the opened computer sitting on the table. At Taylor & Squibb, I had a reputation for being able to read upside down as well as at a distance. At times an executive needs to know what notes her subordinates are passing around behind her back. Yes, there had been a few who didn't like me. Early on in my career, I had been a stickler for detail. I had earned a few colleagues' wrath until I learned to ease up.

On Alison's computer, four Word documents were open. The topmost read: Chocolate Bombs. Right below it was another file, Mother's Chocolate Bombs. I peered at the lower icon bar. All other programs, other than Word, were closed.

I whispered, "Bailey, what was Alison working on?" and pointed at the computer. "Did you get a closer look?"

Bailey edged in that direction. Cinnamon grabbed her arm to thwart her. At the same time, a woman screamed. We all spun to face the front door.

Ingrid Lake, the copyeditor at Foodie Publishing, was clawing Deputy Appleby. "Let me in. Tell me it's not true. Alison?" Ingrid, so reserved at the book club event earlier, looked jittery. Her sculpted hair was in a snarl. Her already pale face looked as white as paper. Her teeth still didn't move, but that was understandable. Fear was making me grit my teeth, too. "Let me in," she demanded. The deputy continued to restrain her.

"Who alerted her?" I asked.

"I called Alison's mother," Coco said. "I thought Wanda should know about"—Coco winced—"her daughter. Wanda must have told Ingrid."

Bailey said, "Ingrid looks like a wreck."

I had to agree. She looked like she hadn't checked herself in a mirror. Neither had I, come to think of it. Was my hair sticking out at odd angles?

"Let me in," Ingrid demanded. "If Alison's dead, I'm second-in-command."

"No, she's not," Coco said to Cinnamon, then whirled on Ingrid. "No, you're not. You're a copyeditor, not a partner."

Cinnamon strode to Ingrid and the deputy. She blocked Ingrid from progressing farther inside. "I'm sorry. You are . . . ?"

"Ingrid Lake."

"You were the company's second-in-command?"

Ingrid's gaze narrowed. "Well, no, not really," she said, her teeth still locked, her lips doing all the work. "Not officially. Not yet. I'm on track to be a partner. Alison was drawing up papers, until . . ." She heaved a sigh and slung a hand in Coco's direction. "Coco is right. For now, I'm just the copyeditor, but there are only the two of us, Alison and me, and with her dead, that puts me in charge."

What about Dash Hamada? Could a photographer be second-in-command at a publishing house? Was he exclusive to Foodie Publishing? Had Alison considered herself anything other than a one-woman operation?

"She did it!" Ingrid stared daggers at Coco. "She killed Alison."

"What?" Coco's voice skipped upward.

Why on earth would Ingrid say something so ridiculous?

"No." Coco wagged her head. "I . . . I was out. On a date. I came back and found Alison like that." She pointed at the body. "The shears were already there, poking out of her, and I—" She slapped a hand over her mouth. "Oh no." Coco swung around to face Cinnamon. "I touched them. My fingerprints will be on them. I mean, they would be anyway because I use them." She splayed her hands. "But, you see, I rushed to Alison. I thought I could help. And I grasped them by the handle. But then I realized I shouldn't pull them out. I've seen the movies. She would bleed more. So I released them, and I . . . I—"

"Don't believe her!" Ingrid shrieked. "She did it."

Coco sank into herself, wrapping her arms around her rib cage. Her chest was heaving. I wished I could comfort her.

Cinnamon held up a warning hand to all of us not to move and drew near to Coco. "What time did you get home, Miss Chastain?"

Coco flushed fuchsia pink. "Just a bit ago. I . . ." She hesitated.

Where had she been? With whom? Coco didn't add more. Why not? Who was she protecting?

"Are those your shears?" Cinnamon asked.

"Yes," Coco said. "They're Messermeister take-apart utility shears."

I owned a pair of utility shears. My aunt had stocked my kitchen with a variety of tools. The shears, in addition to cutting through poultry and snipping herbs, could act as a screwdriver, jar lid opener/gripper, knife, and nutcracker. In my opinion, the knife aspect of the shears would have been a better choice of weapon than scissors.

On the other hand, the murderer would have needed to pull the shears apart, which suggested that he . . . or *she* . . . hadn't had time to disassemble them; the killer had acted swiftly. Had he or *she*—I hated to consider Coco a suspect, but I had to, right?—come into the house to confront Alison, seen the scissors in the knife block, and seized upon the idea to kill her? Was it spur-of-the-moment? Unplanned? Why hadn't Alison twisted around in her chair? Had she been so focused on the documents on her computer that she'd been blind to all other intrusions? Perhaps she had attempted to close the computer, which would explain why it sat nearer the center of the table. What were the documents she had been working on?

"My mother gave me the shears the day I graduated culinary school," Coco went on, still clutching herself like a lifeline. Tears pooled in her eyes. "She . . . she was so proud of me. She was the one who taught me to cook. I stowed the shears in the knife block." She released her hold and flailed a hand in that direction. "Anybody could have used them. I never would have—" She jammed the knuckles of her right hand into her mouth.

Cinnamon strode to the front door and assessed the knob and lock. "The entry has not been compromised. Someone must have used a key to gain access. Are you the only person with a key to this house, Miss Chastain?"

"Yes, I'm the only one with a key, but"—Coco glanced tearfully from me to Bailey to Cinnamon—"I don't lock the front door. Ever. It's a bad habit, I know, but I never use a key."

Was she crazy?

"We live in such a safe neighborhood," Coco added.

In this day and age, that was just darned naïve.

Coco swallowed hard. "Please, you have to believe me. Why would I want Alison dead? We were friends. I didn't do this. Someone is framing me." She swiveled and glowered at Ingrid with such spite that the young woman retreated a step.

"Chief Pritchett," I said, doing her the honor of calling her by her title, not her first name, "what document was Alison working on?"

"Why?" Cinnamon tilted her head. Her eyes narrowed.

"She must have been completely focused on her work not to have noticed her killer." I gestured to the window and explained my reasoning. It was dark out. The reflection worked like a mirror. "If she did see the killer, she trusted whoever it was."

"You see?" Ingrid shouted. "That proves it. Coco did it. She lives here. Alison wouldn't have swiveled in her seat to talk to her."

Though I didn't like the young copyeditor, I had to agree with her. But Alison was familiar with a lot more people in town than simply Coco. On the other hand, anyone other than Coco entering the house unannounced between midnight and now would have been suspect, right?

No, Jenna. Coco did not *do this.*

"I'll bet . . ." Ingrid inhaled sharply, her thoughts coming faster than her breath. "I'll bet Alison told Coco about the cuts she was making."

Coco visibly bristled. "What cuts?"

All heads turned toward her.

"To your latest manuscript," Ingrid said. "You were getting too wordy. Alison said you would throttle her for the myriad cuts she was making."

Cuts. Were the scissors metaphorical? I gazed at Cinnamon, who appeared to be wondering the same thing, her gaze roving from the scissors to Coco and back again.

"Uh-uh." Coco wagged a finger. "We were done with edits on my latest manuscript. We'd already gone through that phase."

"You told her not to edit you at all," Ingrid said. "You told her you had proprietary ownership."

I flashed on the fake fight Alison and Coco had performed at the café earlier. Had there been some truth in their sparring?

"I was kidding." Coco eyed Cinnamon. "Here's how it goes. I turn in the manuscript." She used her hands to explain the process. "Alison reviews it. She makes suggestions. Then I—"

"Made," Ingrid inserted. "*Made* suggestions. Past tense."

Coco snarled but continued using the present tense. "Alison sends them to me. I work on her suggestions and return the manuscript. Then she sends it to Ingrid." Coco glowered at the copyeditor. "It was your turn to review. My latest manuscript should be on your desk. That can't be my manu-script on the computer."

Cinnamon held up a hand to keep everyone at bay and edged toward the computer. Reading from the screen, she said, "Chocolate Bombs. That seems to be the title of a recipe. Is it yours, Miss Chastain?"

Coco blanched and muttered, "Yes, but that wasn't . . . why would she have—"

"There are other documents here," Cinnamon said, lean-ing forward and dragging the documents aside so she could read titles beneath. "A second Chocolate Bombs file. One for Chocolate Desire. Another for Chocolate Macadamia Bites. All yours?"

"Yes, those are my titles, but—"

"There are comments on this topmost document from three different sources in the margins," Cinnamon went on. "*Alison Foodie* in green, *Author* in yellow, and *Copyeditor* in light blue."

"Copyeditor. That's me," Ingrid said then quickly cor-rected herself. "I mean, *I*; that is I. Alison doesn't . . . didn't want her authors to get confused. She used her first and last name so there was no mistake, and then the copyeditor's name was generic. There's only one of me at the company, but even so . . . generic. The author responds first to Alison's comments, then to mine."

"Is that the way it goes, Miss Chastain?" Cinnamon asked.

Coco nodded again, but she looked confused. She piv-oted, as if searching the kitchen for something.

"There are a lot of comments made by you, Miss Lake," Cinnamon said.

Coco spun back and threw out a zinger. "That's because Ingrid makes picayune suggestions."

"I do not!" Ingrid shrieked.

"You do, too!"

"Nothing I do is trivial."

"Ladies," Cinnamon said.

Ingrid didn't heed the warning. "Every comma and colon matters. *Eats, Shoots and Leaves*," she added, citing the title of a humorous book about punctuation. I had read it in college. "Authors don't grasp the value of a copyeditor's expertise."

"Bah!" Coco said. "Even Alison said you were heavy-handed. I wouldn't put it past you to have killed her."

"Me?"

"You were not on track to become a partner."

"I was, too. Besides, I just got here. You did it. A desire for creative control can be a very powerful motive for murder, and you—"

"Ladies, silence!" Cinnamon yelled. "Let's take this outside. Deputy Appleby, snap a few photos, please. The coroner will be here shortly."

I trailed the pack and heard Coco whisper, "If anyone deserved to die, it was Ingrid."

Chapter 6

AROUND DAWN, HEARTSICK for Coco, but mindful of my obligations and knowing I couldn't do anything to change the course of Cinnamon's inquiry, I said I needed to go home. Bailey asked if she could remain behind to support Coco. Just for a few hours. I told her of course. I totally understood. As I was leaving, Deputy Appleby asked if he could have a word with me about my aunt, but Cinnamon intercepted him before we could chat, so I left.

An hour later, after showering and doing something with my hair, I threw on trousers and a cute aqua sweater, downed a necessary meal of oatmeal lavished in sugar and fresh fruit—I made oatmeal once a week and reheated it in the microwave—and, with Tigger in tow, headed to work.

Aunt Vera had arrived at The Cookbook Nook before me. She was already sorting money into the cash register till slots when I entered. She looked colorful in a cardinal red caftan, her hair swept up in a chignon. Her turban rested on the stool behind her. A threesome of tarot cards lay turned up on the vintage kitchen table. I didn't take a peek, but seeing as we didn't have any customers, I figured she was trying to read her own future.

"What's the special occasion?" I asked and set Tigger by the children's corner. He explored beneath the chairs, weaving in and out of the legs as if they were his own private forest, and finally came to rest.

"Whatever do you mean?" My aunt toyed with a hoop earring. Her cluster of silver bracelets jingled.

I twirled a finger. "The getup. I happen to know this particular caftan is your favorite. Do you have a big date with Deputy Appleby today?" The two had gone out on a number of dates in the past three months. My aunt told me it wasn't serious between them, but dating a younger man had done worlds for adding a spring to her step.

"No," she said. "I mean, yes, I have a date, but no, not with the deputy."

"Oho," I said, sounding more like a pirate than I'd intended. "Are you dating more than one man?"

"Um, I'm not seeing Deputy Appleby anymore. My decision."

Aha. Now I understood why the deputy had tried to speak with me earlier. I said, "Care to tell me why not?"

"It's not your concern."

"No, of course not, but I am worried. When I saw him this morning—"

"What?" Aunt Vera turned pale. "You saw him? Where? When? Why?"

I held up a hand. "Alison Foodie was murdered." I told her how I came to be at the crime scene.

My aunt grasped the phoenix amulet she always wore around her neck and rubbed it furiously with her thumb. "What is this world coming to? How will Crystal Cove handle yet another tragedy like this?"

My thoughts exactly.

"How did Bailey know?" she asked.

"Coco called her. Coco was the one who found Alison." I sighed. "Alison was stabbed with scissors."

"Heavens." Aunt Vera gripped my hands and dragged

me to the vintage table. She guided me into a chair and sat as well. "Who did it and why?"

"We don't know yet. I'm pretty sure Cinnamon has her eye on Coco. The copyeditor said Alison was slashing Coco's manuscript to shreds, hence the scissors."

"It's not possible. It couldn't be Coco."

"A number of documents were on the computer. All Coco's. With lots of edits."

"No, that's not what I mean." Aunt Vera batted the air. "If Alison was killed during the night, Coco couldn't have done it. I saw her."

"You did?"

My aunt studied her fingernails for a brief moment.

"Don't hold me in suspense, Aunt Vera. Speak."

"I was at Nature's Retreat last night. Coco was there. I spied her slipping into a room around eleven."

Now I understood my aunt's hesitancy. She must have been a guest at the hotel. She wouldn't have gone there alone, so she must have been with a gentleman—not Deputy Appleby. Well, whoever it was, good for her. I wanted her to be happy. She had suffered her share of heartbreak.

However, back to the matter at hand . . . *Coco was there. At the hotel.*

"Are you sure it was her?" I asked.

Aunt Vera nodded. "She was hard to miss in that alluring dress she was wearing." She outlined Coco's curvy figure.

"Did you see who she met?"

"No, but whoever he was, he wore a wedding ring."

"You caught a glimpse of his hand?"

"As he tugged her inside. She looked positively giddy with delight."

I drew in a deep, slow breath. "Aunt Vera, this is major. You are Coco's alibi." So was the married man, of course. I wondered if Coco had coughed up his name to the police by now. If she hadn't, would he come forward on his own? "Did whomever you were with also see Coco?"

Aunt Vera cleared her throat. "What makes you think I was with someone?"

I offered a knowing glance.

Aunt Vera waggled a hand. "Fine. If you must know, I was with that darling mustachioed manager of the Crystal Cove Inn."

"Hooray." I spanked the table. "I knew you were destined to be together." I didn't add that I was glad she had ended it with the leader of the Crystal Cove Coastal Concern or that I was thrilled she wasn't involved with the deputy any longer, my awkwardness about that whole affair aside. I wanted her to be fulfilled.

"I'm not sure we're destined, dear." Aunt Vera's cheeks reddened. "There is such a fine line between what the universe serves up as destiny and what we do of our own free will." My aunt's beliefs were sometimes hard to pin down. I would swear she believed Fate had a hand in all things, and yet she warned any who asked for her fortune-telling services to take what she said with a grain of salt . . . or *magic*—her word. She stood and smoothed the wrinkles in her caftan. "All I will say is that we do enjoy each other's company. The deputy will have to accept that as . . ." She twirled a hand.

"Destiny," I finished.

"Too-ra-loo." My aunt uttered the carefree expression often. I translated it to mean pretty much the same thing as *que sera, sera*: whatever will be, will be.

"I think he'd like some closure," I said.

Aunt Vera nodded. "Yes, he deserves that. He's a darling man. Better suited to you."

"Because of his age?"

"He's more active than I ever will be. He wants to hike and explore. I'm simply too old."

"Get out of here." I waved her off. "You're in your sixties. Hardly old."

"Hardly young. But enough about me. Back to Coco and poor Alison. Such a fine young woman. What can I do to help? Anything?"

"Call Cinnamon. Tell her what you know."

"I will." My aunt petted my cheek and returned to the sales counter. "By the way, do you know the time of death?"

"Sometime between the end of the book club dinner and when Coco returned home."

"Of course. Hard to pin things down." Aunt Vera picked up the phone but immediately hung up when my father entered the shop with Bailey's mother, Lola, the new love of his life.

Dad was carrying a tool kit and a tube of paper. Lola held two to-go cups from Café au Lait.

Lola said, "Jenna, darling. I heard about Alison. How horrible. And to think I just saw her last night at book club."

Dad nodded his condolences.

"Word is out?" I asked.

Lola said, "You can't keep much from this town once the buzz gets going. Bailey must be torn up."

"She is."

"Where is she?"

"Either at Coco's house or the precinct. She wanted to offer Coco emotional support."

Lola whispered something to my father, handed him his coffee cup, and pecked him on the cheek. Then she hurried out of the shop.

Dad, who was a handsome man in an aging leading man way, grinned with a devilish twinkle. "You've got to admit the woman has get-up-and-go."

"She does indeed." I would never forget the first time I met Lola. I was five. She clutched me to her chest, rumpled my hair, and told me how pretty I was but that I should never rely on my looks. She was going to make it her mission to ensure I became an avid reader. I promised her that my mother and father were already doing that, but she wouldn't let up. Every month, she bought me a Newbery Medal– or Honor–winning book, some with the most exotic titles, like *Island of the Blue Dolphins* or *Red Sails to Capri*. I attributed my love of reading to her. She opened new worlds. She and my father had started dating a few months ago. They were almost as perfect a match as my father and mother had been.

My father finger-combed his silver hair. "I'm ready to be put to work."

"Work?" I said.

Aunt Vera cut in. "I forgot to tell you, Jenna. I've asked your father to do a few tweaks around the shop."

Dad was an expert handyman. After retiring from the FBI and before purchasing his hardware store, he put in a lot of volunteer hours at Habitat for Humanity.

"We have a squeaky door in the stockroom." Aunt Vera ticked the list off her fingertips. "The register drawer gets stuck. And the phone line crackles."

Dad didn't need the income from the handyman work—he had a tidy sum in his savings accounts—but he loved to fix things. Didn't all men? Well, not all. My husband David hadn't. He'd had no knack for that kind of thing. I was pretty sure Rhett could do whatever my father could—he whittled wood like a pro—but he used my father's services instead. He had enough to do, running a thriving business.

"By the way"—Dad jabbed the tube of paper in my direction—"don't you, for one remote second, try to blame yourself for this twist of fate, Tootsie Pop." He loved using the sobriquet he'd dubbed me when I was a tween. I felt somewhat foolish whenever he uttered it, but I would always be his little girl, and face it, what could I do? Tell him to stop? Like he'd listen.

"She wouldn't blame herself, Cary," Aunt Vera said.

I would, but I wasn't. At least I was trying not to. When I was new to town and so many murders had occurred in rapid succession, I'd thought it was somehow my fault. Perhaps I had brought bad luck to Crystal Cove. I didn't feel that way any longer. Maybe I was more like my father than I realized. He, unlike my aunt, was not a believer in hoodoo, as he called it. On the other hand, he did profess that Crystal Cove had a spirit or an essence, if you will. That was about as far as anyone could push him into acknowledging an ethereal influence in his life. Each choice was ours *to grow or blow*—his words. Whenever he couldn't concoct one of his own adages, he could quote a ton of philosophers verbatim to support his theories.

Dad set his tool kit on the sales counter and leaned forward on his elbows. "Tell me about Alison. What happened?"

I gaped. My father rarely liked to bat around ideas when it came to murder. He felt that our police force was one of the best small-sized forces in the state. He had mentored Cinnamon Pritchett in her teens, so he took personal pride in her being a stalwart and perceptive leader.

"You didn't hear at the coffee shop?" I asked.

"Only the fact that she was murdered and the police are investigating. Give me the details."

I told him about the crime scene, the unlocked door, the fact that Alison hadn't swiveled to see the intruder.

Dad hummed as he pondered something. "Seems like a vengeful thing to do, stabbing. Could it be symbolic? Did Alison stab someone in the back business-wise?"

"Tit for tat." Aunt Vera bobbed her head. "That would make sense. Do you know, Jenna?"

"Maybe an author was angry at her," my father suggested. "Seems like everyone has a book in them nowadays. Even I do."

"You do?" I said.

"Yeah." My father buffed the edge of the counter with his hand.

"It's with a small press," Aunt Vera inserted.

"Small presses put out some of our best cookbooks," I countered. "Dad, is it about your life in the FBI?" His work had involved ultra-clandestine stuff. My siblings and I never got the full story about what he did. Would we now find out the truth?

"Heck, no. I can't go blabbing state secrets."

Rats.

"I've written about the beauty of tying a fishing lure and how that relates to life in general."

Aunt Vera rolled her eyes.

I stifled a laugh. "Are you kidding me?"

"I know." My father held up a hand. "It's not your kind of book."

How well he knew me. I no longer read literary novels. Now I devour mysteries and thrillers. In my preteen years, I discovered Agatha Christie: *Appointment with Death*, *Murder on the Orient Express*, *Ten Little Indians*. I swear, after reading all of her books, I imagined myself as an amateur sleuth. In addition, I am also a cookbook fiend. But nonfiction? About fishing lures? *Bleh*.

Dad rubbed the tube of paper on the edge of his chin. "I thought I would have heard from the editor by now, but my critique group—"

"You have a critique group?"

"Online," Aunt Vera offered.

My father shot her a scathing look. "Nothing wrong with online, Vera. My group and I chat every day."

Knock me over with a feather. I needed to spend more time with my father and get to know him—*really* know him. After my mother died, he and I had a falling out, which occurred because my husband died a couple of weeks before, and I was pretty much a loony tune. I couldn't converse. I hid under the covers. I was not a supportive daughter. Three months of intense therapy guided me back to semi-normal. Moving home to Crystal Cove helped with the rest.

"I trade chapters with my group," my father went on. "A few have advised me that it takes time to hear back from an editor. Sometimes a year or more. Which makes me wonder . . ." He drummed the counter with his fingertips. "What if Alison held on to someone's work for a lengthy time, only to finally pass on it, which upset the author?"

"That certainly broadens the suspect pool," Aunt Vera said.

"Or maybe an author didn't like the way she was editing his or her work," my father proposed. "Alison edited the manuscripts, correct?"

"That is the main reason Coco is a suspect," I said. "Alison was stabbed in Coco's house with Coco's scissors. A number of Coco's recipes were open on Alison's computer."

"A killer could have brought up the files to frame her." My father jabbed the tube of paper toward me to make his point. "I'd tell Cinnamon your theories if I were you."

"My—" I cocked my head. "Dad, they're your theories. Why don't you tell her?"

"And incur her wrath for sticking my nose in where it doesn't belong? Not on a bet." My father laughed heartily. Usually he had a reserved laugh closer to a snicker. Perhaps Lola, with her lusty laugh, was rubbing off on him. Yay! "Please, if you see any of Alison's family, pay my respects. Now"—he cleared his throat and struck a pose—"I'll be off to work, mateys."

"Not you, too, with the pirate-ese," Aunt Vera said.

"Aye, 'tis Pirate Week, sister. I've got my . . . me . . . yes, *me* chores mapped out." My father unfurled the tube of paper he was holding. It looked like a pirate's map. X marked the spot at the rear of the shop. "I'll start with the squeaky door." He stopped chortling as he disappeared through the break in the drapes and muttered under his breath, "What is this world coming to?"

"Jenna, dear." Aunt Vera ambled from behind the counter. "Even if your father won't, I am going to talk to Cinnamon. While I'm gone, why don't you spruce up the window display?"

"Is something wrong with it?"

"I'd like the sign reading *Children's Pirate Day* to be bigger. I've had a few parents calling about the event, but not as many as I expected. It is being held tomorrow, after all." She wiggled her fingers in the direction of the display. "And take a look at the fresh load of books we received in this morning's shipment. *Pirate Boy* and *Pirate Pete* seem awfully cute. The artwork in both is terrific. They'd be charming in the display. Perhaps add a couple more chocolate cookbooks, too."

I winked at her. "I'm on it." My aunt had brought me in to be the marketing brain of the operation, but she had been adding her two cents more often. "By the way, did you see the *Luscious Chocolate Desserts* cookbook?"

"I did."

"Did you peek inside?"

"How could I resist? You know what a fool I am for a

good layer cake." Aunt Vera gathered her purse, left her
turban, and headed to the exit. She paused short of the door.
"Silly me. I almost forgot." She dug into her purse and pulled
out bags of foil-wrapped chocolate coins. "I picked these up
yesterday." She flung them at me. "Yo ho!"

I caught them and flashed on last night's thievery. "Aunt
Vera, wait. Have you heard anything from the mayor about
the missing pot of doubloons?"

"Not a word. The playhouse people are quite distraught."
The Theater on The Pier had put the pot of doubloons on
display. "But don't worry your head about it. Mayor Zeller
will set things right. I'm off."

She exited, and Tito Martinez swaggered into the shop,
looking tanned and sporty in a fedora, plaid jacket, pale
yellow shirt, and jeans. I was surprised he wasn't wearing
pirate gear. Given his flair for the dramatic, he seemed like
a perfect candidate.

Tito stopped next to the vintage table and whipped off
his fedora. "*Hola*, Jenna. Forgive me for listening in, but I
know something about the missing pot."

"I heard the photographs of the pot on Mrs. McCartney's
porch went viral online."

"*Sí. Sí.*" Tito scanned the area, obviously on the hunt for
Bailey. "There have been two other sightings. One on the front
steps of the fire station."

"The fire station?"

"This time the note read: *Help!*"

"Did the thief create the note using cutout letters from
magazines?"

Tito nodded. "He also erected a fake blaze using something that looked like opaque orange crinkly paper. Quite
elaborate."

"And the third sighting?" I asked.

"The pot was photographed hanging from a rooftop. Think
of it. Three sightings, all in the same night. What a feat."

What a fiasco, I thought.

"I'm surprised the thief isn't advertising a link to a website or something," Tito added. "It's a great publicity stunt."

"Publicity for what? Don't you believe it's a malicious act?"

Tito snorted. "No way. This is performance art." He fanned the air with his fedora. "Whoever is doing it is trying to get attention." He tapped his temple. "I've got a sense for this kind of news."

"I think whoever did it should be arrested."

"Bah." Tito chuckled. "Harmless fun. Where's Bailey?"

"She's not here yet."

"When do you expect her?"

"I'm not sure." I glanced at the telephone by the counter, willing Bailey to call and bring me up-to-date. As if sensing my distress, Tigger bounded from his spot beneath the children's craft table and leaped onto the stool by the cash register and then onto the counter. He stared at the telephone. No jangle.

"What is going on?" Tito asked. "I've been calling her. I've texted her. She's not responding."

"There's been another murder in town."

"No!"

"Alison Foodie was killed."

"Where?"

"At Coco Chastain's house."

"When?" Tito glanced at the door, the story about the doubloons long forgotten. I could tell he wanted to hightail it out of the shop to scoop the story. "How?"

I hadn't signed any confidentiality agreements with the police. I told him what I had revealed to my aunt and father.

"The shears certainly make a statement," Tito said. "Did an angry boyfriend show up?"

"Alison didn't have a boyfriend."

"An ex?"

"I think Alison lacked a social life. Her career meant everything to her."

"Did she have enemies in business?"

"I doubt it. She was well respected. Besides, she didn't live in Crystal Cove. Why would an enemy follow her here? Why not kill her in San Francisco?"

"Good point. Hey, what about her brother? Maybe he

thought his sister was domineering. You know, too in his face."
Tito demonstrated. He smelled like Juicy Fruit gum. "Maybe
he wanted to cut her out of his life." He jabbed his chest with
his thumb. "Words are my life. The act of cutting. That's what
matters. Trust me." He didn't wait for my agreement. He
donned his fedora and sped out of The Cookbook Nook.

His speculation when coupled with my father's theory
sent a shiver through me. Alison had been editing Coco's
material. Had Coco killed Alison for making cuts to her manuscript?

No matter what, Coco needed a verifiable alibi. I hoped
my aunt could convince Cinnamon that she saw Coco at
Nature's Retreat during the time of the murder. If only Coco
would reveal the name of her paramour. The police would
keep the information confidential, wouldn't they?

A flash of color outside the shop caught my eye.

Chapter 7

NEIL, ALISON'S BROTHER, was charging upstairs to the second floor, leaping two steps at a time. His shoulders were hunched. He wore the same white shirt he'd worn the night before. It was rumpled, the tail loose, the hem smudged with dirt.

I hurried outside to catch up to him. "Neil," I called.

He turned. His eyes looked bloodshot. The usually ruddy color of his complexion was gone. His face appeared more flaccid than ever. His chest was heaving from exertion.

"I'm late," Neil said. "The boss will have my head if I'm not there in one minute."

"Won't he let you have the day off, considering the, um, circumstances?"

"Circumstances?" he echoed.

A pang of sorrow cut through me. Heck, didn't he know about his sister? I hated to be the first to break the news, but someone had to. I forged ahead. "Concerning Alison."

Neil lowered his chin, as if to study his shoes, and wagged his head. "Yeah, I heard she's dead. It's horrible, isn't it?"

Gack! If he knew what had happened, then why was he on his way to work? Was he a miserable, heartless creep?

"She was stabbed," he went on. "Some jerk broke in."

"No. That's not true. No one broke in."

Neil lifted his head and made eye contact. "How would you know?"

"Because I was there this morning. With the police. My friend Bailey—"

"Who works at your store?"

"Yes."

"She was at Vines last night."

"Right." I nodded. "With me. Anyway, Coco Chastain called her. Coco found Alison. She called Bailey, and then Bailey called me. Coco—" I heaved a sigh. "Coco said she never locks the doors. The killer walked right in, easy as pie. Coco also called your mother."

"Yeah, I know. Mom is the one who told me." Neil shifted feet. "It sucks."

I gawped at him. That was it? The full extent of his compassion was *it sucks*? I tamped down my own thoughts of murder.

Neil hitched his thumb toward upstairs. "I gotta go."

"To work?"

"Yeah."

I continued to stare, my heart beating in my chest, my hands balled into fists. It took all my reserve not to wallop him. "I'm sorry, but didn't you call Mr. Butler and tell him that your sister was—"

"Yeah," Neil said. "I did."

"And he told you to come to work?" That didn't seem like the Simon I knew, with an easy grin and easier manner.

"Not *him*, exactly."

"Who then?"

"His wife."

"Isn't she a personal trainer?"

"Yeah." Neil scruffed the back of his neck. "But I guess she's also half owner of Vines."

That was news to me.

"And time off? Today? This week?" Neil kicked the stair. "Nah. It's not happening. Pirate Week is drawing big-time crowds. We're short on staff."

I recalled Simon telling us last night that he was short a waiter, but that didn't warrant him or his wife being so callous. Maybe in the slower economy, the wine bistro simply couldn't afford to cut back. The notion caught me off guard. If something were to happen to Bailey or my aunt, I wasn't sure what I would do at The Cookbook Nook. I couldn't run the shop alone. Note to self: *Hire another assistant as backup.*

"The boss did say she'd let me off for the funeral." Neil twirled a finger and glanced upward. "Whoop-dee-doo."

"How's your mother holding up?"

"A mess. Crying in fits and starts and sleeping, which is nothing new . . . the sleeping." He peeked at his watch. "Look, I really have to run."

I reached for him. "Neil, wait, one question."

"Can't. Wine tasting waits for no man." He wrested from my grasp and trotted upstairs.

Anger swelled within me a second time. Was he colder than a crypt or simply operating on autopilot? For someone who should be grieving, he was certainly being a diligent employee. And a little glib. I tried to cut him some slack. Men could be so different from women.

Pivoting to return to the shop, I caught sight of Simon Butler exiting his BMW at the far end of the lot. He loped toward me. His hair was windblown, his cheeks sunburned. A pair of binoculars bounced on his chest.

I met him beneath the overhang. "Did you hear what happened to Alison Foodie?"

Simon nodded dolefully. His face contorted into a grimace. "What a tragedy." He nudged his round-shaped glasses upward on his nose. "Neil called my wife, who called me. I heard Alison was stabbed. What a shame. You were close, right?"

"Not close, but we were friendly."

"Either way, I'm sorry for your loss. What a curveball that's going to throw into her business."

I didn't blame him for thinking of that; his and many other authors' dreams of being published would be put on hold. I said, "Her brother Neil just ran upstairs to start work. He seemed quite brittle. I hope you'll give him some time off to grieve."

Simon frowned. "Neil said he didn't need time. I can't fault him. As I hinted last night, Alison and he weren't close. Besides, don't let Neil with his jovial demeanor snow you. He's a tough cookie."

Harsher words than those were cycling through my mind. Neil was heartless and obtuse and . . .

I pointed at the binoculars. "Have you been whale watching?"

"Actually, bird-watching. I go to the beach at this time of year to catch sight of black oystercatchers."

"Never heard of them."

"They are by far one of the narrowest ranges of birds in the world, breeding only from Alaska to Baja California, and only in winter." Simon's face grew animated. "They stay remarkably close to the shoreline, not venturing out farther than a few hundred meters. They're often joined by black turnstones and surfbirds."

I would never understand bird-watching. I could sit still for a few minutes occasionally, but spending hours observing birds as they flitted from limb to limb or traipsed across the fields or stretches of sand? Nope. Not for me. I needed my downtime to be more active, or I wanted my nose to be buried in a book.

Simon added, "I also had the pleasure of admiring the pirate ship in the harbor. Have you seen it?" He was referring to a multiple-sailed vessel that was offering sunset cruises.

"I have."

"What a beauty. Wow, I love this town. There are so many things to do."

I adored Crystal Cove, too, except when a crime occurred.

"I'd better get a move on." Holding the binoculars steady so they wouldn't whack his chest, Simon jogged upstairs.

I returned to the shop and dealt with a handful of custom-

ers, many asking about cookbooks that included a pirate
theme. I steered them toward a rare find called *Pirate's Pan-
try: Treasured Recipes of Southwest Louisiana* by the Junior
League of Lake Charles. Compiled in the second half of the
last century, it was a one-stop cookbook, with recipes developed from every part of the melting pot of cultures that made
Louisiana distinctive. Simplistic in style, it included crude
drawings of swords, treasure maps, and more. It offered a ton
of gumbo recipes. I adored gumbo.

Mid-morning, as a pair of customers exited the shop,
Bailey stormed in. She looked decent. Her makeup was fresh
and hair combed. But emotions were churning inside her.
Her eyes were pinpoints of angst. Her gaze flicked right and
left. A hint of perspiration coated her upper lip. The customers peeked worriedly at me; I waved for them to move on. I
could handle my usually bubbly assistant.

"How did it go with Coco?" I asked.

"She's been released on her own recognizance, but Chief
Pritchett . . ." Bailey plucked at the cuticles on her left hand
then screwed up her mouth. "I think she's got a bug up her
you know what for some reason."

"Why do you say that?"

"She's riding Coco hard." Bailey mimed cracking the whip.
"She asked Coco the same questions over and over, putting a
twist on each one, as if to catch Coco in a lie. And yet—"

I gripped her hand to calm her.

Bailey pulled free and began to pace. "I get the distinct
feeling Cinnamon didn't care for Alison Foodie."

"Why would you say that?"

"It's the way Cinnamon says Alison's name. It comes out
as a hiss, and"—Bailey paced between the stockroom and
the counter—"it's as if she's rushing things."

Tigger, who had been hiding from the moment Bailey
marched into the shop, zipped into view and meowed his
concern.

I whispered, "It's okay, Tig-Tig," and then said, "Go on,
Bailey."

"It's as if Cinnamon wants to throw someone—anyone,

namely Coco—in jail, pronto, so she can wrap this sucker up and put the case as far behind her as possible." Bailey stopped pacing and whirled around on the heels of her wedged sandals. "Do you think Alison and Cinnamon knew each other?"

"They did." I recalled Cinnamon answering *yes* when I'd asked the question at the crime scene. One word. Clipped off. No elaboration. "Maybe they went to school together. They were about the same age." What was their history? Was Bailey right to be concerned about a bias on Cinnamon's part?

Bailey beat a fist into her palm. "If only I hadn't put Alison and Coco together. If only I hadn't asked them to come to town for the book club event."

"This is not your fault." I touched her shoulder. "Stop it. Alison is not dead because of you." *Or my karma*, I reminded myself. "And Coco didn't do it."

"Are you sure?"

I wasn't certain about anything, but I wasn't about to fan the fire. "Coco did not kill Alison."

Bailey plopped into one of the overstuffed reading chairs. "If only Alison hadn't stayed at Coco's. She could just as easily have stayed at her mom's house or a nice hotel. Her company makes a good deal of money."

"The killer would have found her at either."

Bailey sighed. "So you don't think this was random?"

"No." I thought about what Bailey had said; Foodie Publishing was a thriving business. I recalled Neil racing upstairs exhibiting virtually no remorse for the death of his sister. "Bailey, do you know who will run Foodie Publishing now that Alison is dead? Will it be sold, or will it fold?"

"I don't have a clue."

"Alison wasn't married. She had no kids. Could her brother be her heir?"

"I doubt it. She wasn't very complimentary about Neil. He's not serious, a kidder. Didn't you hear Simon infer last night at Vines that there was no love lost?"

"If Alison did put him in her will, he would inherit the business. There's motive."

"Wow." Bailey pitched forward and balanced on the edge of the chair.

I told her about my encounter with Neil a few minutes ago. "He was glib, like you say, and unmoved."

"Neil is always like that." Bailey batted the air. "Often sarcastic and quick with a joke. Nothing ever fazes him. And yet . . ." She wagged her head. "I can't imagine he'd want to run the business. He doesn't seem smart enough. What we really need to know," Bailey went on, "is whether the business could be sold at a profit. If Alison did include Neil in her will, he could make off like a bandit."

Tigger scampered to her and nudged her hand with his head. Bailey scrubbed his ears. "Hi, fella. Thanks for the hugs. I need a pet just like you."

"Speaking of pets," I said, "Tito was just here."

Bailey scowled. "That wasn't nice."

"He's texting you and calling you all the time, and he's following you around like a lapdog. Does that make you happy?"

She smiled, albeit the smile was bittersweet. "It doesn't make me unhappy. I sort of like being fawned over. No man has ever done that for me before. Did you tell him where I was?"

I nodded. "But he got wind of the murder and shot out of here like a dog hot on the scent of a fox."

"A reporter's job is to write about the scuttlebutt." Bailey scanned the shop. "Where's your aunt?"

"Wow." I smacked my thigh. "I almost forgot to tell you. Aunt Vera saw Coco at Nature's Retreat last night around eleven."

"That's wonderful." Bailey hopped to her feet. "She can establish Coco's alibi."

"Exactly. She went to the precinct to talk to Cinnamon."

Bailey whacked my arm. "Coco is innocent. I knew it."

"Has Coco told Cinnamon with whom she spent the night?"

Bailey frowned. "Nope. Isn't that crazy? She said she wouldn't ruin his life just because hers was ruined."

"So he is married."

"That's my impression." Bailey squeezed my arm. "But,

now, she shouldn't need to blab, since your aunt can corroborate her whereabouts."

"I suppose."

"No matter what, we'll keep after Cinnamon and make sure she finds Alison's killer, right?"

"Absolutely."

Bailey began to pace again. "I'm starved. Has Katie put any treats out?"

As if on cue, Katie strode down the breezeway connecting The Cookbook Nook to the café. Her toque stood tall on her head. Her chef's coat was spanking white and looked freshly pressed. She was carrying a tray of mini chocolate muffins.

"Perfect timing," Bailey said. "What do you have?"

"Chocolate banana muffins," Katie replied. "Easy to make. Delicious to eat. The recipe is from Coco's first cookbook."

"Perfect. I could use a quick dose of sugar." I downed two. So did Bailey.

"I'm still hungry," Bailey mumbled through a mouthful of food. "Jenna, how about a late breakfast at Mum's the Word?" The Word, which was the abbreviated name for the diner, was known for its comfort food.

I said, "We can go when Aunt Vera returns."

Katie set the tray on the counter and planted her hands on her hips. "What's wrong with eating at the Nook Café?"

Bailey said, "We'll get more gossip if we're not on our own turf."

"Gossip about what?"

Bailey eyed me. "You haven't told her?"

"This is the first I've seen her."

Bailey filled Katie in about Alison's murder.

Tears sprang to Katie's eyes. "I'm so sorry. I really liked her. I didn't know her well, of course, but . . ." She dabbed her eyes with the sleeve of her coat. "Shoot. I'm so horrible."

"Why?" I asked.

"I . . ." Katie faltered.

"Speak," I ordered.

"I was considering sending Alison a cookbook idea. Now . . ." Katie covered her mouth. Through split fingers, she said, "You must think I'm a monster for thinking about *me* at a time like this."

"Of course we don't." I put my hand on her shoulder. "You've got dreams like everyone else. It's normal."

"What can I do to help? Oh, I know." Katie snapped her fingers. "Alison's family will need food. I'll make up some lasagna and some fresh-baked bread."

"There's only her mother and brother," I said.

"Even more reason to show up with a meal." Katie grabbed the tray of goodies and headed back to the café. Over her shoulder she said, "Two people often find a reason to ignore food altogether. They'll starve if they do. I'll make a couple of small portions of lasagna. Pasta . . . it's good for the soul."

"Ingrid is staying with them, too," Bailey called after her.

Ingrid. I wondered what her next move would be. Would she stay in town for the duration of the investigation, or would she return to San Francisco to look for a new job?

Thinking of the tight-toothed copyeditor made me once again ponder the future of Foodie Publishing. Would the company close its doors for good, or would it go up for sale? Had Alison put a plan in place, in the event of her death?

Chapter 8

NO MATTER HOW hungry Bailey and I were, we had to wait until Aunt Vera returned before we could leave the shop. Granted, my father was still in the stockroom working on the squeaky door. He could stop what he was doing, and he would be fine working the register, but he didn't know the merchandise in the shop, and Fridays could be a zoo at The Cookbook Nook. Typically, everyone came in at the last minute in desperate need of something special.

Close to noon, Gran, the eldest member of the Chocolate Cookbook Club, bustled into the store, a mischievous grin on her weathered face. She was fast becoming one of my favorite customers. I couldn't remember a visit where she didn't buy at least two items. At the cookbook club event, she had purchased three of Coco's books, one for each of her daughters-in-law. *Ka-ching*, as Bailey would say.

"Jenna!" Gran wriggled her arm. The silver silhouettes of grandchildren on her charm bracelet jangled.

"Hello. It's so good to see you. I set aside a book for you."

"Wonderful. I heard you have another book that I must

have." Gran pulled a list from her Prada clutch and read, *"The Chocolate Diaries."*

The full title was *The Chocolate Diaries: Secrets for a Sweeter Journey on the Rocky Road of Life*, a nonfiction book that we had brought in recently. Although it was written a few years ago, the true-life stories, often humorous, were au courant. Dozens of women shared tactics about how to achieve a more satisfying life.

"My daughter-in-law suggested it." Gran had moved to town recently. I remembered her first visit with her grandchildren in tow, each chiding her about how many boxes of cookbooks she had brought along in her move. Not only did she collect shawls, she was an avid church bazaar cookbook collector. She claimed she had at least one from every state.

"Which daughter-in-law?" I asked.

"Why, the one I'm living with, silly." Gran winked. "I'm sure there's one particular story she'll want me to read. Possibly about being *less* on the go. She wants me to slow down. Can you imagine? Me?"

She purchased her book and hurried out the way she had raced in. *Never a moment to lose*, I'd heard her say on one occasion.

Bailey sidled up to me. Her stomach grumbled in protest. "It's nearly twelve o'clock. When will your—"

Aunt Vera rushed into the shop. She looked quite ragged. Strands of hair flapped about her face. Her forehead was pinched.

Bailey and I rushed to her.

"It's not good news," Aunt Vera said. "Cinnamon. *Pfft.* That girl." She swatted the air. "She simply refuses to believe that my eyewitness account clears Coco."

Bailey glowered at me. "I warned you."

I hushed her. "Aunt Vera. Go on. Why was Cinnamon skeptical?"

"She asked if I sat outside the room and stared at the door until dawn." Aunt Vera grumbled. "Of course, I didn't, so she said Coco could have slipped into and out of the room without anyone noticing. Nature's Retreat has rear stairs and a path through the gardens. I'm afraid our chief of police will need more corroboration of Coco's whereabouts."

"From Coco's lover."

"Yes."

"And he hasn't come forward?"

"Not to my knowledge. Where's your father?"

"Still in the stockroom."

"He hasn't fixed the telephone line yet?"

"I keep hearing the squeaky door opening and closing," I said. "Bailey and I need to eat lunch. Are you okay running the shop alone?"

"Absolutely. It'll take my mind off—" Aunt Vera flitted a hand again and muttered, "*That girl.* Where are you going?"

"The Word."

"Take flyers about tomorrow's event." My aunt strode through the drapes into the stockroom. "Cary . . ."

I grabbed a batch of flyers, and Bailey and I drove off in my VW. The pirate décor that seemed to have sprung up overnight on Buena Vista Boulevard was fun and frivolous. Flags embellished with skeletons hung from the lampposts. Cutouts of ships or hook hands or tricorn hats adorned the windows of the shops and restaurants.

Along the coast, just short of The Pier, we heard a *boom!*

I tapped the brake. "What was that?"

Bailey pointed toward the bay. "Cannon fire."

An old-fashioned wooden ship with a huge white mainsail adorned with skull and crossbones was anchored in the bay. A string of life rafts looped around the ship. People in pirate outfits were climbing out of the rafts and boarding the vessel. In the last raft stood a bride in a frothy white gown, its train being held up by four young children. Apparently a wedding was kicking into high gear. Fun!

Minutes later, I halted at the entrance to the parking area at The Pier. A gigantic sign read: *Pirates Only, All Others Will Walk the Plank.*

"Will we be ousted for not wearing costumes?" I asked.

"No," Bailey said. "Park."

"Are you sure?"

"Positive. Look out the window."

Throngs of people were making their way across the lot. Only half of them were dressed as pirates.

I parked and pulled the Children's Pirate Day flyers from my tote bag and offered half to Bailey. "Start handing these out."

As we followed the crowd, Bailey said, "Look at everyone, having fun without a care in the world."

"Don't begrudge them their enjoyment. Not everyone knows about the murder." I didn't add, *Nor will they be affected.* Not like us. Keeping to our plan, I said, "What should we ask at Mum's the Word?"

"Did anyone see Coco at Nature's Retreat after your aunt did?" Bailey shoved a flyer into the hands of a mom pushing a stroller.

"Good." I offered a flyer to a father of two.

"Maybe we should ask if someone can identify Coco's lover."

"How about if we ask if anyone has talked about motive for why Alison was murdered?"

"Jenna, stop!" Bailey pointed.

Outside Bait and Switch Fishing and Sport Supply Store, which was a warehouse-sized building at the land's end of The Pier, stood a thirty-foot temporary wall. Rubbery, multicolored, rock-shaped knobs were attached to the wall. Two people hooked into orange harnesses were scaling the wall while a pair of belayers attended to them from below, anchoring ropes that were looped through pulleys. People had queued up behind a line divider rope to wait for a turn. My boyfriend, Rhett, in a flashy blue-and-red pirate costume, directed the next set of climbers to get fitted up.

"We've got to do this," Bailey said.

"You said you were hungry enough to eat two potpies." The potpie at The Word was one of the best I'd ever eaten. The flaky pastry crust was made with cheddar cheese. Yum.

"Look at all those people in line. They're bound to have gossip." Bailey nudged my arm. "C'mon. Exercise will clear our minds and do us good."

Unless I pulled a hamstring. I hadn't stretched this morning. My muscles felt stiff.

"You're in wedge sandals," I protested. "And I forgot to lug along a pair of tennis shoes, in case you hadn't noticed."

"We'll go barefoot. Lots of people are doing that." Bailey prodded me forward. One thing I'd learned over the years: when my pal set her mind on something, she could not be put off. Don't ask me about the time she decided to enter a hot dog eating contest. Not pretty.

The moment we joined the line, Bailey asked the couple in front of us a question. The woman paled. She hadn't heard that there was a murder. Great. Now we were the bearers of bad news. I warned Bailey off our plan, but she wouldn't be deterred. The people behind us were more stalwart. They hadn't been anywhere near Nature's Retreat last night, and they hadn't been in the vicinity of Fisherman's Village after the book club disbanded, so they couldn't offer any insight.

Near the front of the line, Rhett joined us. He pecked me on the cheek. "What a pleasant surprise. Feeling daring?"

"I think we're both in need of a mental break." I explained why.

"Wow. I hadn't heard. I'm so sorry. I remember when Alison used to come to The Grotto with her mother." He offered a comforting smile. "Between you and me, I think they were sizing up the food and trying to determine what could or couldn't be duplicated at her mother's restaurant." Alison's mother used to run a thriving restaurant, which, come to think of it, was called Pirate Cove in honor of their colorful Foodie family lineage. Rhett added, "Alison had a special talent for picking out the different flavors." He shook his head. "What a shame."

"What's even worse," Bailey said, "Chief Pritchett and her posse might not catch the killer."

Rhett raised an eyebrow. "Why do you say that?"

"I don't think she's an Alison Foodie fan." Bailey cocked

a hip. "Say, Rhett, you were tight with Cinnamon once. Do you know why she would have anything against Alison?"

Rhett's mouth thinned. He and Cinnamon had dated for a nanosecond before the fire at The Grotto. Let's just say, the investigation into the arson soured their relationship.

"You do," Bailey said. "Spill."

Rhett tucked his hands beneath his armpits. "Cinnamon and Alison were friends in high school."

"Friends?" I said. "Really? They couldn't seem more different." In high school, Cinnamon had been a wild child—her term. She hung out with a group of rough kids until my father, at my mother's insistence, stepped in and became her mentor. With his guidance, she turned her life around.

"Alison was one of the pack," Rhett said.

"Really? The pack?" Over coffee last month, Cinnamon revealed a bit about the *pack* to me. The group had consisted of six girls. All wore black. All smoked and drank. They pranked other kids. By junior year of high school, one wound up in juvenile detention, one died in a fatal car crash, and one ended up pregnant. Cinnamon hadn't told me their names; she hadn't kept touch with any of them.

"That means Alison had tattoos just like Cinnamon," I said.

Bailey gawped. "Cinnamon has tattoos?"

Rhett grinned. "Yes, but being a gentleman, I won't say where they're located."

"I'll pry it out of him," I promised.

"No, you won't. Loose lips sink ships." Rhett signaled for us to move ahead.

When we came to another standstill, I said, "Rhett, what happened between Cinnamon and Alison?"

"I don't have the full story. Let's just say that when Cinnamon took the road less traveled, Alison didn't want to go along. Words were exchanged that neither could retract. They had a knock-down, drag-out battle. Alison lost a tooth; Cinnamon had to chop off her hair. Glue was involved. Time passed, and ultimately, Alison ditched the old life, went to college, found her calling, and moved to the City." The City was a casual term for San Francisco. "The rest is history."

Bailey said, "So because of some stupid teenage stuff, Cinnamon won't do everything she can to find Alison's killer?"

Rhett shook his head. "I didn't say that."

"But you implied it."

"She's a good cop—"

"Who can occasionally be biased."

"She and I . . ." Rhett hesitated. "That was different, Bailey. She had evidence that she thought proved me guilty. We were involved; it got complicated. It's water under the bridge." Ever since Cinnamon had absolved Rhett, they were on better terms. It did my heart proud that I'd had a hand in the outcome. "Jenna, back me up," Rhett continued. "You know Cinnamon takes great pride in bringing down bad guys." He chucked my chin. "Just like you." He drew his hand along my shoulder and down my arm. A shiver of desire coursed through me. If only I could bottle that feeling and sell it.

"He's right," I murmured.

"I'm just saying," Rhett went on, "trust Cinnamon to do the proper thing."

An attendant called us forward as the climbers ahead of us were wriggling out of their harnesses.

Rhett unlatched the entry cord and gestured for us to move ahead.

The two belayers reset the harnesses on the ground and asked Bailey and me to step into the leg loops. We did as told, raised the harnesses, tightened our waist cinches and then adjusted the leg loops.

"Go," the belayers ordered, one manning Bailey's ropes and the other manning mine.

Gripping a red knob, I pulled upward. Next, I grasped a blue one. I slung my right foot onto a yellow knob then hoisted myself higher and swung my left foot onto a green one.

"Ugh." Bailey grunted, keeping pace with me. "This is harder than it looks."

"Use your core muscles."

"I don't have core muscles."

She was kidding, of course. Bailey, when not working at

the shop, exercised. She kayaked, swam, and bicycled. For a bitty thing, she was mighty strong.

Halfway up the wall, Bailey glanced at the costumed crowd below. "Why do you think people romanticize pirates?"

I told her about a commercial campaign we did at Taylor & Squibb. It was for Habañero Spice, a product from the Caribbean, and involved a horde of Johnny Depp look-alike pirates. "My boss said that he thought people glamorized pirates because pirates lived by their own rules. People forget about the violence pirates did and still do."

"Like the Robin Hood effect?"

"Sort of. Robin really did do good deeds for others. He stole from the rich and gave to the poor. But pirates, not so much. They kept it all."

"You mean they're not all hunky with hearts of gold?"

I snorted. "*Not!*"

"Or darling, like Jake and the Never Land Pirates?"

"Not a chance."

AFTER OUR CLIMB, the two of us hustled to The Word. We sat at the counter, hoping Rosie, a chatty African American waitress with a purple-tinged Afro hairstyle and vibrant purple eyes, would have good information to impart, but she didn't. In fact, she hadn't heard a thing about Alison's murder. She was shocked to learn Coco was a suspect.

"Coco Chastain cooks cheery chocolates," Rosie chirped. She wasn't making fun; she was a fan of mnemonics—a memory enhancer. "If you ask me, she should have called her shop Coco's Candy. Would've made sense. Ah, Coco." Rosie shook her head. Her dangly purple earrings jingled. "I have to admit, that woman baffles me. See, I'm a big fan of Coco's chocolates, and I've visited the candy shop often, but she still doesn't know my name. In fact, she's pretty tight-lipped. Why is that?"

I bit back a smile. Perhaps Coco kept quiet because Rosie was a chatterbox and Coco didn't want to get swept up in a long conversation.

Rosie placed two sets of silverware rolled in napkins in front of Bailey and me. "I asked once about the secret ingredient in Coco's chocolate hearts. Mm-mm. They are deliciousness that I can't describe. But she wouldn't give me the slightest hint. Ha! Like I could ever hope to filch the recipe. I cannot improvise in the least. I need guidelines to cook. Which is why I'm here"—she indicated the counter—"and not there." She jerked a thumb toward the kitchen then handed us menus. "Anyway, Coco promised that the recipe, which is one of her grandmother's, would show up in an upcoming cookbook, but I have every single cookbook. Even her latest. She has a few books for sale at the candy store. But, uh-uh, the recipe is not there." She harrumphed.

"Maybe it'll be in her next one," I said.

"Rosie!" a customer called.

Rosie signaled that she was on her way.

"One more thing before you go," I said. "Would you happen to know the identity of Coco's, um, boyfriend?"

"Boyfriend? Honey, I don't think she has one. I haven't seen her with a soul in the longest time. She comes in here alone, and she's always solo in the shop, except for that little assistant she has." Rosie beat a fingertip on her chin. "You know, she was engaged once to a computer geek. Is that who you mean? Goggly eyes, messy hair. He moved to Seattle with some skinny minny." A gusty laugh burst from her lips. "Lord, that girl was a sorry sight. Bone thin. I blame that on the mother. Don't they teach their daughters that curves are in?" Rosie chortled again. "Sorry I couldn't help you more."

Chapter 9

WHEN BAILEY AND I returned to The Cookbook Nook,
I propped the front door open with a gravel-stuffed
cat to let air into the place. Seconds later, I caught the aroma
of something delicious.

"Katie?" I called. Despite the fact that I'd just downed
an entire potpie, my stomach rumbled.

I hustled to Katie, who was in the breezeway setting goodies on a three-tiered crystal caddy.

"Ahoy! You caught me." Katie grinned. "These are my
first attempt at white chocolate macaroons. Try one. They're
light."

Unable to resist, I nabbed a cookie and bit into it. "Yum!"
They were melt-in-your-mouth heaven. I polished off the
rest of the cookie and resisted taking another.

"What did you find out at the diner?" she asked.

"Nothing that helps." I filled her in.

"What if you track down other friends of Coco's? Maybe
they'll know who her lover is."

"Good thought," I replied, except I didn't know Coco's
other friends. Did they live in Crystal Cove? Did they frequent

Sweet Sensations? Funny how you could be friends with someone for years and not know any of the others who spent time with her.

Out the window, I caught sight of Cinnamon Pritchett exiting her mother's beading shop. Her uniform was crisp and her hat was on straight, but her face was pinched and her movements choppy. The pre-dawn events came swooshing at me: seeing Alison dead at her computer; spotting the scissors in her back; watching Coco and Ingrid go at it.

Pinpoints of angst nicked my eyelids. Why was Cinnamon here? Was something wrong?

Abandoning my urge to take another sweet, I hurried outside. Cinnamon was a few feet from her cruiser. My footsteps must have startled her. She spun around, hand on the butt of her gun.

I reeled back. "Is everything okay?"

Cinnamon lowered her hand and faltered. I thought her knees might give way. I reached to steady her.

She broke free and held up both hands. "I'm okay. It's my mother. She's been feeling a little off balance lately. I think she has an inner ear infection. You know, Ménière's disease. That's where the fluid is out of whack. It makes you feel like you've got vertigo. Mom"—Cinnamon sighed, which conveyed all her pent-up frustration—"won't see a doctor, so I came by to teach her some exercises I learned in rehab therapy."

I gawked at her. "You were in rehab?"

Cinnamon offered a reproachful look. "Not that kind of rehab, you goose. I had vertigo a few years ago. It was due to crystals in my ear. It made me so sick, I had to sleep all the time. My vestibular rehabilitation therapist taught me the Epley maneuver, a way to clear the crystals, which made all the difference in the world." She glanced over her shoulder at Beaders of Paradise. "I came by to teach Mom the moves, but in her cramped stockroom, it wasn't all that easy." She let loose with a raspy laugh. "With her, it probably wouldn't be easy anyplace. I think she's out of whack because she's always bending her head forward to do her work. Her eyes aren't what they used to be, either, but don't tell her I said that."

"Care to come in for a cup of tea and a snack? Katie just put out white chocolate macaroons."

"Sounds great."

We strolled into the shop. I fetched two cups of tea and treats for both of us, and we settled into the chairs at the vintage kitchen table. Bailey, who was pitching a culinary mystery about a Key West food critic to a customer, sent me a pointed look. I nodded, silently assuring her that I would question Cinnamon about everything. In due time.

While Cinnamon downed half of her tea and ate one of the goodies, I toyed with the basket of fruit jigsaw puzzle, which was partially constructed. I grabbed some edge pieces and fitted together the upper right corner of the puzzle.

After a long moment, I said, "My aunt told me her testimony wasn't enough to clear Coco."

Cinnamon set her cup down on the saucer with a clank. "What I said was I needed further corroboration."

"You don't think Aunt Vera's reliable?"

"Don't put words in my mouth." Cinnamon started in on the puzzle, too. Fleetingly, she made eye contact with me. "You and I both know that I rarely accept one person's word. We are questioning staff that works at Nature's Retreat. Happy?"

I continued piecing together edges.

"Don't give me the silent treatment," Cinnamon snapped. "What do you want to say?" She pushed back her chair, as if ready to depart.

I leveled her with a glance. "We're friends."

"Right now, we're acquaintances." Her mouth twitched. Was she trying not to smile? "C'mon. Spit it out."

"You're sort of testy."

"My mother—" She shook her head. "Talk."

"You and Alison Foodie have a history."

"Says who?"

"Says an anonymous source."

"Now you're a reporter?"

"A concerned citizen."

"What if we do . . ." Cinnamon licked her lips and revised. ". . . *did* have a history?"

"Alison was one of the pack. You had a falling out. Why?"

"None of your business." She pursed her lips then exhaled. "It was over a guy, of all things. We liked the same stupid jerk. Neither of us got him."

"You came to blows."

"We said some pretty nasty stuff to each other. She called me rough around the edges. I called her a loser. I wish I could take it all back."

"Then do the right thing and find her killer."

"Whoa!" Cinnamon bounded to her feet. "Do you think I'm slacking off?"

I leaped to my feet, too. My thighs bumped the table. Not smart. "No. I didn't say that. But I do think you might be rushing to conclusions."

"About Coco Chastain."

"You don't want to make a hasty decision. Personal reasons can make us do that."

Cinnamon jammed her hands into her pockets. She assessed me like prey. "You're referring to my relationship with Rhett."

I kept mute. A long silence fell between us.

Cinnamon broke it. "Rhett was the one who told you about me and Alison. Don't deny it. I'm not dense." She pulled her hands free of the pockets. "Serves me right. That's what I get for revealing my past to anyone." Her mouth curled up on one side. "Look, I know you're snooping around, trying to figure out who the killer is."

"I don't snoop."

"Yes, you do. It comes naturally to you. You're good with people, and you care about them."

"That's true."

"You think I don't care."

"I never said—"

Cinnamon held up a warning hand. "I also know you get people to talk. You have a knack."

Not knowing where she was going with this line of—what was it? not an inquiry—I waited for her to continue.

"So here's where we meet on common ground," Cinnamon said. "No matter how much it irks me—and you know it irks me because I'm certain you won't stop investigating—promise me that you'll share whatever you learn."

I was thunderstruck. "You bet." I saluted.

Cinnamon's tough cop act melted away; she actually smiled. "This does not mean I've deputized you."

"I know."

"You are not official."

"Got it."

"But locals gossip. Listen and report back to me."

"Will do. By the way, do you have a time of death?"

"Sometime between eleven P.M. and one A.M."

"When Coco was otherwise engaged."

Cinnamon crinkled her nose, as if weighing her decision. "FYI, I'm doing my job. I've been checking out Foodie Publishing, its authors, its business partners, and any prospective buyers."

"I didn't think Alison had any partners."

"I said *prospective*." Cinnamon reached into her pocket and pulled out her cell phone. A text message was displayed on the screen. From my angle, I couldn't make out the words. Cinnamon caught me trying to sneak a peek. She frowned and drew the cell phone closer.

At the same time, the front door to the shop opened and Coco scuttled inside. She was rummaging in her clutch purse, head down. When she looked up and realized I was with Cinnamon, she drew back. "Oh!" Her cheeks flamed red, a stark contrast to the pink dress and bolero-style pink cardigan she was wearing. "It's you."

"It's me," Cinnamon replied.

Aunt Vera pressed through the drapes leading to the stockroom. "Coco, dear." Arms outstretched, my aunt rushed to Coco and gripped her by the hands. "I'm so glad you came to see me."

Coco looked from Cinnamon, to my aunt, and back at Cinnamon. She withdrew her hands. Her cheeks turned even redder.

Bailey rushed from behind the register. "What's going on?"

Cinnamon said, "It appears Miss Chastain has come to have her fortune told." She eyeballed Coco. "I doubt that will help you with your alibi." She couldn't hide the snarkiness in her tone.

"Chief," I cautioned.

Cinnamon flipped hair off her face. Defiantly. Real adult.

My aunt put a hand on Coco's shoulder. I'd seen her do so many times when a client needed calming. "Don't worry, dear. Your alibi is solid. I saw you at Nature's Retreat."

"Did you happen to see Vera, Miss Chastain?" Cinnamon asked.

"I don't know. No." Coco sputtered. "I didn't. But I was there."

"With . . . ?" Cinnamon said, leadingly.

Coco worried her hands together. "I can't say."

Bailey said, "Coco, c'mon. Spill."

"No."

Aunt Vera patted Coco's shoulder. "You need someone else to corroborate your alibi. The chief thinks I'm lying to protect you."

"I never said that, Vera." Cinnamon sighed. "I stated that you cannot confirm that Miss Chastain was in the suite for longer than a minute. There are no security cameras at that location. No footage."

"The police are interviewing staff," I offered.

"Which means they'll find out who paid for that room," Cinnamon said.

"So he'll have to talk," Bailey chirped.

Aunt Vera continued to caress Coco's shoulder. "Having another person establish your whereabouts would help right now. Isn't that correct, Chief Pritchett?"

Cinnamon said, "Indeed, it would."

Coco shifted feet. She tucked her clutch purse tightly beneath her arm. "I can't. I'm sorry."

Bailey cried, "Coco, he's not worth it!"

Keen to defuse the situation, I said, "Chief, what motive would Coco have to kill Alison? Alison was her publisher. She had a contract. Coco invited Alison to stay in her house." I went on like a prosecutor—an unseasoned prosecutor, not knowing the territory. "They were friends. They were—"

"Not as friendly as you might imagine," Cinnamon cut in. She eyed Coco. "I believe Miss Chastain and Miss Foodie were at odds."

Bailey said, "Are you making that determination because of the documents on Alison's computer?"

I flashed on the theory my father had proposed earlier. "Chief, the killer could have opened those to frame Coco. She—"

"Ladies." Cinnamon held up a hand. "Miss Chastain and Miss Foodie were at odds because Miss Chastain is in negotiations for her next cookbook with a different publisher."

"Is that true?" Bailey asked.

Coco blanched. "Foodie Publishing is a small independent group. To go big-time"—she splayed her hands—"I need a New York publisher."

"The contract is for more money," Cinnamon went on, "but it is also dependent on the sales of the upcoming book. If Miss Foodie was making changes to Miss Chastain's current project, changes that Miss Chastain felt might jeopardize future sales—"

"But, that's just it," Coco said, her voice pleading and strained. "She couldn't have been making changes."

"How can you be so sure?"

"Because Chocolate Bombs is a recipe from a cookbook that came out a year ago titled *Chocolate To Die For.*"

Chapter 10

CINNAMON MOVED TOWARD Coco. She retreated a step and glanced over her shoulder toward the front door of the shop.

"Why would Miss Foodie have that document open, Miss Chastain?" Cinnamon asked.

Coco peered a second time at the exit. Did she intend to flee? Cinnamon would nab her before she could.

Stand still, I silently urged Coco. *Hold your ground*.

"I don't know, Chief," Coco answered. "Because she was hungry?" She chewed her lip. "Please, don't you see, I didn't do it! I—" She shot from The Cookbook Nook as if she'd been propelled by a cannon.

Dang.

Aunt Vera ran after her. Bailey, too. Cinnamon didn't budge, which surprised me. I lasered her with a glare.

"What?" Cinnamon brushed her hands as if ridding herself of guilt. "Don't kill the messenger."

I sneered. "You couldn't have told me about the new contract earlier?"

"I just learned about it myself." Cinnamon held up her

cell phone to show me the recently received text message. It spelled out the contract issue.

In the parking lot, Coco had stopped running and was slumped against the driver's door of her Sweet Sensations–logoed SUV. Her face was buried in her hands. My aunt stood next to her, mouth moving. No doubt she was trying to reason with Coco to return inside.

I rapped Cinnamon on the arm and gestured to Coco. "Does she look like a guilty woman?"

"I don't know what she is, but she has more explaining to do." Cinnamon's cell phone rang. She answered and moved toward the exit. I followed. Her forehead drew down, forming a deeply etched number eleven between her eyebrows. "Where? When?" She ground her teeth together as she listened. "Aw, heck. On my way." She glanced at Coco and back at me. "Two pirates are going at it on The Pier. Blood has been drawn. I've got to go."

"What about Coco?"

"Do that voodoo you do. Talk to her. Get her to come to the precinct and spill her guts out of her own free will. Things will go much more smoothly. Promise."

"She didn't kill Alison."

"I need the name of her lover." Cinnamon hurried out of the shop and sped off in her cruiser.

Coco looked up as the cruiser hightailed it past her. She gazed at me. I beckoned her inside. She tucked her chin and nodded. Bailey and my aunt flanked her and guided her to the vintage kitchen table.

Aunt Vera released her and said, "Talk to the girls, dear. It will help much more than a tarot card reading right now." Aunt Vera pecked Coco's cheek, then said she had to pop into the café for a bowl of soup. She would return shortly.

Coco nestled into the chair Cinnamon had vacated. Bailey sat beside her. I took the chair opposite them. Tigger, wanting in on the action, scrambled beneath the table and nuzzled my ankles. I chucked his chin with my fingers. He turned in circles and finally settled on the floor.

Coco, like so many others, picked up a piece of the jigsaw

puzzle. She twisted it to the right and left, then discarded it. "It's hopeless."

"Let me help," I said.

"Not the puzzle, you goon," Bailey hissed.

"The whole affair," Coco said. "Alison." Tears welled in her eyes. "I didn't kill her. You have to believe me."

"Of course we do," Bailey said.

Did I? I just told Cinnamon that I did, but Coco's finger-prints were on the murder weapon. Alison was killed at Coco's house. *Stop it, Jenna. She's innocent.*

"Nature's Retreat," I said, encouraging her to elaborate. "You met a man."

She nodded once.

"A married man," I stated.

"Jenna, I can't—"

"He has to come forward."

"He . . . we . . ." She gulped in air. "He promised we . . ." More air.

I patted her back. "Breathe. Slowly."

"Did Jenna get it right?" Bailey asked. "Is he married?"

"He's going to divorce her," Coco whispered.

I knew it. "And he promised to marry you. Have I got that much right?"

Coco moved her head up and down. Tiny jerky movements.

"She doesn't get him like you do," Bailey said.

"Yes. Yes." Coco gazed at Bailey with appreciation and relief. Someone was *finally* understanding. "She bullies him."

I gasped. "Are you saying she beats him?"

"No. Not physically. But verbally. She's a shrew."

In addition to Bailey, whose relationship with a married man had ended badly, I had known a number of women who had engaged in affairs. Only one had worked out. But it wasn't my place to counsel Coco about matters of the heart.

"Yoo-hoo. Hello, ladies." Faith Fairchild, the twin of the woman who ran Home Sweet Home, one of my favorite homemade collectibles stores, hurried into the shop. Unlike her sister, who wore her long hair in a braid Faith wore her hair in spiky abandon, like she had run her fingers through it because that was all she had time for, and yet she'd had plenty of time to apply makeup. A heaping amount. "Help! I need a cookbook gift, pronto." Faith raced to the counter.

Bailey glanced at me. I hitched my chin for her to tend to Faith. I was the boss, after all, and she was the assistant. Bailey scowled and mimed: *Fill me in.* I blinked that I would.

After she left us, I said, "Coco, you've got to talk to your lover. Tell him to go to the precinct. The police will keep his testimony confidential. He has to give you a verifiable alibi."

Coco dug into her purse and pulled out a tissue. She dabbed her teary eyes. "I must look a fright."

"You look fine," I assured her.

"Oh." Coco hiccupped. "Poor Alison." She covered her mouth with the tissue, took a deep breath, and blew her nose. She wadded the tissue into her fist. "She didn't deserve to die, Jenna. Alison was a good lady. Smart. Independent. And a good publisher."

"You were ending your contract."

"That's not true. Not yet. My other publisher and I . . . we're discussing options. You know how it goes. Nothing is final until there's ink on the page. And Alison, well, I told her. She understood."

"She did?" I said. Coco was one of Alison's biggest sellers. She wouldn't have relished letting her go. "You two fought the night she died. At the book club event."

Coco tilted her head up, her gaze toward the ceiling as if she was trying to remember when they had battled. The memory dawned on her. "Oh, that. It was staged. We told you so."

"But the words you used. You argued about Alison taking too much creative control. Was there truth in that?"

Coco heaved a sigh. "Alison . . . what can I say? She could be dastardly when it came to editing, so, yes, there was some truth, but she was not cruel, and she wasn't indiscriminate. She was excellent. In the end, I trusted her choices."

I shifted in my chair. "Tell me about the new contract."

"I have so many more cookbooks in me. Alison"—Coco

crammed the used tissue into her purse and pulled out a new one—"could only publish so many. She was a one-woman operation."

"She had Ingrid."

Coco sniffed. "Ingrid. *Pfft*."

Okay. That summed up her opinion of the copyeditor's worth. "You told Alison about the contract. How did she react?"

"She wasn't thrilled, but she knew that I had to spread my wings. I have high hopes of becoming the next Ina Garten or Martha Stewart." Coco sighed. "Alison had dreams of growing her business. She wanted to expand. But—" Coco jammed her lips together.

"What?"

"Alison could be controlling. To the point of martyrdom. She could do it faster, better. Why hire someone else? She had the best eye for editing. She had the best eye for art. Honestly, that slows things down."

I thumped the tabletop. "Back to Ingrid. She said she was Alison's second-in-command. Is that true?"

"No, but if Alison was thinking about taking on a partner, then Ingrid, as much as I don't like her, would be a wise choice. She's very smart. Very detailed. But she and Alison were oil and water." Coco sat taller. "Hey, did I tell you I saw the two of them exchanging words after the cookbook club meeting?"

"No. Why didn't you bring that up when we went to Vines?" Better yet, why hadn't she mentioned it to the police? "What were they arguing about?"

"I only caught a snippet. They were standing near Alison's car. Ingrid was shaking a finger. She hissed—" Coco sniggered. "You've noticed she hisses, right? Those teeth of hers! Anyway, she said. 'You promised—' but Alison cut her off with, 'I did not . . .' I didn't listen to the rest. It wasn't my business. And I was in a hurry to catch up to you and Bailey." Coco glanced toward the parking lot. "You know, Pepper Pritchett might have overheard them. I saw her lingering about."

According to Cinnamon, her mother was under the weather. Would Pepper remember what she had heard?

"Alison and Ingrid argued on numerous other occasions," Coco went on. "One time, I heard Ingrid claim she could run the business better than Alison. Of course, Alison took umbrage. Ingrid said Alison should expand not only the number of cookbook authors she handled, but also the number of nonfiction authors, too. Like I said, Alison was against too much expansion. Taking on too many authors or titles could lessen the impact of the imprint and cripple a small independent publisher."

We'd had the same problem at Taylor & Squibb. If we took on too many new clients, other accounts might suffer. Employees would be overloaded. Creativity could flounder.

"On the other hand," Coco continued, "I know Alison has a number of books lined up for publication, so maybe she had taken Ingrid's suggestion to heart. Dash has a book on Alison's desk. Bailey's mother, too."

Not to mention Simon Butler and so many others, I mused. All of them would have wanted Alison alive to fulfill their dreams. Who had wanted her dead?

"Poor Alison," Coco repeated. "She had so much life ahead of her. If only . . ." She sighed.

"If only what?"

"If only she and the guy she was dating had gotten together."

"I thought you said she didn't have a boyfriend."

"She doesn't . . . *didn't*. Not currently, but she did. He died of a stroke about a month ago."

"Wow. That stinks."

Coco nodded in empathy. "He wasn't forty yet. Tragic. She was heartsick."

"Who was he?"

"She wouldn't tell me. Whenever she talked about him, she sounded dreamy. I think he lived in San Francisco. He might have been an investment banker. Or an entrepreneur."

"Was he married?"

"I don't know."

"That seems to be the reason of the day to keep a man's identity secret."

Coco glowered at me. "He had money, I know that much.

Alison had hoped he might invest in her company and help her grow. But he didn't. You know, it's possible"—Coco gripped my wrist—"that Alison was pregnant."

I gawped at Coco and then glanced at Bailey, who was at the sales counter ringing up Faith Fairchild. Bailey must have sensed me looking her way. She mouthed, *What?* I wagged my head and said to Coco, "Why would you think that?"

"I'm not positive, but Alison mentioned wanting a child, and well, when her boyfriend died, she lost all control. She either cried or she slept. Nonstop."

"I lost it when my husband died." Actually I was a wreck, screaming, kicking, and yelling at nothing and nobody, just to get through the anger, but I didn't need to tell Coco all that. "Losing control is not unusual."

"Lately—I'm just saying friends notice these things— Alison has . . . *had* . . . been feeling out of sorts. Morning sickness is my guess. And the night before the cookbook club dinner, when she and I went out, she didn't have a lick of wine. Alison loved a glass or two of wine."

Someone knocked on the front door of the shop, even though it was propped open. I twisted in my chair. Simon Butler entered with his hard-bodied, horsey-faced wife, Gloria, who had dressed in a riot of color: tight yellow gym pants and tank, aqua blue purse, purple lace flats, turquoise fingernails. Her burgundy hair added to the full-color-spectrum effect.

Coco stiffened.

I whispered, "Don't worry. I don't think they overheard us talking about Alison being, you know . . ." I twirled a hand.

"Hey, Jenna." Simon nudged his glasses higher on his nose. "My wife was asking about your Chocolate Cookbook Club. She wants to join. She's sort of shy about these things."

Gloria was anything but shy. She was an in-demand personal trainer who could command anyone into shape. Why on earth would she want to join the club?

"Do I have to fill out a form?" Gloria asked in an assertive, definitely-not-shy voice.

"There isn't a form," I said, "but let me get some particulars." I gestured for her to follow me to the checkout counter.

Simon moved toward Coco. "I'm sorry about Alison."

"Thanks," she mumbled.

Simon uttered something else, but I couldn't make it out because his wife said, "I know you think I'm nuts to join the club, Jenna. I can see it in your eyes, but I adore chocolate. Ultra-dark chocolate. As little sugar as possible, of course."

"Of course." I tilted my head, trying to figure out her angle. Perhaps she was hoping to score more clients from the group. Many of our book club members could use an exercise regimen. At the hundred-dollars-an-hour fee Gloria charged, she wouldn't need more than a few appointments a week to make well in excess of fifty thousand a year.

"What do you need from me?" Gloria asked. "Phone number, e-mail? Here's my business card, which has everything you should need." The card was as colorful as Gloria. Her name and telephone number were printed in a bold font. The full-body picture of her in the upper right corner looked just like her. "By the way, I simply have to own Coco Chastain's last cookbook." Gloria eyed Coco. "Simon is buying it for me as a Valentine's gift."

So much for giving her a surprise. Maybe he planned to cook her a romantic meal using the recipes.

"Where is it?" Gloria asked.

I pointed to the pile of books attractively displayed to her left. How had she missed seeing them? Coco's face figured prominently on the front cover.

Gloria grabbed one, hurried back to Coco, and thrust it at her. "Would you autograph it for me? It's spelled G-L-O-R-I-A, just like Van Morrison wrote it in the song."

Was there any other way to spell it? I wondered. Perhaps with a *y*.

Coco took the book, fetched a pen from her purse, and signed the title page. She finished her signature by drawing a heart with an arrow through it, and handed the book back to Gloria, who opened it and immediately scanned the inscription.

"Aww," she whispered. "Sweet."

Simon tapped Coco's arm. "How is Alison's family doing? I mean, her brother seems to be coping."

Coping? I nearly laughed. Neil had taken no time off to mourn, which made him colder than an icicle, in my humble opinion, or in desperate need of a paycheck.

I said, "By the way, Coco, have you touched base with her mother?"

She shook her head. "Ingrid called me. She said a doctor stopped by to see Wanda."

"Ingrid." Gloria screwed up her mouth. "That's the copy-editor, isn't it? The one with the long torso, short legs. She asked for my card yesterday."

"Yesterday?" Simon raised an eyebrow. "You were on a plane to Vegas."

"At eight in the evening. She caught me right before I hopped in the car to head to the airport." Gloria addressed Coco and me. "I'm like a speeding bullet lately. In and out of town on a moment's notice. I attended a crack-of-dawn seminar for gym equipment and was back on a plane by nine this morning. Thanks to my darling husband. He registered me for the event. Gym equipment. Can you imagine? I'll tell you, testosterone was teeming." She snorted out a laugh. "Want to know what the latest is? An abdomen roller wheel. It really works. See, you get on your knees—" She started to crouch, as if she were going to show us on the floor.

Simon tapped her shoulder. "Hon, you're doing it again."

Gloria rose to her full height. "Am I? Forgive me. I have a tendency to proselytize. But the core matters." She outlined her firm torso. "My husband doesn't work on the core."

Simon rubbed his knuckles along her arm. "Or the neck, or the spine."

"He watches birds." Gloria sniffed her disapproval. "What a frivolous waste of time."

Simon's mouth turned down. "Not to me."

"There's no exercise value in it."

"But there's aesthetic value. Moving on." Simon twirled a finger to end the discussion.

Faith sidled up to us, a Cookbook Nook bag looped over her arm. "Excuse me. I couldn't help overhearing. Were you talking about that woman with the tight teeth? Ingrid, is that her name?" She drew back her lips, which made her look, other than the hairstyle, strikingly similar to Ingrid Lake. "I saw her in Vines last night."

"I didn't see her," I said. "Or you."

Faith bobbed her head. "I came in around ten forty-five. I'm a night owl."

Hmm. If asked, I would have sworn Faith was a morning person. On the other hand, she was single, and according to Bailey, forever on the hunt for a mate.

Simon frowned. "I didn't see you, either."

"That's because you weren't around, silly." Faith batted Simon's arm. "The waitress with the wavy hair said you'd gone to the store to pick up more peanuts."

Was Faith flirting with Simon? In front of his wife? Gloria grumbled; her teeth looked as tightly gritted as Ingrid's. Coco cleared her throat, I'm pretty sure to catch my attention. We exchanged a bemused glance.

Simon must have realized what was going on. He moved a half pace away from Faith. "Right. We ran out of nuts around ten."

Oblivious to her gaffe, Faith stepped toward him like a supersonic train, in fast-forward with no inclination to slow down. "I've got to say, something seemed odd about Ingrid. She wasn't with anyone, yet she ordered a bottle of wine for herself. Indulgent, if you ask me, but"—she tittered—"you didn't."

Gloria shifted feet.

"Maybe Ingrid was working off some anger," I offered. "Coco saw Alison and Ingrid arguing after the cookbook club meeting."

"Anger can make you hotter than a pistol," Gloria said. "Trust me, I know." She eyed Faith with outright hostility then skewered her husband with a similar look. "Speaking of which, *whew!* It's hot in here. Honey, I'm going outside to cool off." She fanned herself with Coco's cookbook. "Pay for this, will you?" She shoved the book into his hands, strode outside, and paused on the sidewalk, foot tapping.

"Say, Gloria," Faith shouted, "hold up! I've got a new client for you." She traipsed outside. Whether or not she did have a client didn't matter. Gloria's mood lightened. Perhaps Faith hadn't meant to hit on her husband.

Simon drew near to Coco and me. He lowered his voice. "Hey, you two, you don't think that Ingrid—" He halted.

"Go on," Coco said.

"What if, after Ingrid and Alison argued, Ingrid got drunk and went to your place to have it out with Alison?" Simon nodded, concurring with his own theory. "It's worth pinning down her alibi, don't you think?"

"Simon," Gloria called from the doorway. Faith had departed. "Let's get a move on, darling. We have three errands to run before I have to meet my next client. You know Miss Chubby Dumpling hates to be kept waiting."

Coco and I exchanged another glance—an appalled one. Did Gloria really talk about her clients that way? Yipes.

Simon smiled at Coco. "Keep your chin up." Then he edged to the checkout counter, paid Bailey cash, and, without waiting for one of our shopping bags, hurried off with Coco's book.

Coco watched him leave then turned back to me. Her face was flushed, her eyes glistening, and at that moment I knew. *Knew!* Simon was the man with whom she was having an affair. The glances, the softly exchanged words, the caress to her arm, the way he had complimented her at Vines the other night, her statement that he went to her shop all the time to taste the wares. Until now, I'd missed the signs. Dumb me. With his wife going out of town regularly for business, Simon had the freedom to play. And play he had.

I gripped Coco's wrist and whispered, "Either you tell Cinnamon Pritchett about Simon or I will. And while you're at it, tell her to check whether Alison was with child."

Chapter 11

M OMENTS AFTER THE shop cleared, I filled Bailey in
about Simon being Coco's lover—she was stunned—
and the possibility that Alison might have been pregnant—
she was doubly shocked—and the fact that Cinnamon said
it was okay for me to *investigate* . . . well, not investigate, but
to *listen* and *report*.

Bailey's mouth fell open. "Honest to gosh?"

"Scout's honor." I held up three fingers.

Next, we discussed what I . . . *we* . . . might be able to do
at this point, which was nothing. Coco had to tell Cinnamon
everything about her lover—name, height, and social security number if she had it. After that, Cinnamon would have
to take the lead. Bailey and I were done trying to help Coco.

The afternoon came at us in a rush. Customer upon customer arrived looking for cookbooks. Because of the pirate
craze in town, Caribbean-themed cookbooks were in demand.
Repeatedly I recommended one by Rita Springer, simply
titled: *Caribbean Cookbook*. When it first came in, I had
pored over the book. Written in 1979 but reprinted and raved
about by readers, it contained not only tidbits of history about

Caribbean cuisine, but also tasty recipes for coconut bread and conkie, a sweet, cornbread-based dish baked in banana leaves.

By closing time, my voice was hoarse from talking, and I was beat on my feet. I settled onto the stool beside the register and slugged down the contents of an entire bottle of spring water.

Bailey sidled up to the counter. "Look sharp, girlfriend. We've got a hot double date." She tapped her watch. "Ten minutes."

"A date?"

"Don't you remember? You promised to go on a sunset whaling adventure with Rhett. I'm going with Tito. They'll be here to pick us up in a few minutes."

I bounded off my stool. Nothing revived me more than seeing Rhett. I didn't care how tired I was. Tigger mewed from the floor. I scooped him up. "Aunt Vera is taking you home. She'll spoil you with fish treats."

He meowed again.

"That's right. Fish treats and lots of love. Be good." I bopped his nose with my fingertip. "No poking around in her closets or messing up her decks of tarot cards." The last time my aunt had cat-sat, Tigger had played master snoop. I don't think he had many more lives before she would beg off sitting for the little imp, and I needed her to do so if I wanted to have a social life. I didn't believe in letting a kitten hang out in the cottage by his lonesome for hours on end. Some might call me a helicopter cat-parent, but I didn't care. I set him back on the floor and hurried to the stockroom to freshen up.

A half hour later, Bailey, Tito, Rhett, and I, all dressed warmly, boarded a sleek ship specially brought into the harbor for Pirate Week dubbed the *Victory*, a small trading-style vessel about 140 feet in length, with multiple sails, a foresail, and eight cannons.

The captain had allowed a maximum of one hundred passengers on board. Each passenger wore a pirate hat or bandana, which the crew had handed out to us while boarding. In addition, each passenger was now holding a cocktail of some sort. Mine was called Pirate's Poison, a delicious rum and fruit juice concoction. The sun had not yet set, although it hung low in the sky. Huge swipes of pink and orange sky spanned the horizon, but dark clouds were amassing way far out, foretelling a coming storm.

"Where are the whales?" Bailey asked.

"Be patient," Tito chided and bussed her on the cheek.

Whales commonly migrated south in the winter and were often sighted from Washington to Baja. They were known to be more active on blustery days. The roiling water seemed to drive them toward the surface. However, the captain had assured us that even today, on a fairly calm ocean at sunset— given the impending storm, it would not be calm in a few hours—we were bound to spy a few. He would use radar to explore the ocean to see where whale activity was heaviest. He was already playing music below deck, a tried-and-true way to lure whales closer to the ship, though not closer than coast guard regulations allowed.

Soon we were cutting through the water. I took up a position near the aft of the boat and gazed out over the water, vigilant for activity. A gentle breeze wafted across the deck. I shivered and pulled the poncho I had thrown over my jeans and sweater tighter.

Bailey sidled up to me. "Thinking about Alison?"

"And Coco." She hadn't called Bailey or me. Had she gone to the precinct? Had Simon come forward on her behalf? Had Cinnamon exonerated her? "I feel guilty being out here while her fate is in question."

"Tell me about it, but there's nothing more we can do."

A heavy silence fell between us.

After a moment, Bailey said, "So what do you think?"

"About Coco?"

"About Tito." She nodded toward the men.

Rhett, who looked extremely handsome in a cable-knit sweater and jeans, with his tricorn hat tipped rakishly down over one eye, had chosen to stay seated near the portside railing. A veteran fisherman, he was immune to the allure of watching for whales. When one was sighted, he would rise to his feet and cheer with the rest of us, but until then, he would relax. Tito, seated beside Rhett, was regaling him with an obviously humorous story. Rhett caught me staring at him laughing, and he smiled. I smiled back.

"Rhett likes him," I said. "That says a lot."

"You don't think Rhett is simply being nice?"

"Rhett's pretty opinionated. I think if he didn't enjoy Tito, he'd move away."

Bailey grinned, pleased with my answer. "You know what I love about Tito?"

I elbowed her. "Love? Did you say *love*, girlfriend?"

"Like. What I *like* about him?" She blushed. "He's always up-to-date with the news."

"That's his job."

"Yes, but he's on top of the latest stories. Not just here in little old Crystal Cove. In California. The U.S. The world."

Tito slapped his leg. Loudly, he said, "Exactly!"

Bailey nudged me toward them. "Enough watching for whales and thinking deep, dark thoughts. Move. Lighten up, if even for two hours."

When we arrived where the men were sitting, Rhett patted his knee for me to perch on it. My cheeks warmed. I liked modest public displays of affection. A peck on the cheek or holding hands. All good. Snuggling? Uh-uh.

Bailey picked up on my hesitancy. She batted her eyelashes and said to Tito, "What are you two laughing about?"

"There was another pot of gold doubloons sighting," Tito announced.

"You're kidding. Where?"

"Online, on a new blog called *Fun Times*."

"Stupid move," Bailey said. "The police can track down the creator using a web address."

"Not likely." Tito swatted the air. "The blog has already been removed, just like the others. It went up, and within thirty minutes, gone. *Poof!* But the picture remained in Google Images."

"How is that possible?"

"People shared via Pinterest and Facebook, so it went viral, yet again."

"Why would someone do that?" I asked.

"Exactly!" Tito said, the same way he had to Rhett. "To get attention."

I shook my head. "Unless the sightings are driving business the thief's way, it doesn't earn him anything. Why do it?"

"Street cred," Rhett said.

I raised an eyebrow. "Whoa, listen to you. *Street cred*. Tough guy."

"Rhett is right," Tito said. "The thief is doing this so he can tell tales. And get this, before the blog vanished, he said whoever figured out his name first would get two free tickets."

"To what?" we asked in unison.

"That's just it." Tito grinned. "He didn't say."

"Two free tickets directly to Jail," Bailey joked. "Do not pass Go."

"It's all very curious," Tito added. "He's piqued my interest."

"How do you know it's a he?" I asked.

Bailey smacked Tito's chest. "Is it you?"

"Me? Are you nuts?" Tito chortled. "I only wish I'd thought of it. I would like to expand my audience. Readership for the paper has floundered. If I could bolster our sales, who knows where that might lead? Editor? Owner?"

Bailey elbowed him. "Keep that swelled head in check, *amigo*."

Tito wrapped an arm around Bailey and kissed the side of her head. The sight warmed me. I had never seen Bailey so openly affectionate with a guy.

Rhett said, "If you'd wanted to bolster readership and you were the thief, wouldn't you have left the blog up? It doesn't make—"

"There!" a crowd of people shouted. "Aft!"

Off the starboard side of the boat, a whale surfaced. Every guest on the ship hurried to watch. The whale swam parallel to the ship, its back cresting the ocean. As it glided along, it raised a fin and spanked the water. People squealed with delight. The whale repeated its performance three or four times then disappeared. None of us budged an inch. We waited with bated breath. And then suddenly, out in front of the ship, the whale breached. The upper portion of its mammoth-sized body rose straight up, then the giant beast plummeted into the water. The crowd heaved a collective sigh of regret. Once a whale breached, it would not resurface for a long time. The show was over.

Soon the sky grew dark, and the captain turned the ship around. We debarked from the ship and walked along the boardwalk, ready to find someplace to eat dinner.

"How about Mum's the Word?" Tito said.

Bailey shook her head. "Jenna and I ate lunch there. How about Tacos To Go?"

"Done."

While the two ran off to fetch dinner, Rhett and I strolled ahead. The Pier was crowded with tons of revelers. I would bet nearly everyone in town was there. Some were *walking the plank* across a board set atop an expanse of paper painted blue to resemble water. Others were lured into paying a dollar to throw a ring on a pirate's hook to win prizes. Most rings fell short.

A crowd of people stood in a semicircle around a pirate-clad man showing off his trained seal, also in pirate gear. The seal, using its nose, played catch with the pirate. After each toss, it barked. A hat filled with dollar bill tips sat on the boardwalk in front of them. Whether or not the artist had placed the dollars there to encourage more tipping was any-one's guess.

Among the seal and pirate onlookers, I spied Dash Hamada in full pirate regalia. He held a camera and was snapping off pictures in rapid succession. He whirled around and took photographs of people exiting The Theater on The Pier. The first of the evening's performances of *The Pirates of Penzance*, the show that the red and blue pirates had advertised at The Cookbook Nook, had just let out. Dash moved on and paused at The Pearl, a jewelry store. He aimed his camera at something inside, but he didn't depress the button. He released the camera, letting it hang on its strap around his neck, and swiped a finger beneath his eyes. Was he crying?

Poor guy. I understood why he was still in town. He had tagged along with the others from Foodie Publishing so he could experience Pirate Week. Did the event have the same allure now that Alison was dead? Did Dash miss her? How would her death affect his career? Did he have new jobs lined up?

The owner of the jewelry store, a slight man with dark curly hair and enough pierced jewelry in his ears to set off security alarms at the airport, emerged from the store and joined Dash. He put a hand on Dash's shoulder and said something, then he looped an arm around Dash and drew him into the store.

I recalled the conversation Coco and I had at Vines. Was she right and I wrong? Was Dash gay? Did it matter? No, not really.

I spied Pepper Pritchett heading toward us carrying a blue pastry box. She raised a hand as if trying to get my attention. I snuggled into Rhett, doing my best to ignore her signal. Pepper tugged up the collar of her overcoat and veered away.

"Hey, Jenna. *Psst.*" Bailey caught up to me and offered me a taco. I passed. My appetite was nil. "There's Ingrid Lake," she whispered. "She's exiting the Seaside Bakery. See her?"

Ingrid looked like she had come straight from a dry cleaner, clad in a crisply pressed gray jacket and skirt. No color; no spunk. She, too, was carrying a blue pastry box.

"Go talk to her," Bailey urged.

"Why?" I asked, sotto voce, not wanting Rhett to hear us.

"Remember what Simon Butler said at the shop? You know"—she twirled a hand—"that whatever Ingrid and Alison were arguing about might matter. Ask her for her alibi last night."

"You do it."

"No way. Cinnamon told you to investigate."

"Wrong. She said I could listen and report back."

"C'mon. The time is right." Bailey knuckled my arm.

I veered into Rhett.

He juggled his taco and steadied me. "Are you all right?"

I grunted a *yes*. "Give me a second." I didn't add, *Or Bailey will never leave me in peace*. "I need to speak with that woman over there."

"About her alibi," Bailey chimed.

Rhett cocked an eyebrow. I knew what that meant. It wasn't that he didn't want me to get involved—he trusted my intellect and my instincts—but he didn't want me to get hurt. Period.

"Go!" Bailey warned. "She's getting away."

Tito, unlike Rhett, was not against the idea. "Can I listen in?"

"No!" I barked then hurried off to accost . . . *question* . . . Ingrid. I caught up to her beyond the diner and smiled. "Hi, Ingrid. I thought you would have gone back to San Francisco by now."

"No, I'm still here." Her voice was lackluster, her teeth still tight.

"How are you holding up?" I placed a comforting hand on her elbow.

Ingrid pulled away. "Fine. I guess. I can't believe Alison is gone."

"Who are the cupcakes for?"

"Alison's mother. Not her brother. He doesn't eat—"

"Sugar," I completed the sentence. "He's diabetic. Did you get the meal my chef and I sent over?" I might as well take some credit for the idea. After all, the food had come from my café.

"We did. It was very good. That was sweet of you."

"How long are you planning to stay in town?"

"I don't know. I couldn't leave now, not while the murder goes unsolved. It's not like I have another job to go to. Besides, Mrs. Foodie is so kind, and she's"— Ingrid's voice caught—"in deep emotional pain. The doctor doesn't think she should be left alone, and I agree."

Coco had heard Ingrid taunting Alison, claiming she could run the business better than Alison. Was Ingrid hoping that as a stand-in for Mrs. Foodie's daughter, she might have some sway with the future of Foodie Publishing?

"Neil . . ." Ingrid paused to lick her lips, proving her teeth did, indeed, move. "Let's just say that he isn't much help."

Neil. For some reason, the guy irked me. His sister had died, his mother was suffering, and yet he hadn't taken a second off to grieve. Granted, people handled sorrow in different ways, but I had to wonder about him. Did he stand to inherit the business? Where was he when Alison was killed? What time did his shift end?

Ingrid's gaze darted to the right. Was she looking for an escape route?

Now or never, Jenna. Focus on the matter at hand. Get Ingrid's alibi.

"Ingrid," I said. "What were you doing last night?"

Ingrid tilted her head; her eyes narrowed. "I've already answered to the police, but if you must know, after I left the book club meeting, I went back to the Foodies' house, and I watched television in bed."

Liar, liar. "You were seen at Vines."

"Oh, right." Ingrid tugged down the hem of her jacket and stretched her neck. "After Alison dropped me at her mother's house, I went out for a glass of wine."

Faith Fairchild said Ingrid had ordered a bottle of wine, but I wouldn't quibble with details. I said, "We were there, too, Bailey, Coco, and I, but I don't remember seeing you."

Ingrid sputtered. "I didn't go right away. Like I said, I watched a little television with Mrs. Foodie and then—"

"A second ago you said you watched TV in bed."

"That was later. First, I watched with Mrs. Foodie—an episode of *CSI*."

Reruns of *CSI* played day and night.

"Wanda dozed off," Ingrid continued. "Wanda is Mrs. Foodie."

"I know." I'd met Wanda. She had come into the store a time or two. She had a particular fondness for spicy dishes.

"I got bored, so . . ." Ingrid twirled a hand to elaborate without adding anything more.

"Someone heard you arguing with Alison after the book club meeting." How I wished I had taken Pepper up on a chat a few minutes ago. If she had overheard the dispute—

"Who?" Ingrid demanded.

She didn't deny it. That was a start.

"A friend," I said and glanced over my shoulder. Rhett stood at the edge of The Pier. Tito and Bailey huddled nearby. None of them were talking. Bailey's gaze was riveted on me. Rhett checked his watch. If I didn't wrap this up quickly, he might leave. I didn't want to end the night on a sour note. On the other hand, Ingrid was being responsive. I wanted to learn all I could. "What did you disagree about?"

Ingrid raised the pastry box and clutched it in front of her torso with both arms, like a shield. "It was nothing."

I remembered a time at Taylor & Squibb, while working on the Bandy's Candies account. An associate said he thought there might be a glitch in the campaign. When I asked him what, he'd said, *It was nothing.* It turned out that the copywriter we'd hired had written a similar campaign for another advertising firm. It wasn't *nothing.* It had turned into a lawsuit.

"Sometimes nothing can matter," I said. "Care to share?"

Ingrid shrugged. "We were talking about the books Alison was putting on the back burner. Dash's book and Coco's latest."

"You didn't think they should flounder?"

"I didn't say that." Ingrid pursed her lips, which made her look like a duck.

"Did you argue about anything else?"

"Alison thought I was being too fastidious about some edits. She said I wasn't letting a few of her authors' voices come through."

"Like?"

"Dash and Coco, to be specific."

At the crime scene, Coco had called Ingrid's editing style picayune, which had almost brought them to blows.

"You didn't agree?" I asked.

"Does an employee ever agree with the boss?" Ingrid

attempted a smile. It looked painful. "I listened. After a bit, she calmed down. But you know Alison. She could run hot and cold."

"Were you friends?"

"No, not really. We didn't hang out. But she trusted me enough to let me stay at her mother's house, if that's any indication. She was grooming me."

My ears perked up. "Grooming you for what? Partnership?"

"That, and more." Ingrid fitted a lock of hair behind her ear and smoothed her hands over the whole hairdo. Everything in its place, I mused. "She was grooming me to do her job so she could retire."

Okay, that was news. "Why would Alison want to retire?"

"She wanted to get married. Travel. Have a life. Up until a month ago." Ingrid leaned in. "The guy she hoped to marry . . . he died."

That concurred with what Coco had said.

"Ingrid, this is a very personal question," I said, "but was Alison pregnant?"

Her eyes widened. "Hmm. You know, she might have been. Recently, she changed her diet. She started eating lots of yogurt, and let me tell you, she hated yogurt. In addition, she was downing handfuls of vitamins packed with folic acid."

"How do you know that?"

Ingrid blushed. "We share an office space. Even though she declared a cabinet off-limits, I snooped. You need to understand, I was worried because"—she smoothed her hair again—"I had no desire to work for someone who was popping pills. My mother is a drug addict. I need stability."

Hence the tight teeth and buttoned-down personality. And the desire for a new, kindly mother figure like Wanda Foodie. Got it.

I gazed past Ingrid and caught sight of The Pearl jewelry store, which made me think of Dash. Now the question of whether he was gay or straight mattered, because if he was straight and in love with Alison, what would he have done if he had found out she was pregnant with another man's baby?

Chapter 12

ON THE DRIVE back to Fisherman's Village where I had left my VW, Rhett and I didn't speak. He surprised me when he pulled into the lot and didn't utter a sound while swerving out of the way of an exiting car. He often muttered at bad drivers, as if that would make them see the error of their ways.

"Oops. I left the lights on in the shop," I said, trying to make small talk.

Rhett didn't counter. He pulled in front of The Cookbook Nook and left the engine idling.

I unbuckled my seat belt and swiveled to face him. "Are you mad at me?"

"No."

"Concerned?"

"Yes."

"Because I'm sticking my nose into things."

"Because you can't seem to help yourself."

I didn't argue. Bailey had pushed me into a situation, and I hadn't put up any resistance. Yes, I had picked up good information from Ingrid, and yet I wasn't sure whether she was lying or guilty or both.

"I get it," Rhett said. "Coco is your friend, and you were friends with Alison Foodie, too. You want to do right by them. Heck, I wouldn't be cleared of wrongdoing and on an even keel with our chief of police if not for your bullheadedness. I'm just—"

I ran my hand along his arm. "I've always been stubborn. That's not going to change. But I'm persistent with a purpose."

He laced his fingers through my hair. "Jenna." His voice was husky and filled with emotion. He pulled me close and kissed me tenderly. "Be careful."

"Always."

Bailey and Tito arrived a minute after Rhett drove off. I doubted that she had received the same treatment I had. Tito probably grilled her for information with an eagerness bordering on zeal. Bailey couldn't have revealed anything, because after talking to Ingrid, I'd corralled everyone and said, "Let's get going."

I slotted the key into the shop's front door and called for Tigger until I remembered Aunt Vera had taken him home.

Bailey sprinted in after me. Alone. "Spill. Blab. Talk. Now."

I recapped every facet of my conversation with Ingrid.

When I finished, Bailey scowled. "That's garbage. Ingrid actually said Alison was *grooming* her? I don't buy it. As for the pregnant thing, we have to find out for sure whether Alison was pregnant, and we have to find out what Dash knew and when he knew it."

"If he was into Alison."

"You think he was, so he was. You've always had a well-developed sense of these things."

"Have I?" That was the first she'd ever mentioned it to me.

The door to the shop squeaked open. Bailey and I spun around. Pepper stood in the doorway.

"I'm sorry," I said, fully expecting her to lambaste me for snubbing her earlier.

"For what?" she asked.

"On The Pier . . . you were carrying a pastry box. You waved at me. I—" I didn't finish; how could I admit I had ignored her on purpose? "What did you buy at the bakery?"

"I purchased mini cupcakes for the beading club."

I didn't even know she had a beading club, although I knew she taught classes on the weekends.

"We ate them all," she added, "or I'd offer you one."

Now I really felt embarrassed. "Short meeting," I murmured.

"We were only setting next month's schedule. It was a ten-minute get-together."

"How are you feeling?" I asked. "How is the vertigo?"

"I can be quite a dizzy broad," Pepper said and winked. When had she developed a sense of humor? Was she on goofy drugs for her condition? Maybe, thanks to our teaming up a few months ago to catch a killer, she had finally realized that I was a friend, not a foe. "All kidding aside, I have to lie down occasionally, but that's not why I'm here."

"Did you need to talk to me earlier?" I asked.

"It's about that girl you were talking to on The Pier."

"Girl. You mean, Ingrid Lake?" She was hardly a girl. Closer to my age, maybe older. "Did you overhear her arguing with Alison on the night of the murder?"

Pepper nodded. "Yes. How did you know?"

"Coco thought she'd seen you." I didn't add *lingering.* "Go on."

"I had gone outside to get a bag of beads from my car. Metallic gold acrylic beads. Beautiful. Faith—you know Faith Fairchild." Pepper outlined Faith with her spiky hair. "Quite spirited." She pumped her arms like a locomotive.

"And a flirt," Bailey added.

We all seemed to have an opinion about Faith.

"She ordered them," Pepper said. "She's making a necklace for her grandmother, who is one of our beaders. The woman is ninety-eight years old, can you imagine? Good genes. Anyway"—Pepper fluttered her fingers in the air—"Faith didn't want her grandmother to see the beads, so I had them sent specially to my house instead of to Faith. I'd forgotten to bring them inside."

"The argument," I prompted.

Pepper pursed her lips. "That Ingrid. She speaks in a very thin voice."

"Yes, she does. She talks through clenched teeth."

"She wagged a finger and said, 'You promised.' Alison tried to cut her off, but Ingrid pressed on. 'Yes, you did. You promised me I'd own half the company,' to which Alison responded, 'You're dreaming.' Ingrid countered. 'You said you were drawing up a contract.'" Pepper chopped one hand with the other. "That was when Alison said, 'No, it's not happening. Not now. Not ever.'" *Chop*, *chop*, *chop*. "And then she fired her."

I gasped. "Alison *fired* Ingrid?"

Pepper nodded. "I quote, 'You're done. Finished.' But Ingrid said, 'I have legal rights.'"

"Wow," Bailey said. "There's motive for murder."

I agreed. "And not at all what Ingrid told me on The Pier."

Pepper said, "Next, Alison shook a fist at Ingrid."

Bailey said, "I thought *Ingrid* shook a fist at Alison."

"No," I said. "She wagged a finger."

Pepper lifted a shoulder. "Who knows who did what? They're about the same height."

Alison and Ingrid were completely different sizes, but I kept mute. Pepper's credibility when it came to her eyesight was tenuous at best. Hopefully her hearing ability would stand up in court.

"Anyway," Pepper went on, "Alison said Ingrid wasn't doing her job well. She said she, Alison, had needed to go over all manuscripts of late. She—Alison—said Ingrid wasn't worth her salt and certainly not worth the salary Alison was paying her. At the last, Alison said Ingrid was to clean out her desk," Pepper said with finality.

Later that night, did Ingrid go to Coco's house so she could lay into Alison one more time? Did Alison open up Coco's old manuscript on the computer to make a point?

I thanked Pepper for her information and promised her a fresh batch of her favorite zesty dark chocolate as soon as I had time to whip it up.

Before Pepper hurried off, I said, "Wait. Did you tell your daughter everything you told me?"

"No."

"Why not?"

Pepper jutted her chin. "Because she's babying me. I don't like it."

Uh-oh. Had she chosen me to be the recipient of her information to pit me against Cinnamon? Those could be treacherous waters. I'd have to tread carefully.

Speaking of water, as I headed home, the storm that had hung on the horizon throughout the whale-watching cruise arrived. Tenfold. Rain didn't just start falling. It pummeled my car. I tried calling the precinct on my cell phone, but the squall made it impossible to get a signal.

I drove to my aunt's house to pick up Tigger. I never carried an umbrella. The precipitation in our area was rarely icy cold, and like most people living in a beach community, I didn't mind getting splashed by a spritz of water. But this? I covered Tigger with my poncho and darted back to my VW. He stayed dry; I didn't.

After getting the cat settled in the cottage, I shrugged off my wet clothes and hurried to the telephone on the bed stand to call the precinct. I lifted the receiver. No dial tone. Dang! A month or two ago, I had called my provider about the reception. The service representative informed me that old lines were the culprits. Humidity got in; squirrels ate them. The provider would no longer replace old lines. At some point I would have to upgrade. Now, I wish I'd done what she had recommended.

The good news? Ingrid wasn't going anywhere. She was feeling quite comfy and cozy living with Wanda Foodie.

SATURDAY MORNING, I woke with a start. Rain teemed down in sheets. I closed all the windows, took a quick shower, threw on jeans and a silk turtleneck sweater, grabbed an energy bar, and drove to work.

Rain pelted the pavement as I cut across the parking lot and entered the shop. Same as last night, Tigger stayed dry; I got drenched. Oh well. I set Tigger on the floor. "Go play." He rumbled his disapproval at my wet hand. I tweaked his nose. "I promise. I will invest in an umbrella." Fortunately, I had a backup outfit hanging in the stockroom. At least I'd planned ahead that much. A girl never knew when she might snag a sweater while opening a box of books, or worse, like today, get drenched and look like something the cat dragged in.

Ten minutes later, I was dry and I had refreshed my makeup, but there was nothing I could do with my hair. It hung stick straight.

Next, I queued up music for the day. Usually, we played food-related music in the shop, but for Pirate Week, I'd made a special mix that included "I Am a Pirate King!" from *The Pirates of Penzance* as well as silly songs like "Shiver Me Timbers" from *Muppet Treasure Island*.

A flash of red caught my eye. My aunt was darting across the parking lot, umbrella overhead. Heaven forbid she allowed one of her gorgeous caftans to get sopping wet. At the entry, she pumped the umbrella a few times to rid it of water, then dropped the hem of her ruby-red caftan.

"This is to be the first of many storms, I fear," she said. "*C'est la vie*. Rain brings flowers."

"And shoos away customers," I added.

"*Yo ho*. Not today. We have children scheduled to come in at one P.M. for our special event, and I promise they will beg, plead, and wail if their parents don't bring them. You'll see. I heard a number of people talking about the flyer you handed out." She set her umbrella in the stockroom then returned to me and fetched a bowl of Hershey's Kisses from beneath the counter. She set it by the specialty bookmarks and craned an ear. "Why are we playing those songs?"

"It's Pirate Week."

"Don't we have any candy-themed music, like "Sugar Pie Honey Bunch" or "Sugar, Sugar"? Or how about "The Chocolate Song"? It's an obscure one, but it is, after all, Chocolate Month. And we are featuring chocolate cookbooks."

"I'll get on it after this round of music plays." I skirted behind the sales counter.

Aunt Vera straightened the display of mini inspirational books on the stand, an item she insisted we carry, food-related or not. With titles like *Believe in Yourself* or *Live,*

Love, Laugh or *Seize the Moment*, how could I refuse? Everyone needed an inexpensive pick-me-up.

"By the by," Aunt Vera said, "Mayor Zeller called me. She's putting up a reward for the return of the pot of doubloons."

"A reward?"

"One thousand dollars."

"You're kidding."

"Nope. Old Jake is footing the bill. Z.Z. said he's up in arms at this scallywag—Jake's word—making a fool of the mayor." Old Jake is a local legend. Once a drifter, now a millionaire. "I think Jake's sort of sweet on the mayor."

"He's thirty years her senior."

"Don't judge, lest ye be judged." My aunt threw me a chastening look. "Z.Z. is posting flyers alerting the public. She asked us to put one in the window. She sent you an e-mail with the attachment. Hope you don't mind."

I opened the e-mail file, printed the flyer, and handed it to my aunt.

She taped it in the sidelight window next to the front door and returned. "Now, let's get cracking. Where's that Peter Pan book we ordered?" She wandered off in search.

For Children's Pirate Day, we had cleared the table in the children's section so the kids could make pirate hats and maps. My aunt planned to read *Peter Pan* aloud—the real *Peter Pan* by J. M. Barrie, not the modified and, frankly, toned-down Disney version. Barrie had created a deep character, filled with darkness and selfishness. The adventure Peter Pan and the children go on is fun, but it's also quite scary. Our advertisements warned parents about the theme of the reading. I didn't think the warning would scare anyone off.

"Ahoy, mateys!" Bailey trotted into the shop carrying a darling blue-swirled umbrella—smart girl—and a cat in her arms. It was gray and black, with only a splash of white around its nose and whiskers, at least a year or two old.

"Who's your new friend?" I asked.

"I haven't named him yet. Tito gave him to me."

I gaped. "And you accepted?" Bailey had never owned a pet. Her mother had been too busy to have cats or dogs or even an easy-to-take-care-of goldfish. Once Bailey was grown and had a thriving career, she had become too busy, as well. She had no idea how much attention a cat required. Not as much as a dog, of course, but even so. I said, "He's very athletic looking."

"Isn't he? He's an American shorthair, descended from European cats. Tito's sister couldn't care for it anymore."

"Tito has a sister?"

"In Fresno. She stopped in last weekend and handed the cat over to Tito."

"And he dropped him on your doorstep?"

"Yes, and I've fallen in love." Bailey went to nuzzle the cat with her nose. He recoiled. Uh-oh. He didn't seem very friendly. Bopping between owners could take its toll, I mused.

"Did Tito's sister give the cat a name?"

"Tom." Bailey sniffed. "But I am *not* calling any cat Tom. What do you think about Simba or Zeus?" She eyed the bowl of Hershey's Kisses on the counter. "Or Hershey?" She giggled. "You know how much I love chocolate. And it's February. National Chocolate Month. Perfect, right?"

"Hershey," I said. "I like it. Just don't give him any chocolate."

"I won't. I'm not dumb." Bailey lifted the cat to her face. "You are so *lick*able," she cooed. "Yes, you are."

He drew back. Bailey leaned in. He recoiled farther. Wow, he had a flexible neck.

"Uh, Bailey." How was I supposed to broach the next question? "Does this mean Tito is permanently in your life?"

Her head snapped around. "Huh? What? No. I mean . . ." She glanced at Hershey and back at me. "Are you suggesting that by taking the cat, we are bonded together?"

"Something like that."

Bailey held Hershey at arm's length and studied him, then pulled him close to her chest. He frantically chugged his hind legs, but she didn't release him. She whispered, "You're mine. We'll work out the other details and visiting rights soon." She glanced around the shop. "Is it okay if I put him down? Will Tigger take to him?"

"Let's see."

Bailey set Hershey on the floor and gave his rump a push.

Tigger darted toward him and acted as if he'd found a long-lost friend. Hershey wasn't so certain. He reared up. Tigger got the cue. He backed away and sat patiently. Hard to do for a kitty. Bailey didn't seem to notice Hershey's antisocial behavior. I'd have to keep my eye on the cat to make sure he didn't trounce Tigger.

Sotto voce, Bailey said, "Did you contact Cinnamon and tell her that Alison fired Ingrid?"

I shook my head. "I couldn't. The rain played havoc with my cell phone and the landline. I'll call her after we get the shop up and running for today's event. Did you think of a way to confirm whether Alison was pregnant?"

"No." Bailey sounded dejected. "If we can drum up her address book and call her doctor—"

"The doctor would never break client-patient confidentiality."

"Right." Bailey slumped against the counter.

I pricked her arm. "We'll get to the truth. Promise. For now, down to business. Why don't you set up the children's corner with the paper and glue the children will need for hats and maps."

"Aye, aye."

Mid-morning, I rang the precinct, but Cinnamon wasn't available. I left a message. Close to noon, I headed to the café to chat with Katie about adding some extra snacks to the menu. A few days ago, I'd found a number of children's pirate treats in a variety of cookbooks, darling items like apples and cheese fixed together with toothpicks and decorated with pirate flags to look like boats, or halved red grapes skewered with stick pretzels to resemble swords. Of course, it being Chocolate Month, we had to have chocolate cupcakes decorated with pirate faces. For a beverage, I thought nonalcoholic grog made with apple cider, orange juice, brown sugar, and a bunch of fun spices would do the trick.

On my way into the café, I nearly bumped into Neil Foodie, who was on his way out of the restaurant carrying a to-go bag. Neil looked pale. His nose was chafed and red. He caught sight of me and bolted out the door.

Chapter 13

I SPRINTED AFTER Neil, taking the steps to the second floor of Fisherman's Village two at a time. I caught up with him near the top and tapped his back.

He spun around, a sheepish look on his face. "Hiya. Did you want to talk to me?"

"Yes."

He held up his to-go bag like a prize. "Soup. Navy bean, in honor of Pirate Week."

"Katie makes great soup."

"So I've heard. What do you want?"

"How are you doing?" I asked.

"Oh, is that all?"

What had he expected?

"I'm fine," he said. "Just fine."

"Are you sick?"

"No."

"Been crying?" I pointed to my nose, indicating the redness of his own.

He frowned. "Okay, no, I'm not fine. I'm lying through my teeth. Yes, I've been crying. I miss Ali—" He drew in a sharp breath. "And Mother is—" Another breath. "We're having a funeral."

"When?"

"Tomorrow morning. It's going to be private. Just the three of us."

"Three?"

"Mother, me, and—" He sighed.

Alison. I offered a consoling smile.

"Mother doesn't want a lot of fuss. She's . . ." Neil shimmied tension out of his shoulders. "Mother is usually stalwart. She always has been. But Alison's death has shaken her to the core."

"And you?"

"I try not to dwell. I keep my feet moving. Fred Flintstone, at your service." He trotted in place, as if he was the cartoon character in his footmobile.

Recalling how Bailey said Neil often resorted to corny humor, I did my best to cut him a little slack for his goofy behavior. "Have the police—"

"No," he interrupted, then added, "Yeah, like, I'm sorry. That was rude. You were going to ask whether the police have found Alison's killer. If they have, they haven't told me. They're looking at Coco Chastain."

Coco still hadn't touched base with me. Why not? Had Cinnamon locked her up? Why hadn't Cinnamon returned my call?

"But I don't think Coco did it," Neil went on. "Alison was stabbed in the back, and to quote Oscar Wilde, 'True friends stab you in the front.' Coco and Alison were not just true friends, they were great friends."

My mouth fell open. Neil was well-read? Given his peculiar sense of humor and the way he talked, using the casual form of *yeah* and *nah*, I'd never have guessed. "What about Foodie Publishing?" I asked. "Will it go up for sale?"

"Maybe, but I don't expect there to be any buyers. There's no value in it. Alison told me it was running in the red. She barely made payroll month to month. There might be some back stock to sell and a contract or two to cancel. We'll have to talk with her attorney."

"We?"

"My mom and me." He checked his watch. "Gotta go. See ya."

"Wait. Neil . . ." I didn't want him to leave quite yet, not until I pursued one more line of questioning.

Neil shifted the to-go bag to his other hand. "What?"

"Did Ingrid have a stake in the publishing company?"

"Ingrid, as in Ingrid Lake? Miss Uptight of the Century?" Neil guffawed. "You're kidding, right?" His tone led me to believe there was more to his taunt than him not liking the woman. Had he made a pass at her? Had she rebuked him? "To answer your question, nah, not that I know of."

"Are you positive?"

"I haven't seen any formal paper yet, so I could be wrong. Like I said, we'll have to talk to the attorney." Neil sounded worn-out by the mere thought. "At one time, Alison had an investor, but he died."

"Her boyfriend?"

"Yeah, him."

"Did you meet him?"

"Nope. Never. Alison could be secretive."

Alison was certainly cagey if her brother, her friend, and her employee had never met the guy. Again, I wondered if the man had been married. Had Alison, like Coco, kept his name private because she hadn't wanted to ruin his life?

"There could've been more partners, I suppose." Neil tapped his temple. "My sister never let me in on the aspects of her business. I'm not smart enough." He offered a weak grin. "Some people say they've never seen such a small mind inside such a big head before." He yukked at his put-down, then glanced at my face. I must not have hidden my dismay well. I hated when people ridiculed themselves. He offered a cockeyed grin. "Not funny, huh? Yeah, I'll have to work on that. Gallows humor doesn't translate sometimes." He pivoted to leave.

"Neil, one more thing." Before calling Cinnamon a second time, I wanted to corroborate Pepper's account; not that she would lie, but she might have misheard. "Do you know if Alison intended to fire Ingrid?"

"You're asking me?" He aimed a pointer finger at his forehead. "Remember, this brain is empty."

"Ingrid said she was home watching television with your mother the night Alison died, but someone else saw Ingrid at Vines. Did you?"

Neil scratched his chin. "Come to think of it, yeah, she was there for like a nanosecond. Why?"

"Was she at home when you got off work?"

"Um . . ." He shifted the to-go bag back to the other hand.

"What time did you get off work?"

"At eleven, but I didn't go home right away. Not until early morning." His tongue worked its way around the inside of his mouth. Had I caught him off guard? Had he, like Coco, gone on a clandestine date, or was he fashioning an alibi?

I peered hard at him. "Where did you go?"

Neil backed up a step and aimed a finger at me. "Oho! Here we go. I've heard about you. I know what you do."

I frowned. "What are you talking about?"

"You investigate."

"I do not."

"Yeah, you get people talking. A few months ago"—Neil held up three fingers—"three people died in a matter of weeks."

Four people, I thought, if you counted a suspect in one of the murders who wound up dead at a motel. The memory made my stomach wrench.

"You were in at the finish each time," Neil continued. "You figured it all out."

"That's not true. The police solved the murders."

"Uh-uh." He wagged his head. "You did it. Upstairs"—he pointed toward Vines Wine Bistro—"we talk. We know how it went down."

I didn't know whether to be appalled or flattered. Would

Cinnamon be ticked off or pleased? She had told me to listen and report back.

"Look," Neil said, "I'll tell you where I was, but you've got to keep it hush-hush." He lowered his voice. "I was at a nightclub in Santa Cruz called Laugh a Minute. See, I'm trying to be a stand-up comedian."

Aha! That was why Neil was always trying out jokes. He wasn't naturally funny like a few of the comedians I'd used in commercials while at Taylor & Squibb, but then, not all comedians were funny. Some were dour, bordering on anti-social.

"Do you have a demo reel?" I asked. "Is it on your website?"

"Uh, I don't have a website yet, but believe me, I've got some really fresh material. It's got to be fresh. Novice comics like me can't come in with stale stuff, but I can't advertise it, see, because I've got to be careful. Other comics steal material like that." Neil snapped his fingers to make a point, then peeked up the staircase. "I also can't let my boss know I'm doing this."

"Why?"

"I'll get fired. All of us at Vines are supposed to be lifers."

"Lifers?"

"Yep. No kidding." The guy shuddered.

"Restaurant staff, other than chefs, are rarely in it for the long haul," I reasoned.

"I know. It's a stupid expectation, right? But I've been warned."

I gaped. "Simon threatened to fire you?"

"Not him."

"Who then, Gloria?" I remembered Neil claiming that Simon's wife was half owner.

Neil didn't respond, but by the way he was trembling, I could see he was truly afraid of losing his job. Was that the real reason he hadn't taken time off to mourn his sister?

I said, "You must need the job badly."

"Yeah, I've got debts." He jerked his shoulder. "Everybody does."

Actually, not everyone. I didn't. I liked paying cash for things. My deceased husband's habits did not match mine. "So, getting back to my initial question, Neil, you can't verify Ingrid's whereabouts at the time your sister was killed."

"Nope, but I can tell you this. Ingrid wasn't there when I got home at four A.M. I know because my mother's car was gone." Without offering more, Neil ditched me and ran upstairs.

I headed to the kitchen in the café and found Katie pacing like a drill sergeant, a towel bunched in her hands, her toque askew.

"Get those appetizers ready," Katie commanded her crew. "The cheese is over there."

I caught up with her and said, "What's wrong? You look a wreck."

"My mother."

"What's wrong with your mom?" Katie's mother had Alzheimer's and was living in a twenty-four-hour care facility just north of town.

Katie rubbed a finger beneath her nose. "She's been shouting at the nurses for the past two hours. Nobody is sure what happened. She doesn't recognize anyone. I've got to go to her."

"Of course." Katie's father, a miserable man, only visited her mother once a year. Even in his early years, he wasn't a warm and fuzzy guy.

Katie pointed at a lean man in a chef's coat. "Chef Phil will be tending to everything this afternoon. He's got the specials menu down, and snacks for the kiddies at your event are no problem. Everything's good to go. There shouldn't be any hiccups."

I smiled. Asking for extra items was out of the question. I gave her a hug and wished her the best.

Tears pressed at the corners of her eyes. "Ah, moms. Can't exist without them."

Chapter 14

I HURRIED BACK to the shop and was surprised to see a group of parents and a band of children in costumes already assembled at the rear of the store. The happy chatter was intense. What a hit!

Under Bailey's supervision, each child was cutting, pasting, sprinkling glitter, or doodling. Aunt Vera, wearing an eye patch slung over one eye, had taken up a position in the corner. She was reading aloud from *Peter Pan*. I felt a tug on my heartstrings watching the children, wondering if someday I would have children while at the same time aching for Alison and the possible loss of her child. Had she been pregnant? Did Cinnamon have a clue?

Confident the Children's Pirate Day event was running smoothly, I slipped into the stockroom and put in a call to the precinct. I had so much to tell Cinnamon, but she still wasn't available. The clerk asked if I wished to be transferred to Deputy Appleby. I passed. I didn't know if my aunt had contacted him; I certainly wasn't in the mood to answer questions about her if she hadn't.

Seeing as there was nothing in regard to the murder

investigation that I could do until Cinnamon called me back, I returned to the party. Tigger, the imp, was having a field day lurking beneath the table, trying to nab falling snippets of yarn and paper. Hershey wanted none of the infantile action. He had tucked himself into a comfy reading chair and was refusing to give it up to an elderly woman. I intended to fix that. I marched toward the grumpy cat.

Before I reached him, Bailey charged up to me and hooked a thumb. "What was that about?"

"What was what about?"

She prodded me to the sales counter. "Outside. On the stairs. You and Neil."

I told her in less than thirty words.

"Did you believe him about where he was?"

"You're the one who told me he's always cracking jokes."

"Sure, but that doesn't mean he was really at the comedy club." Bailey folded her arms. "He admitted he has debts. Did you ask why?"

I hadn't.

"Maybe he's a gambler," she said.

"Or he's simply spending beyond his means."

"He lives at home!"

Like that made a difference. The thirty-something son of my boss at Taylor & Squibb still lived at home and spent wild amounts of money.

Over Bailey's shoulder, I spied Dash Hamada entering the store. He wore a plumed tricorn hat and a pirate-style coat, which hit his jeans mid-thigh. He'd slung a couple of local shopping bags over his shoulder. His pockets overflowed with a map of the town, flyers, and photo contact sheets, making him look like a walking advertisement for Crystal Cove. How many pictures had he taken of the place?

"Ahoy!" Dash raised a hand in greeting. In his other hand, he held a Beaders of Paradise gift bag. I recognized the ornate figure of a parrot on the outside. Dash seemed a whole lot cheerier than he had when I'd seen him on The Pier last night. It never ceased to amaze me how people coped with sadness. Grief came in waves. It had for me when my husband went missing, and again when my mother passed away. On some days at work, I had barely muddled through. On other days, I had been downright hilarious.

I whispered to Bailey, "I'll be right back," and I approached Dash. "Hey, there. You sure look festive."

"Got to get in the spirit."

"Why are you still in town?"

Warily, he tilted his head. "Do you mean, why am I not holing up in my apartment, pining away now that my employer is dead?"

"I didn't—"

"It's okay." Dash swiped the air with his hand. "It's Pirate Week. Alison wouldn't have begrudged me having fun. She knows . . . *knew* how much I liked this stuff. Such a loss," he added, then wheezed out a sigh.

I eyed the bag in his hand. "What did you buy at Beaders of Paradise?"

Dash brushed his scraggly hair over his shoulder. "I'm going for the total pirate look at Pirate Cosplay. Beaded braids. Johnny Depp chic."

Typically, cosplay was the practice of dressing up as a character from a movie, book, or video game, and acting out the character. Pirate Cosplay, which was going to be held on The Pier on Tuesday night, would cap off the events for Pirate Week. The experience was for adults only; children, per the mayor's instructions, were forbidden. Pirates could get rowdy. Rhett and I were planning to attend. We also had tickets to go to The Theater on The Pier for some karaoke. I'd been piecing together a pirate costume based on a cult-favorite farce I'd read, *The Legendary Adventures of the Pirate Queens* by James Grant Goldin, which featured a woman, circa 1718, who had to pretend to be a man to find her long-lost love aboard a pirate ship. Rhett said he wouldn't care if I dressed like a guy. He thought I would look downright sexy in tight pants tucked into boots.

"Why have you come into the shop?" I asked Dash.

"I'm looking for a book with tattoos. The title will come to me. My friend, the guy I'm staying with, said you had it."

"Sterling?" The fellow with the multipierced ears who owned the jewelry store.

"Do you know him?"

"A bit." I hadn't spent any time in his shop. I didn't have enough information to know whether he was gay. "How's that going?"

"Beg your pardon?"

"Coco said you and he have a *thing*."

"Huh? No way. I'm straight." Dash's jaw ticked with tension for a split second, but then the tension melted away. "*Very* straight."

"I thought so," I let slip and felt my cheeks warm at my faux pas. "In fact, I told Coco you liked Alison."

"I—" Dash studied the knuckles on his hands. "No. We were colleagues. Nothing more." His eyes flickered; he was lying. I was sure of it. Had Alison known how much he cared? Had she rebuffed him? Dash flipped his hands over and assessed his palms, then he smacked them together. "Back to the book I'm looking for. It starts with the word *pirate*. *Pirate*-something. It's got temporary tattoos in it."

"You don't have enough tattoos of your own?"

"It's for personal reference."

"Maybe you're talking about *The Pirate Tattoo Book*?" I walked him to the display and lifted a copy. "It has twenty-four temporary tattoos and a ton of interactive stuff to do."

"That looks a bit young for me."

It was definitely skewed toward children. "How about *Pirateology*?" I picked up that book, perfect for young explorers and possibly older ones, as well. An inset compass adorned the front cover. The back cover had an inset ruby. "It's filled with extraordinary pictures."

"*Arrr.* That's it."

"I don't think it has tattoos, however. It has maps." We had sold over a dozen copies of the book so far.

Dash flipped through it—no tattoos—but that didn't seem to bother him. He carried it to the checkout counter and laid down cash.

I skirted around the sales counter, completed the transaction, and stuffed the book into a striped bag with our logo. I added a number of the shop's bookmarks and handed the bag to Dash along with the receipt. "Dash, about Alison. Do you know if . . ." I let the sentence hang. I couldn't ask him outright whether he knew Alison was pregnant. I didn't know for sure myself.

"Do I know what?"

"Nothing."

"Alison—" He halted. His eyes flickered. "She will be sorely missed. She believed in my work. She intended to publish my tattoo book as part of her nonfiction line. But now . . ."

"I'm sorry."

"Don't be. I'll find another publisher, but Alison will never—" He swallowed so hard his Adam's apple slid up and down in his throat.

I was sure I was right. He had loved her. Did she cut him out of her life? Did he then *cut* her out of his?

"Man, Alison was talented at what she did," Dash said. "She had an eye for a good book, and she had a knack for making a successful business."

"Successful? Her brother said the business was in the red."

"Not a chance. It was running a profit."

I flashed on a previous thought. About Neil. Was he Alison's heir? Would he have killed her for her money?

"Are you acquainted with Neil Foodie?" I asked.

"Sort of. He rarely came to the city, and he seldom visited the publishing house, but if you want my two cents, what I saw of him, I didn't like. He's shallow. No, that's not right. He's"—Dash snapped his fingers—"callow. Foolish. Always making jokes."

"Would Neil have any reason other than money to kill his sister?"

Dash looked right and left. "Between you and me, he said stuff that made me wonder if he was jealous of her. He intimated that Alison had it all: the brains, the talent. And he said, with a bit of bite, that she was lucky to get out from under their mother, unlike him who was stuck taking care of her. I remember him saying he wished he could cut bait and run." Dash ground his teeth. "Can you imagine? Abandoning your mother? My mom is the best. You'd never hear me say anything like that in regard to her."

"I didn't think pirates had mothers," I teased.

"Most do." Dash offered a wicked smile. "In fact, I'm pretty sure all did at one time or another."

A long silence fell between us. Finally, I said, "I can't help thinking if only Alison—"

"Yeah." Dash nodded. "If only one of us had been with her, right?"

"No, that wasn't what I was going to say. If only she had stayed at her mother's house."

"That wouldn't have solved anything. The killer would have found her there, too." Dash ran his hand down the buttons of his jacket. "*If only.* Sadder words were never said. I would imagine we all have a wealth of *if only*'s in our memory banks. If only I didn't leave the cookbook club dinner and go to the piano bar. What a fool."

"You sing?"

With robust abandon, Dash joined in with the song playing in the queue, "Yo Ho a Pirate's Life for Me," thrusting a bent arm whenever he sang the words *pillage* and *plunder.* When the song finished, Dash doffed his plumed hat and said, "I'll take my leave." Then he spun on his heel and exited the shop. Watching him go, I realized I liked him more each time I saw him. Was he snowing me? Was he a killer?

Needing to lighten my spirit, I moved to the children's table. I asked Bailey to man the sales register and deal with the regular customers, and then I dove in.

Over the course of the next hour or so, I helped children complete projects. A tricorn hat wasn't hard to make. We had posted easy-to-follow, origami-like instructions on the wall next to the table. I made a hat for myself and fashioned an origami-style parrot. When I attached that to my shoulder, the children laughed. How I loved the sound. I helped kids create hooks for their hands using paper cups and foil.

After that, we constructed treasure maps using brown packing paper. I circled the group, asking each child what special booty he or she might stow in a treasure chest. With black felt-tip pens, we plotted where they would stash their booty—X marks the spot—and what safeguards they would put in place to keep looters from stealing it.

The afternoon flew by. When the queue of music started to play "A Professional Pirate," also from *Muppet Treasure Island*, I gonged a bell that I'd bought for the occasion. "All right, Aunt Vera. Story time is over. Kids, moms, dads, grandparents, and special friends. Listen up! It's time to search for the hidden goldfish. So far no child has found it." Bailey had done a fantastic job of hiding it. I scanned the shop for Bailey. She wasn't at the register. Where had she gone? It didn't matter. No regular customers roamed the shop. "And then, kids," I continued, "it's time to parade around the shop so we can choose the best pirate costume. The winner will win dessert for four at the Nook Café."

A chorus of *whee!* rang out.

Ten minutes of chaos ensued until a freckle-faced redhead girl shouted, "I've found it!" She waved the goldfish overhead.

"Phooey!" another girl cried. "Where was it?"

"Tucked inside an oven mitt!"

Aunt Vera directed the winner and her redheaded father to a table of books from which she could choose her free book.

I wielded a gong. "The rest of you, it's time to follow me!" I banged the gong in time to the music. "March!"

Kiddies lined up behind me, each giggling or chatting with excitement. Aunt Vera clapped along with the gong. When the music ended, I yelled, "Freeze!" The children stopped in place. I patted heads, one by one, and said, "Sit down." When I came to a girl sporting an eye patch and dressed in a black-and-white striped bandana, black-lace bodice, and a swatch of black-and-white striped material over a red skirt, I said, "The winner!" I awarded her the certificate for the Nook Café desserts.

While Aunt Vera and I doled out the bags of gold foil–wrapped chocolate coins, Bailey broke through the curtains from the stockroom. "Jenna!" She raced to my side. "Neil," she rasped. "I called."

"Called who?"

"That stand-up club. He wasn't there the night Alison died."

"What?" I said, my voice skating upward.

"The owner didn't see him. He wasn't scheduled to do a routine."

"Maybe Neil meant he was in the audience."

"Uh-uh. The owner asked around. He said his employees know Neil by sight. He wasn't lying about being a regular there, but he wasn't at the club *that night*. Not between eleven and one. Not ever." Bailey gulped in air. "So where was he? Why did he lie to you?"

Chapter 15

A FTER WE CLEANED up, my aunt went to the Nook Café
for dinner and Bailey left with Hershey—she had a hot
date with Tito. I called the precinct again. Cinnamon still
wasn't in. The clerk advised me that the chief of police had
been following leads all day. She didn't know when her boss
would return. She assured me she had given Cinnamon my
messages.

Grabbing Tigger, I closed up the shop and headed to my
car. In the rain. Remembering the promise I'd made to my
darling cat to pick up an umbrella, I stopped at Artiste Arcade,
a cluster of high-end jewelry and fashion shops not far from
Fisherman's Village.

I parked on the street—not a lot of people were out and
about in the downpour—and assured Tigger I'd be right back.
Racing to the arcade, I got damp but not soaked. Minutes
later, I exited Adorn Yourself carrying a stylish umbrella à
la Van Gogh's *Starry Night* painting. I popped it open and
strolled to my car. On the way, I caught sight of Simon Butler.
He was standing outside Sweet Sensations, peering in through
the plate-glass window. I waved, but he didn't see me. The

shop lights were out. Where was Coco? Incarcerated? Free on bail? Why hadn't she called me? Simon looked forlorn. Had he hoped to steal a moment with Coco before starting his night shift at Vines? Was Coco right? Did he intend to leave his wife for her? I remembered a line by Chaucer that my mother used to quote: "Time and tide wait for no man." She advised me to always seize the moment. Would Simon? Would Coco finally be with her true love? Would Gloria blow a gasket?

Rain blasted the windshield all the way home. The moment I arrived at the cottage, I exited the car, opened the new umbrella, tucked Tigger beneath its protection—he purred his appreciation—and hurried inside.

Over the course of the next hour, I fed the cat, poured myself a glass of Chianti, nibbled on a piece of Manchego cheese, and threw together a turkey meat loaf—one of the easiest comfort foods that even I could manage. I set the meat loaf into the oven to slow-bake at 300 degrees and eyed my cell phone, which was sitting on the counter.

Why hadn't Cinnamon returned my call? I had updates. Was she avoiding me? I chided myself for acting like a teenager. When a boy in high school didn't call me back, what were the questions I would ask myself? *Was I coming on too strong*? *Was he getting ready to dump me*? Gack. Cinnamon was busy; she would contact me when she could.

I needed to do something to occupy my mind. I stared at the painting I had going for Bailey. Nearly three months ago she had asked me to create something for her new apartment. Her only caveat—no dancing ballerinas. To date, I'd finished the base blue, a few waves, and some sketches of palm trees and a bluff. I eyed the Ching cabinet. My palette of oils sat inside the double doors, but I didn't feel the urge to paint. I was stuck wishing I could chat with Cinnamon. I tried to convince myself solving Alison's murder wasn't my problem, it was a police issue, but my mind wouldn't stop cycling with theories.

Did Neil kill his sister? He told me he had debts. Was Alison's estate, whether big or small, enough reason to murder her? Had there been a rivalry between Neil and Alison, as suggested by Dash as well as Simon? Neil, not as bright; Neil, not as successful; Neil, not taken as seriously as his sister, saddled with an aging mother.

What about Ingrid Lake? Fired employee. Angry wannabe partner. Did she kill Alison? Had Cinnamon believed Ingrid's iffy alibi? Maybe Cinnamon wasn't calling me because Pepper finally caved and told her daughter about Ingrid's argument with Alison. Cinnamon had the information she needed; she didn't require my input.

In an effort to redirect my thoughts, I scooped the slightly damp mail out of the wicker box beneath the door slot. While sorting through the mail, I remembered that I'd promised to bring cupcakes to tomorrow night's family dinner. Every Sunday, my aunt, my father, and whomever else we invited would dine at my father's or aunt's house. The tradition was fast becoming one of my favorite reasons for returning to Crystal Cove. I loved the camaraderie and conversation.

What to make? I set aside the mail and collected a few cookbooks from the bookshelf. I flipped through them. When I landed on a double dark chocolate cupcake recipe with a picture that made my mouth water, I knew I had a winner. The recipe was in, of all things, *The How Can It Be Gluten Free Cookbook* by America's Test Kitchen. Katie touted the wonderful recipes she had discovered within its pages. She said loads more people were trying to eat healthier by avoiding gluten. The authors of the cookbook had given all sorts of tips and hints as to how to make something gluten-free taste nearly the same as goodies made with regular flour. Along with the cookbook, Katie had provided me with gluten-free flour and a binding agent called xanthan gum so I would be prepared to bake upon a moment's notice. Like now.

I assembled the ingredients on the counter and fetched another slice of cheese. Tigger traipsed behind me, hoping for a dropped tidbit.

"Uh-uh, kitty," I cooed. "Not a chance." I handed him a couple of tuna morsels and set them in his bowl. He ate them, albeit reluctantly, and eyed me with disfavor. "Tough."

After whipping up the mixture and using an ice cream scoop to pour dollops of batter into greased cupcake tins, my cell phone rang. The readout said: *Cinnamon Pritchett*.

I stabbed the word Accept. "You got my message."

"Yes," she snapped. "Why else would I call you?"

"I don't know. Perhaps for a weather update. Perhaps to tell me Bucky and you are tying the knot. You know, girl talk." I pretended to be lighthearted, but my nerves were firing inside me. What did she know? Was Neil the killer? Had Pepper—

"Jenna, stop."

"Stop what?"

"I need you to stop playing the concerned citizen."

"*Playing the*—" Whoa! Talk about coming out of left field. "I'm not *playing* anything. You said for me to call if I had information."

"I've changed my mind."

"Changed—"

"Look," Cinnamon cut me off. "I don't need you touching base with me daily to give me updates."

"What happened to your command that I *listen* and *report* back to you?"

"I rescind it. I need you to butt out."

"Hold it." Frustrated, I waved a hand in the air. "Why are you so ticked off at me? What did I do? Does this have anything to do with Bailey and me asking you about your relationship with Alison?"

"No."

"Why then?"

Silence.

"Cinnamon," I pleaded. "C'mon, talk to me. We're friends, right? Be honest."

She sighed. "I'm getting complaints."

"From whom? Who's calling you?"

"Actually, they're texts."

"Texts."

"Telling me to do my job and not to rely on the locals to do it for me."

"Who's sending these texts?"

"I don't know."

"What?" The word burst from my mouth. "You're laying into me because of some anonymous texts that could have come from a prankster using a burner phone?"

More silence.

I flashed on Neil. He was a practical joker. Was he sending the messages? Was he scared that I would dig deeper?

"My team is on this, Jenna."

"Maybe Neil Foodie is sending you those texts," I said. "He's an aspiring comic. He—"

"Stop. Please. We know about Neil Foodie. We know about a whole lot of things."

"Do you know who inherits Alison's estate? Like possibly Neil?"

She didn't respond.

"Do you know whether or not Alison was pregnant? Or whether the argument Alison had with Ingrid Lake—"

Cinnamon heaved a sigh.

"Fine," I said. "Be that way." Sheesh, I sounded petulant. Moments ago, I was moping about like a teenager, and now I was acting like a two-year-old. *Grow up!* But, honestly, couldn't Cinnamon be a little more receptive? I had valid information.

"Good night, Jenna." She clicked off.

I stared at my cell phone with outright anger. So much for our budding friendship. If Cinnamon were standing in my kitchen, I'd give her a piece of my mind. But she wasn't. All I could do was scream. Tigger yowled his displeasure.

"Hush," I muttered.

I removed the meat loaf from the oven, but my appetite had flown the coop. When the meat loaf cooled, I would store it in the fridge. In the meantime, I baked the cupcakes with lackluster enthusiasm. I would decorate them tomorrow.

Around midnight, I went to sleep. I left the windows open during the night so I could hear the rain and feel a cool breeze. Despite those attempts to bring calm into my world, I slept fitfully.

At dawn Sunday morning, the caw of seagulls woke me.
The rain had abated, although moisture still hung in the air.
I could run if I chose to, which I did. Barefoot. I love the
feel of sand beneath my feet. Even wet sand. It makes me
feel like I'm communing with the earth.

A couple of times, I paused to watch a rare sighting, a
snowy white egret wading in the shallows of the ocean,
stalking its prey. If more humans than just little old me had
been around, the egret would have been scared off. Lifting
one foot slowly, it moved forward, barely making a ripple.
Then *bam!* It lunged for breakfast—a fish.

At that same moment, the sun ascended over the crest of
the mountains behind me. Sunlight cut through a clump of
clouds and highlighted the egret. Perfect for picture taking,
if only I had a camera. I'd left my cell phone at the cottage.

Church bells chimed, signaling that I had spent more
time on the beach than I realized. I raced home, showered,
and threw on a nifty pair of jeans, a ribbed cotton sweater,
and flip-flops. I downed a quickie breakfast of a hard-boiled
egg and a handful of grapes and headed to work.

When Tigger and I entered The Cookbook Nook, we
found Bailey dusting shelves. I set Tigger on the floor. Bailey's American shorthair, Hershey, was yet again nestled in
the cozy reading chair. Tigger meowed at Hershey and ran
off, daring the cat to join him in a game of *catch me if you
can*. Hershey, who looked like he could lose a pound or two,
couldn't be bothered. Tigger, no matter how hard he tried,
was not going to be hired as the cat's personal trainer.

"Morning," Bailey said without glancing my way. She
didn't look like she had slept any better than I had. Her hairdo
was spikier than usual. Her makeup looked slapped on.

"Is everything okay?" I asked.

"Yes."

"Did you have a fight with Tito?"

"No. We never fight. It's . . ." She gazed at Hershey.

I understood the look. Ah, the joys of being a new pet owner.

Bailey said, "Did you hear from Cinnamon?"

I recapped our terse conversation.

"What's her problem?" Bailey said. "Why is she such a control freak?"

"Don't be too hard on her," I said, having told myself the same thing last night while I applied ice to my post-crying-hissy-fit puffy eyes. "Cinnamon is a woman in a man's world. She wants respect. And she wants to set the pace."

"Pace-schmace," Bailey muttered. "Did you ask her whether she arrested Coco?"

"I didn't get the chance."

"Let's go find out for ourselves. Your aunt is here. We won't open for another hour." On Sundays we opened at 10:00 instead of 9:00 A.M. "How about I buy you a morning pastry at Sweet Sensations?" She grabbed her purse. "Vera! I'm taking Jenna out for a quick coffee. We'll be right back."

Before I could argue, Bailey muscled me out the door, and we jogged to Sweet Sensations. Flip-flops, by the way, are not very good for jogging.

Sun peeked through big pillows of clouds, warming an otherwise cool day, and shone down upon a cluster of people that were huddling outside the candy shop. Everyone seemed to be eyeing treats in the display window. More folks were crowded inside the shop.

"Is there a sale going on?" I asked Bailey.

"Got me."

When we finally made our way into the pink-on-pink shop—pink-striped wallpaper; pink-and-white checkerboard floor; pink countertops on all the glass cases—we realized what the lure was. Coco was, indeed, free, and she was having a chocolate-tasting party. She had thrown one the last time she released a cookbook, too. Dozens of trays of candy lay on top of the glass cases. Each tray held at least six different kinds of candies: sparkling pink fudge, chocolate-glazed squares, thin bark-like chocolates, two different colored suckers, and, specially for Pirate Week, Pirate's Booty fudge.

Coco spotted us and hurried from behind the counter, leaving her assistant, who was a chunky young woman with a fondness for all things Hello Kitty from her sweater to her jewelry, to tend to the customers.

"Bailey! Jenna! I'm so thrilled to see you." Coco had poured herself into another *va-va-voom* dress that fit her figure like a glove, this one 1950s' style, with a tapered bodice and pleated skirt. Her apron and the skirt beneath flounced as she moved.

Bailey said, "We're thrilled to see you, too. You're not in jail. Obviously, Chief Pritchett doesn't suspect you any longer."

"Isn't it wonderful?" Coco grabbed our hands and squeezed. "I didn't think, since Alison's funeral was so private, that a party was too gauche of me. Do you think it is?"

What could we say? Her customers didn't seem to mind. Perhaps the temptation to learn more about the murder intrigued everyone. Maybe they were here simply because Coco made the best chocolate around.

Bailey withdrew her hand and petted Coco's shoulder. "It's fine."

"What did Cinnamon say when you went to the precinct?" I asked.

"Once I explained why I hadn't wanted to reveal who I was with—you know, to protect him—she was very sympathetic. Well, not sympathetic but considerate."

"But this time you told her it was Simon, right?" Bailey asked.

Coco nodded and beckoned us to follow her to her office at the back of the shop.

The office was bigger than a bread box, but not much, and it was cluttered to the max. Crates, boxes, and a pair of file cabinets lined the walls. A teensy pink desk stood in the middle of the room. On top of the desk sat piles of papers, magazines, recipe cards, recipe boxes, and containers holding pens in every pink hue imaginable.

"Welcome to my workroom." Coco blushed. "It's nothing like my kitchen, which is pristine. I guess this is where the real pack rat in me comes out. I never get rid of any paper. I know I should streamline and do everything on the computer, but I can't. Part of my process is writing everything down. You should see how many recipe cards have notes on them.

Add more of this; use a little less of this. I tweak until it's just right. My grandmother and mother did the same thing. How I treasure their recipes." She pressed a hand to her chest. "Here, let me show you one." She leafed through a category in the recipe box. "My *bunica*'s Chocolate Bombs, the recipe Alison made . . ." Her voice caught. She cleared her throat of what had to be overwhelming emotion remembering that night. "Boy, are these sticky." She rubbed her fingers on her apron and resumed her search. "Hmm." She screwed up her mouth.

"What's wrong?" I asked.

"That one's missing. Guess I took it home. I'll have to look for it there. But, here, look at this one." Coco plucked a card from the grouping and twirled it so we could read it. "Vanilla fudge. It's to die for. See the notes down the side and wrapping around to the other side of the card? My grandmother was adamant that I use cream of tartar. But not too much. At first a quarter teaspoon, but then an eighth, and then my mother revised it to just a pinch. See?" She giggled. "It's funny, isn't it? I can hear them speaking to me through these cards." Coco replaced the recipe card and set aside the box.

Bailey patted Coco's shoulder. "We were discussing Chief Pritchett and your alibi."

"Oh, right." Coco pounded her fists together. "The chief said she wouldn't approach Simon's wife as long as he came in and backed up my account."

"And did he?" Bailey pressed.

"I don't know. We haven't spoken. We thought . . ." Coco licked her lips. "*He* thought that we should cool it for now."

Uh-oh. Maybe that was why I had seen Simon lurking outside her shop last night. He intended to tell her he couldn't come forward.

Coco jammed the pointy heel of one shoe into the checkerboard floor. "He's right, of course. I just miss him. That night . . ." She rolled her eyes in a dreamy way. "It was our first time, our first official date. Well, not official, since it was clandestine." Coco flamed the same color as her pink dress. "Simon has come into the shop so many times. To sample the wares. He's such a flirt."

I didn't get that impression. I'd seen Simon in action with Faith Fairchild, trying to keep his distance at all costs. Perhaps out of view from his wife, with Coco in the privacy of her shop . . .

"I fell hard for him," Coco went on. "Yes, I know he's married, but I don't care. I mean, I do. But I want him and he wants me. We tried not to cross the line, but when he called, how could I say no? The night was . . . magical." Coco blanched. "I'm sorry, that was crass of me. It was the same night that Alison—" She gasped for breath.

I gripped her shoulder. "It's okay. Go on. Simon."

"I can't even describe how I feel around him. He's like no one I've ever met. He knows wine, and he adores people. Have you ever seen him talk to the clientele at Vines? He's so charismatic. And he reads just about everything, from bird-watching to politics. His wife." Coco sniffed. "She doesn't get him at all."

"So you said the other day," Bailey chimed.

"She's so bossy."

"I'm not sure *bossy* is how I'd describe her," I said. "The words *self-sufficient* and *commanding* come to mind."

"Why do men choose women like their mothers?" Coco asked. "He can't do enough to please her, either. His sister gets all the praise. And now that she's had a baby? Argh! He'll never hear the end of it from his mother. Gloria wouldn't dare have a baby. It'd hurt her figure. Me? I'd love to have ten babies." She sighed. "And Simon's book, the one that Alison is going to publish?"

Was going to might be a more apt phrase. Who knew what Foodie Publishing would do at this point?

"Simon told me all about it," Coco gushed. "It's wonderful. He draws on the family's history, his mother's family in particular. Her grandfather owned a vineyard in the old country. Very Italian." Coco stabbed the air. "But is his mother impressed that he got a publishing deal? No, she is not! And Gloria . . . don't get me started. She needs him to *do* more, to *be* more." Coco sucked on her lower lip in a girlish way. "I think that's why he likes me. I'm not bossy in the least. Sure,

I run my own company, but I'm not in-your-face overbearing. We've fallen in love and, well"—she fanned her neck—"that's why he asked me to spend a night at Nature's Retreat."

"When his wife was out of town," I said, stating the obvious.

"I know." Coco pouted. "I shouldn't have said *yes*. I should have waited until the divorce is final, but how could I? I adore him."

Bailey offered a skeptical look, like a girl who had drunk that same fairy-tale tea but was now immune to the stuff. "Does Gloria know?"

"She must."

I said, "Friday, at the shop, she didn't seem like she was preparing for a life alone."

"You're wrong. Didn't you see how she ordered him around? Didn't you see the looks he was giving her?" Coco shot a finger at me. "I know you did, Jenna. That's why you told me to go to the precinct."

"You have to admit that he seemed quite attentive to her."

"It's all an act. For the public."

"Sweetie," I said and instantly regretted the use of the word. I didn't mean to be dismissive. "He ran his knuckles down her arm. They made eye contact. There were sparks in that exchange."

"He's leaving her." Coco slumped into one hip. "You should have seen how attentive he was to me at Nature's Retreat. We made love and then he ran a bath for me. A bath! No man has ever done that. And he brought me champagne and hand-fed me chocolates . . . that I'd made, of course. It was so romantic."

I'll bet, which convinced me further that this was purely an affair and not a lifelong commitment. No man could romance a woman with that kind of dedication, day in and day out.

Bailey exchanged a knowing look with me and said, "We'll have to see, won't we? But no matter what, you're innocent. So let's put our heads together. Who else might have wanted Alison dead?"

Chapter 16

C OCO, BAILEY, AND I batted around theories for quite a while. We ended our discussion when Coco's assistant begged for Coco to return to the counter. The crowd had swelled. All were clamoring for more of the Pirate's Booty fudge. By Valentine's Day, Sweet Sensations was bound to be overwrought with orders.

Bailey and I headed back to the shop, and throughout the remainder of the day, we continued theorizing. By the time I entered my aunt's house for dinner, my mind was awhirl with possibilities.

"Cupcakes," I announced as I moved through the foyer of her one-story beach home, past the marble-topped console table, to the hall. Tigger trotted in behind me. He didn't embrace the outdoors like most cats, but he could make his way from my cottage to my aunt's without panicking. Quickly he found his favorite velveteen footstool in the adjoining living room and leaped onto it for a nap.

My aunt exited the kitchen and met me halfway down the hall, arms extended. She bussed me on the cheek then eyed my works of art and smiled. "I think you're getting the hang of this."

"I used a pastry tube fitted with a starburst tip to pipe the chocolate frosting."

"Very pretty. Nearly professional." She chuckled. "However, perhaps you were heavy-handed with the sprinkles."

I glanced at the tray of cupcakes and had to agree. "It's a carryover from yesterday. The kids loved pouring glitter on their creations."

Aunt Vera took the tray and jutted her chin toward the back of the house. "Your father and Lola are on the deck. I've put out some Caribbean-themed appetizers. All are easy enough for you to make."

A crisp wind off the ocean hit me as I opened the exterior door and walked outside. I was glad I'd donned the ribbed sweater and not something flimsier. The sun, a stunning ball of orange, was halfway submerged over the horizon.

I drew in a deep calming breath. "Hi, Dad. Hi, Lola."

The porch was set up in a cozy conversation style, with a wicker settee and a half dozen matching chairs, all facing one another. My father and Lola were sitting on the settee. On the coffee table in front of them sat platters of colorful appetizers, including a spicy dip encircled with chips, shrimp-stuffed mushrooms, and chicken-pineapple kebabs. Aunt Vera could whip up a gourmet meal almost as fast as Katie could. On a side cart stood wineglasses and a bottle of white wine in an icer. My father and Lola each held a glass of wine.

"Jenna, welcome," Lola said. She was a vision in a silver sweater, silver leggings, and silver sandals. "You look peaked." She rose from the settee and embraced me. "Aren't you getting any sleep?"

"Not really. This thing with Alison . . ." I sidled to my father and pecked his cheek.

"Dear Alison," Lola murmured. "She was a lovely woman. I had nothing but utmost respect for her. She had a talent. She knew exactly what to pare from the cookbooks she published on my behalf."

"That's what I keep hearing."

"Did you know Alison loved to bake? She learned at the age of five. Her mother taught her. She had fond memories of those times."

"She told Bailey and me the same thing at the book club event."

Lola peered past me. "Where is my daughter?"

"Present and accounted for!" Bailey clomped through the door, her wedge sandals making a racket on the wooden porch. She carried a bottle of red wine in her hand. "Did you tell them?"

"Tell us what?" Lola looked from Bailey to me. "Did the police catch the killer?"

"Not yet," I said. "But Bailey and I have been batting around ideas about who killed Alison." Even if Cinnamon didn't want my help, she couldn't prevent me from theorizing.

Bailey set down the wine and removed the cork. She poured herself a glass of merlot and asked if I wanted one. I opted for the white wine, a scrumptiously oaky chardonnay.

"What theories?" Lola asked. At one time, Lola had practiced law with some of the sharpest, toughest minds in California. She had given up her illustrious career for a simpler life in Crystal Cove and was thrilled with the choice. Otherwise, she never would have wound up with my father.

Bailey plopped onto a chair, took a sip of her wine, and said, "First of all, Coco is innocent. She's got a verifiable alibi."

"Verifiable," I inserted, "when *he* comes forward."

"If he hasn't already," Bailey said.

"He, who?" Lola asked.

"Can't say." I mimed zipping my lips.

Lola looked to Bailey, who also mimed locking her mouth.

My father grunted and leaned forward to dunk a chip into the bowl of dip. He crunched as loudly as he had grunted.

I shot him a dour look. "What, Dad? Got something to say?"

"Nope. Nothing."

"Don't you like the spices?" I taunted. "Too pungent for you? *Arrr*, matey. You could do with some spice."

Lola grinned. Dad scowled.

"C'mon. Out with it," I said. "You have an opinion."

"Not one I'll share." Dad held up a hand as if he was ready to swear in court. "I am not an authority."

"Neither am I, but that doesn't mean I can't speculate."

"Here we go," he muttered.

I heaved a sigh. "Dad, let's not do this every time."

"That's just it, isn't it?" he said. "Here we are with another *every* time. Another murder, in our town, and somehow you've landed in the thick of it."

"Because a friend of ours died."

"You barely knew her."

"Bailey knew her very well, and I help my friends!" I nabbed a chicken-pineapple kebab and wielded it like a sword. *Parry, lunge, thrust. Take that, you scalawag.* "Aren't you the one who said, only last week, that Crystal Cove is as susceptible to crime as, say, big, old Los Angeles?"

"Jenna."

"Cary!" Wow. Had I uttered my father's first name? Out loud? Sassy is fine; impudent is off the mark. *Cool your jets, Jenna.* I bit off the top portion of a kebab and purred my appreciation. Aunt Vera had made a deliciously tangy pepper-infused sauce.

After a long silence, my father said, "Don't put words into my mouth."

"Fine." I sounded calmer . . . *quasi* adult. "What did you say, exactly?"

"What I said was, 'You must not lose faith in humanity. Humanity is an ocean; if a few drops of the ocean are dirty, the ocean does not become dirty.'"

"I like my loose translation," I muttered.

"Who am I citing?"

"Mahatma Gandhi," I conceded. Dad could always best me in a game of who said what, but I had memorized pretty much all the quotes he'd put before me over the years. I nestled onto the wicker armchair, set my skewer on a napkin, and eyed Bailey. "Let's not talk about our theories tonight."

"No, no." Lola settled beside my father and elbowed him hard in the ribs. "Let's *do* talk about them."

Aunt Vera joined us on the deck and, while rubbing her phoenix amulet, drew in a deep breath. "Isn't the view incredible tonight?"

We all chimed, "Yes," then glanced at my aunt. Had she been listening to our discord? Had she stroked her amulet to work her magic on us and bring us into harmony? She was crafty beyond sly. We didn't have any Gypsy in our family line, as far as I knew, but at times I wondered if my aunt could channel pixie or something elfin.

Aunt Vera kissed her fingertips and blew bad karma toward the sea. "Now, tell us, Jenna, who do you suspect the most?"

"Neil," I said.

"Aha, the brother." Aunt Vera waved a hand. "Go on."

"Neil told me he was at a stand-up nightclub when his sister was killed."

My aunt said, "I always felt that boy had too much of the rascal in him, cracking jokes at inappropriate times. Did you know he toilet papered the church when he was in high school? Stand-up." She harrumphed as she settled onto the arm of the settee. "Yes, that suits him."

"But he wasn't at the comedy club," I said. "He lied."

"Did you ask him where he was?" Lola asked.

"No. I tried to tell Cinnamon that he fibbed, but she advised me to butt out. She said she and her team were on the case."

"There." My father spread his arms apart as if the case was officially closed.

Bailey bounded to her feet. "No, not *there*. The police can be on the case all they want, but if the case isn't solved, it's not solved. We have information. That *they* should want." She eyed me.

I glanced at my father. He leveled me with a glare. If I could have retreated like a tortoise into its shell, I would have.

Bailey continued, "Neil has motive and, now, with no alibi, opportunity. First, the motive." She held up an index finger. "To inherit Alison's estate."

Lola said, "Which consists of . . ."

"I would imagine her condo in San Francisco"—Bailey ticked off her fingertips—"and her business and who knows what else."

"But you're not sure." Lola rose and began to pace as if addressing the court. "This must be determined."

I said, "Neil admitted to me that he's in debt."

"Not everyone will kill to pay off a debt," my father argued.

Lola agreed. "Who else makes the suspect list?"

My father grunted again, but I could tell he was becoming engaged in the discussion. His eyes were bright, and he was leaning forward, forearms propped on his thighs.

"Ingrid Lake," I said. "The copyeditor."

"I don't trust that girl," Aunt Vera said. "She's wound as tightly as a top."

I explained that Ingrid and Alison had argued that night and, later, she was seen at Vines Wine Bistro, drinking alone.

"What did they argue about?" Lola asked.

"Apparently, Alison fired her," I said.

"Which you told Cinnamon," my father inserted.

"She didn't let me. She hung up on me." I was still seething from her treatment.

Bailey waved a hand. "There's more. It's possible Ingrid and Alison were disputing ownership of the company. Ingrid claims she was on track to becoming a partner. She was awaiting a contract."

"Aha!" Lola said. "A broken promise is a good motive."

"And then there's Dash Hamada," I stated. "The photographer. I'm certain Dash had a thing for Alison."

"He told you this?" my father asked.

"Not in so many words."

He cocked his head. "Now you're a professional profiler?"

Lola swatted my father's thigh. "Cary, cut it out. You know you love Jenna's mind. You've told me so time and again."

He had? News to me. My boss at Taylor & Squibb had been just as taciturn as my father until I quit my job. Then he gushed about how he hated to lose his prized executive. Too little, too late.

Lola said, "Cut her some slack, Cary."

My father glanced at me sideways. His mouth twitched at the corners. Was Lola right? Had he been provoking me on purpose? The devil. Was that how he had cajoled Cinnamon into changing from an errant teen into a law-abiding do-gooder?

"Go on, Jenna," Lola said.

"I think Alison was pregnant. And not by Dash. I did mention that possibility to Cinnamon. Who knows whether she'll follow up."

Dad said, "She'll follow up."

"Anyway," I continued, "if Dash found out the baby wasn't his—"

"Were they an item?" Aunt Vera said.

"No." I waved a hand. "That's just it. I think he worshiped her from afar."

"Don't you see?" Bailey cut in. "If he loved her and found out she was in love with someone else and was going to have a family with that person, he might have lashed out."

"Except that guy died," I added quickly, "of natural causes. So, in truth, Dash could have made a move on Alison and become the kid's stepfather."

"If there was a child," my father reasoned.

"Whatever." Bailey held up her wineglass. "That's all we've got. Three suspects."

Lola swirled her glass of wine. "Don't forget Coco."

"But she's been exonerated," Bailey cried.

My father offered an ingratiating look. "Has she? Really?"

"Dinner!" Aunt Vera announced.

Bailey and I helped unfold the bay windows so the dining room was open to the patio and, therefore, the beach. The sun had fully set. The sky was awash with orange-tinged clouds that would quickly turn gray with night.

I lit candles. Afterward, Bailey and I set out platters of Caribbean-style food including whitefish and plantains, jerk chicken wings, rice and beans, and an appetizing cucumber salad. I took a chair facing the sunset and drank in the beauty. Ever since returning to Crystal Cove, I couldn't get enough of staring at the ocean. For the first few months, all

I could imagine when looking at the water was my husband dying on his sailboat. Now, I turned to the ocean for inspiration and hope.

Through dinner, we chatted about normal life, not murder. However, over dessert, while my father and aunt were praising my cupcakes—Dad hadn't realized they were gluten-free—Bailey said something to her mother . . . quite loudly.

"You're wrong, Mother."

"Wrong about what?" Aunt Vera asked.

Lola didn't respond.

"Bailey?" Aunt Vera said, rubbing her amulet with her thumb and forefinger.

"Coco would never have used scissors to kill Alison."

"In a fit of passion," Lola said.

"There were knives, Mother, which are much easier to wield."

I had thought the same thing.

"And Coco wasn't upset with Alison's cuts to her latest work," Bailey added.

Aha. So Lola had made the connection between scissors and an editor's cuts.

"That's the scuttlebutt at The Pelican Brief," Lola said.

"Local gossip is not always correct," Bailey snapped. "You of all people should realize that!" Lola had been suspected of murder a couple of months ago. At the time, the town had teemed with rumors about Lola and the victim. Bailey jabbed a fork into a bite of her cupcake. I couldn't ever remember her eating a cupcake like a normal person. Slicing it up like a big piece of cake, she claimed, made it taste more decadent. She held up the fork and waggled it, cake and all. "Coco talked glowingly about how good an editor Alison was. She loved Foodie Publishing and the product it put out."

"Then why does she have a contract with a bigger publisher?" Lola said over the brim of her coffee cup, "If Coco has a better possibility on the horizon, perhaps Alison didn't want to let her out of her contract."

"Can't an author work for two publishers?" Bailey asked.

"It would depend on the contract stipulations," Lola responded. "Back to the married man with whom she's having an affair."

Bailey protested, "I didn't say she was having an affair."

"Darling, you didn't have to. He must not have come forward or, I assure you, I would have heard about it at the diner."

"Not true, Mother. The police promised confidentiality."

Lola petted her daughter's cheek. "You are such an innocent."

Was she? Was I? Was Coco? Why had Cinnamon exonerated Coco? Perhaps it was a ploy. Maybe Cinnamon had let her go free, hoping Coco would slip up.

Chapter 17

ON MONDAY MORNING, panic shot through me. We had so much to do at the shop. So many boxes to unpack; so many books to put on shelves. As soon as Wednesday, we would have to deconstruct the Pirate's Week theme and put up something for Valentine's Day. Yipes! I had already assigned Bailey the job of cutting out cupids and hearts for the window display. Luckily, in addition to all the chocolate-themed cookbooks we had on hand, I'd thought ahead to order dozens that focused specifically on Valentine's Day. I had even remembered to stock a number of children's fiction books like *The Day It Rained Hearts*, which was all about sharing, and *Pete the Cat: Valentine's Day Is Cool*, complete with poster, punch-out valentines, and stickers. Parents and grandparents would come in droves to purchase those for their little darlings.

Around noon, concerned about Katie and how her mother was faring, I called her. She told me she was hanging in, though she wasn't great. Her mother was struggling with balancing her medications. Katie promised she would return by Wednesday. I assured her Chef Phil was doing just fine and to take her time. It wasn't a lie; business was cooking at the Nook Café.

Soon after, Mayor Zeller bustled into the shop, her arms filled with a ream of heavy-stock paper.

"Hi, Z.Z.," I said. "Are you all right?"

She was perspiring. Her blouse was only half tucked into her trousers. "I'm fine. On a mission." She pulled off a sheet of paper and handed it to me. It was another poster regarding the missing pot of doubloons. I'd nearly forgotten the pot had been stolen. "Will you replace the notice in your window, Jenna?"

On the poster, she'd printed: *Reward for Return of the Pot of Doubloons—$2,000.* Twice the amount she had been offering. Beneath the announcement, she had inserted one of the Internet pictures of the absconded pot and added, *Thief! Enough of this silly business. Own up to your mistake, and you will not be punished.*

"Really?" I said. "No punishment?"

The mayor chortled. "Aw, Jenna, I can tell this hoax is all in fun. People all over town are laughing about it."

"What if the thief turns the pot in? Will he or she get the two thousand dollars?"

"Heavens, no!" The mayor's gaze narrowed. She scanned the poster. "Oh, I see what you mean. Hmm. Too late now. I've put up over fifty of these."

As I was removing the first poster from the window, I caught sight of Neil Foodie heading across the parking lot with the sassy waitress from Vines Wine Bistro on his arm. Today, her curly hair was tucked into a sporty ponytail. She was laughing at something he said.

Seeing Neil made me wonder whether Cinnamon was following up on him. He had lied about his alibi, and yet he was still at large. I stepped outside and hailed him. "Hey, Neil, hold up. How was the funeral?"

The waitress wiggled her fingers, sang out, "See ya," and trotted upstairs.

Neil grew respectfully serious. "Fine."

"How's your mother?"

"Sleeping." He spied the poster in my hand. "Yo ho. The mayor is offering a reward? Some lucky stiff is going to be happy."

"Do you have a clue who stole the pot?"

He frowned. "Nah. Do you?"

"No." Why would I have asked?

Neil started toward the stairs.

"Before you go," I said and tapped his arm.

"What?" He spit out the word with such venom, a shiver shimmied down my spine.

I backed up a step. "Quick question. You said you were at the comedy club the night your sister died. However, I called." I wasn't going to bring Bailey into the matter.

"Why would you—" Neil chewed his teeth then clicked his tongue against them. "Yeah, so?"

"The owner said you weren't there."

"Sure I was. I . . . I . . ." He sputtered. "I was in costume. Pirate costume. Big plumed hat. Fake nose. I even used a phony name. No one recognized me."

I peered into his eyes. Truth or lie? I couldn't tell. His gaze was flat.

"I told you, I was trying out new material," he went on. "Real fresh stuff."

"Fresh."

"Yeah. I came up with this great idea. But like I told you the other day, I didn't tell anyone because I didn't want some joker to steal my routine. Comedy isn't copyrighted. You snooze, you lose."

"Even if they didn't know it was you, someone in the audience could steal the material, Neil."

He lasered me with an edgy stare. He was lying. I was sure of it. But I couldn't prove it. Shoot.

"Gotta go." He flew upstairs.

Midway through the afternoon, I had a craving for a latte and a snack. I headed along the breezeway toward the café, but I paused when through the plate-glass window I caught sight of Beaders of Paradise. Feeling surprisingly maternal, I wondered whether Pepper could use a pick-me-up. I went to check on her, but I hung back when I heard footsteps pounding the second-floor landing.

A woman shouted. "It's your mother we're talking about!"

At the top of the stairs leading to the second floor of Fisherman's Village, Simon and his wife appeared. Simon was leading and doing his best to ignore his wife. Gloria, who was clad in a cheery lemon yellow outfit, looked anything but joyful.

"You have an obligation to her," she continued while pursuing him, her voice so shrill it made my teeth chatter.

"I don't owe her a dratted thing," Simon countered, over his shoulder.

"It's her family's history. You promised. Before she died. She's on death's door."

"I told you, it was shelved."

"Well, un-shelve it. I swear, Simon, you are a recipe for disaster. What do I have to do to keep you on target? Tell me, honestly, what? You have all this intelligence running around in that marvelous brain of yours"—she waved her muscular arms overhead—"and yet you waste it by putting things on ice."

Simon whirled around. "I didn't postpone anything."

Gloria poked him in the chest. "Do not *ever* tell me I'm wrong. I know better than you. I always will."

Gack! Coco was right. Gloria was a bully.

Gloria breezed past Simon and across the parking lot. Not keen for her to catch me overhearing their spat, I hurried back to the shop. I would do Pepper a favor another time.

Once I was safely installed behind the counter and my teeth stopped clicking like an out-of-control Geiger counter, I thought about mothers. Mine. Katie's. Simon's. I wondered how Alison's mother, Wanda, was doing, too. Her son wasn't the warmest, most caring soul. Had Neil consoled her or tended to her needs in the slightest after the funeral? Wanda had put her daughter—her eldest—in a grave.

I hailed Aunt Vera and said I'd like to check on Wanda Foodie. Bailey heard me and begged to come along. My aunt was more than willing to man the register. Business was often slow around this time in the afternoon. Typically our customers were picking up kids at school or doing last-minute grocery shopping.

WANDA FOODIE LIVED in a modest home, which, like so many homes in Crystal Cove, was painted white with a red-tiled roof. The garden was well tended. A beautifully sculpted wooden dolphin stood in the center of the grass.

I strode up the path to the front porch and came to a halt. I tugged on the hem of my sweater, finger-combed my hair, and then rang the doorbell.

Bailey pulled alongside me. "I'll bet she knows who killed Alison. She must. Mothers know everything." The words sped out of her lightning fast. "You were so smart to come here. If she can tell us—"

I put a hand on her forearm to calm her.

Wanda didn't answer the door. Ingrid Lake did. She attempted a smile. With her teeth wedged together like always, she reminded me of a sneering cornered dog.

"She's sleeping," Ingrid said when I asked to see Wanda. "She does that a lot. Neil says not to wake her whenever it happens. It's just a nap. I'm sure she'll rouse soon. Come in." Ingrid escorted us into the well-appointed foyer, complete with an antique console, ladder-back chairs, and an array of blue silk flowers in a ceramic vase. She slid the door closed. In a hushed voice, she said, "I'm glad you stopped by, Jenna. I have news about what we were talking about."

"What we were—"

"In regard to Alison. On The Pier. You know what I'm saying." The words came out in a hiss.

I shook my head.

"She wasn't *PG*," Ingrid offered cryptically.

"How can you be sure she wasn't pregnant?"

"I have proof." Ingrid peeked around the corner of the foyer into the living room. I followed her gaze.

The room consisted of a large couch, a couple of brown Barcaloungers, end tables, a modest coffee table, and a television atop a console. Wanda Foodie, big-boned and almost the spitting image of Alison except she had gray-streaked hair, lay asleep in one of the Barcaloungers; her mouth hung open. The television was switched on but muted. Beyond the Barcaloungers stood a dinette set. A desktop computer sat on the dining table. A web page for Neil Foodie was open on the screen. Didn't he tell me he hadn't constructed a website yet? Had Ingrid been checking him out?

Ingrid tapped my arm so I would refocus on her. She said, "I wasn't being a snoop, I want you to know. I was emptying the guest bathroom trash, and through the plastic bag, I saw what looked like the remnants of a First Response kit, so I opened the bag. The test strip hadn't changed color, which is indicative of a negative result. I know because, well, you understand. *Phew*, right?" Ingrid twirled a finger in front of her abdomen, hinting she had tested for pregnancy at least once.

An image of Ingrid trying to kiss a guy with her teeth clenched caused nervous laughter to bubble up inside me. I tamped it down.

"How did the kit get there?" Bailey asked. "Alison was staying at Coco's."

"She was staying there the second night," Ingrid explained. "The first night, Alison bunked here. She came in a day early to have dinner with her mother. She vacated so I'd have a place to stay."

I recalled Alison saying the same.

"She must have taken the test that night." Ingrid plucked at the bow of her silk blouse. "By the way, Jenna, I saw Dash on The Pier earlier. I was thinking about him after you and I talked. I don't know if it's right for me to tell you, but he got mad at Alison once."

Pointing fingers seemed to be a hobby of just about everyone this week. I said, "Go on."

Ingrid's eyes blazed with fervor. "It happened about six months ago. He came into the office hopping mad. He was brandishing a vegetarian cookbook we published, *Smart*

Eats: From Avocado to Zucchini. He'd provided photographs for about twenty of its recipes. Well, it turned out, Alison didn't like the work he did, so she took her own photos and installed them in the book. She had given Dash the credit, which made him furious. He said her work was subpar, and why on earth would she do that without asking him? He would have gladly reshot anything she didn't like. She said she didn't have time." Ingrid toyed with the tails of the bow. "Alison was often in a hurry. *My way or the highway*, that's what she would say. Dash said she could have ruined his reputation. I've never seen him so mad."

"Did it ruin his reputation?"

"You'd have to ask him. He has lots of irons in the fire, I think."

"Speaking of disputes," I said, "I heard you and Alison argued on the night of the book club event. She fired you."

Ingrid's eyes widened. "Would you like tea while we wait for Wanda to stir?" She didn't hang around for a response. She strolled away.

Bailey gave me an exaggerated eye roll.

I nudged her to follow.

The kitchen was as comfortable as the living room, decorated with granite counters and chocolate-colored appliances. Bailey sidled onto a stool at the island in the center. I continued to stand. Ingrid filled a teakettle, lit a flame on the gas stove, and set the teakettle over it. Then she strode to a cabinet and fetched three pretty china cups.

I repeated, "Alison fired you."

Ingrid hiccupped out a laugh. "She fired me weekly. Do you think I killed her over a silly thing like that? It was no big deal."

Had she drummed up that response while making tea?

"You threatened you had legal rights," I said.

"Yes, that's my go-to defense." Ingrid withdrew three Earl Grey tea bags from another cabinet and placed them in the cups. "You see, Alison promised on more than one occasion to give me a stake in the company, but she never drew up papers. She could be quite mercurial. I nagged her and told her a woman's word is her bond. She thought that was hysterically funny."

"Why would she have wanted you as her partner?"

"Because I'm good."

No lack of confidence there. I said, "Alison claimed you were too meticulous. She had to redo your work."

"That had to cost her time and money," Bailey added.

"It didn't." Ingrid fluffed a hand in the air. "I got the work done in a timely fashion. Always."

"Some of Coco's recipes were open on Alison's computer," I said. "Do you know why?"

"Yeah," Bailey backed me up. "Was Alison intent on pointing out your previous mistakes?"

Ingrid whirled around, fury in her gaze. At the same time, the teakettle started to jiggle and whistle. Ingrid cut a hard glance at the kettle, and then, just as quickly as she had come to a boil, she cooled to a simmer. She retrieved the kettle and poured steaming hot water into the three cups. "Sugar or honey?" she asked over her shoulder.

"Honey," Bailey said.

"Neither for me," I replied.

Ingrid squeezed a dollop of honey into one teacup and stirred it with a spoon.

"Well?" Bailey pressed. "Answer me."

Ingrid clanked the spoon on the rim of the cup. "I have no idea why those recipes were on the computer. I didn't go to the house. We didn't talk. They are as much a mystery to me as they are to you."

Ingrid picked up a single teacup, removed the tea bag, dropped it in the sink, and returned to the living room. Bailey and I did the same. In silence, we sipped tea for a half hour. When Wanda still didn't waken—she was snoring like a longshoreman—we headed out.

At the door, I turned back to Ingrid. "By the way, I was talking with Neil."

"Mama's boy." She sniffed her dislike.

"He said something that concerned me. You claim you

went home to watch TV the night Alison died, and then you went to Vines. Neil said you borrowed his mother's car."

"I did."

"Well, he didn't see it in the garage when he got home. At four A.M." I let the time hang in the air. "Where were you?"

Ingrid folded her arms across her chest. "My, my. Small towns. Does everyone around here know everyone else's business?"

I waited patiently. Bailey, not as tolerant as I, tapped her foot.

"I only sleep a few hours each night," Ingrid said. "I can't watch TV all the time. Boring. So I went to Vines. I told you that, but I certainly didn't want to drink more than a glass of wine, so I drove around."

"You ordered a whole bottle," I said, remembering Faith's energetic and gossipy account.

"It's cheaper that way if you want a good glass of wine. They corked the rest. I put it in the trunk of the car. Want to see the bottle? It's in the fridge." Ingrid stabbed a finger toward the kitchen.

She was feisty; I had to give her that. "Where did you drive?" I asked.

"Up and down the coast."

"All night long?" Bailey blurted.

"Well past four A.M. I find driving clears my mind, important in my line of business. Editing can be quite tedious."

"Witnesses?" I asked.

"I almost ran into an old guy on a tractor. Around midnight, if that matters."

Yes, it mattered. A near accident around midnight would provide her with an alibi.

"He came out of nowhere. Just north of The Pier. I honked like crazy. He spun around and nearly did a wheelie. He had a gnarly face."

Ingrid was referring to Old Jake. He volunteered to sweep the beaches at night. He wasn't likely to forget an incident like that.

Chapter 18

THE REMAINDER OF the day dragged on. I created to-do lists up the wazoo. My aunt told two fortunes. Bailey tried, repeatedly, to get Hershey to sit in her lap, and Tigger attempted to lure Hershey into a game of chase. The cat wasn't friendly to human or feline. After work, I slogged home, ate leftover meat loaf—it warmed nicely in the microwave—and nearly fell into bed.

The next day, Tuesday, was my day off. Crystal Cove was a resort type of town, and souvenir buyers were at a maximum pretty much every day of the week. We stayed open on weekends; however, in order to keep our sanity, we closed the shop and café on Sunday at dusk, and we closed it one full day a week, as well—Tuesday. When I was at Taylor & Squibb, I had worked twenty-four-seven, with very little time off for good behavior. Once I returned to Crystal Cove, I made a sensible decision not to live like that ever again.

I rose late and went out for a walk, not a run. I was simply too exhausted from Monday's rash of activity, and I needed energy for the evening's event—the finale for Pirate Week. Sunlight shone down on me, but I didn't worry about it burning my skin. I'd put on a long-sleeved shirt, long linen pants, and a sun hat. An hour later, I returned home and baked easy-to-make chocolate scones.

After pulling the goodies out of the oven to cool, I whipped up a creamy batch of scrambled eggs. I fixed a plate with my meal, poured myself a cup of tea, and moved to the mini patio to dine. Tigger followed, excited to get whatever treats I might add to his bowl. I didn't disappoint. I had stocked the cupboards with grain-free snacks that he adored.

While I dined on the patio, I dug into *The New Wine Country Cookbook: Recipes from California's Central Coast.* There were over 120 wine-friendly recipes, but the photographs alone were enough to draw me inside the cover. Over the past few months, I had fallen in love with the stories of how cookbook authors came up with recipes. Often I would lap up the author's descriptions of the dish. *Zippy*, *zesty*, and *zingy* were some of my favorite adjectives. At times, the way the author laid out the recipe was what grabbed me. Was it easy to understand? Did the author have a sense of humor when relating the steps necessary to complete a complicated dish? Did those words inspire me to take the plunge? These things mattered to my customers and now to me.

After breakfast, I set up an easel on the patio and focused on Bailey's painting, making more headway than I thought I would. Creativity doesn't always come when beckoned, so when it does come, I never waste it. I painted for three hours. By the time I quit, my wrists and forearms were sore.

Following lunch, I took a luxurious bath, dried my hair, and concentrated on my costume for the evening. A few items needed pressing. I hate to iron, but one or two days a year, I can manage.

Rhett arrived before dusk. He was dressed in the same debonair red-and-blue pirate's costume he had worn at the climbing wall. "Wow, me lass," he said, taking me in his arms and planting a firm kiss on my lips. "Aren't ye the sleekest beauty on which I've ever laid eyes."

"Ahem. I'm a guy."

"Oh, right." He cleared his throat. "Ye make a fine-looking pirate. Nice outfit for a mate."

"Thank you, me hearty."

I had visited a used-clothing store to purchase pieces for my costume. For the top half, I'd bought the perfect black velvet jacket, nipped at the waist. I had sewn ecru lace on the cuffs and added gold buttons in two rows down the front. Beneath, I wore a white blouse, fastened at the neck. For the bottom half of the costume, I'd settled for leggings tucked into thigh-high black boots.

I swiveled to let him admire my backside.

He grinned. "Indeed, a fine mate."

I put on a black tricorn hat that I had adorned with gold trim and a giant black feather, and we were off.

On The Pier, a wealth of people in costumes paraded the boardwalk amid freestanding white canvas sales stalls. At one stall, you could purchase scarves and shawls. At another, you could paw through a treasure trove of glitzy jewelry. Food carts catering to all tastes abounded, as well.

Someone tapped on a microphone. *Thump, thump.*

"Testing!" A woman's voice radiated through amplifiers.

I swung around and spied Mayor Zeller standing atop a raised stage midway down The Pier. A moderate-sized crowd surrounded her. I grabbed Rhett's hand and hurried toward the gathering.

"Who among ye has stolen the pot of doubloons?" The mayor shouted in a raspy pirate accent while brandishing one of her latest posters. She looked poured into her brown-toned innkeeper outfit.

Many in the throng waved their hands then laughed uproariously. "Just kidding," a few quipped.

The mayor said, "I'll have ye know, we know who ye are. If ye come in now, ye'll not suffer. If we have to nab ye, ye shall suffer for your crime."

"Make him walk the plank!" an observer shouted.

"Off with his head!" yelled another.

"Don't be chiding me." The mayor wagged a fist and

scanned the throng. "Beware, matey. Beware!" She switched off the microphone and climbed off the stage.

I drew near. "No luck yet, Z.Z.?"

The mayor shook her head. "I'm holding on to hope."

Rhett and I moved on. Near The Pearl jewelry store, I caught sight of Dash, who looked every bit as flamboyant as Johnny Depp in *Pirates of the Caribbean*. Black braids, black leather jacket, black trousers and boots. He was taking a photograph of Sterling and another handsome guy who was much taller and heftier than the jewelry store owner. Both were poking their heads through holes in a life-sized cutout of a pair of pirates and looking at one another adoringly.

"Hold it. That's it," Dash said. "Say cheesecake!"

Just beyond the scene stood two carny guys I had dubbed Mutt and Jeff a few months ago. I still didn't know their names. Mutt was huge and furry; Jeff was so skinny I wondered how his trousers, sans belt, stayed up. They were eyeing Sterling and his friend with unconcealed disgust. *Who were they to judge?* I mused. Only a few months ago, Mutt had been at Jeff's throat when he believed Jeff was having an affair with his wife. Love was nothing if not unpredictable.

I glanced back at Dash, wondering about the story Ingrid had told me. Did Alison replace his photos with subpar photos she had taken? Did Dash lose his temper? The dispute happened six months ago. Would Dash have held a grudge this long? Did that give him a second motive for murder, the first being unrequited love? I watched him taking photographs of Sterling and his friend from all angles, and another—less dire—thought occurred to me. Was Dash the gold doubloons thief? The pot had disappeared the night he arrived in town. Directly afterward, photos appeared on the World Wide Web. I recalled Alison saying Dash was Internet savvy; his website was deep and thorough. Could he have managed to create and delete blog after blog for the pure fun of taunting our beloved mayor and Pirate Week–loving crowds in Crystal Cove? On the other hand, everyone on the boardwalk was taking pictures, and I would bet there were plenty of shrewd Internet users among them.

A swell of people started pushing past us, heading toward the far end of The Pier. Each was chatting excitedly. I spotted Rosie, the waitress from Mum's the Word Diner, among the throng and hurried to her.

"What's going on?"

"The pot of gold doubloons turned up."

"Did the thief hand it over?" Maybe the mayor's campaign and her announcement a few minutes ago had done the trick.

"Yep. An anonymous caller"—Rosie flapped a hand—"told the mayor to look under the stage. Voilà. There it was! Z.Z.'s ready to award the pot to the winner! I hope it's me." Rosie waved her ticket as enthusiastically as the children with the golden tickets in *Charlie and the Chocolate Factory*.

I eyed Rhett. "Do you have a ticket?"

He grinned. "Nope. Can you believe it? I handed them all out at the store and forgot to keep one for myself. Did you get one?"

"What do I need with a fake pot of doubloons?"

"Bragging rights."

We neared The Theater on The Pier, and the door opened. Loud music, not pirate fare, spilled out. Bucky Winston, a handsome-as-all-get-out fireman—the guy could be the poster boy for volunteers—emerged and waved to Rhett. "Hey, me hearties! You're late." Bucky was bare chested beneath his pirate jacket and looked downright devilish. He and Cinnamon had started dating a few months ago; it was Cinnamon's first serious relationship after the breakup with Rhett. What she hadn't realized when she fell for Bucky was what good friends he was with Rhett. "Hurry up, you old sea dogs!" Bucky gestured for us to run. "Get your bods in here!"

So much for having the time to see who won the pot of doubloons. It had been recovered. That was all that mattered.

The Theater on The Pier was set up like an old dance hall or saloon. All patrons sat around cocktail tables. The red brocade cushions on the cane-backed chairs matched the other plush décor. Turn-of-the-century-style footlights jutted up from the apron of the semicircular stage and cast a warm glow across the area.

The stage could hold about ten people, but tonight, there was only a piano, a mustachioed pirate piano player, a singing pirate, and a hornpipe player—a hornpipe is a clarinet-like instrument that was often used on old ships; I knew because we had used a hornpipe player in a Salty Seadog Potato Chips campaign. The singing pirate wasn't exactly dressed as a pirate. He looked more like an Elvis impersonator in foppish clothes. He peered into the distance at a television monitor situated over the antique bar on which words were scrolling. His huge swoop of dark hair bounced as he sang his heart out to "Suspicious Minds." The guy wasn't half bad. His entourage, an aging octet of gaudy pirate wenches with a combined number of face-lifts and breast enhancements enough for the entire female population of Crystal Cove, whooped and hollered their support. Every time he sang the chorus, the wenches joined in.

I nudged Rhett and asked telepathically, *What have we gotten ourselves into?* He chuckled.

"Care to sing?" a slim woman in a corseted getup trilled as she sashayed by us. She was carrying a bowl filled with tickets. "Anyone? Take a number."

"We'll pass," Rhett and I said together.

Bucky steered us to a table where Cinnamon, who had curled and tousled her typically straight hair and looked ravishing in a red dress, one shoulder exposed, sat sipping a glass of water. Rhett and I settled into chairs opposite her. A redheaded waitress, also dressed in a corseted outfit, took our orders.

When she departed, Cinnamon eyed my costume. "Really? You're a guy?"

"Not exactly." I explained the inspiration.

"I would have preferred to wear your outfit," she said. "Why didn't you cue me in?"

Yeah, right. Like we had communicated a lot lately. I didn't think now was the time to mention that. Why spoil the mood?

"But darlin'," Bucky cut in. "You're yar."

"*Yar?*" Cinnamon retorted. "Are you comparing me to a sailboat?"

Bucky gently clipped her cheek with his knuckles. "Ye handle well."

She batted his hand away and blew him a kiss.

I had to admit, I enjoyed seeing her having fun and did my best to put aside the grumblings about how shabbily she had treated me of late.

Our drinks arrived: a glass of wine for me, two Dos Equis, and a nonalcoholic margarita for Cinnamon. I raised a toast. "To you, Cinnamon, and the truth."

Cinnamon raised a skeptical eyebrow.

"Thank you for believing Coco and exonerating her," I said.

"Ahh." She sipped her drink.

"I assume you did it, based on"—I lowered my voice in an effort to keep Coco's secret confidential—"Simon Butler's corroboration."

"Nope. He hasn't come forward yet," Cinnamon whispered back. "And he's not returning calls."

"Really? Then why—"

"I believe her. For now. Let's stay positive."

As composed as Cinnamon seemed, I wondered whether she had solved the case and was simply waiting for more corroborative evidence before making an arrest. She took another sip of her cocktail. I followed suit while thinking about Simon's wife, Gloria. Had she laid into him because she found out about his dalliance with Coco? Had she forbidden him to offer testimony on Coco's behalf? Cinnamon's cryptic words *for now* clanged in my brain. What if *for now* vanished and Coco was once again the main suspect in Alison's death?

Elvis finished singing and bowed repeatedly as his age-defying female fans whooped it up.

The piano player called out, "Seventeen. Come forward, you lucky landlubber!"

Cinnamon glanced at what turned out to be a ticket jutting from beneath her cocktail napkin and bounded to her feet. "That's me!"

My aunt had told me Cinnamon sang like an angel. After her rebellious high school years but prior to serving as the chief of police, Cinnamon had appeared in a number of local theater programs.

I turned to Bucky. "What's she going to sing?"

"Heck knows. She's been mum all day. Saving her voice, she said."

Was that why she hadn't called me back?

Cinnamon climbed the steps to the stage and, lacking any nervousness at all, chatted with the pianist. He murmured something to the hornpipe player, who began to beat time with his foot. The pair launched into a rhythmic number.

After a few bars, Cinnamon joined them in a jazzy rendition of "Ac-Cent-Tchu-Ate the Positive." My mouth dropped open. Wow! She hit every note with gusto. An angel? My aunt was wrong. Cinnamon was a chanteuse. A diva. I chortled and Bucky glowered at me.

"What? I'm not making fun. I'm aghast. In awe." I raised my glass again. "To Cinnamon. She's good. Not just good. Great. I'm truly blown away."

When Cinnamon concluded, the audience went wild. Many chanted, "Chief, Chief, Chief." I think most of them were as amazed as I was that our chief of police had so much talent.

Cinnamon returned to the table, flushed and out of breath. Perhaps she was more nervous than I had allowed. Bucky gave her a peck on the cheek and told her how marvelous she was. Rhett offered a wink.

"Where is our waitress?" Bucky said. "We need champagne." He rose out of his chair.

"No champagne for me," Cinnamon said. "It'll go right to my head. Perrier, please."

Rhett said, "I'll go with you, Bucky."

Once the men left the table, I said to Cinnamon, "Great job."

"Do you think so?"

I gave her a curious look. "You know you're excellent."

"I'm not bad."

"Humility becomes you."

"I'll never make singing my profession."

"Good. We need you here. Speaking of which . . . I didn't get to tell you everything last time we spoke." I didn't add, *Because you hung up on me.* "There's something you really need to know."

Cinnamon rolled her eyes. "Not now."

"Then when? You don't call," I sassed. "You don't write."

She lasered me with a stern look. "Fine. Go ahead. Make my day."

"Alison fired her copyeditor, Ingrid Lake, right after the cookbook club event. Your mother overheard the conversation."

"Why didn't my mother tell me?" Cinnamon clenched her teeth. "Never mind. I know why. What else?"

"When I visited Mrs. Foodie yesterday—"

"Why did you do that?"

"Because it was the neighborly thing to do. I was thinking about my mom—about all moms—and I thought of her. I was worried. Ingrid Lake was there. By the way, she found a First Response kit. Alison was not pregnant, just in case you hadn't found out."

"We had. I told you we're on top of things." Cinnamon's gaze flared with exasperation. "Anything else?"

"Yes. Back to Ingrid . . ." I replayed Ingrid's account of how avid she was to tell me that Alison and Dash argued over a photo spread. "According to Ingrid, Alison put Dash's name on photos she took and used them in a cookbook."

"And that's bad, why?" Cinnamon asked.

"Because Dash's reputation could suffer if the photos weren't good. Luckily for him, he has a solid alibi. He was here singing at the piano bar that night. Lots of people must have seen him. As for Ingrid's alibi—"

"Hold it." Cinnamon stopped me with her palm. "Dash said he was here?"

"Uh-huh."

"Funny. I was here that night. Until closing. And I don't remember seeing him."

Chapter 19

CINNAMON LEFT THE theater to track down Dash. Rhett and I hung around on The Pier. We gobbled spicy dogs and snuggled close to watch the fireworks. Spectacular. Afterward, we returned to the cottage for a nightcap. The evening ended with some lovely kisses. He drove home, and I slept better than I had in a week.

On Wednesday morning, I awoke feeling chipper and eager to tackle the day. After throwing on a bright red sweater and my favorite pair of twill trousers, I fed Tigger, gulped down a honey-laced fruit smoothie—heavy on the fruit—and headed to work.

"Good morning, Jenna, dear," Aunt Vera said as I entered The Cookbook Nook. She was sitting at the vintage table shuffling a deck of tarot cards. A client sat opposite her. "Come near." She stacked the tarot cards on the table, tapped the top card with a fingertip, and bid me closer.

I set Tigger on the floor, slung my purse onto the sales counter, and joined my aunt.

She clutched my hand. Hers were clammy. "I nearly called you at midnight," she said in a raspy whisper.

"Why?"

"I had the most unnerving dream. You were in it, dressed in pirate costume, and running as fast as you could. You were glancing over your shoulder."

My heartbeat kicked up a notch. So much for my good night's sleep. My smoothie threatened to make a reappearance. *Down, down.* I urged myself to remain calm. I didn't usually overreact when people said they had bad feelings about some aspect of my life, but when my aunt did, I took heed. "What else?"

"Soon, the dream filled with people singing and lights exploding. Pop, pop, pop!" Aunt Vera released me and flicked her fingers with each *pop.* "Is something troubling you?"

"No." At least not as far as I knew. I cycled through my thoughts—was my brain ever at rest or empty?—and repeated, "No."

"Is anyone stalking you?"

A shiver ran down my spine. "Double no."

"Hmm." My aunt frowned. "Then it was nothing." She shooed me away.

Of course, saying it was *nothing* didn't reassure me. Now I was revved up. My aunt's dreams, like mine, could be colorful and often prophetic. Shoot. I hated tiptoeing around, looking over my shoulder. There was no reason for anyone to stalk me. I tried to shrug off my aunt's concern. Perhaps thinking about Alison's tragic end had triggered her dream. Unless, of course, she was picking up some psychic message, like Alison's killer thought I knew something that could implicate him or her. Did I?

"Yo ho!" Bailey entered the shop. She sounded chipper, but her face looked drawn and her hair was limp. She carried Hershey tucked under her arm. "Hello, winsome lass."

I raised an eyebrow. "Are you okay?"

"Am I trying too hard?" she asked.

"Perhaps a touch. Besides, Pirate Week is over. It concluded last night. I repeat, are you okay? You look, um—how to put it nicely?—ruffled."

"Cat troubles." She held up Hershey and wiggled one of

his paws as a greeting. He growled. "Hush, you," she ordered. "He didn't want to leave the apartment."

"Why not?"

"I haven't a clue. He cried all night. Is that what cats do? Cry?"

I read that cats have about one hundred vocalizations, which they sling together to try to make us understand them because humans don't pick up on their body language. Tigger makes all sorts of noises. A trill, which was halfway between a purr and a meow, means: *Happy to see you*. A growl? Definitely means *back off*. A chattering sound, similar to that of a squirrel? Yes, Tigger chatters at the window whenever there's a bird outside. It means he wants out. Now!

I said, "Maybe Hershey is feeling a little anxious. Cats need to get used to their environs."

Bailey shuffled Hershey around in her arms so she could stare into his eyes. "Is that what's bothering you?"

He yowled.

Bailey flinched. "What does that mean?"

"That's a final warning. Usually before a fight begins."

She stretched out her arms. "Take him." Hershey's legs dangled beneath him. "Help me."

I grabbed the cat. He craned his head, his gaze aimed at the floor. Tigger stood beneath us. "Aha!" I said. "Perhaps Hershey is feeling intimidated because he has to share space with another cat. Don't worry. He'll find his niche." I set him on the floor.

Tigger pounced toward him. Hershey darted in the opposite direction and leaped into his chair. He tucked his tail around him.

"Tigger," I said. "Cool it."

My kitten hunkered down, head lower than his haunches. He wanted to play, but he would wait for Hershey to come around. He had learned a tad of self-control around children.

Bailey tossed her purse onto a shelf beneath the sales counter. "Wow! I never knew a cat could have so much attitude." Over her shoulder, she said to Hershey, "You'll have to move when the children get here, buddy." The cat didn't deign to look her way. Bailey huffed and slumped forward, both elbows on the counter. "Now what?" she said to me. "Is it something I did?"

"No. Sometimes cats are aloof."

"I want a friendly cat. Like me. Like Tigger."

"Leave Hershey be," I said. "He's either like you, or he isn't. You can't change him."

She grumbled her disappointment. "What do you need me to do around here?"

For the next hour, we straightened and dusted bookshelves. Mid-morning, as I organized the trays of chocolate swirl muffins in the breezeway that Chef Phil had brought in for our guests, I spied Dash entering the café with a raven-haired, statuesque beauty. Why was he still at large? Apparently, Cinnamon hadn't apprehended him.

I said to Bailey, "Back in a sec," and I hurried to the café. No, I didn't plan to make a citizen's arrest, but I did want to find out if Cinnamon had interrogated him and cleared him.

The aroma of fresh-baked muffins, cornbread, and croissants filled the air. My salivary glands went into high alert. If given the opportunity, I would've devoured an entire basket of the goodies. A smoothie was not enough to keep a girl going.

Across the room, the hostess was showing Dash and his date to a table for two. Dash was wearing the same outfit he had worn when I first met him. His date sported a summery number more appropriate for one hundred degree, not fifty-five degree, weather. Dash gallantly pulled the chair out for his date. He sat in the opposite chair. He said something to the hostess and grinned.

The hostess's hand flew to her chest. She did a U-turn and raced to the podium. She reached for a pair of menus.

I stopped her and said, "I'll deliver those." I wasn't sure what I would say to Dash; I'd wing it. I approached the table with the menus. "Good morning," was all that came out of my mouth. How clever. Not.

Dash acknowledged me with a nod.

I handed out the menus. "Say, Dash, has Chief Pritchett

contacted you?" Again, real slick. Where had my gift of gab gone?

Dash raised an eyebrow. "No, why would she need to?"

"I think you should touch base with her."

"What about?" He set his menu aside and seared me with a look.

I glanced around the café. Business was good. Diners filled all the tables. Dash wouldn't assail me with this many witnesses around. Not that he would need to hurt me. He very well might be innocent. "You and Alison argued," I said, feeling comfortable telling him what I knew. "She published a cookbook using her own photos and attributed them to you."

"Yeah, so?" Dash lifted a water glass and downed half of the contents. "That was months ago. What's your point?"

"Your reputation was on the line."

Dash set the glass down and leaned back in his chair. "Are you asking whether that made me angry enough to kill her?"

His date's eyes fluttered.

"It's okay, lass." Dash leaned forward and patted her hand. "I didn't kill anybody." He returned his gaze to me. "Look, what Alison did was wrong, but it didn't cost me a job. Not one. Her photos weren't good—in fact they stank— but in the end, I was able to convince a couple of employers that they weren't mine. Big deal."

"Why would she do that to you?" I asked.

He shrugged. "I asked her the same thing, and she said, she had wanted different angles, ASAP. I was working on another shoot and wasn't available. Publishing is all about meeting deadlines." He shrugged again. "She made a mistake. I forgave her and put it in the past. 'As the Lord has forgiven you, so you also must forgive.' Colossians 3:13."

I wasn't sure what impressed me more, that he could forgive Alison or that he knew biblical passages by heart. "You forgave her because you liked her."

"Yeah."

"A lot."

"I told you—"

"A *lot*," I repeated. "In fact, you loved her."

Dash ran his tongue along his teeth and clicked at the end. "Yeah, so?"

"Did you love her enough to forgive her when she put your book about tattoos on hold?"

"Where did you hear—" Dash scrubbed his chin. "Never mind. I know where. Ingrid Lake. She's got a mouth, that girl does. What a conniver. Always plotting, always planning." He thumped the table with his palm. "Look, Alison put a ton of books on hold. Bailey's mom's book. The Wine Country book. Another book by Coco Chastain. Some vegetarian piece of garbage by a well-known chef. Postponing projects isn't a big deal. Contracts are made; contracts can be broken. Alison was paring back. The erratic economy is making the publishing business quite volatile." Dash folded his arms across his chest. The tattoos on his forearms bulged. "I understood, and I was willing to be patient. Alison was my biggest, steadiest employer when it came to my photography work. What was I going to say? I'd walk? Fat chance."

"At the cookbook club event, she touted your work. What happened?"

"During dessert, she made a snap decision. She pulled the plug. Who knows what got into her? She could be quite impulsive. Funny thing. That's what I liked—" Dash hesitated. "*Loved* about her." He pitched forward and handed a menu to his date. "I didn't hold a grudge. Alison agreed to give me back the rights so I could shop it elsewhere. Like in *The Godfather*, it's 'just business.'"

Actually, Michael Corleone said to Sonny that it was "*strictly* business." My husband had been a *Godfather* aficionado—I must have seen the film fifty times—but I wouldn't quibble. I said, "Coco found another publisher to publish hers."

"Bully for her. I've already got a few bites of my own." Dash gestured to the menu. "Now, if you don't mind, I'd like to order, then I'm hitting the road. Back to San Francisco. Back to the real world." He shoved his hand into one of the outside pockets of his photographer's vest to fetch a pair of glasses.

When he reached into another for a swatch of silk to rub smudges off his glasses, I flashed on the night I had met him at the café. He was taking pictures of Coco and Alison nonstop and paused only to wipe the lens of his camera. Soon after, Tigger, the scamp, slipped into Dash's pockets and stole strips of contact prints. Dash snatched them back. What was on them? Something incriminating? I saw a set of strips peeking from an inside pocket of his vest. I recalled Alison saying Dash wouldn't go anywhere without them. He was paranoid that someone might swipe them.

"I'd like to see those contact prints." I pointed.

"Show me your badge," Dash said.

I made a move toward them.

He tossed the menu to the floor and gripped my wrist like a vice. "Don't!"

I winced. His grip was strong. His eyes blazed with fury. *You're in a public place* cycled through my head. *Relax.*

"Dash, let me go."

"Why should I? You've got some nerve."

His date shocked me by sliding her hand across his chest and reaching into the pocket. She pulled out the contact prints and gasped. "What are these?" She flashed the images at me.

I caught a quick glimpse. There were myriad black-and-white images of Alison in various states of undress, as seen through gauzy curtains or slatted shades.

"You pervert," the date said.

"No," Dash protested. "You don't understand."

There were also images of Alison the night she died, her back to the camera lens. She was sitting at her computer, staring at the screen while bracing her forehead with her left hand.

"Wow," I whispered. Dash hadn't been simply in love with Alison; he had been obsessed with her.

"I understand enough," the date hissed and hurled the contact prints at Dash. "Good-bye and good riddance." She bolted from her chair and hurried out of the restaurant.

Dash glowered at me while shuffling the contact prints into a stack. "You," he muttered.

"Did Alison realize you were taking those photographs of her?" I said. "Did she threaten to expose you? Is that why you killed her?"

"I didn't do it." Dash's voice grew gruff and full of emotion. "I told you. I have an alibi."

"Which can be debunked. The chief of police was at the karaoke place the night Alison was killed. She didn't see you there."

Dash's gaze turned as dark as the ocean at midnight. "Okay, I lied. I wasn't there. I was photographing Alison, but I swear I didn't kill her. You've got to believe me. I loved her."

"You are a voyeur."

"No. I . . . okay, yes, but only of Alison."

"Why her?"

"Because she *got* me." His voice flooded with emotion. "She understood me. Every aspect of me. She didn't mind that I was offbeat. She didn't mind the multiple tattoos and my weird quirks."

"Did you tell her about this?" I shot a finger at the contact prints in his hand.

Dash's eyes fluttered. "That night, after I took these photos, I went back to Sterling's house to develop them. I intended to tell Alison the next day. I was going to admit my feelings and show her the photos. They're gorgeous shots. They're art. Look at them. Closely." He spread them, using his thumb. "Alison didn't think she was beautiful. She felt she was too large, too mannish looking. I wanted her to know how exquisite she was." A sob escaped his throat. "I thought seeing herself as I saw her might make her feel, you know . . . good."

Or downright creepy.

"Can Sterling corroborate your whereabouts?"

"No. He was out with his new boyfriend." Dash's mouth turned downward. "Ah, man. If only I'd stuck around Coco's house that night. I might have seen the killer."

Chapter 20

I WASN'T SURE I believed Dash, but it wasn't my job to determine the truthfulness of his claim. My duty was to inform the police of his whereabouts. I hurried back to The Cookbook Nook and fetched my cell phone from my pocket to dial the precinct.

Bailey bolted to me and gripped my wrist. "Not so fast. Put down the phone. What is up with you running off again?"

I told her about Dash's contact prints.

"Ew." She squinched up her nose. "He is definitely a perv. Okay, call."

"Thank you for your permission."

I couldn't reach Cinnamon; I settled for Deputy Appleby. He listened patiently and said he was *on it*.

After I disconnected, I dumped my phone back in my pocket and rounded up my aunt. She, Bailey, and I set about dismantling all the pirate things we had put out for Pirate Week.

Aunt Vera moved the Caribbean cookbooks to the foreign food section while Bailey collected the pirate-themed books and set them on a special sales table. We couldn't send them back to the publishers; they were nonreturnable. A discount of fifty percent would make them popular. If not, we would store them for next year's Pirate Week festivities. Cookbooks never grow old. Well, of course, some do, like those from the Middle Ages, but who needed a recipe for roasted peacock cooked over an open hearth? Actually, I knew a couple of clients who might love a Middle Ages cookbook, and made a mental note to track one down.

I eyed the wealth of craft items we had amassed in the children's section and decided instead to tackle the deconstruction of the display window.

While I was boxing up the seagull that had dangled over the seascape, Coco sashayed into the shop in a snug pink dress. A pink Prada tote hung over her shoulder. Out of the top of the tote spilled pink-embossed envelopes.

Coco plucked an envelope from the collection and handed it to me. "Here's your invitation."

"To . . ."

"Sweet Sensations' Valentine's Day Lollapalooza, of course."

I grinned. "What a mouthful, worthy of a cookbook title." I removed the invitation from its gorgeous envelope and perused the text. "Why are you having another event? You just threw a delicious chocolate tasting on Sunday."

"A shop can never do enough to lure customers."

How true. "When is it?"

"Tomorrow! Gotta nab that fresh batch of tourists." Coco blew out a gust of air. "Boy, oh, boy, I can't tell you how much I hate publicity! I am an artist. I bake. I glaze. I ice. I don't want to go around town doing *this*." She whacked her tote.

"Especially in those heels," I joked. She was wearing precipitously high, spiky heels.

"But you and I"—she waggled a finger between us—"both know how important it is to make sure the locals know what's going on, face-to-face. I couldn't ask my Hello Kitty–loving assistant to do the dirty work, could I?" She barked out a laugh. "Honestly, I don't think that girl ever learned the art of communication. She's the one-word-answer queen." Coco pulled a couple more invitations out of her bag. "And don't get me started on how much I despise doing social media stuff."

"But you're so good at it," I said.

"Only because I have to be. *Friend* me; *like* me; show me the love!" She snorted. "Ah, yes, the Internet. It's the way of the world. At least I don't have your worry."

"What's that?"

"No one will ever digitalize the taste of chocolate. People will always be coming to Sweet Sensations for a morsel. You can't e-book that."

I winced. Yes, we had to worry about what the digital age might do to our cookbook sales, but customers—*our* customers—still loved the feel of paper. They enjoyed flipping through cookbooks. They treasured collecting them and filling their home shelves with them. I wasn't too worried about a drop in sales. Yet.

A police car pulled into the parking lot. At the same time, I caught sight of the vivacious waitress from Vines Wine Bistro hightailing it toward Buena Vista Boulevard. She was a blur of orange. Her hair, cinched in a ponytail, wafted behind her.

I raced outside and yelled, "Is there a fire?"

"No fire," she responded, "but there are storm clouds on the horizon."

The sky was a gorgeous blue and cloud free. What the heck was she talking about?

"Neil quit," she went on. "He came into some money. A couple thou." She pointed upward. "That upset Gloria, and then Simon said something to her—I'm not sure what—and she went ballistic! I'm out of here."

I looked in the direction of her aim. Gloria was charging down the stairs that led from the second floor to the ground level of Fisherman's Village. Clad in a clingy black top and leggings, her burgundy hair hidden beneath a black knit hat, her typically colorful accessories exchanged for black ones, she looked like a ninja ready to attack. A pair of black binoculars on a black strap bounced on her chest. Had she gone bird-watching with Simon after all her complaints about it?

What do you bet she suspected Simon was cheating on her, which would explain why she was spending so much time at Vines as well as with him. She didn't want to let him out of her sight. Pity the poor fool who crossed her path right now.

Gloria stole a look in my direction, and I blanched. Her face wasn't filled with anger about Neil quitting. It was streaked with tears. What had her husband said to her? Did he admit he was in love with another woman?

A door slammed. Across the parking lot, Deputy Appleby was exiting the police car that had pulled in moments ago. He headed toward the café and looked longingly toward The Cookbook Nook entrance. Was he still regretting that my aunt had broken off their relationship? Hadn't she had a heart-to-heart with him yet? After acknowledging me, he charged inside the café.

Coco peeped out the front door. "What's going on?"

I moved inside the shop and jabbed a finger toward Gloria, who was climbing into a Cadillac SUV. "Someone isn't happy."

Coco breathed high in her chest. "Is she . . . did he . . . tell her he was leaving her?"

"I think he might have."

Gloria yanked the door of her car closed.

Coco nearly vibrated with anticipation. I didn't think anyone could look so gleeful over the prospect of divorce. "I've got to go to him." She nudged her tote higher on her shoulder.

"Wait, Coco!" I held her back.

Gloria was reopening the door of her SUV.

Coco gasped. "Oh no. She's coming back. She's going to plead with him. She's . . . oh, *phew!*"

Gloria yanked on her purse strap, which had gotten caught on the door handle. She tugged and jerked again, and finally released it. *Slam!* She closed the door a second time.

The moment Gloria peeled rubber out of the parking lot, Coco said, "I'll be right back," and she sprinted upstairs to the wine bistro.

A few minutes later, Deputy Appleby exited the café with Dash Hamada. Dash wasn't putting up a fuss.

A quarter of an hour later, Coco hadn't resurfaced. Who knew what Simon was telling her? I worried about her, but I couldn't fix it, no matter what *it* was. Simon and Coco were adults. Gloria, too.

I was busy fitting various items from the display window into a storage box, reserving the four-foot-long toy ship with the three masts for last, when Wanda Foodie shuffled into the shop. Wanda had donned exactly what Alison had worn to the book club meeting—a red shawl over red sweater and plaid slacks—and I was struck, yet again, by how much she looked like her daughter. If not for the typical signs of age, they could have been twins, except Wanda's face looked drawn, her eyes puffy.

I hurried to her and gave her a hug. "Mrs. Foodie."

"Call me Wanda. How many times do I have to tell you that, Jenna?" Although she had visited the shop a few times, I'd never noticed that she sounded as throaty as Alison.

Bailey stopped primping the sales table and hastened to join us. She gave Wanda a hug. "You look good."

"Nonsense. I'm a disaster." Wanda flicked the air with a finger. "I heard you two stopped by the house to check in on me. That was sweet of you." She offered a thin, tired smile.

Aunt Vera strolled to Wanda and took her by the hand. "Wanda, dear." My aunt stroked gently, doing her best to infuse good energy into the beleaguered woman. "I'm so sorry for your loss."

Wanda pulled her hand free and raised her chin in a stately manner. "We carry on. We must, mustn't we, Vera?"

"Why have you come in?" I asked.

"I wanted to thank you for your consideration."

"You shouldn't have gone out of your way—"

"It wasn't an inconvenience." Wanda fussed with the shawl. Her fingers shook. "I've also come to pick up my son. His car broke down yesterday. What a heap he drives. He had to meet with his boss. Now, I have to take him home to change clothes before we visit Alison's attorney. What a chatty man he is. We have quite a few matters to settle in regard to Alison's estate, he tells me."

I was stunned. Alison hadn't been dead a week. "So soon?"

"Time marches on. The attorney would like to get this over with as quickly as possible. He informed me that Neil and I are the only two named in the will. Of course, funds won't be released for quite some months."

I glanced out the front door, recalling what the ponytailed waitress had said about Neil coming into some cash. Where did he get off quitting if he wasn't getting inheritance money right away? He told me he had debts. "Wanda, I heard a rumor that Neil gave notice at Vines."

Wanda nodded. "Yes, he quit. That's why he came in early today."

"Did he get a paying stand-up comedy gig?"

"A what?" Wanda shot me a curious look.

"He—" I hesitated. Perhaps he hadn't shared that facet, or any facet, of his life with his mother. Deftly, I switched topics. "What will happen to Foodie Publishing? Will you hire someone to run it? Like Ingrid Lake?"

"Ingrid? Why I . . ." Wanda covered her mouth to hide a yawn. "I don't believe she could handle the pressure. Besides, the attorney said he has buyers lined up, if we are of the mind to sell."

Bailey said, "Um, Wanda, forgive for me saying this, but I'm surprised that Alison included Neil in her will."

"Why wouldn't she? He's family."

"Yes, but—" Bailey blanched. She eyed me. I kept mum. All I knew was hearsay. I had never seen Neil interact with his sister.

Wanda drew taller. "Years ago, I convinced Alison to take pity on her brother. He is an innocent soul. He's not as bright as she was, it's sad to say, but he is kind beyond words."

Ingrid's words *Mama's boy* rang out in my head, except, from Wanda's account, I deduced Neil was not her favorite child. Alison had been. Simon's and Dash's comments that Neil had resented Alison replayed in my mind. Had Wanda revealed to her son how weak she thought he was? Did bile boil inside him until he lashed out at his sister? Why not

kill the mother instead? Because he loved her. Needed her.
Wanted to be her one and only.

Wanda added, "Sweet Neil will be lost without Alison.
Like a ship without a mooring."

Did she really believe that? Was she deluding herself?

Returning to the previous thread of conversation, I said,
"What will Neil do now that he's leaving Vines?"

"He's going to return to his old job."

"Doing what?"

"He used to be a computer technician. He's very good
at it."

Yipes! How had I not put two and two together? The
waitress from Vines said Neil had come into a couple of
thousand dollars. Did he receive the reward money for
returning the pot of doubloons? I'd already theorized that
the thief who absconded with the pot of doubloons was a
tech-savvy person. I'd considered Dash the culprit because
of the timing of his arrival to town and the fact that he had
an in-depth website, but Neil, if he was a computer geek,
could have orchestrated the whole thing. He claimed he
hadn't constructed a website, and yet I had seen one—
whether or not it was up and running—on the computer on
his mother's dining table. Why would he steal the pot? He
said he needed *fresh* material for his stand-up comedy routine. Was his plan to tell funny stories about the theft? None
of his competition would be able to duplicate the tales of
his caper. He even had photos he could share with his audience, photos that he had put up and taken down on illusive
blogs. *Fresh*, indeed!

Did his antics absolve him of killing his sister? Not necessarily. Though he was traveling from site to site to take
photos for the blogs, he could have made his way to Coco's
house, in between location shoots, to kill Alison. His
motive? Jealousy and money. Was Alison's estate sizable?
With no rent and a mother, whether doting or not, to shuttle
him around town, Neil wouldn't need more than the two
thousand dollar reward and a modest-paying job to survive

until Alison's estate settled. I remembered how he had tried to convince me that he was at the comedy club the night his sister was killed. Perhaps he lied about that because he didn't want to admit that he had been roaming Crystal Cove with the pot of doubloons, capturing it in its many resting places on film. *One lie leads to another,* my father always says. Would Neil lie again or finally confess to what he had done?

No matter what, I had to alert the mayor to let her know the person Wanda called an *innocent soul* had duped her. I would also leave a message for Cinnamon. The other night, she said she knew about Neil Foodie, but did she know everything?

Wanda gave each of us a hug and thanked Bailey and me again for dropping by her house to check on her. Her voice, thick with emotion, caught as she said, "Good-bye." Then she exited.

Seconds later, a pair of regulars entered the store. "Cheerio!" one called. She was very British, very proper.

"Bailey," I said. "Can you see to the ladies?" I pulled my cell phone from my pocket and dialed.

At the same time, Katie rushed down the breezeway. "I'm back," she yodeled, the word *back* taking about three syllables to conclude.

The mayor's telephone rolled over into voice mail. I left a hurried message, texted Cinnamon, plunked my cell phone back into my pocket, and crossed to Katie. She looked cheery in a yellow-striped dress. Her cheeks were flushed; her eyes, animated.

"How's your mother?" I asked.

"Doing so much better. This morning she recognized me and her regular attending nurse." Katie kissed the fingertips of her hand, a habit she'd picked up from my aunt, and blew a blessing into the air. "The meds are helping. She's sleeping a tad more than usual, but the doctor said, 'Sleep is the great healer.' At least she's comfortable." Katie hugged me and pushed apart. "Now, what's on the schedule? Bailey said the Chocolate Cookbook Club is going to have a gathering tonight."

"Tonight? Why?" I glanced at Bailey. "The first Thursday of the month is when we usually meet."

"It's Pepper's idea, and you know her. When she gets her mind set on something . . ." Bailey wagged a hand. "She wishes to grieve for Alison. She believes others might want the same opportunity."

"But it's Wednesday."

"Don't be a stickler," Bailey said. "Besides, Pepper called my mother, who called me. The two of them cleared it with many of the club members, and now it's all arranged. That's why I contacted Katie."

"Okay," I said. "I'll go with the flow."

Katie tapped her cheek with a finger. "Now, what shall I cook? Jenna, come help me plan a menu." She hooked her thumb and bustled down the breezeway toward the café.

"Go," Aunt Vera said. "Bailey and I have the rest of this handled." She waved at the boxes of pirate-themed items. "I'll finish packing up the window display. Bailey will tend to the children's corner. It'll do you good to see how Katie puts together her masterpieces, and"—she winked—"you can keep an eye on her. She's quite fragile."

I scooted after my friend. The café was turning over for the lunch crowd. The kitchen staff rushed around doing prep work.

For a half hour, Katie and I nibbled on grilled winter pear and blue cheese sandwiches and perused the various cookbooks she kept on metal shelves above the sinks. All of the chocolate-themed cookbooks were tucked in with the dessert cookbooks at the far right. In addition to the standards like *Better Homes and Gardens*: *Chocolate* and *The Ghirardelli Chocolate Cookbook: Recipes and History from America's Premier Chocolate Maker*, she had *Adventures with Chocolate: 80 Sensational Recipes* and *Couture Chocolate: A Masterclass in Chocolate*.

She grabbed the latter. "Every chef I know raves about this cookbook," she exclaimed. "Have you flipped through it?"

I had. The author had provided excellent instructions on how to deal with chocolate. The book included a fabulous section on the origins of chocolate, and there was a chapter devoted to how to taste chocolate. Until I scanned the book, I didn't have a clue there could be up to four hundred aromas in one piece of chocolate. It was to be savored like wine or cheese. Bliss!

Thumbing through the *Better Homes and Gardens* book, I said, "How does chocolate rum cheesecake sound? Or mocha mousse? Or a tri-level brownie?"

Katie offered an impish grin. "We could serve a chocolate and whipped cream omelet as an entrée."

I smirked. "That sounds scrumptious but not very substantial. How about braised beer and pork with chocolate sauce?"

"Whoa. Where did you see that? In that book?" She snatched the cookbook I was holding and fanned through the pages.

"No. I remember eating something like it at a restaurant in San Francisco. It was tantalizingly good."

"Hmm." Katie slapped the cookbook closed, replaced it on the shelf, and scanned the titles of her remaining books. "I think I've seen a recipe like that in a Michael Symon book." She had a number of the famous Cleveland-based chef's books in her collection, including *Michael Symon's Carnivore: 120 Recipes for Meat Lovers.* "Aha, here it is." She grabbed Symon's book and opened to the index. Flip, flip. "Nope, not here." She smacked that book closed, too. "But you've got me thinking." She nabbed one of her many recipe boxes and pulled out a card. "Aha. This will do." She knuckled me on the shoulder. "You've inspired me." She flashed the three-by-five card at me, which read: *Pork with Port Sauce.* "A couple of tweaks, and we've got it."

My cell phone buzzed in my trousers pocket. I tugged it out and scanned the text from Bailey: *Coco is here. She's upset. Hurry back.*

I wished Katie luck putting together tonight's book club meal and scuttled through the café. Outside, beyond the diners and plate-glass windows, the ocean and the sky were brilliant shades of blue. A family of seagulls whisked by the window and dove toward the ocean. A box kite rose into view, its tails fluttering. The entire scene looked so inviting and brought a smile to my face. But I couldn't dally.

I was rounding the corner to enter the breezeway when I heard, "Tootsie Pop. Over here!"

My father and Old Jake—just *Jake*, I reminded myself; he hated being called *old*—sat at a table by a window. They seemed an unlikely pair, Jake so gnarled and weathered and my father supremely fit. Despite their age difference, they were fast friends. When my father was twelve, Jake, a rover with no roots, had saved my father from drowning. My grandfather had taken Jake under his wing and taught him how to invest; hence, why Jake was the wealthiest guy in town. Now that my father had retired from the FBI, he took Jake to brunch or lunch at least once a month to catch up. He wouldn't let Jake pay. Ever.

Seeing Jake made me think of Ingrid Lake and her alibi. I knew I'd forgotten to tell Cinnamon something at karaoke night. Would she care? She hadn't seemed particularly interested in Ingrid as a suspect, probably because, directly after I related Ingrid's account about Dash and the clash with Alison over photos, I mentioned Dash's alibi, and Cinnamon took off after him.

Dad beckoned me over.

I glanced toward The Cookbook Nook. Bailey could handle Coco on her own, couldn't she? Bailey loved playing therapist to girlfriends. She said it was like being a fan of soap operas; after watching the train wrecks, Bailey always felt happier with her own life choices.

My father pulled out a chair so I could join Jake and him.

I waved him off. "Can't stay." I kissed him on the cheek. Bubbling beverages sat in front of both of them. Jake had set one of each item from the breadbasket on a side plate. "Hi, Jake. How are you?"

"Great. Couldn't be better. You're looking mighty pretty today, Jenna." He said that to everyone. I knew for a fact I looked frazzled. I never left the café kitchen without feeling like I had spent time in a sauna.

I tucked a loose hair behind my ear. "Thanks."

"I hope you have wonderful things planned for yourself." Jake offered that greeting to everyone, too.

"I do. Sir, could I speak to you about something, possibly confidential?"

"Shoot." Jake took a sip of his drink.

I could feel my father's gaze on me; I ignored it. "A lady in town might owe you an apology."

Jake chortled. "There might be a few ladies to whom I owe an apology."

"She said she nearly ran a guy on a tractor off the road the night Alison Foodie was killed, around midnight. I can't think of anyone else who drives a tractor that late"—I winked—"can you?"

"Balderdash!" Jake didn't raise his voice. He naturally said things like *balderdash* and *poppycock*. No one was quite sure where Jake came from. He had drifted into town; he never spoke about his past. His wife, the love of his life, had taken the personal secrets she had known about him to her grave. "The woman's lying," Jake said. "No one ran me off the road."

"*Nearly* off the road," my father inserted.

"Last Thursday night," I added.

Jake set down his glass. "Now look here. I realize I've been known to take a ten-second snooze every once in a while on the old girl." *Old girl* was what he called his tractor. He missed his wife something fierce. I think driving his tractor at night gave him the opportunity to talk to his wife beneath the stars. "The eyes get tired. I just need to rest 'em. I always put the tractor in park. I don't drive when I'm nodding off. And, by the way, young lady, I'm not the only one who snoozes. Why, I've seen your father taking a quick nap at that hardware store of his."

My father bit back a laugh.

Jake went on. "But I have a clear recollection of last Thursday, and I didn't sleep a wink. Not one wink. That's when the schooner came to harbor."

"The *Victory*?" I asked.

"Indeed." Jake tapped the table with his index finger. "I know I was wide awake and bushy tailed because I downed three cups of coffee so I could stay awake long enough to see the ship arrive. My, what a beauty she is."

"Yar," I said.

"Yar, indeed."

The schooner was scheduled to leave harbor this afternoon.

"After I took a gander at the boat," Jake went on, "I went about my nightly chores." He offered his sand-sweeping services for free. It was his way to give back to the community. He wanted a clean beach like the rest of us. "So you see, I'd have known in an instant if someone made me swerve. Whoever made this claim is a bald-faced liar."

"Who told you this, Jenna?" my father asked.

"A woman with motive to kill Alison Foodie. Jake is her alibi."

"I repeat, she's a liar." Jake stabbed the table again. "A conniver. A fraud. Who does she think she is, trying to wrangle me into corroborating her whereabouts? Did she think I was so old I wouldn't remember? Why I ought to—" He pushed back his chair and stood.

My father said, "Sit down, Jake. Don't get your nose out of whack. Jenna will take care of this."

Dad gave me a supportive look . . . or what I interpreted to be a supportive look and not a chastising one. A girl has to pick her battles.

Chapter 21

WHEN I RETURNED to The Cookbook Nook, I found Bailey sitting with Coco at the vintage kitchen table. Coco's eyes were puffy and her face tearstained. My aunt lingered behind the sales counter, rubbing her phoenix amulet while looking on. The children's corner was still chaos, with Pirate Week stuff scattered everywhere. The display window was the same, unpacked. Luckily, no customers roamed the shop, and even if there had been a few, most would have understood a changeover day.

"Over, finished, done." Coco shook her head. "Before it even began. Ooh." She gripped her abdomen. "I feel like I could die. Just die."

A breeze gushed through the open door and chilled me to the bone. I closed the door and hurried back to the vintage table. "What's over, Coco?" So much for me having a moment to contact the police about Ingrid.

"Simon and me." Coco hiccupped and covered her mouth. "I apologize. My insides . . ."

I knew what nerves could do. For months after my husband's death, my stomach was in knots.

Bailey threw me a concerned look. *Do something*, she mouthed.

"His wife . . ." Coco leaned forward on the table, arms crossed. "He told her about us. She threatened to leave him, and then she ran off crying. He . . . he said seeing her like that—so vulnerable—he realized he still loves her. He can't let her go. He said he's sorry, as if that's enough. *Sorry!*"

Bailey said, "What did you expect?"

"You already said that," Coco sniped. "Five minutes ago!"

"I thought maybe you hadn't heard me."

Coco sniffed. "Of course I heard you. I'm not deaf."

"Honestly, believing that Simon will love you forever if he leaves Gloria is sort of naïve, too. There's no guarantee he'll stick around."

"Okay, I get it, Bailey Bird. Stop talking!"

"Ladies," I said. They shot me scathing looks. I threw up my hands. "Do either of you want tea?"

"No!" Both of them. In chorus. Like harpies.

"Ooh," Coco moaned. "I'm going to be sick."

"Do you want something fizzy to drink?" I asked.

"No!"

I settled into a chair and gazed at Coco. "What did he say?"

Bailey rolled her eyes like she didn't want to hear the story again. I ignored her. She was the one who had dragged me into this little tête-à-tête by texting me to hurry back to the shop. What did she want me to do, usher Coco out by the elbow and throw her to the curb? *Puh-lease!*

"Coco, talk to me," I said.

"He cried. He said it was wrong of him to ever involve me in . . . in . . ." Coco held her quivering lip in check with her teeth. "He said he was a cad and selfish. I agreed, of course. He's all of those things and more! He swore that our night together meant something special to him, and he wouldn't trade that for anything, but he had to preserve his marriage." She hissed through tight teeth. "*Preserve*. Does that mean he loves her? No, it does not. He's staying with her because he *has* to. He doesn't love her."

"He took a vow," I offered. "Some men are faithful that way."

"She doesn't like wine," Coco said. "I do. She doesn't go bird-watching with him. I would."

Actually, Gloria had gone with Simon, if those binoculars around her neck were any indication, but I wouldn't throw fuel on the fire.

"Simon told me Gloria didn't understand him. Why does he want to be faithful to a woman who doesn't get him? I—"

Bailey cut in. "They all say that."

Coco held up a hand to quiet her. "You don't have to preach. I've seen the movies. I've read the books. Heck, I've sucked up all the advice columns, too. I thought he was different. I thought I was special enough that Simon would—"

"You are."

"Then why did Simon do an about-face?" Coco snapped her fingers. "Like that! Why?"

Bailey kicked me under the table and eyeballed me. *Chime in anytime.*

What could I say? I had never dated a married man. I had never even dated a guy who was in a relationship with someone else. I had a boyfriend in college; we broke up; and then I met David. I fell head over heels in a matter of seconds. He had felt the same. We never considered looking at, let alone dating, anyone else.

Bailey booted me again.

"I don't know," I said feebly.

Bailey rasped, "You'll find someone special, Coco. You will."

"When? My fiancé left me for a stick. The boyfriend before that dumped me for an eco-nut."

"Soon," Bailey promised.

"Here? In Crystal Cove? Ha!" Coco's sharp laugh could have cut diamonds. "I should pack up and leave. Move to a big city where—"

"No!" Bailey and I cried in unison.

Tigger raced over to see what was the matter. Hershey sat up in the chair he had chosen as his throne.

"Why not?" Coco asked.

Bailey and I flushed pink, embarrassed by our simultaneous outbursts, but I could see in my friend's gaze that neither of us wanted Coco to take away our favorite sweet shop. We wanted Coco to stay, too, of course.

"You're hurting; you'll heal," I said lamely, as if those words were comforting. They hadn't helped me when I learned David disappeared in the ocean. They definitely hadn't helped when I found his suicide note. I wove my hands together and studied my thumbnails.

"Jenna's right," Bailey said. "I found someone here. You will, too."

"Tito?" Coco coughed.

Bailey bridled. "What's wrong with Tito?"

"Nothing. He's darling. He adores you. It's just—" Coco opened her pink Prada tote bag and suddenly burst into heaving, sloppy tears. "Oh my. Oh, Alison."

"Alison?" Bailey bolted from her chair, grabbed a box of tissues from the sales counter, and raced back. She thrust the box at Coco, who drew two and mopped her face. "What about Alison?"

"This." Coco wadded up the tissues and extended her Prada purse. "Alison . . . gave this to me. She said . . . it was the first of many. She said"—Coco hiccupped—"that we would make so much money together, we would each need an extra closet to store all the beautiful things we could buy with our loot." Coco giggled in a hysterical way. "I miss her so much!"

And then she vomited into her purse.

COCO OPTED OUT of coming to the cookbook club meeting. She needed to distribute her invitations, then go home and figure out her future . . . and recuperate. She hoped her sour stomach was simply due to nerves. She couldn't afford to have the flu. She had to fix up her shop tonight for tomorrow's Valentine's Day Lollapalooza. Bailey and I offered to hand out the rest of her invites, but Coco wouldn't hear of it. She shuffled out of the shop, the weight of the world on her shoulders.

For the remainder of the afternoon, Bailey and I decided to ditch revamping the store and chose, instead, to compile a batch of chocolate-themed cookbooks to share with the book club. I selected some reasonably priced books so that the cost wouldn't break the bank for our book club members. *Crazy for Chocolate* was a good primer that beginning cooks could use to understand everything about chocolate. *Hershey 4 Cookbooks in 1: Bars, Brownies & Treats; Cookies, Candies & Snacks; Cakes & Cheesecakes; Pies & Desserts*, a horribly lengthy title, was a spiral-bound cookbook, recommended highly by all its readers for the abundance of great recipes. I must have sold a dozen of those in the last week alone. In addition, I included *Adventures with Chocolate: 80 Sensational Recipes* by the British chocolatier Paul A. Young, famous for his unique ideas. Who could pass up an exotic recipe like Aztec Hot Chocolate or Caramelized Red Onion and Rosemary Truffle? Sure, the author pushed the envelope when it came to *quirky*, but according to him, cooking with and eating chocolate was meant to be fun, delicious, and daring. To the growing stack I also added a few of the cookbooks I had seen in the café's kitchen earlier when I'd helped Katie compile a menu.

Close of business rolled around in record time. Bailey and I checked on Katie, who was happily in her element, whistling as she whipped, baked, and taste-tested. She promised the braised pork with chocolate was going to be a hit. I had no doubt.

We didn't close the restaurant for the book club event because we hadn't scheduled an author to give a chat. Instead, we set an extra-long rectangular table where the club could gather.

Lola arrived first. She had left The Pelican Brief Diner in the good hands of her chef and was flush with excitement for a dinner with her daughter and friends. Her face dropped, however, when Bailey quietly told her about Coco's heartbreak. "Poor thing," Lola said, "but we all know what happens when you get involved with a married man."

Bailey put up a hand. "Yes, Mom, we know."

Lola sighed. "I'm sorry, love. I didn't mean to open an old wound. Will Coco be all right? Should we check on her?"

"She's fine, Mom. She's a big girl." Bailey pinched her lips together. I could tell she was doing her best not to add that she, too, was a big girl, and her mother should *mind her own beeswax*—Bailey's snappy comeback since the time we were six years old.

Next, Cinnamon and her mother strolled into the café. I was glad to see they had made up. Pepper couldn't stay ticked off at her daughter for long, no matter how meddlesome Cinnamon was. Pepper was wearing a sweater beaded with a pair of frogs—she loved the little green creatures. Cinnamon had changed out of her police uniform and looked refreshed, casual, and approachable in jeans and a formfitting T-shirt.

I hurried to them and welcomed them to the club. I asked Pepper how she was feeling. She told me in her typically crisp fashion that she was fully recovered from her illness and to stop prying.

Cinnamon surprised me by thanking me for alerting the police to Dash Hamada's whereabouts today. "We searched for him last night, but he wasn't at his friend's home. Your heads-up was invaluable."

The book club soiree maxed out at sixteen; a number of members hadn't been able to attend. Keeping out of the way of other diners, we hovered around the table without sitting. A waitress mingled among us, offering tiny wedges of a grilled panini sandwich made with dark chocolate and mozzarella. We each took one.

"Do you still have Dash in custody?" I nibbled the panini appetizer. Divine. It tasted like a cheesecake sandwich.

Cinnamon nodded. "He's copped to being a voyeur. He won't admit that he killed Alison." She bit into her tiny sandwich and hummed her approval.

"Can I give you another heads-up?" I asked.

"Can I stop you?"

I filled her in on Ingrid's bogus alibi. "Also do you know that Neil Foodie lied about his whereabouts on the night of

the murder?" I revealed my suspicion that Neil was the doubloons thief, and paused as an image niggled at the edges of
my mind. Of Neil. At Vines.

"I know that look." Cinnamon mimicked my expression,
wrinkling her nose and squinting her eyes. "What's going
on in that brain of yours?"

"It's probably nothing."

"I'll make the determination of whether it's nothing."

Was she once again trusting my instincts? Doubtful.

Our waitress asked us to take our seats. I perched on the
chair at the north end of the table; Bailey settled at the opposite end.

Cinnamon chose the chair next to me. "Go on."

"At the book club event last Thursday, Alison was texting
someone. She was frowning as she stabbed in the letters.
Did you check her text messages?"

"We did. There was only one to her mother."

"All others were erased?"

"What others?"

I replayed the scene from that night. "What if the killer
texted her? What if the killer planned to meet Alison?"

The waitress returned with a bottle of pinot grigio. She
apologized for interrupting and asked me if she could pour.

I signaled her to go ahead and turned back to Cinnamon.
"What if the killer erased that communication with Alison
after stabbing her?"

"Then we have nothing."

"Maybe you do. I saw Neil Foodie that night at Vines."

"You went to Vines? When?"

"Right after you and the mayor left to track down the
doubloons thief."

Cinnamon screwed up her mouth. "Didn't you just tell me
that Neil was the doubloons thief? How could he be running
around town and working at Vines at the same time?"

"He could have stolen the doubloons earlier, taken photographs, and then posted the photographs from work. But that
doesn't matter right now. I'm telling you, I saw him texting
someone that night. He was being quite cagey about it."

Cinnamon shook her head. "How can you be sure he was texting and not e-mailing?"

I couldn't. Rats. "Have you checked his cell phone for text messages?"

"We had no cause to."

Mayor Zeller sidled up to the table and plunked into the chair next to Cinnamon. "Sorry I'm late."

Cinnamon offered a formal nod. "You look exhausted, Z.Z."

"It's been a trying week." The mayor took a sip from her water glass and sighed. "Oh, that tastes good. I needed to wet my whistle. So, Jenna, did I overhear you talking about Neil Foodie?"

"You did." I explained my theory. He stole the pot of doubloons and concealed the pot under the stage at The Pier, then acted as if he'd discovered its whereabouts to reap the reward.

"The sneak," the mayor said.

"Indeed." I grinned.

The mayor shook her head. "The poor child needs therapy, I'm afraid. Moments ago I received a phone call from his mother."

Cinnamon looked intrigued.

"You know Wanda is one of my dear friends," Z.Z. went on. "We go way back. I fronted her the money for her restaurant. Our families' lineages are intertwined."

"Do you both have pirates in your history?" Cinnamon teased.

"Not pirates. Men of the sea."

"Uh-huh." Cinnamon winked at me.

Usually I liked to hear the history of the people in Crystal Cove, but right now I was too eager to know what the mayor had to say about the Foodies. "Why did Wanda call you?"

"She and Neil went to meet with Alison's attorney," Z.Z. said. "They heard the reading of the will, and an hour later—get this—Neil took off in his mother's car, without his mother. He left her stranded on the sidewalk. Can you believe it?" The mayor shook her head. "Needless to say, Wanda is distraught."

"He stole her car?" I eyed Cinnamon. "He killed Alison to inherit her estate, and now that the will spells it out, he knows he'll be your number one suspect. He's on the run."

"Heavens!" Z.Z. yelped. "You think Neil killed his sister? No, no. It's not possible. Didn't you just finish telling us he was out and about moving the doubloons from location to location, and he was posting photos on all those blogs? That little prankster had to be way too busy to kill somebody."

"Not necessarily," I said. "Don't you understand how easy it is to keep current on the Internet thanks to handheld devices? Neil would have had plenty of time, after work and in between capers, to kill her. Cinnamon, you've got to put out an APB."

Chapter 22

CINNAMON BELIEVED MY argument had merit and left the café in a hurry. The mayor accompanied her. I stayed at the café to run the book club meeting. Naturally, the remaining club members plied me with questions, only a few of which I could answer without compromising the investigation.

Bailey put an end to the questions by raising a glass in a toast. "To Alison Foodie. May she rest in peace."

We observed a quiet minute, and then we moved ahead with our meeting, sharing titles of cookbooks we had recently discovered and citing recipes in each that were truly remarkable. All of the club members enjoyed browsing the cookbooks I had brought as well as tasting Katie's sensations. For dessert, Katie had made a scrumptious Irish Cream pie using Oreo cookies as the base, and she had concocted a Kahlúa dessert drink that was truly decadent. I wanted to lick the bottom of the glass. After selling nearly the entire stock of cookbooks, we adjourned the meeting.

Katie nabbed me before I could return to The Cookbook Nook to fetch Tigger. She was perspiring from her hard work in the kitchen, but she looked elated.

"Major success," I said. "Everyone wants you to print out the recipes you used."

"Will do." She removed her toque and fluffed her curly hair. "Got time for a drink upstairs?"

I wasn't sure I could fit another sip of anything into my stomach, but I could see she needed to talk. Her forehead was pinched; her eyes, pained. I hoped her mother hadn't taken a turn for the worse. I said to Bailey, "Do you want to join us?"

"I can't."

"Hot date?"

She smirked. "What do you think?"

All pirate decorations at Vines Wine Bistro were gone. The place looked normal and intimate again. The pert waitress with the cascading hair—no ponytail tonight—showed us to our table and provided menus. While perusing the special wine selections, I noticed Simon standing at the far end of the bar with his wife, Gloria. She looked pale. Was she ill? Simon was clutching her elbow and stroking her hair. He said something, and she smiled lovingly at him. Apparently she had forgiven him. Had there truly been a moment when he wasn't in love with her? I thought about calling Coco to see if she was still in a funk. I considered asking her to join us to buoy her spirits, but that would be cruel. There was no need for her to watch Simon doting on his wife. Gloria pecked Simon on the cheek and slogged toward the ladies' room. Simon retreated into the kitchen.

At the same time, to my surprise, Neil Foodie exited the kitchen, in waiter uniform, carrying a tray set with hors d'oeuvres and a carafe of nuts.

"Ready to order?" our waitress asked.

"I thought Neil quit," I said. In truth, I thought he had fled town.

"Yeah, about that." The waitress smirked. "He slinked in an hour ago and begged the boss to rehire him. Simon is such a softie. *Forgive and forget* seems to be the message of the day."

Where had Neil gone? Would he have returned if he were guilty of murder?

"So, what'll it be?" the waitress asked. We gave her our orders. She set out cocktail napkins and strolled away.

I watched Neil as he delivered the treats to a table where an intense-looking couple was talking nose to nose.

Anxious to find out whether Cinnamon had caught up to him before now, I excused myself from the table and met him halfway to the bar. "Neil."

He spun to greet me. His smile turned into a frown when he realized it was little old *me* and not a customer from one of his tables. "Yeah?"

A fine welcome. I said, "Did you talk to the police?"

"No." His eyes grew wary. "Why?"

"You drove off in your mother's car and left her on the sidewalk."

"I needed time to think."

"I thought you quit here and got another job."

"I'm not going to take it. The pay is better at Vines, and like I said, I've got debts. I need the extra bucks." Neil moved the tray he was holding to his left hand and glanced over his shoulder. "Look, I've gotta get back to work before the boss reconsiders his decision."

"Wait," I said. Simon wasn't paying attention to us. Gloria hadn't returned from the restroom. "Didn't you get the finder's fee for returning the pot of doubloons?"

"How'd you know about that?"

"Your colleague over there"—I thumbed at our waitress—"said you came into a couple of thousand dollars. I did the math."

"Yeah, well, I couldn't keep it."

"Couldn't because you were the one who stole the pot?"

"I—" He sucked his lower lip. "I should've guessed you'd figure it out. Lucky you. You get two free tickets."

"To?"

"My next stand-up gig." Neil winked. "Okay, let's just say, I borrowed the pot."

"For your *fresh* comedy material."

He snickered. "It was funny. I'll slay 'em with the stories the next time I get a gig."

"How about all those photographs?" I said, baiting him.

"Heh-heh. Yeah. I got a boatload of those."

"How did you manage to do it and work at Vines that night?" I asked. "Did you take the doubloons and snap off a few photographs at different locations before your shift, and then load them while you were here?"

"You're pretty clever."

"So are you." I had no compunctions about falsely appealing to the guy's ego as I led him down a path to a confession.

Neil shifted feet. "Yeah, the hardest part was going house to house."

"Or firehouse, in one instance."

"Yeah, without anyone catching me. By the time four A.M. rolled around, I was sweating like a pig." Neil stiffened. His doughy face went still.

"Neil?" I waved a hand in front of his face.

He blinked and roused and took a quick peek around the bistro. He zeroed in on Simon, who wasn't looking our way. In a cold, almost ghostly voice, Neil said, "I've got customers to attend to."

"One more thing. This is important, Neil." I tapped his forearm. "Your mother is worried."

"Why?"

"When you took her car, she thought you might be on the run." It was a small lie.

"On the run because . . ." His eyes widened. "Aw, cripes. She thinks I killed my sister? Do you? Dang. Nah. No way. I went back and forth all night, from the photo shoots to home, to check on my mother. She didn't wake up, so she doesn't have a clue."

"Why did you need to check on her? Was she sick?"

"No, she's—"

"Getting on in years."

"That's not it, either. She's . . ." Neil worked his tongue inside his mouth. "Heck, it's not a crime. My mother has narcolepsy. She falls asleep pretty much at the drop of a pin. It's why she quit the restaurant business. It's why I can't take the computer job."

"Do you have narcolepsy, too? Do you zone out, like you did a second ago?"

"Nah. I can't do the day job because I need to be with Mom during the daylight hours. At night, like now, once she's out, she's *out*. That's how she was the night Alison died. *Out*. Shoot." He scuffed his shoe on the floor and looked a third time at Simon. "Man, I need to talk to my mom, but I can't ask to go home right now. I just got here." Neil drummed the empty tray with his palm. "I need this job."

A patron passed by us to use the facilities. After he disappeared into the restroom, I said to Neil, "What about Alison's estate? That should bring you an income. Why do you need to work here?"

Neil snorted. "What estate? It turns out Alison poured every penny into her company. She was flat broke, like I thought."

"The business has got to be worth something."

"In name only. It's buried in debt."

That didn't correspond with what Wanda had told us. "Your mother said the attorney has buyers lined up."

"Buyer. One. Lake Enterprises."

"As in Ingrid Lake?"

He nodded.

My skin tingled pins and needles. Did Ingrid murder Alison so she could descend upon Alison's unassuming family and purchase the publishing company for a song?

Neil added, "Don't worry. I'm not selling to her. She doesn't have an ounce of creativity in her little finger."

"Why do you care?"

"Foodie Publishing was my sister's baby. Her company shouldn't be run further into the ground by some tight-teethed know-nothing."

He spoke with such vehemence, and yet something about his passion seemed off. I would bet he was an adequate comedian. Was he a decent actor, too? He seemed intent on convincing me of his loyalty to family. Was it possible he murdered his sister to set the sale of her company in motion?

"I've got to call a friend to check in on Mom." Neil

tucked the serving tray under his arm and fetched his cell phone from his pocket.

Seeing him with his phone zinged me back to my conversation with Cinnamon earlier. "Neil, the night Alison died, she was texting someone. Was that you?"

"Nah. I never text."

"Sure you do. I saw you texting that night. Here, at Vines."

"Uh-uh, I don't text."

"Over there." I pointed. "You were lingering by the entrance to the kitchen, leaning against the wall and punching the buttons of your telephone."

He grinned, but there was no warmth in his gaze. "Man, you are observant, but nah, I wasn't texting. I write down jokes on a cyber notepad as they come to me. Here." He opened an application on his phone and thrust it at me. "Check, if you don't believe me."

I glanced at the screen. Jokes appeared on the notepad app—ordinary jokes, nothing with pizzazz. The date and time on the note synched with what he was saying. I clicked on his text message app. There was nothing there. Not even one text.

"Hand back the phone now," he said.

Another thought occurred to me. Boldly, I moved away from him while hitting the telephone icon.

"Hey." Neil followed me and batted my arm. "Give it back."

I spun around. His face was a fit of rage. What did he intend to do? Wrestle me for it? What was he hiding? I pressed on the Recently Called list.

"Don't," he hissed. "Stop."

I saw a record of phone calls with only two numbers dialed repeatedly, each of which had a designation: his mother and Vines. I suspected the killer had erased all communication from Alison's phone. Wouldn't Neil have been diligent enough to do so on his own phone? Was he innocent after all? If so, why was he so adamant that I relinquish the phone?

"Please," he pleaded. "If the boss sees me with my cell phone out, I'm toast."

"You're lying. You just said you pulled out your phone to call a friend to check on your mom."

"I was going to make one call. Back there. Out of sight. C'mon, hand it back."

I did.

Neil stuffed the phone into his pocket and said, "Keep your distance from me from now on, okay?"

"You need to talk to the police."

"Yeah, yeah." He shuffled away.

When I returned to the table, Katie was sipping a glass of wine. Half of it was already consumed. She had ordered me a glass of the same. I took a sip and sighed. It was a cool and crisp Riesling, perfect after a heavy meal.

"Is everything okay?" Katie asked.

"I thought Neil might have killed Alison, but now, I don't think so. He isn't smart enough. Whoever killed her was savvy." I swirled the wine. Thin streams of the gold liquid trickled down the insides of the goblet. I took another sip and thought about Ingrid Lake. She wanted to purchase Foodie Publishing. Was that enough motive for murder?

"Hello," Katie said. "Where did you go? La-la land?"

I flicked the air with my fingertips. "I'm here. I won't dwell on it anymore. Did you eat?"

"I tasted everything that went out of the café kitchen earlier. That's plenty of food for me." Katie ran a finger down the stem of her glass. "Besides, I'm not very hungry, with my mother . . ." She bobbed her head. "You know. I'm sort of wondering how much longer she can go on like this. I've studied the statistics. She's in the four percent of people under age sixty-five who have Alzheimer's. Most can live a long life, but does she want to?"

"What is the alternative?"

Katie leaned forward on both elbows. "It's draining."

"I wish your dad would help."

"Me, too." Katie offered a rueful smile. "I remember learning to cook at my mother's side. She was marvelous. Did I tell you? She could whip up stuff in a blink of an eye. Add a little this, remove a tad of that."

"My mother did the same." Which was one of the reasons I had never learned to cook until now. Why try when there was a great chef at the helm?

Katie polished off her wine and signaled the waitress to bring her another. "What do you think about Bailey and Tito?"

"Why do you ask?"

"Do you think they make a good match?"

"It's early yet, and for Bailey, that means it'll probably end soon."

"Wow. Aren't you the cynic."

"She'll find a reason to end it."

"Why do you say that?"

"Because she's nervous about *forever*. I think it has to do with the fact that her mom and dad got divorced."

"It's better to get divorced than live a lie, like my parents." Katie sighed. "Besides, Bailey's mother is completely in love with your father. That's got to show her there's an ideal to strive for."

Our waitress appeared with a second glass of wine for Katie. She took a sip and nodded. The waitress departed.

"What about you and Rhett?" Katie asked.

"What about us?"

"You seem destined."

My cheeks warmed. "*Destined* is a big—" My cell phone buzzed in my pocket. I fished it out and looked at the readout. No name. I answered anyway.

"Jenna!" Coco cried. "I—" She inhaled. "I'm sorry to bother you. I—" She sobbed.

"What's wrong? Are you sick? Throwing up? Do you need to go to the hospital?"

"No, I'm fine." She moaned. "I tried calling Bailey, but she's not answering. Can you come to the shop? Quick!"

Chapter 23

I VEERED MY VW into a parking spot in front of Sweet Sensations and skidded to a stop. I told Tigger to sit tight, and I rushed inside. The place was a mess. Fresh baked goods littered the floor. Trays of candies lay overturned inside the glass display cases. I found Coco in the kitchen retrieving the precious recipe cards that the perpetrator must have strewn on the floor. Flour and sugar were scattered everywhere. A carton of broken eggs lay in front of the walk-in refrigerator. Wet paper towels clung to the walls and dripped from the edges of the sink and off shelves. Ugh!

Coco raced to me and grabbed me in a fierce hug. "Thank you for coming. I didn't know—" She released me and fanned herself with a fistful of recipe cards. "I didn't know who else to call."

"The police," I suggested.

"Yes, of course." She buffed the tip of her nose with the back of her hand. "We must."

I pulled my cell phone from my pocket and dialed the precinct.

"Who would do this?" Coco muttered.

A kid, I thought. The mess had all the earmarks of a TP-type job, mean and childish in its intent, carried out in a matter of minutes.

"Crystal Cove Police Department," a clerk said on the other end of the line.

I explained the problem. She patched me through to Detective Appleby, who was driving in the location. When he answered, I recapped what I had told the clerk. The detective promised he would arrive soon and disconnected.

"After distributing the invitations," Coco said, "I was so grimy and still nauseous, I went home to take a shower. Then I laid down for a couple of hours. I need to feel refreshed before I make candy."

"What time did your assistant close up shop?"

"I would assume the normal time. At six. When I arrived, the lights were out. I switched them on and found this"— Coco brandished her hand—"fiasco." She returned to the chore of retrieving recipe cards. I bent to help. Many of the cards had frayed corners. Some were stained with oil and other unidentifiable cooking items, like milk, oil, chocolate, or juice. I tried to categorize the cards but realized my sorting pattern might not be Coco's and decided to stack them instead.

"You don't think it was someone who hates Valentine's Day, do you?" Coco asked.

"Why would you say that?"

She pointed. Someone had shredded the sparkly, pale pink heart decorations Coco had yet to hang in the windows.

A siren whooped outside.

I set the recipes I'd collected on a counter and hurried through the saloon-style swinging doors to the main shop. Coco followed. A patrol car pulled up behind my VW. The light rotating on top of the car bathed the shop in red. Deputy Appleby lumbered out of the driver's side. A younger deputy, wafer-thin in comparison to Appleby, scrambled out of the passenger side.

Appleby paused inside the front door of the shop and

scanned the area. "Nasty," he muttered. To his colleague, he said, "Take pictures."

I rushed to the deputy and shook his hand. "Thanks for coming."

His mouth quirked up on one side. "Might I ask why you are at yet another scene of the crime?"

"I'm Coco's friend. She called me." I gestured at the chaos. "Is there any way to figure out who did this?"

"The door looks intact." Appleby eyed Coco, who had followed me from the kitchen. "Miss Chastain, don't tell me you leave this door unlocked, too?"

"Of course not, Deputy."

"Does anyone else have a key?"

"No, but my assistant might have neglected to lock it. She's a hard worker and dedicated, but she can be"—Coco pressed her lips together—"a bubblehead."

Appleby sauntered to the kitchen and paused in the doorway; his gaze seemed to be taking in every detail. "The delinquent must have seen her leave and then made his move."

"Why do you think a delinquent did this?" I asked.

The deputy jerked a thumb at the wet paper towels in the kitchen sink. Then he indicated the eggs on the floor. "Kids love making messes." He pivoted and resumed examining the main shop again. "I'd bet you're missing a bunch of stock, Miss Chastain. The chocolate truffles in the glass display case look pretty picked over."

Coco sighed. "All the cake pops are gone, as well. All that work—"

"Yep. Teens," the deputy said. "We'll file a report, but there's not much else we can do."

"Can you lift fingerprints?" I asked.

"That won't help if the culprits aren't in the system." Appleby scrutinized the upper corners of the shop. "You don't seem to have any security cameras, Miss Chastain. You might want to install some for the future."

Coco shook her head, dismayed. "I pay Crystal Cove Security Patrol to keep an eye on the place."

"Worthless," Appleby mumbled. "If they're not in the vicinity at the time of the crime, they can't do a blasted thing. This wreckage took less than ten minutes, tops."

Exactly what I had calculated.

"I'd bet the teen had been plotting his move for weeks," he added.

"Or *her* move," I said, believing a local teenage girl who loved to create chaos might be the culprit. Poor thing didn't have a mother; her father didn't keep her in tow.

When the deputy and his associate were done with what little they could or *would* do, I said to Coco, "I'll stay and help you clean up."

"You don't have to."

"No arguments."

Appleby strode toward the exit. He paused and cleared his throat. "Jenna? A word?"

Uh-oh. I joined him, my senses on hyperalert.

"How is your aunt doing?" he asked.

I knew it. He wanted me to spill family secrets. *No way.* I smiled. "She's fine, Deputy."

"Has she mentioned . . ." Appleby shrugged. "You know."

"You? Yes. She hinted that you're no longer dating." I could say that much. No harm, no foul.

"Do you think she'll change her mind?"

"Why should she?"

His face twisted with love that looked painful. "Because she's my soul mate."

"Says who?"

"My mother."

I bit back a giggle. His mother?

"Mother says it's in the cards," Appleby continued.

Honestly? Another chuckle threatened to surface. *Keep cool, Jenna.*

"She reads tarot, like your aunt," Appleby added.

Aha! Now I understood the attraction.

"Mom did a reading for me." Appleby rotated his hand as if flipping over cards. "She turned up the Lovers, the Two of Cups, and the Four of Wands."

I knew the significance. I'd learned from my aunt that there were ten top love cards. All three in the deputy's reading were included in the ten; the Lovers being the ultimate. I said, "Do you believe in that mumbo jumbo?"

"Don't you?"

"Not really. It's fun, and I know my aunt believes in it, but I feel we create our own fate. Anyone can alter their outcome by making different choices." My reasoning didn't seem to be swaying the detective. "Look, if you feel this confident about changing the tide, be bold. Ask my aunt to tea. Tell her your hopes and dreams, but don't expect miracles. Once a Hart woman's mind is made up, it's hard to change it." I weighed whether to say more, and decided *why not*? "By the way, how would your kids feel if they had a stepmother in her sixties?"

"My children are in their thirties. They won't get a say."

I gawped. "Are you joshing me? Did you have them when you were twelve?"

He grinned. "I'm fifty-eight."

"Really?" Wow! I thought the guy was in his early forties. He was closer in age to my aunt than I had imagined.

"Good genes," Appleby said, "plus I don't eat a lot of starch." He offered a two-fingered salute. "Thanks for the advice."

COCO AND I spent the better part of two hours cleaning up Sweet Sensations. During the process, she professed repeatedly that nobody, not even an angry, deviant kid, could sidetrack her. A delinquent could plot and loot, but he—or *she*, I reminded her—would not keep Coco from having her Valentine's Day Lollapalooza. No, sir.

When I woke the next morning with only five hours of sleep, I was dog tired. Somehow I had to drum up the energy to finish decorating my own shop. *Too-ra-loo*, as my aunt would say. One day at a time. I skipped my morning exercise routine, slugged down a strong cup of coffee, loaded up with a homemade energy bar packed with sunflower seeds, honey,

and oats—my aunt made them, not me—and I headed to
The Cookbook Nook.

Bailey was already there. She had revamped the children's
corner, decorating with strings of hearts and miniature
cupids. On a typical day, we always put out coloring books
and crayons on the circular table. Today, she'd added a bucket
of scissors, construction paper, and glue sticks. Her cat Hershey was nestled in the reading chair. I waved at him, but he
didn't bat an eyelash.

"Good morning," I said.

Bailey didn't respond. After a date with Tito, I had
expected her to be glowing, but she didn't look all that good.
She was dressed entirely in black—a rarity for a woman who
adored color. She wasn't wearing makeup or jewelry. And
she was mumbling to herself. Call me crazy, but given her
mood, I didn't feel I should tell her about Coco's disaster
right off the bat.

"Good morning," I repeated and slung my purse onto the
sales counter. I set Tigger on the floor. He romped into the
stockroom and back out, as frisky as all get-out. He stared
at Hershey, who still hadn't roused, and made a beeline
for me.

"It's okay, Tigger," I cooed. "Don't take the rejection personally. Hershey has issues."

Tigger raised his head and whisked his tail, asking me to
follow him. I did. He romped to the children's corner, ducked
beneath the table, and yowled. I knelt down and spied a few
maps from Pirate Week scattered on the floor.

I collected them and rose to my feet. "Bailey, uh, girlfriend,
yoo-hoo. Did you hear me? What's up?"

Bailey muttered something that sounded an awful lot like,
"I'm so stupid."

"Are you talking to yourself?" I asked.

"No!"

"Did you and Tito break up?"

"Why would you say that?" she snapped. "We are fine with
a capital *F. Comprende*?"

I shot up my hands to defend against slings and arrows. "I understand. *Sí.*"

"Sorry." Bailey exhaled through her nose. "I didn't mean to bark at you. Tito and I are in great shape. The best. In fact, I think I'm in love."

"You're kidding."

"Not a whit. He's cute and funny and smart."

"We're talking about Tito Martinez, right?"

Bailey swatted my arm. "Cut it out."

I had to admit, ever since Tito subbed for a magician who bowed out of one of our special events, my opinion of him had changed. I liked him. "So what's wrong?"

"The cat."

Hershey raised his head and leered at her.

"Yeah, you," Bailey snarled then choked back a sob. "He doesn't like me. I'm not savvy when it comes to cats, and he knows it."

"How could he possibly know that?" I unrolled a map that was tied with raffia ribbon and admired the handiwork. A parent must have helped a child. I slotted it at the top of the pile I'd amassed.

"Tito says it's my nose."

"Huh? You have a darling nose."

"No, not my *nose* nose. Yes, I do have a pretty cute one." Bailey tapped her nose with a finger. I was pleased to see her sense of humor was still intact. "Tito says I wrinkle my nose whenever I get near the litter box."

"So do I. Yuck."

"I also squinch it whenever I pick up the cat. I don't do that with dogs. I stick my nose right in their fur and breathe deeply. I must be a dog person." She sighed. "I'm so stupid."

"You're not stupid. So, you're not a cat person." In truth, she was a cat person; she did with Tigger exactly what she was describing she did with dogs. The problem was Hershey, but Bailey had to come to that realization on her own.

"Tito offered to take the cat," she said. "He adores him."

Hershey lifted his head again and, I swear, gave a satisfied

Cheshire Cat grin, as if he had planned all along to be returned to Tito. Did cats have a say in the matter? Tigger glanced at me, and I laughed. Obviously, they did. They picked their human, not the other way around.

"I have to go with the flow," Bailey said. "It's not what I planned, but—"

"Whoa!" I yelped.

"What?"

I stared at the maps in my hand as an idea formed.

"*What?*" Bailey repeated.

"He said she wasn't home."

"He *who*? Which *she*?"

"She admitted as much." A line on the topmost map swooped downward and ended at a big red *X*. I flailed my fistful of maps at Bailey. "*X* marks the spot."

"What spot?" Bailey cried. "Will you please make sense?"

I plunked into a chair beside the table and laid down the maps. I stabbed the *X*. "She must have known about Old Jake's sleeping habit."

"I repeat, she *who*? What are you talking about?" Bailey perched on one of the other chairs. "Speak English."

"Neil Foodie said Ingrid wasn't home at four A.M. Ingrid said she was driving around, and maybe she was, but I think she planned, or *plotted*, if you will, to kill Alison. It wasn't spur-of-the-moment. She wanted to be a partner at Foodie Publishing. Alison kept dangling the carrot, but she never drew up a contract."

"If Ingrid is to be believed."

"Right." I grabbed a piece of construction paper and a crayon from the supplies on the table and explained my theory while drawing my own kind of map, outlining where and when Ingrid went on the night Alison was murdered. "Ingrid and Alison argued after the book club meeting. Alison fired her." I wrote *The Cookbook Nook* on the map. "Ingrid went back to Wanda Foodie's house." I added *WF house*. "I imagine Ingrid sulked at first, then she got angry. Steaming mad. That's when the idea to kill Alison must have come to her. She went to Vines for fortification." I drew a line from *WF house* to *Vines*.

"Ingrid ordered a bottle of wine, but she only drank a glass; that was enough to solidify her resolve. She returned to Wanda's to give herself an alibi, but Wanda Foodie was already asleep, and Neil was out of the house." I quickly explained that he was the pot-of-doubloons thief. "So, to cover the time span, Ingrid claimed she went for a spin." I drew a line that doubled back to *WF house* and another that zigzagged around Crystal Cove. "Ingrid said she nearly ran into Old Jake, which made him drive off the road."

"She forced Jake off the road?"

"No, that's just it. She didn't. I'll bet she learned through the grapevine that Jake often pulls to the side to *rest his eyes*, as he says. It's common knowledge. It's no big deal. He's never hurt anyone. Except Jake didn't fall asleep that night."

"How do you know?"

"I saw him at the café. He was having his monthly meal with Dad. I asked him about the incident. He said he knew for a fact that he had not been run off the road or dozing because he drank three cups of coffee to stay awake so he could see the *Victory* pull into the bay." I flashed on the mess at Sweet Sensations. "Could it have been Ingrid who turned Coco's shop topsy-turvy?"

"What? What? What?" Bailey squawked sounding like a macaw stuck with a one-word vocabulary.

Oops. I hadn't told her about the break-in yet. I recapped last evening.

Bailey spanked the table. "That's all Detective Appleby did? Make a report? Sheesh. Why didn't Coco call me?"

"She did. You, um, didn't answer. You and Tito . . . I would imagine . . ."

Bailey scruffed the back of her neck. "Talk about feeling guilty."

"Don't. Coco wasn't in danger. It was vandalism, pure and simple. Or at least I thought so. Now I'm wondering whether it could have been a deliberate message."

"Why would Ingrid tear up Coco's place?"

"Because she was angry at Coco. She knew Coco had

Alison's ear. Coco was her prized cookbook author." I paused. "You heard Ingrid lash out at Coco at the crime scene. She said Alison was making cuts to Coco's latest manuscript. Coco denied it. Maybe Ingrid believed Coco had drawn the line with Alison: *Enough with the hypercritical copyeditor. Either Ingrid goes or I go.* Coco had, after all, pursued another publisher." I flashed on the multiple recipes open on Alison's computer. "What if Alison had Coco's older recipes on her computer screen because she was revisiting Ingrid's editing work? What if she determined Ingrid was being unduly harsh on Coco?"

"Hold it." Bailey raised a hand. "There's one flaw to your theory. Ingrid didn't know Coco was going out that night."

"Maybe she did." I pictured the three of us having drinks at Vines after the book club meeting. Simon and Coco had flirted. I didn't realize that was what they were doing at the time. Did Simon contact Coco later? "Ingrid went to Vines after us that night." I jabbed the crayon on the word *Vines* on the map. "What if she overheard Simon on his cell phone setting up the tryst with Coco?"

"Oh, that's good. That makes sense." Bailey nodded. "So Ingrid went to Coco's and watched her leave."

I added *Coco's house* to the map. "Maybe she even saw Dash hanging around, taking photographs."

"When all was clear, Ingrid went inside."

"Right. The door was unlocked. Alison didn't turn around when Ingrid entered because she could see Ingrid's reflection in the darkened window. She didn't feel threatened. Ingrid grabbed the shears, stabbed Alison, and drove around for a few hours, hoping to establish her alibi."

"That settles it." Bailey spanked the tabletop again. "I'm going over to Wanda Foodie's house to confront Ingrid."

Chapter 24

BAILEY LURCHED TO her feet. Both cats startled and yowled. Bailey didn't seem to care; she darted to the sales counter to fetch her purse.

"Wait." I bolted off the miniature chair and nabbed Bailey by the elbow. "Let's call the precinct."

"And get the same runaround Coco got from Detective Appleby last night?"

"Cinnamon will listen."

"No, she won't. Not to theories. She needs facts." Bailey slung her purse over her shoulder and sprinted toward the exit. "For Alison's sake, I've got to make sure Ingrid doesn't get a foothold with Wanda Foodie."

"She won't have a shot at taking over the company. Neil is onto her."

"But Wanda isn't." Bailey tore out the door.

Actually, Wanda was; she didn't think Ingrid could handle the pressure of running Foodie Publishing, but my opinion wouldn't make my pal change course. I stared after her, wondering what I should do. Bailey was usually rational, but not always. I remembered a time at Taylor & Squibb when an ad campaign for Beat the Heat lemonade was in full cycle. Bailey, who was in charge of monitoring television, magazine, and Internet campaigns, went on a rampage, from cubicle to cubicle, yelling at everyone because a station had messed up airing the ad. She felt responsible. Beat the Heat, the first product from a local start-up company, was a product she believed in. Everyone, from the big boss down to me, assured Bailey it wasn't her fault, but she lost it. Fond feelings for the company's president might have been involved. After her scream fest, she buried herself under a blanket for nearly a week. I couldn't let her go off half-cocked now, could I?

Aunt Vera entered the shop. "Hello, dear." The draped folds of her red-and-black caftan billowed behind her.

"Perfect timing," I said and rushed past her to apprehend Bailey. I nearly bumped into my father.

"Perfect timing for what?" Dad asked.

I quickly explained the situation. I shot a finger at Bailey's retreating figure.

Aunt Vera said, "Don't go yet. Let me do a reading for you."

My father wagged a finger. "Don't stall her, Vera. Go, Jenna. No time to waste."

Wow. Wow. Wow. Did my father just jump to my defense?

"I saw that young Lake woman packing a car," my father continued. Wanda Foodie's house wasn't far from my father's. "Go!"

I paused. "Why are you two together?"

"We went to breakfast," my father said. "We're starting a new tradition. Once a week, every Thursday."

Something quivered at the pit of my stomach. My father was a person of habit, but my aunt was not. For her to set a regular date with my father made me leery. Was she sick? Was Dad? Were they trying to make the most of their last days together?

Gack, Jenna, stop it. Don't overreact.

"Is everything okay?" I said.

My father grinned. "Yep."

"Your health is good?"

"Yep."

I looked to my aunt. "Yours, too?"

"Yep," she said as briskly as my father.

"What's going on?" I asked.

"Nothing," they said and exchanged a look.

"Uh-oh. Is this weekly powwow intended to discuss me?"

"Darling," Aunt Vera said. "That sounds entirely para-noid."

"Though astute," my father said.

"Swell." I didn't have time to ask why they were chatting about me. They were family; they would discuss my fate forever.

Eager to divert the conversation from me, and feeling somewhat puckish, I said to my aunt, "By the way, that darling, delectable Detective Appleby wants to have a chat with you."

She gawped. "When did you see him?"

"At Sweet Sensations, after it was trashed."

"Trashed?" my father said. "How could you not tell us that the moment we walked in?"

"Later!" I ran after Bailey while yelling over my shoulder, "By the way, the deputy's mother reads tarot, too! It's fate."

"Jenna, wait!" my aunt yelled to no avail.

I stopped Bailey before she could hightail it out of the parking lot in her Toyota RAV4. "I'm going with you."

"Get in."

She didn't give me time to put on my seat belt before roaring forward.

We arrived at Wanda Foodie's in less than eight minutes. Ingrid Lake was, indeed, piling her things into a yellow taxi. She gave a pillow a shove, tossed in a dark blue over-nighter, and headed back up the path without closing the door to the car.

Bailey and I parked in a hurry and snaked up the winding brick path. The front door hung open. We walked inside and found Ingrid returning to the foyer with a wheeled suitcase. She shrieked and braced a hand on the antique console abut-ting the wall. The ceramic vase of silk flowers teetered.

Ingrid steadied the vase then shimmied to her full height and dusted off her pencil skirt. "You startled me." Her lips moved; her teeth didn't. She balled her hands into fists.

Bailey took a step toward her, looking feistier than all get-out.

Ingrid crowded back against the console. "What's your problem?"

"Where are you going?" Bailey asked.

"Why do you care?"

"Ingrid, dear, who's here?" Wanda Foodie appeared in the hall from the direction of the kitchen. She was carrying a china cup set on a saucer. The liquid in the cup was steaming. As before at The Cookbook Nook, she seemed fragile. Her face looked puffy from crying. "Oh, Jenna and Bailey, it's you. Come in. Sit down." She gestured languidly toward the living room. "Did you come by to send Ingrid off? Would you care for some coffee or tea?"

I shook my head and remained in the foyer. "We're not staying, but thank you. We came to speak with Ingrid."

"What about?"

"Her alibi for the night Alison was killed doesn't hold up."

"Oh my." Wanda teetered. Her eyes grew moist.

I hated to bring up her daughter's murder again, but until the case was solved, she would have to find the courage to face facts.

"Let me explain." Bailey reiterated Old Jake's account as if she had been the one to hear it directly. "Care to revise, Miss Lake?" Her tone was just shy of take-no-prisoners.

"I told you"—Ingrid scowled at Bailey and then me—"I was with Wanda. Watching television and then—"

"Were you?" Wanda squinted, as if trying to remember. "You fell asleep."

Wanda yawned and covered her mouth with the back of her fingertips. "Yes, I probably did. What did we watch?"

"*CSI.*"

"My favorite."

"I know," Ingrid said. "You chose it. I prefer food shows."

Wanda yawned again. Neil's claim about his mother's health zipped through my mind and summoned a previous thought about how similar Wanda and Alison were. I said, "Wanda—"

"Yes, dear?"

"Did Alison have narcolepsy, too?"

"What do you mean, *too*?" Bailey cried.

I recapped Neil's account. Was it possible that Alison hadn't defended herself from an attack because she had fallen asleep at the computer keyboard? If so, anyone—not just Ingrid or Coco—could have sneaked up on her.

"Is the ailment hereditary?" I asked.

Wanda hesitated. "Yes."

"Does Neil have a form of it? He zones out, though he won't admit it."

Wanda frowned. "I don't believe so. He's simply over-worked. It's my fault."

Ingrid set a hand on Wanda's shoulder. "I'm so sorry. I had no idea."

"What a crock," Bailey sniped. "You knew. You counted on her falling asleep so she would be your alibi."

"I did *not* know," Ingrid protested.

"You had to." Bailey spoke like Ingrid did, through tight teeth. "Alison was conscientious. She would have warned you to be on alert in case her mother needed help."

"Alison didn't. I swear."

Bailey shot a finger at Ingrid. "Your eyelids are fluttering. You're lying. If Alison didn't tell you, Neil did."

"Neil never tells me anything." Ingrid spit out the words with such venom that I wondered again whether there had been a relationship between them. Had they dated and bro-ken up? Was that why Neil was so adamant that Ingrid not be able to buy the company?

Bailey pressed on. "When you went to Coco's house that night, you counted on Alison being dead to the world."

I winced at her choice of words.

"I did no such thing," Ingrid shouted. "I came home and then I went to Vines, and . . ." Ingrid swung her gaze between Bailey and me. "I wasn't lying when I said I drove around, but—"

"You lied about running Jake off the road." I jutted a finger.

Ingrid threw up her hands. "I needed something concrete. Who would believe me otherwise?"

"You're right about that!" Bailey snapped. "Especially now that you've put in a bid for Foodie Publishing."

"How do you know about that?"

"You want to buy the company?" Wanda blurted.

Ingrid looked ruefully at the woman who had put her up for a week. "No, Wanda . . . Mrs. Foodie. I mean, yes, I want to, but Neil won't let me." She glowered at Bailey and me. "Do you honestly believe I would kill Alison so I could make a run at the company? Get real."

"You didn't know Neil would stalemate you," I said.

Ingrid smirked. "That's true. I have to admit I was surprised he had a say in it. I thought Alison would have cut him out of any portion of her estate. She hated him." Ingrid glanced at Wanda, who looked as if Ingrid had mortally wounded her. "It's true. He hated her, too. He said—" She cut herself off.

"What did he say?" I asked. "Are you and he involved?"

"Involved? Ha!" Ingrid sniggered. "Neil and I went out one time to a comedy club because a friend of mine was the main attraction. Neil got snockered."

"He doesn't drink," Wanda said.

"Sure he does. He's rather sloppy. He starts running off at the mouth. Let's just say he was not complimentary about Alison."

Wanda's hand shook. The cup and saucer rattled. She reached out with her other hand as if groping for something to steady herself.

I guided her to a ladder-back chair on the far side of the console and said, "Sit." I took the cup and saucer from her and set it on the console. "Do you want some water?"

Wanda shook her head. "Go on, Ingrid, tell us everything."

"There's nothing more to tell." Ingrid shrugged. "Neil

and Alison were not allies. Leave it at that. It doesn't matter now. Neil gets the business. He'll run it into the ground."

I said, "Neil claims you would do the same."

"I wouldn't. I have a head for business, and a passion for what I do."

"And a bent for being persnickety when it comes to editing," Bailey sassed.

"It's not a crime to seek perfection." Ingrid ran her fingers along the lapel of her suit jacket. "If that's all, I'm leaving."

"I'm calling the police," Bailey said.

"Go ahead. You have no proof that I killed Alison, which I didn't."

"Don't move."

Ingrid cocked her head. "Are you planning to cuff me?"

"I would if I could."

Bailey would, too. I'd never seen her this aggressive. Without taking her eyes off Ingrid, she pulled out her cell phone and stabbed in 911.

I eyed Ingrid's suitcase. "Where were you planning to run to?"

"I wasn't running." Her chest heaved with the exertion. "I was heading back to the city. I have to downsize. Without a job—"

"Did Neil fire you?"

Wanda said, "He wouldn't dare," and reached for Ingrid's hand.

Ingrid didn't budge. "It's all right, Wanda. This will be my fresh start."

Not if she was in jail, I thought.

A deputy arrived in minutes. Bailey, brimming with steam, filled him in. Ingrid, still professing her innocence, went willingly to the precinct.

Chapter 25

WHEN BAILEY AND I returned to The Cookbook Nook, I could barely contain her. Ordering her to sit down fell on deaf ears. Pacing alongside her exhausted me. My father, the voice of reason, was no longer at the shop, but my aunt, who waited out Bailey's ranting, finally corralled her.

I spied Rhett entering the Nook Café. Alone. Knowing Bailey was in good hands, I hurried through the breezeway and caught up with him at the hostess's stand. I tapped his elbow. He pivoted and a smile spread across his face. He pecked me on the cheek, letting his lips linger a tad longer than appropriate. I loved it. A warm shiver of deliciousness ran through me.

"Got time for a bite?" Rhett said.

"I can't. Too much to do, but I was hoping you might join me this afternoon at Sweet Sensations."

"What's going on there?"

"Coco's having a big bash. I want to show my support, seeing as this week has been horrific for her." I told him about last night's break-in. He was sympathetic. "Free candy," I added.

"I'm in. I love her truffles."

I rubbed his arm and hurried back to the shop, ready to fine-tune the Valentine displays.

With Aunt Vera's help, we moved the boxes holding the Pirate Week window display items to the stockroom. Tigger traipsed behind me, trying to play with the heels of my flip-flops. I had to be careful not to stomp on him.

"*Psst*, move, Tig-Tig."

He romped ahead and leaped over my foot, dragging his tail across my toes.

"Stop," I warned him. "That's tickle torture!"

Aunt Vera, arms now free, scooped him up and nuzzled under his chin. "Bailey told me all about your encounter with Ingrid Lake."

"She's a piece of work." I looked for a place to set the box that held the toy ship and sighed at the lack of level space. We were accumulating a lot of decorations in addition to a ton of books. Pretty soon, we would have to consider renting a storage space. For the time being, I balanced the box on top of a teetering mass of books, out of harm's way, and started collecting Valentine-appropriate items.

"Do you believe Ingrid?" Aunt Vera asked.

"She's told so many lies, I don't know what to believe." I scooped up the cupids that Bailey had attached to yarn, and then I fetched a couple of copies of *Deadly Valentine*, the sixth in the Death on Demand mystery series by Carolyn Hart. Her latest books were easier to obtain, but how could I have resisted the title during the season of love, right? I added children's books to my pile, including the darling *Happy Valentine's Day, Mouse*, a simplistic board book geared toward babies and not toddlers. Moms would go gaga for that one.

Aunt Vera said, "It made me nervous when you ran off to interrogate Ingrid, Jenna. It made your father anxious, too."

"But he's the one who told me to go."

"Only because he knows he can't control you."

"It's about time he learned that." I grinned. "Don't worry, Aunt Vera. I won't do anything rash. Bailey and I were together, and we did inform the police."

Aunt Vera muttered what sounded like a harmony blessing.

"Yoo-hoo!" Katie poked her head into the stockroom. "Come out here and see what I've created."

Aunt Vera set Tigger on the floor and patted his rump. He scampered into the main shop. We followed.

Katie flaunted a tray filled with chocolate cookies. "Fresh from the oven. They're Coco's Chocolate Cookies. The recipe is right out of her first cookbook. Are you picking up the aroma of nutmeg?" She flapped a hand over the plate to help the scent waft toward me.

The whiff caught me up short and made me zip back to the night Alison died. She had baked cookies flavored with nutmeg. Why did she feel the need to cook after the lavish meal we'd eaten at the book club event? Was she actually hungry? And why did she have so many of Coco's older recipes open on her computer? Ingrid was adamant that Alison hadn't been reviewing her work. Had Alison been looking for the perfect recipe to satisfy a craving?

I nabbed a cookie and bit into it. "Hmm."

"Taste the coffee?" Katie asked. "That's the secret ingredient."

Another memory came to me in a flash. When Bailey and I visited Coco at Sweet Sensations on Sunday, Coco went searching for one of her grandmother's recipes and couldn't find it. She thought she might have taken it home. Had someone stolen it? Why?

"They contain triple the chocolate," Katie went on. "A half teaspoon of nutmeg per batch and a tablespoon of brewed coffee." She pivoted and moved into the breezeway to set up a platter of treats for our customers.

I took a second bite of my cookie and returned to my thoughts about Alison. Had she been flipping between recipes on the computer? The topmost was titled Chocolate Bombs, from Coco's cookbook *Chocolate To Die For*. The one beneath was Mother's Chocolate Bombs. Why the altered title? Did it have a different ingredient? While Coco was having her tryst with Simon, was Alison fiddling with Coco's recipes, tweaking one or two and retitling them so she could include them in

Coco's next manuscript—was that what publishers called a cookbook? Alison had messed with Dash's photographs; would she have done the same to her authors' work?

A dastardly scenario shot through my mind. What if Coco returned home from her date and caught Alison in the act of rewriting? I flashed on the spat Alison and Coco had enacted at the book club event. Coco railed at Alison for making cuts to her material. Was there some truth in the skit they had created?

No, I could not—*would* not—believe Coco was guilty. She was a good person, a friend. And she had clearly spent that night with Simon.

I thought again about the recipes on the computer. Why were there so many layered on top of one another? Coco claimed they were recipes from previous cookbooks. If I returned to her house, maybe I could peer at the computer, and the notion that was niggling at me would come to light.

Quickly, I dialed Coco's cell phone number, but she didn't answer. My call rolled into voice mail. Why wasn't she answering? Perhaps she was too busy preparing for her big bash. I left a message asking her to return the call, and then remembered she never locked the doors to her house.

Bailey sidled up to me and whispered, "You look transfixed. What's going on in that brain of yours?"

"Why, nothing."

Bailey sniggered and said, in a Southern accent, "Why, darlin', I do declare you sound like you were born and bred in the Deep South. *Why, nothing,* indeed! Should I get you a fan to flutter? You're perspiring."

"I am not."

"Are, too. Talk to me."

"I was just wondering . . ." I replayed my theory.

"Are you saying that Alison changed perfectly good recipes just because she had the power to?"

"No. Maybe. I'm not sure. If I could take a peek at the computer . . ." I flailed a hand.

Bailey clapped me on the shoulder. "Let's go. I'm sure your aunt can handle sales on her own for a short bit."

Aunt Vera, who was sorting cash from the register, wasn't pleased with our plan, especially after our most recent discussion. This time, she refused to let me leave without doing a one-card tarot reading. She didn't have my father to dissuade her.

Complying with her wishes, I sat at the vintage kitchen table, pushed aside the jigsaw puzzle, and drew a single card—the Sun card, which I knew was not just a *good* card, but a *great* card. It is associated with attained knowledge. The image on the card is of a child holding a red flag, while riding upon a white horse. Overhead, a big yellow sun with a human-type face looks down upon the child, which symbolizes accomplishment. I couldn't have been happier with the draw.

Aunt Vera's forehead pinched with frustration. She knew she couldn't detain me now. She rose from her chair and rubbed her amulet with passion. "Be safe."

AS EXPECTED, COCO'S front door was unlocked. Amazingly, she had learned nothing about safety following Alison's murder.

Bailey entered first and called out, "Coco?" She didn't answer. Bailey strode to Coco's bedroom and peeked inside. "Not here. Bed's made."

A chill shot through me as I crossed the threshold. I recalled everything about the morning I arrived at Coco's house, starting with Deputy Appleby acting like a sentry and Cinnamon with her no-nonsense glare. I remembered how pink everything was, from the kitchen to the utensils to the couch and lamps. And then there was Alison, in red, slumped forward on the table, the scissors sticking out of her back, the reflection of everyone in the darkened window beyond her.

Bailey hurried back to me. "Hey." She touched my arm. "Are you okay?"

"It's horrible. I don't know how Coco can sleep here."

"Some people have more grit."

"Or nowhere else to go."

The memory of the night after I learned my husband drowned scudded through me. I went home to the apartment. Alone. The place didn't smell the same. Food lacked appeal. The cottage was so cold that I had bundled up in two comforters for warmth.

"Jenna." Bailey had moved into the kitchen and was peering in cabinets and behind doors. "The computer's not here."

"Of course it isn't." I moaned. What a dolt I was. "The police must have taken it as evidence. We should have realized that before coming here. Shoot."

Bailey folded her arms over her chest. "Now what?"

"We leave."

"No, wait. Call her."

"Coco?"

"Cinnamon. Ask her if she noticed what you noticed."

I gulped back a laugh. "Yeah, like she'll tell me."

"She knows you're checking things out. She told you to listen and report back."

"And subsequently rescinded that order."

"C'mon. Are you chicken?" Bailey clucked. "Cinnamon should be pleased to tell you what she's doing on behalf of solving the case."

This plucky attitude . . . this *spunk* . . . is what I love about Bailey. She assumes she is always right, and most of the time, she is. When she's not, she bluffs like a champ. Her mother trained her well.

I pulled my cell phone from my pocket and dialed the precinct. The clerk put me through to Cinnamon, who answered after one ring. At least my call didn't go to voice mail.

"What's up?" Cinnamon said.

"I . . ." Why was I nervous? She had listened to my theories at the recent book club meeting. *Be bold. Speak.*

"Jenna, are you there?"

"Yes." Surely, Cinnamon had found what I was trying to uncover. On the other hand—

"Just spit it out. You called me, remember?"

Man, she sounded like my father. Terse and to the point.

Cinnamon sighed. "Let me help you. I'm assuming you've got something to convey about Alison Foodie's murder, but you don't know how to tell me. You're afraid I'll jump all over you."

I chuckled. "You're on the right track."

"I won't be mad. Do you want to know why? Because I've got nothing."

"You've got Ingrid Lake." In my present scenario, was it possible that Ingrid was the killer? Why would she have messed with the recipes? "And Dash Hamada."

"Dash is innocent," Cinnamon said. "His film is time-stamped an hour before she died, and his host—"

"Sterling," I cut in.

"Yes. He came home while Dash was developing film. Dash didn't see him. Given travel time to and from Coco's house, Dash is off the hook. I've released him. I've set Ingrid Lake free, too."

I gaped. "But she lied about her alibi."

"She lied because she was scared. It happens. As it turns out, witnesses have come forward, corroborating her whereabouts between eleven P.M. and two A.M."

"Who?"

Cinnamon clicked her tongue. "A couple that attended a wedding on the pirate ship. After the ceremony, they snuck off to Lovers' Lane Overlook."

The overlook near the lighthouse wasn't really called Lovers' Lane. It was La Buena Vista, but the nickname took hold because the overlook was *the* place to neck in the dark. I remembered a time, years ago, when David and I sneaked out there.

Cinnamon continued. "The couple remembered seeing a woman fitting Ingrid's description when they arrived. She was huddled down in Wanda Foodie's car, crying her eyes out."

"Because she'd been fired."

"She was still there when they left a few hours later."

"Why wouldn't she say that?"

"Who knows?" Cinnamon paused. "So now who's on your list? And why?"

Deep breath, Jenna. One fact at a time. "I'm at Coco Chastain's house. I came to take a peek at Alison Foodie's laptop."

"Which we took."

"I realize that now." I laid out my theory.

Cinnamon muttered, "I don't understand why seeing the documents would help you."

"I thought I might pick up something from one of Alison's comments." Whenever I did an ad campaign, I made notes in the margin to remind me about what I needed to tweak or change. Sometimes I doodled grocery or to-do lists. Perhaps Alison had left some kind of note that would reveal why she was baking. Maybe she was doing a compare and contrast on a pair of documents. I told Cinnamon as much.

"I'll have our guys take another look-see. Satisfied?"

"Yes. Thanks."

"Jenna," Cinnamon added, "Ingrid said if I spoke to you—I guess she assumes we're good friends—"

"Aren't we?"

"We could be if you weren't always trying to do my job."

"I'm not—"

She chortled in a semi-sarcastic way.

Lucky for me she couldn't see me stick my tongue out on the other end of the receiver.

"Anyway," Cinnamon continued, "Ingrid said to tell you she was lying about Neil."

"Lying how?"

"He liked his sister, and Alison liked him, too. Ingrid isn't sure why she said those things to Wanda and you earlier. It was cruel."

"Simon and Dash said similar things about Neil not liking his sister. The vibe must have been there."

"Or they were making assumptions." Cinnamon cleared her throat. "It doesn't matter. And now, Jenna, good-bye."

"Coffee soon?"

"We'll see."

Chapter 26

B AILEY DROVE MORE sanely on the way back to the shop, taking turns at a decent speed and halting completely at stop signs instead of doing what people call *California stops*—sliding through at about five miles per hour, believing the word *stop* was only a suggestion. On Buena Vista Boulevard, many shop owners were changing out the Pirate Week displays. Halfway along the road, I caught sight of clusters of multi-shaded pink balloons, which were tied to an awning and bouncing in the breeze. Beneath the awning, a long line of people headed into Sweet Sensations.

"Oh my gosh," I cried. Coco's Valentine Lollapalooza was already in action. Time was flying by. "Park!" I shouted at Bailey and aimed a finger at the last parking spot on the street.

Bailey didn't glower at me or question me. In one deft maneuver, she swerved her Toyota into the spot. "What about your aunt handling the shop on her own?"

"It looks like the whole town might be here. The Cookbook Nook must be empty." Coco's warning that shop owners constantly needed to be on the front line of promotion hit me like a mallet. Perhaps I ought to consider some kind of big bash for the shop and café, bigger and more adult than Children's Pirate Day. Because Katie had taken a couple of days off to tend to her mother, I had forgotten to put together a chocolate-making demonstration last Saturday; that would be a nice treat for the adults. The larger the crowds, the merrier the sales. We were doing fine business-wise, but I had a competitive streak in me. I liked to excel.

Jazzy music greeted us as we entered Sweet Sensations. A female fiddler playing with fervor stood just inside the door. I was surprised to see how many people the candy shop could hold. At least a hundred were milling about, most tasting the wares on the various trays of candies set on the counters, others eyeballing the goodies displayed in the glass-enclosed cases. Coco had replaced the pale-pink paper hearts that she'd intended to hang, the ones the perpetrator had shredded, with larger, hot pink versions. Each dangled on a ribbon tacked to the ceiling.

Huddling near the sales register stood a few of the Chocolate Cookbook Club members, including Lola, the mayor, the owner of Home Sweet Home, and Gran, the enthusiastic cookbook purchaser.

"Tito's here." Bailey gestured to her right.

Tito, looking casual in jeans, white shirt, and photographer's vest, was taking snapshots of the party. He fiddled with the zoom lens before each picture and shot at quirky angles: tilted and sideways and upward from the floor.

"I'll be right back." Bailey moseyed to him and tapped his shoulder.

He spun around, and his eyes lit up with good humor. He wrapped an arm around her waist and pulled her close for a kiss, which Bailey didn't seem to mind. Big shock. Like me, she was not typically into public displays of affection.

I glimpsed Dash among the crowd. I was surprised to see the raven-haired beauty beside him, her hand in his. She had seemed pretty disgusted with him yesterday. He must be a smooth talker.

The book club ladies waved to me and beckoned me over.

Lola drew me into the clique. "Darling, don't you look wonderful."

I wasn't so sure about that. I had thrown on the first thing I'd touched in my wardrobe—a lacy red sweater over a red ruffled skirt. The reds didn't entirely match.

"Very Valentine-y," Lola said. "Me?" She gestured to her eye-popping electric blue jumpsuit. "I look horrid in red."

Coco's Hello Kitty–loving assistant waltzed up to us. Even the bows in her hair were Hello Kitty. "Try this." She thrust a white chocolate–coated truffle at me. On top was a teensy embellishment of a raspberry.

I bit into it. "Divine." I adore anything raspberry. I'm not a huge fan of the seeds, but the flavor always makes me think of summer days when my mother and I would go berry picking.

The assistant threaded through the crowd to other customers.

"Don't miss the cherry brownies," the mayor said. "They're to swoon for." She looked quite mussed, as if she had bumped and battled her way into the shop. She adored food; she went crazy for *free* food.

Lola could tell what I was thinking. She grinned and then snagged a shot glass filled with a pink quaff off a tray and handed it to me.

I took a sip. "Yum." The concoction tasted like iced strawberries.

"Coco is quite the talent, isn't she?" Lola said.

I looked around for Coco and spied her lingering by the swinging doors that led to the kitchen. Simon, looking dapper in a pale shirt, sport coat, and slacks, stood close to her. One arm was braced on the wall beside the door; his head and body were tilted forward; his mouth was moving. Coco nodded and plucked at her beaded pink necklace. Gloria was nowhere to be seen. Last night at Vines she had seemed under the weather. Was she still feeling ill? Did she know Simon was cuddling up to Coco? Simon nudged his glasses higher on his nose and leaned closer. I thought of a scene in one of my favorite movies, *While You Were Sleeping*, when Sandra Bullock's smarmy landlord *leaned* in, not in a good

way. Coco put a hand on Simon's chest to keep him at bay.
He backed up a smidge.

The mayor said, "Jenna, we were just discussing whether
these recipes will find their way into another of Coco's cookbooks. With Foodie Publishing going under—"

"It's not going under, Z.Z.," I said.

"It's not? But with Alison gone . . ." The mayor twirled
her hand.

"Her brother and mother are looking for a buyer," I said.
Now that Ingrid, per our chief of police, was cleared of
murder, would she make another bid for the company?
Would Neil Foodie respond favorably this time?

"I hope so," Lola said. "I would hate for my latest cookbook
to be shelved. I don't have it in me to look for another publisher.
Not that it really matters. I have the diner to keep me busy. But
Coco"—she gestured toward my friend—"must be distraught.
All of her works have been released through Foodie Publishing,
and with the other contract being cancelled—"

"Cancelled?"

"Didn't you know? The New York publisher passed on
Coco's next manuscript."

I glanced back at Coco. She pulled a handkerchief from
beneath the sleeve of her pink jacket and dabbed her eyes.
Was she crying? She put a hand on the swinging door and
looked like she was exiting to the rear of the shop. Simon
clutched her shoulder and swiveled her to face him. She
shimmied free of his grasp. Sensing she might need my support, I weaved through the crowd toward her.

Drawing near, I heard Simon rasp, "I'm sorry. How many
times can I say that? I truly didn't mean for you to suffer."

"Whatever," Coco muttered.

"I'm a jerk. I admit it."

Coco grunted, obviously agreeing. Simon traced a finger
down her arm. She shivered and recoiled.

After a stilted silence, Simon continued. "What a shame
that teens in this town would wreck your shop. I'm glad you
were able to put the place back together."

Coco offered a half smile. "I was lucky that Jenna—"

She caught sight of me and relief swept over her face. "Jenna, over here," she beckoned.

I joined them.

Simon nodded to me, but he looked sheepish. Was he worried I would tell his wife that he was hanging around Coco? Didn't he realize there were a whole lot of other witnesses at the party who might blab? He apologized one more time to Coco and hurried away.

Coco pinched her lips together and trudged toward the kitchen. I trailed her and stood just inside the saloon-style doors to make sure no one could enter.

"Are you okay?" I asked.

"Fine." She sniffed, using both pinkies to wipe away tears before they could fall. "Simon—" Another sniff. She pulled the hankie from beneath her sleeve. "I wish he hadn't come here. Not during the—" She blew her nose into the hankie and stuffed it out of sight. "I must look a wreck."

"You don't."

"I'm probably blotchy."

"People will think you're flushed."

She tittered. "Yeah, right."

"Why was Simon here?"

"He heard about the break-in last night. He felt sorry for me." Coco hissed air through her teeth. "I'm such a cliché. I fell in love with a man who . . ." She clicked her tongue. "I thought I was smarter than that. Why didn't I see it coming?"

I wanted to say, *Because you were single and lonely and impressionable.* What I said was, "Maybe he really cared for you until he was faced with a decision."

"No. I could see it in his eyes just now. There wasn't any warmth. Part of me thinks he asked me out because he had it in for Gloria, like he wanted to hurt her. I was the easiest sap he could seduce, and . . ." Coco sank back against the prep table. "So stupid." She gazed up at the ceiling and heaved a sigh.

"I heard about the New York publisher passing on your next project. I'm sorry."

Coco grimaced. "Yeah, when it rains it pours."

I peered over the swinging doors. The crowd seemed to have doubled. "Your guests are really enjoying themselves."

"They should be. It's costing me a mini-fortune, but what can you do? Like I said before, publicity. You've got to do it to thrive."

"Tell me about it."

We shared a halfhearted laugh.

I said, "Did Detective Appleby figure out who trashed the place?"

"Not as far as I know. I didn't see any of our law enforcement in the crowd, did you?"

"No."

"They're probably ashamed to show their faces."

Or busy. Pirate Week may have drawn to a close, but Crystal Cove was still bustling. Petty crime was always an issue.

Speaking of petty crime . . .

"Coco, by the way, if one of your neighbors calls and says a couple of women stole into your house today, the culprits were Bailey and me. You've got to start locking your door."

Coco raised an eyebrow. "Why?"

"Because it's not safe."

She flapped a hand. "I know it's not safe. It was an oversight. But that's not what I meant. Why did you steal into my house?"

"I wanted to know why Alison had four documents up on her computer."

"For review."

"But you said they were all older recipes. Chocolate Macadamia Bites. Chocolate Bombs. Mother's Chocolate Bombs and—"

"Hold it." Coco pushed herself away from the prep table. "That last one isn't the title for one of my recipes."

"You told Chief Pritchett it was."

"No. I distinctly remember her saying there was one called Chocolate Bombs and a second one called Chocolate Bombs. She never said the word *Mother's*."

She was right. I had seen the word *Mother's* and had inserted it instinctively.

"My recipe in *Chocolate To Die For* was handed down from my grandmother. I never would have named it *Mother's*."

The notion that Alison had been toying with Coco's work flitted through my mind again. "Maybe Alison retitled it so she could reuse it in your new cookbook. Is that allowed in your contract?"

"No. Uh-uh. It wasn't, and she wouldn't." Coco chopped the edge of one hand against the other. "Alison demanded that everything be fresh. No duplicates. She was such a stickler that she would search the Internet to make sure none of her authors' recipes matched anyone else's. She asked me to sign legal documents saying I owned the rights to what I wrote. Maybe she was concerned because another author had a title similar to mine, and she was comparing the two."

I thought again about what Alison was doing that night— baking. Was she concerned that whoever had delivered the recipe called Mother's Chocolate Bombs had ripped off Coco's recipe? Was that a crime worth killing over? How appropriate would that be during Pirate Week, someone stealing Coco's *booty*? I recalled the aroma I had detected when I'd entered Coco's house that night. "Does your Chocolate Bombs recipe include nutmeg?"

"Yes. A hefty dose. However, just so you know, a list of ingredients for a recipe is not copyrightable." Coco used her fingertips to clarify. "You can't own the list, because a recipe is essentially a chemical process requiring basic elements, unless, of course, you've patented the recipe."

I nodded, grasping the concept. During my brief stint as a cookbook store owner, I have seen many recipes with the same ingredients; after all, how many ways can you make sugar cookies?

"I haven't patented anything," Coco said. "Only the verbiage used in the directions of a recipe is proprietary, which is why I am so adamant about my editor not changing what I write. It's my voice, and that voice is what gives my recipes life and verve."

"Coco, remember the other day when Bailey and I were here. You said your grandmother's recipe card for Chocolate

Bombs was missing from your recipe box. You were going to check at home. Did you find it?"

"Now that you mention it, no."

"Is it possible someone stole it, and days later, put it back while trashing Sweet Sensations? Recipes were strewn everywhere."

Coco hurried to the recipe box and sorted through it. After an extensive search, she removed a card and said, "I'll be darned. Here it is. But . . . but . . ."

"What?"

"Now I can't find my *bunica*'s holiday cookie recipe. Help me." She thrust the oversized box at me. Her hands were shaking like crazy.

"Could you have misfiled it last night? You were in such a state."

"I . . . I don't know." Coco gripped her hands to steady them. "Oh, Jenna."

I thumbed through the recipes, noting what I had before. The stains, the blurry handwriting due to age. "I don't see it."

"I can't lose it. It's the first one my grandmother ever gave me." Coco raced to a locker, spun the combination, and retrieved her purse. "I've got to go home. It must be there. It has to be."

Rhett rapped on the swinging door. "Jenna? Is this a private party?"

Before I could address Coco's fears, she fled through the doorway that led to the alley behind the shop. The door clacked shut.

Rhett pushed through the swinging door. "Was it something I said?"

"No, it's . . ." How could I explain Coco's passion for her family memories? "I'm glad you came."

"I can't stay." Pain flickered in his eyes. "My mother called me. I have to go to Napa." Rhett's parents owned a renowned restaurant in Napa Valley called Intime. For quite some time, Rhett and his father had been estranged because, at the young age of eighteen, Rhett had eloped with a woman against his father's wishes. It didn't help that Rhett also struck out on his own instead of following in his father's footsteps. His father disinherited him and banned his mother from seeing him. Rhett had been communicating with her and his two sisters clandestinely.

"Is your mother ill?" I asked.

Rhett raised an eyebrow. "Why would you say that?"

"Because your mother has put off seeing you in the past and yet you're racing up there. Why the urgency? She must be sick; otherwise—"

Rhett pulled me to him and gently tucked a hair behind my ear. "You, my sweet, are a fatalist."

"Pragmatist."

"Who has seen too much grief in her young life."

I poked him in the chest and grinned. "You sound as ancient as Old Jake. My *young life*. I'll be thirty in a few months."

"Luckily, I believe in the French dating system. You can date a woman half your age plus seven years."

"Hold on a sec. Does that mean you can date someone as young as twenty-four? I'm way too old for you then," I teased.

But Rhett didn't smile. The edges of his eyes twitched with worry.

A pang gripped my heart. "There is something wrong."

He clasped my hands, pressed them against his chest, and kissed my forehead. "I'm not sure. I'll call you when I find out."

Chapter 27

BAILEY WAS BUZZING with happy vibes when we returned to The Cookbook Nook. She'd had such a good time with Tito at Sweet Sensations. Being hand-fed candies can do that to a girl. I, on the other hand, was now not only worried about Coco, but about Rhett as well. I hadn't told Bailey about either. How could I spoil her bliss?

To put my mind at ease regarding at least one of my concerns, I hurried to the telephone at the sales counter, ready to dial Coco. My cell phone in my purse jangled. I fished it out, slung the purse beneath the counter, and answered.

"Jenna." It was Coco. My aunt would call the timing kismet. "I found the recipe. It was in the box at home. *Phew.*" She sounded breathless. "I'm sorry I ran out on you."

"Don't worry about it."

"I'm thinking about taking the rest of the afternoon off."

"Why don't you? Your assistant looked in her element when I left the lollapalooza. Nearly all the candy and treats in the shop had been devoured or sold."

"That's good. Um, Jenna?"

"What?"

Coco was silent for a long time. "Nothing. Thanks again for listening." She disconnected.

Needless to say, I felt a little uneasy about the end of our conversation, but I convinced myself she simply needed time to heal. Simon, by showing up at her shop, had thrown her a curveball.

The afternoon sped by. With Aunt Vera's and Bailey's help, we set up the Valentine's window display, all of us laughing at the whimsy as well as the florid colors. Raspberry. Strawberry. Hot, hot, hot pink. The combination made me recall a campaign we'd done at Taylor & Squibb for sunscreen. Every person in the commercial was made up to look like they were beet red. You know the color—you've seen people at theme parks and beaches who have forgotten to apply lotion. How people can do that to their skin with all we've learned about sun damage is beyond me.

Aunt Vera tapped her watch. "Quitting time, girls. Go home or go on a date."

"A date?" Bailey carped. "Yeah, right. Tito has a deadline. I won't see him until tomorrow or maybe a week from now."

My aunt petted Bailey's cheek. "Now, now, don't get sour so early in the relationship."

"I'm not sour. This is the first time I've wanted to see a guy so badly. All the time. Eek!"

Was she really talking about Tito? Ah, love. Go figure.

"See you in the morning," Aunt Vera said and left.

Bailey stretched. "I'm starved."

"Me, too," I said. "Let's go to the café for a bite."

"A *bite*? No way. If I go there, I'll be tempted to eat way too much." She patted her belly. "Did you see Katie's special prix fixe menu? Beef Wellington, potatoes Dauphinoise, Caesar salad with Parmesan crisps, and triple-decker dark chocolate cake drenched in icing and whipped cream. Uh-uh. How about we go upstairs to Vines and get a simple cheese platter or veggies and dip?"

"Sure." I checked on Tigger and Hershey, who was still acting like king of the hill, roosting in his favorite chair and shunning my kitten. Bah! I wondered when Tito would take possession of the prickly cat. "Back soon," I whispered to Tigger. "Hang tough." I chucked him under the chin.

VINES WINE BISTRO was active. I recognized many of the faces I'd seen at Sweet Sensations earlier. Nothing like having a glass of wine after a sugar rush. We ordered a carafe of the house cabernet sauvignon and a cheese platter, with a selection of three cheeses, from the same wavy-haired waitress who had served us over the course of the past week.

She returned in a timely fashion. Right after she filled our glasses from the carafe and headed off, the door to Vines opened and in sauntered my aunt with Deputy Appleby. They weren't holding hands, but they moved as one, their upper arms brushing together. Oho, I thought. Perhaps my encouraging words to the deputy had helped him find the nerve to woo my aunt a second time. If he were successful, there would be one sad mustachioed hotel manager.

I said, "Bailey, look. There." I pointed at the happy duo.

Bailey swiveled in her chair. "No wonder your aunt wanted to close shop right on time. Good for her." Bailey's cell phone hummed in her purse. She fished it out and glanced at the readout. Her eyes brightened. "I've got to take this." She pressed Accept. "*Hola*, Tito!" I couldn't hear the other end of the conversation, but Bailey's cheeks flushed and her foot started to tap in a happy way. She said a lot of *uh-huh*s, and finally, "You're on." When she hung up, she eyed me guiltily. "Um, he finished early, so do you mind if—"

"Go." I'd never seen her so smitten with a guy. "I'll pay the tab."

"I'll fetch Hershey."

"Do you want me to take him for the night?"

"Would you? Could you? I mean—" She pressed her lips together, obviously embarrassed to sound so enthusiastic. "I'm blathering."

"Go." I laughed. "Maybe spending a little time at my cottage will help the stinker warm up to Tigger."

Bailey exited, and I signaled the waitress to bring our

check. While waiting, I spied Simon, sport coat removed, at the specials board. He erased the top two items, nudged his glasses higher on his nose with the back of his wrist, and, referring to a note card, began to write in substitutions. Gloria was not in attendance.

Off to my right, I caught sight of Neil Foodie. He wasn't serving customers. He was doing, of all things, a card trick for a couple. What in the world? Had he given up his comedy act and was now working on a magic show? Neil fanned a deck of red-toned cards toward the woman. She tapped a card. Neil nodded and began to shuffle the cards. He pulled them apart like an accordion, but as he attempted to restack them, they fluted upward and spewed everywhere. Neil turned the color of the deck of cards and apologized profusely. He bent to retrieve the mess. While crouched, he whipped his head right and left. Was he worried that Simon would fire him on the spot? And why shouldn't he? Neil was neglecting his duty. A number of customers tried to snag Neil's attention.

Our waitress appeared with the bill tucked into a leatherette folder. "Don't mind Neil," she said, setting the tab on the table. "He can be a goofball. Have you ever seen him pull the gallium spoon trick?"

"The what?"

"Gallium spoon trick. Gallium is this super soft metal that can be molded into a spoon shape, but when the spoon heats up, it melts and disappears into a beverage. Poof!" She showed me with her hands. "Neil just about lost his job over that. His mother would have been ticked." The waitress laughed and moved away.

I didn't laugh. His mother? Mother's Chocolate Bombs. Ingrid had called Neil a *Mama's boy*. Neil had moved home. He was taking care of her. Was it possible he wanted to get into the cookbook business to please his mother? Did Neil, a semi-delinquent, steal into Sweet Sensations and swipe some of Coco's recipe cards? Not all of her family recipes were published in one of her books yet. Did he hope to pawn them off as his own? Had his sister figured it out?

I drummed my fingertips on the table. No, Neil was a wag, a comedian. Yes, he was a thief; he'd stolen the pot of doubloons. But I doubted he was an aspiring chef, and deep down, I didn't think he was capable of murder. He wasn't sly enough.

Neil rose and fanned the playing cards again. Simon glanced in Neil's direction. His face ticked with anger. He tucked the note card to which he'd been referring into his shirt pocket, rubbed his fingers against his pant leg to rid them of chalk dust, and started for Neil.

The action triggered a vivid memory. As an advertising executive, I'd had to pay attention to what we in the business referred to as *continuity*. We might shoot a commercial out of order, but the action had to remain coherent. An actor couldn't pick up a full glass of wine in one shot and hold a half-empty glass in the next. An actress couldn't tuck a hair over her right ear in the master shot and then slip it over her left ear in the close-up. Details mattered.

I ran my finger down the stem of my wineglass as I imagined facets of Alison's murder that I hadn't been able to make sense of before.

It's in the cards, Deputy Appleby said at the Sweet Sensations crime scene. He hadn't been talking about recipe cards, but right now, that was what I was thinking about—specifically the mess of cards after the break-in as well as the temporarily missing cards from Coco's private stash.

Coco's mother and grandmother had handed down the recipe cards. Someone had filched a few, and, if my intuition was right, had replaced them. Why?

I peeked at Simon. Brushing chalk off his trousers.

That's it, I thought. Not the chalk. The action. Swiping his fingertips against his pant leg.

Coco's family recipe cards were old; stains were inevitable. Would new stains be noticeable? Would a lab be able to determine whether any stains were caused by, say, peanut oil? If there was oil on the Chocolate Bombs recipe card, it wouldn't have come from Neil's fingertips, because he was allergic to peanuts. But it could have come from Simon's hand. He handled peanuts on a regular basis at Vines. Would the recipe card or cards that had magically reappeared at Coco's shop be contaminated with not only peanut oil but also Simon's DNA?

No, my theory was off. Simon had been with Coco at the time of the murder. Their rendezvous lasted until the wee hours of the morning. Or had it? Yes, it must have. Coco wouldn't have lied about that. She had been over the moon to spend time with him.

I sipped the last remnants of my wine as a more sinister scenario came to me. Did Coco and Simon carry out the murder together? No, even in teetering heels, Coco walked with clod-stomping loudness. Her entrance would have awakened Alison from her nap. Simon, on the other hand, was stealthy. I recalled observing bird-watchers outside my cottage the other day as they sneaked up on the egret. Simon was a bird-watcher, trained to be quiet. He could have tip-toed to Alison and stabbed her in the back long before she roused.

Simon came across as an easygoing soul, but he had stepped out on his wife. He wasn't good to his mother, either, according to his wife. During the argument with Gloria on the steps outside The Cookbook Nook, she had blamed Simon for letting his mother down. Gloria ranted that Simon was a *recipe for disaster*.

The conversation with the book club ladies at Sweet Sensations a few hours ago rang out in my mind. Lola mentioned that her cookbook at Foodie Publishing might be *shelved*. Gloria had chided Simon about a project being shelved. She ordered him to *un-shelve* it.

I flashed on another exchange. With Dash. A few days ago. He told me Alison was halting production on a number of books, including the Wine Country book. Was that Simon's work? Simon's great-grandfather owned a vineyard in the old country.

Had Simon included recipes in his manuscript? Did he run out of ideas? Did he turn to Coco for inspiration? Simon visited Coco at her workplace. Often, she said. Did he make a play for her in order to steal one of her recipes? Did he then break into and trash Sweet Sensations so he could reinsert the cards he had pinched?

What if Simon incorporated the notes from Coco's mother and grandmother into his own anecdotal account and claimed them as his own? Alison was smart. She would have figured out the truth. Based on her assumption, did she tell Simon she was shelving his work? Prior to her visit to Crystal Cove?

Yes, that made sense. He planned to kill her when she arrived. That was why Simon had enrolled his wife in an out-of-town conference, and that was why Simon had chosen the book club night to cement his relationship with Coco.

I remembered Alison texting someone at the book club event. The killer had erased Alison's text messages. If they could be recovered, would they prove Simon was the killer? Did Simon, in a text message, challenge Alison to prove his guilt? Was that why she had gone back to Coco's, pulled up the recipes on the computer, and baked cookies?

I balked, yet again, over the fact that Coco had been with Simon that night. I didn't think she had lied about being with him. My aunt saw her enter the room at Nature's Retreat. How could Simon have crept out unnoticed? I swiveled in my chair and glanced at Simon. He glimpsed me peeking and tilted his head as if questioning my interest. Quickly I plucked a credit card from my purse, popped it inside the leatherette folder without looking at the charge, and waved the folder.

Smooth, Jenna.

Simon winked at me, acknowledging my request. He pressed a hand at the arch of the hostess's back and gestured toward me with his chin, after which he grabbed his sport coat from a hook and shrugged into it. He grabbed a bottle of wine from a slot by the bar and waggled it at the hostess. "I'm putting this baby in safekeeping."

The hostess nodded, and Simon exited the bistro. His departure seemed hasty. Where was he off to? If he realized what I'd figured out, was Coco in danger? She was his alibi.

I thought about calling Cinnamon, but what if I was

wrong? What if Simon wasn't the killer? Cinnamon had been pretty curt with me at the end of our last conversation. I yanked my cell phone from my purse and dialed Coco's number instead.

"Yeah?" She sounded hazy, like she had been drinking.

"It's me. Jenna."

"Whazzup?"

"Coco, are you okay?"

"Uh-huh. Sure. Just lonely."

Now I understood why she hadn't wanted to return to Sweet Sensations. She'd needed to indulge in a pity party. I had celebrated enough of my own. I wouldn't judge. I said, "I need you to focus."

I heard a slapping sound, as if Coco was smacking her cheeks to wake up. She said, "Go ahead."

"On the night Alison died—"

"The night Simon used me?"

"Exactly." He'd *used* her. "I think Simon might have killed Alison."

"What?" Coco rasped. "No. He couldn't have. Wait a second. You don't suspect me, too, do you?" She wasn't so loaded that she had missed that possibility.

"No."

The hostess picked up the leatherette folder and departed.

"Coco, what time did you meet Simon?"

"Around eleven."

"What did you and Simon do?"

"You know what we did." Coco tittered.

"Did you stay the whole night together?"

"Until four thirty. Then I headed home to change for work and found Alison, and I . . ." Coco clicked her tongue but added nothing further.

"Did Simon ever leave the room?"

Silence. Coco seemed to be weighing the question.

"Coco, is it possible he slipped out?"

"No. At least—" She inhaled deeply.

"What? Tell me. I want a play-by-play."

Coco inhaled sharply. "Jenna, I can't."

"Not that kind of play-by-play. I want to know the timing of everything. From the beginning."

"Simon paid for the room. When I arrived, I called from downstairs. He told me the room number. I went up the elevator."

The hostess returned with the bill. I removed my credit card from the leatherette folder and signed the charge, and she left again. Adrenaline was rushing through me. I tapped the corner of the credit card on the tabletop. "Keep going, Coco. Then what?"

"We drank champagne. We tore each other's clothes off and made love. I took a bath around midnight. I might have fallen asleep in the tub."

"Might have or did?"

"Did."

"You fell asleep? How long were you out?"

"I don't know. An hour. Why?"

"Did you feel drugged?" Date rape drugs were often used to make people forget an incident.

"No. I'm a lightweight when it comes to champagne."

In the deep recesses of my brain, I remembered her saying that at the book club event.

"I get weak in the knees," she went on. "I can drink hard liquor with no problem, but—"

"Does Simon know?"

"That I'm easy?" Coco snickered, then sniffed.

"About the champagne."

"I might have mentioned it, but Jenna, he was there when I got out of the bath. I think you're wrong. He didn't do this."

I quickly explained my theory about the recipe cards. "You said Simon visited the store."

"A number of times."

"Did he ever go into the kitchen or the office at Sweet Sensations?"

Coco sighed. "Yes. We, um, necked back there."

"When did he set up your tryst?"

"I hate that word," she hissed.

Call a spade a spade, I thought. "When?"

"After the book club and the three of us went to Vines. It was so spur-of-the-moment. I couldn't help but say yes." She bit back a sob. "I know it was wrong, Jenna."

"Coco, stop it. It's not your fault. If it makes you feel any better, I think he invited you to the hotel to establish his alibi."

"I can't believe he's the killer." Her voice crackled with emotion.

I felt for her. No woman ever wants to think the person she loves is a bad guy. I certainly didn't, but David was.

"Listen, Coco, Simon left here a few minutes ago. If he calls, don't answer. Lock your doors and windows."

Coco whimpered. "You're scaring me."

"Call the police."

"He wouldn't hurt me."

"Don't be naïve."

Chapter 28

I SCANNED THE bistro for my aunt and Deputy Appleby. They had left during my conversation with Coco. Not willing to dally any longer, I headed back to The Cookbook Nook to fetch Tigger and Hershey. On my way, I set aside my hesitation about being wrong about Simon and called the precinct. Cinnamon wasn't on duty. Risking the end of a beautiful friendship, I decided to call her on her cell phone. She answered after one ring.

"Are you busy?" I asked.

"It's late."

I heard background noise. The news on TV. I dove into my spiel, outlining my thoughts about Simon stealing the recipe cards.

"Is that why you needed to see what was on the computer?" Cinnamon asked.

"Yes. Do you recall who the author of the document called Mother's Chocolate Bombs was?"

"Not offhand, but I'll check it out."

"I believe it was Simon. I think he altered one of Coco's recipes to pawn it off as his own."

"Why steal something that has already been published?"

"Because he was running short on good recipes for his cookbook," I said. "He needed a few tried-and-true."

"Aren't recipes copyrightable?"

I explained what Coco had said to me, that the directions for the recipe and the *voice* of the author were proprietary, not the ingredients. Therefore, if Simon changed the instructions and altered the wording, voilà. The recipe was *his*. Except Alison was no dummy. She knew he'd stolen recipes from Coco.

Cinnamon said, "Where are you?"

"At the shop and then on my way home."

"I'll call you back."

I disconnected, a smile on my face. At least she hadn't labeled me crazy. I unlocked the front door of the shop and heard a high-pitched yowl. Panic cut through me. I called Tigger's name. He didn't come.

"Hershey!" I yelled. "Whatever you're doing, stop it." I raced past the breezeway leading to the café—the door was always closed and locked at end of business—and past the antique kitchen table and sales counter. I pushed through the drapes into the stockroom and saw Hershey, his hind legs stiff, his rear end raised, and his back sloped downward toward his head. He was holding Tigger at bay in a corner. Tigger's tail was wrapped protectively around his body. His eyes were dilated with fear.

I shrugged off my purse and stepped cautiously toward them. I didn't want Hershey attacking Tigger just because Tigger's human had arrived.

"Hershey, it's okay, fella. Let's play nice."

He hissed again. There seemed to be no reason for his aggression. There was no female cat in the area; both food bowls were full. What had Tigger done to earn Hershey's wrath, or was Hershey simply mean-spirited?

"Time out, Hershey," I said, hoping words would work with cats like they do with people.

I heard a door creak open. "Bailey!" I called, thankful she'd had a change of heart and was here to collect the cat. "I'm in the stockroom. Your cat—"

Hands shoved back the drapes. Simon Butler entered.

What the heck? I thought he'd left the vicinity for the night. My insides clenched. I pressed down the fear rising up my throat.

Simon's face was pasty white and covered in perspiration. His arms dangled at his sides. In one hand, he held the bottle of wine he had told his staff he was taking for safekeeping. Prisoner Blindfold. I recognized the label.

Hershey, sensing something was wrong, stood stock-still. Like an owl, he swiveled his head to look at the intruder. Tigger scampered to me and nudged my ankles with his head. I toed him away and made a slight gesture, warning him to stay put.

"Hello, Simon," I said. "Fancy seeing you here." Honestly, *fancy*? I never said fancy. Was my voice shaking? "Why are you here?"

Simon didn't say anything. The words *Cat got your tongue?* flitted through my mind. I bit the corner of my lip to keep from blurting anything idiotic. No need to stir the pot. Simon looked somewhat confused. I recalled a time when I'd house-sat for my boss at Taylor & Squibb. I was working in his office one morning when—surprise, surprise—his thirty-something alcoholic son appeared in the doorway with a huge knife in hand. My boss hadn't told me the guy was staying there. Big oops. It turned out the son had been cutting melon in the kitchen and heard sounds. *Me.* He'd come to investigate the intruder. Thanks to the alcohol he had imbibed the night before, he was in a bit of a trance. I'd had to feign all sorts of calm in order to coerce him back to his bedroom. Simon looked like that crazed son. Tousled. Unsure.

Hershey mewed. I shot him a cautionary glance. Tigger slunk to Hershey's side to buddy up. Hershey didn't hiss. *Better the enemy you know . . .*

"Is that wine for me, Simon?" I extended a hand, hoping he would hand over the bottle. "I heard Neil talking about that particular wine the other night. I've been meaning to taste it. I bet it would've gone great with the cheese platter I ordered." And never ate because Bailey abandoned me. If only she hadn't run off to see Tito. "How much is it? I'll pay you in cash." I edged toward my purse.

"Don't!" Simon ordered.

I froze.

"You know," he said in a menacingly low voice.

"What do I know?"

"You figured it out."

I made my face go blank. Might as well have him spell it out.

"You were staring at me upstairs, Jenna."

"It's a bad habit," I said. I do stare. I wasn't lying. "I apologize."

"You. Know." Simon spit out the words. He shifted the wine bottle to his other hand.

Did he intend to cudgel me with it? If so, I needed a weapon, pronto. A pencil sharpener sat on the cluttered desk. It would make a fine blunt object. Even a sharp pencil had some merit. The pair of children's scissors were worthless.

No, calm down, Jenna. Simon hasn't made a move toward you. The wine bottle is probably getting heavy. Control the conversation.

"You look tired, Simon. Why don't you go home and get some sleep? Let's chat tomorrow after you've rested up."

"You called Coco."

Aw, heck. Did Coco phone Simon and alert him to my suspicions? What universe of denial was she living in?

"You were staring at me," he added.

"I already apologized."

"Something I was doing at the chalkboard made you suspect me."

I had to give him credit. He was good at reading me.

"Tell me," he ordered.

No way. I was not blabbing that the note cards he had been holding triggered a memory. That I pictured the mess of cards on the floor at Coco's shop. That when he wiped his hand on his pant leg—

"You didn't expect me to show up here, did you, Jenna?"

Nope. Not in a million years.

"I left Vines, but I doubled back," he went on. "You didn't see me reenter the bistro. I heard you call Coco."

Hooray. She hadn't phoned to warn him. It was wrong of me to even jump to that conclusion. But, wow, Simon had taken craftiness to a whole new level. How had he hightailed it out of the bistro and returned to where I couldn't see him? Did it matter?

"You know," he repeated.

I sighed, realizing he wasn't going to relent. "Yes, I know. You killed Alison Foodie because she decided not to publish your book. That made you mad. Actually, it made your wife mad, and she shamed you into doing something about it. For your mother's sake. Before your mother dies."

"My mother." Simon said the word with such disdain.

Mama's boy popped into my head. Neil wasn't the only one.

"Coco told me your book is good. It's about your great-grandfather. It includes some of your mother's recipes. Why did you need Coco's recipes, Simon?"

"My mother's weren't enough."

As I had surmised.

"Alison wanted more," he hissed. "She said cookbooks aren't simply about the pictures and the historical accounts. They're about the recipes. I couldn't wrangle any more of my mother's or even my grandmother's recipes out of my sister. She has control over everything. She hates me. She wants to see me fail."

A fleeting concern about Rhett, off to see his mother, darted through my mind. I pushed it aside. No matter what was wrong, he would survive. He was a survivor.

So was I.

"Simon, tell me about Coco." I had to keep him talking while I figured out a plan of escape. With the cats. "You envied the relationship she had with her mother and her grandmother, didn't you?"

Simon didn't respond.

"You seduced Coco. You knew how needy she was for your love."

He kept mute.

"Your fatal mistake, Simon, was when you swiped a recipe that Coco had already published in a previous book. Alison realized it. She called you on it. What I don't understand is why kill her? Why didn't you admit you made a mistake and move on?"

"I did admit it. Weeks ago. We agreed to pull some recipes, start fresh. But last Thursday, Alison texted me. She said she couldn't follow through. She said I couldn't be trusted. She vowed to tell others. My reputation. It would be ruined. I couldn't have people thinking I was a phony and a liar. Rage overtook me. I was insane."

"Uh-uh. An insanity plea won't work. You mapped out your plan to kill Alison long before she came to town. You registered your wife for the conference to get her out of town. Then you set up an alibi with Coco. That was pretty clever."

He smirked.

"You brought champagne to your tryst. You're a wine bistro owner. Coco was a regular at Vines. You knew what champagne did to her. Just in case the champagne didn't make her sleepy enough, for the pièce de résistance, you suggested a bath."

Simon shifted the wine bottle to his other hand. His dominant hand. Uh-oh.

I glanced again at the desk. How about a letter opener as a weapon? That would be poetic justice. Stab the person who stabbed Alison. Too bad it was out of reach. My purse, which I'd set on the floor while dealing with the cats, was heavy and would pack a punch, but I'd have to bend over to reach it. If I did, the back of my head would make a perfect target.

What else could I use? *Think, Jenna.*

"You tiptoed out," I said. "You went to Coco's house. It was just around the corner from Nature's Retreat."

Simon stepped toward me. There were tons of books to my right, but none readily accessible. Shoot.

I said, "You saw Alison inside the house. Alone. You slipped inside."

"No. First, I spotted Dash. Loitering outside. Snapping

photographs like a fanatic paparazzo. Loser." Simon sniggered. "So I waited. When he left and I finally got to make my move, lo and behold, Alison was asleep at the computer. I'm ashamed to say it was like child's play. It couldn't have been easier. I felt like a tiger with a kitten."

Tigger and Hershey hissed in unison.

"I entered the house, grabbed the scissors—"

"After you killed Alison," I cut in, "why didn't you delete the recipes off the computer?"

"I tried to, but she had so many darned files open. I erased at least a dozen. Then I heard a sound. I thought Dash had returned. I ran."

"You cleared Alison's phone of text messages."

He didn't contradict me.

"You trashed Sweet Sensations so you could put the recipes back in the box. You knew that if Coco ever came to her senses she would realize you had arranged the affair to provide yourself with an alibi. If you put the recipes back, it was one less loose thread."

"Smart girl." He slinked toward me.

I inched backward. "I should've figured something was up when your wife started hovering over you, not letting you out of her sight. She even went bird-watching with you. She loathed bird-watching."

"She hates pretty much everything I do. I make her sick."

"Speaking of sick, Coco was ill the night Sweet Sensations was trashed. She got nauseous right after she flew upstairs to talk with you that afternoon. She threw up in her purse. Come to think of it, your wife was ill that same night. Did you give them something that upset their digestion so they'd be out of your hair while you trashed the candy shop?"

Simon sneered. "Arsenic is so easy to get your hands on. Slipping it into a piece of cheese was easy. I didn't give either enough to kill them."

I cringed. The man had no shame.

"And now for you." Simon hoisted the bottle of wine, ready to strike.

"Wait!" I squeaked. "I called Chief Pritchett."

That made him pause.

"I told her about the duplicated recipes."

"Liar."

"She's checking out Alison's computer right this minute. She said she'd call me back. If she doesn't reach me—"

"Dead men tell no tales. *Arrr*."

Man, I hated Pirate Week.

"Enough parrying." Simon swung at me.

I ducked and pivoted. Out of the corner of my eye, I spied the box of pirate décor. The four-foot-long, three-masted metal galleon with the lethal-looking bowsprit was poking out of the top. I leaped to it and pulled the ship free. I swooped around and, wielding the ship like a sword, lunged at Simon.

He raised the bottle of wine as protection.

I shoved the bowsprit beneath and into his chest. The tip didn't penetrate, but Simon careened backward and plunged to the floor.

Hershey dashed at him. Claws bared, he bounded onto Simon's face and latched on. Tigger, taking his cue from his former enemy, did the same, landing on Simon's groin. Simon yowled at the top of his lungs.

Serves you right, I mused.

I wrenched the bottle of wine out of his hands, planted a foot on his abdomen, and wielded the bottle with a two-handed hold. "Don't move!"

The front door squeaked open. "Jenna?" a man called.

"Rhett!" I'd never been so happy to hear his voice. I mean, I had, but considering the situation . . .

The front door banged shut. I didn't turn around. I didn't dare lose my hold on Simon.

"In here!" I yelled.

Rhett pushed through the drapes and drew alongside me. He gazed down at my quarry. "What the—"

"He killed Alison." I quickly recapped Simon's confession.

Rhett bent down, nudged Hershey off Simon's face, and landed a punch squarely on Simon's jaw. Simon's head rocked to the left. His eyes fluttered closed. *Out for the count.* Too bad his count wasn't anything like Alison's.

Hershey joined Tigger at his lower-region post. The two nuzzled chins.

Rhett caressed my face. "Are you all right?"

"Yes. What are you doing here?"

"I wanted one more kiss before I left town."

As he leaned in, I heard the front door whoosh open and bang closed.

Bailey yelled, "Jenna!"

I pushed apart from Rhett and cried, "In here!"

Bailey rushed into the stockroom, followed by Tito. Bailey gaped at Simon. "What's going on? Is he . . . Did he . . ."

I nodded. "He murdered Alison. What are you two doing here?"

Bailey smirked. "Tito missed seeing Hershey."

The cat heard its name and sprinted to Tito. He bounded into the reporter's arms.

The front door to the shop opened again. Footsteps pounded the floor. The drapes split apart.

Cinnamon Pritchett took in the scene, drew her weapon, and aimed it at Simon, who was rousing and moving his jaw. "Is there a party I wasn't invited to?" she quipped. "Jenna, how many times have I told you to answer your cell phone when I'm calling?"

I grinned at Simon. "Told you she'd check up on me!"

Chapter 29

CINNAMON HANDCUFFED SIMON, read him his rights, and marched him out of The Cookbook Nook. He demanded a lawyer. Cinnamon promised to comply, but she warned him his prospects of being set free in his lifetime were between nil and none.

The next day started out busier than ever. Before opening the shop, the delivery guy showed up with the balance of items we had ordered for Valentine's Day: cookbooks, fictional foodie books, red- or pink-themed kitchenware, aprons, and decorations. Thank heavens. The special day was a mere two days away. Customers would be frantic to purchase the best, most unique gift for their loved ones.

Bailey nabbed the pink heart-shaped sun catchers and hung them in the display window. Sunlight shot through them. Rays of pink light radiated across the shop. Perfect.

I arranged groupings of spatulas and mitts and salt shakers and pepper mills on tables already filled with Valentine-themed books. I set a Ghirardelli Chocolate cookbook on a metal cookbook holder that had an adorable heart-scrolled top, and placed *The Sweet Book of Candy Making: From the Simple to the Spectacular—How to Make Caramels, Fudge, Hard Candy, Fondant, Toffee, and More!*—perhaps the longest title I'd ever read on a cookbook cover—on another cookbook holder. It was more of a technique book than a recipe book, but who couldn't use help with technique? Namely, me! I hung a couple of retro red polka-dotted aprons on the hooks by the front door. I stood there for a moment, fingering an apron, which reminded me of the apron my mother used to wear. Where had it gone? Did my sister have it? I decided to buy one for myself and plucked it off the hook.

"Sale!" I announced.

Bailey laughed.

Aunt Vera had thought ahead and stocked up on a couple of Wilton classics like the heart-shaped Bundt pan and heart-shaped springform pan. She'd also found a darling decorative heart pan by Nordic Ware with a tooled bottom. A single-layer chocolate cake would look fabulous baked in it. In addition, she had remembered to purchase do-it-yourself kits for children so they could make their own bookmark valentines using felt, glue, and paper clips. Quite clever. Tigger had his nose and one paw in the box with the kits.

"Tig-Tig, no!" I chirped.

Tigger offered an impish look. At times, I think he believed he was invisible. Silly cat.

I was setting up the register for the onslaught of customers we expected when Coco hurried into the shop carrying a shopping bag from Sweet Sensations. Her makeup was perfect, her cotton candy–pink dress stylish to the max. Her eyes welled with grateful tears. "I heard about Simon. I can't believe it. I simply can't. But if it's so"—she batted the air with her free hand—"then it's so. The bigger fool am I. I brought you something." She pulled a pink-beribboned box out of her shopping bag. "One for you." She thrust it at me and pulled out another. "Bailey, this is for you." She fetched a third. "Vera, for you."

"For me?" my aunt said. "I didn't do anything."

Coco's eyes twinkled. "I saw you rubbing your amulet

on my behalf." She slung the bag over her forearm. "They're truffles. White chocolate raspberry."

"My favorite," I said.

"I know." She turned to leave.

I said, "Coco, wait."

She spun back. The tears that she had been keeping at bay seeped from her eyes.

"We're always here for you." I gestured between my aunt and Bailey. "Anytime you want to talk."

"What I want to do is go through life with eyes wide open from now on."

"What about your next cookbook? What's going on with that?"

"I don't know. Time will tell. One mustn't crave what one can't have." She said it so wistfully. Had she found the slogan in one of our mini inspirational books? "And now I must get back to the shop. We're overrun with orders." She hugged us and raced away.

Soon after, a number of the cookbook club women, including Lola, the mayor, and Pepper showed up, each eager to hear what had happened.

Pepper was quite vocal about how she had never trusted Simon. His shifty eyes had tipped her off.

Lola told us Gloria had already put Vines Wine Bistro on the market. She hated the place. The mayor believed Gloria would move to the Wine Country to take care of Simon's aging mother. There was a huge population up north that needed an exercise guru.

"So much for stand by your man," Bailey quipped to me.

I knuckled her and said, "I'm sure she'll return for the trial."

"I'll make you a bet."

"You're bad."

"But honest."

Bailey guided the book club ladies to the table holding the new Valentine's Day books, and I returned to the sales counter.

I was plunking in a stack of five-dollar bills when Wanda

and Neil Foodie sauntered into the shop. I cut around the counter and hurried to Wanda. She gave me a hug. Neil hung back.

"Jenna, dear," Wanda said. "You have been such a godsend. Thank you for figuring out who killed my Alison."

"Bailey was as much a part of the solution as I was." I gestured to Bailey. She left the group of ladies and joined us.

Wanda hugged her fiercely. "Alison adored you."

"And I adored her," Bailey said.

"I'd like the two of you to be the first to know, we're keeping the business." Wanda reached for her son. He sidled toward her. "C'mon, Neil, get over here. Don't be shy, son."

He moved beside her.

Wanda brushed her hand along his shoulder and down the top few buttons of his shirt. Primping. "Neil came up with the brilliant idea to hire someone already in the publishing business to run it." She petted his cheek.

Neil blushed.

"Dash recommended the woman to us," Wanda went on. "She's a New York editor who wants a quieter life and smaller responsibilities." Wanda grabbed her son's hand and squeezed. "She adores Dash, so he'll continue to be part of the team."

"What about Ingrid Lake?" Bailey asked. "Will she become a partner in the firm?"

"We'll have to see." Wanda glanced at Neil. "She's a good girl. A little uptight."

"A little?" Neil jibed.

Wanda *tsk*ed. "Ingrid needs some grooming."

"Which mother has decided to do." Neil rolled his eyes.

"Don't worry. She is not taking the place of your sister," Wanda assured him. "No one can."

"And you, Neil?" I asked. "What are your plans?" If Vines was closing and he couldn't take a day job because of his mother's illness, where would he work at night?

"Neil," Wanda said, answering for him, "will be going back to school. If he wants to be a performer, he needs more training. There's a wonderful stand-up comedy teacher in San Jose."

Wow. Wanda was supporting her son's dream to become a comedian? I said, "Doesn't Neil need to tend to you?"

Neil eyed his mother. "She won't let me. She's hiring a day person."

Wanda beamed. "My son shouldn't be bound to me by a ball and chain. He should be encouraged to follow his soul. I did. His sister did." She released his hand. "Well, girls, I must tell the mayor. She'll want the full scoop." Wanda steered Neil to the book club clique.

Bailey raised an eyebrow. "Close a door, open a window."

I agreed. "Expect rainbows at the end of rainstorms," I added, quoting something my mother used to say to me.

Aunt Vera sidled up to Bailey and me while brushing her hands free of remnants of cardboard boxes. "Bailey Bird, you have something you want to say."

Bailey spun to face her. "Um, no I don't, Vera."

"Yes, you do."

I eyed Bailey, who looked like the cat that swallowed the canary. If she opened her mouth, a bird would most certainly trill.

"What?" I poked her in the ribs.

"Ow!" Bailey backed up.

Lola split from the book club group and joined us. "What's going on?"

Aunt Vera rubbed her amulet and peered at Bailey. "Your daughter has some news."

"About that cat?" Lola frowned. "I told you it wasn't going to work out."

"Now, Mom, don't start. It's not about the cat. Tito's—" Bailey pressed her lips together.

"Tito's keeping the cat," I finished.

"Yes," Bailey replied, "and—" She sealed her lips again.

"And what? Out with it," I ordered. "Aunt Vera is sensing whatever you're giving off. Blab! Please don't tell me you're moving back to San Francisco. I couldn't bear it."

"No." Bailey looked trapped. "It's—"

Tito swaggered into the shop and stopped with his feet apart, hands on hips. He reminded me of a young Yul Brynner in *The Magnificent Seven*, surprisingly handsome and manly. He strode to Bailey and pecked her on the cheek. "Well?" he asked her.

"Well, what?" Lola and I asked in chorus.

"Did you tell them, *mi amor*?" Tito asked.

"Tell us what?" Lola demanded.

Bailey blushed. "Um, Tito has asked me to marry him."

I clasped her in a hug. Aunt Vera tweaked Bailey's ear and said a quick blessing.

Lola gasped. "I didn't even know you were dating."

Bailey nodded enthusiastically. "We have been for three months."

Lola sniffed. Her lower lip trembled. "I'm the last to know?"

"Mom!"

"Are you pregnant?"

Bailey yelped. "No!"

"Then why so fast? Why the rush to the altar?"

"Because for the first time in my life, I am truly, one hundred percent in love." Bailey slung an arm around Tito's back. Her eyes sparkled with outright adoration.

"What about the cat?" I asked.

"Tito's going to take care of all its needs." Bailey addressed her mother. "May we have your blessing? Please?"

Lola's peevishness melted away. She grinned and opened welcoming arms. "Absolutely."

Bailey and Tito crowded into them. Tito muttered, "Mom."

Lola cracked, "Don't push it!"

My cell phone jangled in my pocket. *Rhett*. My heartbeat kicked up a notch. I moved to the stockroom to take the call. "How is your mother?"

"Fine."

"How about your father?"

"Relax." Rhett's voice was warm and husky. "Everyone is healthy."

"Then why did your mother summon you?"

"Because she finally got through to my dad and convinced him to see me. She didn't want too much time to pass in case he changed his mind."

"Rhett, that's wonderful."

"Yeah, it is." He chuckled. "The old codger and I had a sit-down. He's hard as nails, but he said he loves me, and he forgives me."

"Do you forgive him?"

"I never begrudged him a thing."

A train whistle blasted in the background.

"Where are you?" I asked.

"Still in Napa."

"When are you coming home?"

"Actually, I was going to ask when are you coming up here?"

"What?"

"My family wants to meet you. We've got a reservation for dinner at Intime tomorrow night at eight. Are you available?"

His family wanted to meet me? Gulp!

"Jenna?"

My heart filled with love. "How could I ever say no to you?"

Recipes

From Jenna:

This recipe is from Coco's very first cookbook. She got it from her bunica, her grandmother. Katie made them for me, and I adored them. The browned butter adds a nice nutty flavor. The coffee adds a delicious zing. These would be perfect for a care package gift. They are definitely recommended for your next book club. By the way, if you'd like to make these cookies gluten-free, substitute out the regular flour for your favorite gluten-free flour (Katie tells me a good combo is sweet rice flour mixed with tapioca starch), and add 1 teaspoon of xanthan gum to the gluten-free flour mixture.

Coco's Chocolate Cookies

(makes 24 to 30 cookies)

> 1 cup (2 sticks) unsalted butter, browned
> 2½ cups flour
> 1 tablespoon brewed coffee
> 1¼ teaspoons baking soda
> 1 teaspoon salt
> ½ teaspoon nutmeg

1¼ cups dark brown sugar
7 ounces sweetened condensed milk
1 egg, room temperature
2 teaspoons vanilla extract
1½ cups dark chocolate chips

In a sauté pan, heat the 2 sticks of butter on medium low for a few minutes until the butter froths up and turns golden brown. Don't let it overcook. Burned butter is NOT good. Turn off the heat and allow the butter to cool.

Meanwhile, in a small bowl, mix together the flour, coffee, baking soda, salt, and nutmeg. Set aside. (If you are making this gluten-free, this is where you would substitute out the regular flour, and add xanthan gum.)

In a large bowl, using a whisk, combine cooled browned butter and brown sugar. Add the sweetened condensed milk, egg, and vanilla. Whisk until smooth and satiny.

Stir the flour mixture into the butter/sugar mixture until all the flour is mixed in.

Pour in the dark chocolate chips and stir until combined. This will be a thick mixture, like any chocolate chip cookie recipe. Refrigerate the dough for a half hour.

Meanwhile, preheat the oven to 350°F. Line a cookie sheet with parchment paper.

On a cutting board, roll the dough into 1½-inch balls, about the size of large walnuts. Place the balls on the cookie sheet. Set them 1 inch apart because they will spread. Press down slightly until flattened.

Bake the cookies for 13–15 minutes (know your oven), until the cookies are slightly browned.

Cool for 5 minutes on the cookie sheet, and then transfer the cookies to a cooling rack or to paper towels to completely cool.

From Cinnamon:

I'm learning to bake. Step-by-step, sort of like Jenna. These are so easy to make. Just a few ingredients, just a few steps. Delicious, easy. I told a friend who needs to eat gluten-free about them, and she went ballistic with joy! Bailey's mom, Lola, who has been coaching me in the kitchen, recommended that I use the best cocoa possible. I used Penzeys, which is really rich, in my humble opinion. Enjoy! And stay safe!

Cinnamon Chocolate Meringues

(naturally gluten-free)

(makes 24 to 30 cookies)

1 pound powdered sugar
¾ cup unsweetened cocoa
½ teaspoon salt
4 large egg whites
1 teaspoon vanilla
1 teaspoon cinnamon
1½ cups dark chocolate chips

Preheat oven to 350°F. Line 2 cookie sheets with parchment paper.

In a large bowl, whisk powdered sugar, cocoa, and salt.

In a separate bowl, whip the egg whites, vanilla, and cinnamon to a gentle froth. Add the egg whites mixture to the sugar-cocoa mixture. Stir with a spoon. Then fold in chocolate chips.

Drop dough by rounded tablespoonfuls, about 1–2 inches apart onto the parchment paper. They will spread and merge into one another a bit, so beware. ☺

Bake 13–14 minutes. They will look glossy and crackly. Do not overbake. Let the cookies cool on cookie sheets for a couple of minutes, then carefully transfer to paper towels or wire rack to cool. Store in an airtight container.

From Jenna:

Yet again, how easy can this be? So few ingredients. These are light, delicate cookies, perfect for a luncheon or tea and absolutely divine for a wedding. Do any of you have wedding bells in your future?

White Chocolate Macaroons

(makes 5 dozen)

    5 egg whites, room temperature
    ¾ cup ground almonds
    5¼ cups flaked coconut, toasted, divided
        (*see below)
    ½ teaspoon vanilla extract

1⅓ cups sugar
6 ounces white baking chocolate, chopped

Bring the egg whites to room temperature. This takes about 30 minutes.

Grind the almonds and set aside. [I used my food processor.]

To toast the coconut, lay parchment paper on a 15-by-9-inch jelly roll pan. Spread the coconut on the parchment paper and toast in a slow oven, 300°F, for 15 minutes, until lightly browned. Remove from oven and cool. Set aside ¼ cup of the toasted coconut for garnish.

Meanwhile, place the egg whites in a large bowl. Add vanilla extract. Beat the mixture on medium until soft peaks form, about 3–4 minutes. Gradually beat in the sugar on high, until stiff glossy peaks form, about 4–6 minutes. Gradually fold in 5 cups of the toasted coconut and ground almonds.

Line the jelly roll pan again with a new sheet of parchment paper. Drop the mixture by rounded tablespoons full, 2 inches apart. Bake the cookies at 275°F for 20–25 minutes, until firm to the touch. Remove the cookies to wire racks or paper towels to cool completely.

Meanwhile, in a microwave-safe bowl, melt the white chocolate, at half power, for about 30 seconds at a time until it can be easily stirred. Do not over-zap.

Spoon ¼ teaspoon of melted white chocolate onto each cookie. Sprinkle with the reserved toasted coconut. Refrigerate for approximately 1 hour, until chocolate is set. Store in airtight container.

From Katie:

These croutons are so simple. They dress up any salad. My favorite is a green salad with a simple olive oil–vinegar dressing. You can doll up the salad even more if you add some orange slices dipped in melted chocolate.

Cocoa Brioche Croutons

(serves 4)

> 4 slices brioche, crusts removed and cut into cubes
> 4 tablespoons butter
> 2 tablespoons high-quality cocoa powder
> 1 tablespoon powdered sugar (confectioners' sugar)
> ½ teaspoon salt

Preheat the oven to 350°F and place the cubed brioche in a bowl.

Melt butter in a saucepan. Add the brioche cubes and toss until well coated.

Place the brioche cubes on a shallow 15-by-9-inch jelly roll pan. Toast the cubes in the oven until golden brown, about 15 minutes.

Meanwhile, sift the cocoa powder and powdered sugar into a large bowl.

When the croutons come out of the oven, toss them immediately with the powdered mixture and season with salt. The croutons should be served warm on top of a crisp salad.

From Jenna:

This is so easy to make. It's Katie's recipe, but I'm the one plugging it, because according to my father, it was one of my mother's favorite desserts. Rich, decadent. This was one of the desserts she made regularly when having guests for dinner.

Bailey's Irish Cream Pie

(serves 6)

> 28 Oreo cookies
> ½ stick of butter (4 tablespoons) melted
> 1 cup milk chocolate chips
> 8 ounces cream cheese
> 2 cups heavy cream
> 1 cup Bailey's Irish Cream
> 1 good quality chocolate bar, frozen [I use
>   Ghirardelli]

In a food processor, crush the Oreo cookies until they are fine crumbs. Dump the crumbs into a large mixing bowl and mix in the melted butter. Press the mixture into the bottom of a 9-inch pie dish. Cover the dish and chill for at least 1 hour.

Meanwhile, in the microwave, set on medium to medium-low, melt the chocolate chips for 1 minute. Stir and, if necessary, heat for another 30 seconds. You do NOT want the chocolate to overcook. Set the melted chocolate aside.

In a large mixing bowl, beat the cream cheese for 2 minutes using an electric mixer. Scoop out the cream cheese and reserve in a smaller bowl. Then in the same mixing bowl whip the heavy cream and ½ cup of the Bailey's Irish Cream until the cream forms stiff peaks. Now fold in the melted chocolate, the reserved whipped cream cheese, and the remaining ½ cup of Bailey's Irish Cream. Pour the mixture into the prepared pie dish.

Cover and chill the pie for at least 4 hours or overnight. You are almost done! Remember that frozen chocolate bar?

Before serving, using a vegetable peeler, take the frozen bar of chocolate and peel off curls of chocolate onto a sheet of plastic or parchment paper. Sprinkle the chocolate shavings on top of the pie. Yum!

From Coco:

I love fudge. There's something about the texture of fudge that is like no other candy. It melts in your mouth but has substance. And when you add all sorts of goodies into it, it's a texture explosion. For the pirate's booty, I have added some of my favorite treats, extra chips and nuts. But if you're not in the mood for that, add your own goodies, like extra marshmallows or even chopped fruit. Booty means treasure. What does your heart desire? Little side note, just in case you need to know, if you can't eat gluten, make sure you find a gluten-free marshmallow cream or marshmallows, okay? Arr, matey! Wouldn't want you ailin', now, would we?

Pirate's Booty Fudge

4½ cups sugar
1 12-ounce can evaporated milk
3 12-ounce packages chocolate chips
7 ounces marshmallow cream

1 cup (2 sticks) butter, melted
1 tablespoon vanilla
½ cup white chocolate chips
½ cup butterscotch chips
2 cups chopped pecans or almonds, if desired

Line a 13-by-9-inch pan with parchment paper. Make sure the paper goes up and over the sides. Butter the parchment paper.

In a large saucepan, mix the sugar with the evaporated milk. Bring the mixture to a rolling boil and boil for 7 minutes, stirring often. Do not let it boil over the rim.

In a large mixing bowl, stir the chocolate chips, marshmallow cream, and melted butter together. Pour the hot sugar-milk mixture over the chocolate mixture. Stir well.

After the chocolate has melted, stir in the vanilla. Now, quickly add the white chocolate chips and butterscotch chips, and add the chopped pecans or almonds, if desired. The chips will melt a bit, but not entirely.

Pour the mixture into the prepared 13-by-9-inch dish. Spread evenly. Chill in the refrigerator.

Just before the mixture is "firm," cut the fudge into squares. Chill again. Remove squares with a spatula. Store in an airtight container.

Marshmallow cream substitute: You can buy a bag of mini marshmallows, about 4 cups, and melt them in the microwave on medium for 1 minute. Stir well.

From Katie:

There's nothing quite like a fun nightcap. This one is dessert in a glass. When I used to work for Old Man Powers, he liked a toddy at bedtime. It didn't have to be hot. It could be cold. But no matter what, he wanted something different every night of the month, so I started to get creative. This is what I call my graduating-from-college pudding drink. Chocolate, through and through, with a splash of soda.

Kahlúa Cream Nightcap

(makes 1 drink)

> 1 ounce Irish Cream (Bailey's is the best bet)
> 1 ounce Kahlúa
> 3 ounces Dr. Pepper or preferred cola
> 2 tablespoons heavy whipping cream
> 1 swirl whipped cream

In a highball glass, stir the Irish Cream, Kahlúa, Dr. Pepper, and heavy cream. Add ice. Stir. Top with a big swirl of whipped cream. Bottoms up!

Dear Reader,

For those of you who don't know, I write two culinary mystery series under two names—my real name, Daryl Wood Gerber, and my pseudonym, Avery Aames. Avery writes the Cheese Shop Mysteries. The seventh book in the series, For Cheddar or Worse, *debuts February 2016. I thought it would be fun for fans of the Cookbook Nook Mysteries to have a taste of cheese at the end of* Fudging the Books. *It will keep you from over-loading on chocolate!*

If you're not familiar with the Cheese Shop Mysteries, let me introduce you to Charlotte Bessette. Charlotte is the pro-prietor of Fromagerie Bessette—or, as it's more commonly known by the residents of small-town Providence, Ohio, The Cheese Shop. Ever since Charlotte moved in with her grand-parents, under her grandfather's tutelage, she learned to relish all things cheese. Charlotte adores cheese. She also adores family and friends. Because Charlotte is a fixer, she often finds herself solving crimes because someone she loves is involved.

In For Cheddar or Worse, *Charlotte and her grandmother are helping the town sponsor its first annual Cheese Festival. There will be cooking classes, farm and creamery tours, and, as a finale, a cheese competition. In addition, a few cheese makers and distributors will hone their cheddar cheese-making skills at a local farm owned by one of Charlotte's good friends. The attendees, who are staying at the inn on the farm, get more than they bargained for when an attendee is found murdered in her room. The windows are sealed shut; the door is locked from the inside. Like the police, Charlotte is puzzled, but she won't rest until she helps her friend put the horrible nightmare behind her.*

I hope you will join Charlotte and the cast of lovable characters as Charlotte once again seeks to right a wrong. Perhaps you'll even find a new cheese or a great recipe to share with friends.

For those of you who love the Cookbook Nook Mysteries, take heart. There will be more of those to come, too! The fifth installment will be released next summer.

Keep reading for a preview of the next Cheese Shop Mystery: For Cheddar or Worse.

Savor the Mystery!
Daryl Wood Gerber

I STOPPED DEAD in my tracks and listened, on full alert: a leaf fluttering in the early morning breeze, a creature skittering across the pavement; footsteps. I whirled to my right, but I couldn't see a thing. Dang. It was inky black out. The crescent moon had disappeared over an hour ago. *It's always darkest before the dawn*, my grandfather would say.

"Anybody there?" I whispered.

As if, I thought. As if someone wishing me harm would cry out, *Yes!*

Breathe, Charlotte. I did my shallow best and glanced at Rags, my adorable Ragdoll cat. I could make out the white of his dappled fur. He wasn't acting antsy, which meant I shouldn't, either, but sometimes the dark scared the bejeebers out of me. Why was I so jumpy? I couldn't put my finger on it. The month of May was a lovely time of year. The temperatures were growing warmer. Birds were building nests and feeding newborns. Tourists were flocking to our fair town, which meant sales at Fromagerie Bessette were good. No, not just good . . . booming.

"Let's go," I said to Rags and tugged on his leash. He

was one of the few cats I knew that had taken to one. I think a leash made him feel safer.

If only some big, strong person had hold of my leash.

A breeze kicked up behind me. A chill shimmied down my spine. I spun again but didn't see any sign of danger.

"Think lovely thoughts," I muttered. "Raindrops on roses." We were on our way to the shop, walking instead of driving, as we often did. What could go wrong? Maybe I should have put on something warmer than a lacy sweater and trousers. Ah, who was I kidding? A jacket, mittens, and an ear-flapped snowcap wouldn't have been enough to warm me right now. Something was getting to me. What?

Then it dawned on me. It was the date my parents died. My shoulders tensed, my skin flushed red-hot. Every year it happened. The memory of their deaths slammed into me like a thunderbolt. Over thirty years had passed, and yet that fleeting moment when the car went out of control and we crashed changed my entire world.

A sudden death or two will do that, I thought wryly and mentally kicked myself. *Buck up!*

I forced the sound of screeching brakes and my parents' shouts from my mind and hurried ahead. I unlocked the front door of Fromagerie Bessette—what the locals of Providence called The Cheese Shop—and allowed Rags to cross the threshold first. "Let's switch on all these lights," I said to him. "We'll drum up good vibes. No wallowing."

I roamed the shop, drinking in the luscious aroma of cheese, drawing strength from what I, thanks to my grandparents, was able to call my own. Though the two darling people who raised me were both alive and in fine health, when my grandfather decided to retire, he turned over Fromagerie Bessette—Bessette being the family name—to my cousin and me. Ever since I moved in with my grandparents, under my grandfather's tutelage, I learned to relish all things cheese. Prior to joining me in this venture, my cousin was a well-respected sommelier. He managed the wine annex portion of our shop.

"Not much to do, is there?" I said to Rags. Before leaving

last night, I had straightened the boxes of crackers and jars of jam on the shelves, and I'd rearranged the displays on each of the slatted wine barrels. Decorative cheese knives and colorful plates nestled among the crystal wineglasses. Cheese graters stood beside chalkboard-style cheese markers, all set atop a huge wheel of Grafton Cave-Aged Cheddar, one of my favorite cheeses when paired with a dark chocolate like Olive and Sinclair's Southern Artisan chocolate.

Rags meowed. I was pretty sure he thought his plea was packed with meaning that I could interpret. I couldn't, of course. I wasn't even good at sign language.

"Hungry?" I asked. I took him to the office—his home away from home—and freshened his water and treats.

Rags circled on his pillow once and settled into a ball. Not hungry.

"What should I make for today's special quiche?" I said as I wakened the computer on my desk. Rags offered no inspiration. "Maybe I'll add some secret item or spice that no one can figure out. Ooh, I know! I'll make it with peanut butter and apples and a dash of nutmeg. I'll use a simple Havarti." A good melting cheese. "That combo will throw Pépère for a loop." My grandfather loved trying to guess ingredients. "Don't you think?"

Rags couldn't be bothered. He was already snoring.

Every day at the shop, in addition to the vast array of cheeses we had to offer, we sold slices of quiche and specialty sandwiches. When the items sold out, we didn't make more. We weren't trying to compete with the Country Kitchen diner across the street. We just wanted our customers to feel they had plenty of time to browse the shop. If they cared to, they could slip into the wine annex and eat their items at one of the mosaic inlaid café tables.

I clicked on the e-mail icon and reviewed all the entries. A couple of orders topped the list. There was also an e-mail from Jordan, my husband of three months. Subject: *I adore you*. He must have sent the note the moment I left home. *Our* home. At least, we were in the process of making it *ours*. We were revamping some of the bedrooms by repainting and switching out the window coverings, and we were upgrading the kitchen. New appliances were on order. Jordan loved to cook. So did I.

I typed a quick response. *Love you, too*, and I headed to the kitchen at the back of the shop.

An hour later, as I was removing the quiches from the oven, Rebecca, my twenty-something assistant, entered the shop.

"Charlotte," she called. "Mmm. Smells fantastic. You'll never guess what I did!" Rebecca, relentlessly perky, bopped into the kitchen while tying the strings of her gold apron.

"You cut your hair."

Usually Rebecca wore her long blonde hair in a ponytail. Not anymore. A swath of bangs swooped across her forehead. She swiveled to reveal the back of her head, fringed in an A-line at the nape of the neck, not all that different from the style I wore.

"It's darling," I said. "Who made you so bold?" I remember her saying that she would never cut her hair. Ever. "The deputy?" Rebecca had been dating the very handsome Deputy O'Shea for a few months. I don't think they had gone past first base, which was so sweet and refreshing. I adored the way they gazed at each other.

"No. I won't let a man dictate how I wear my hair."

"My, my. Aren't you sassy today?"

Rebecca grinned. "I cut it because I saw this blog online—"

"I thought you weren't going online anymore."

"To *shop*. And I haven't shopped. But I like to read. The blogger wrote that a woman should make a change to her look every few years, to keep life fresh and fun."

When I hired Rebecca, she was an innocent right off an Amish farm, ready to spread her wings and taste all life had to offer. Within a month, she fell in love with the vastness of the Internet. She discovered clothing sites, home decorating sites, and more. Then she found TV reruns and became a mystery junkie. After that, she discovered books—everything from mysteries to classics—and movies. She was like an empty vessel ready to be filled. She had seen every film starring Barbara Stanwyck, Meryl Streep, and Reese Witherspoon. Now she was lapping up movies featuring foreign-born actresses. I think Kate Winslet was her latest favorite, which might explain the inspiration for her haircut. Kate had cut off her curly tresses a month ago.

While I wrapped slices of quiche, Rebecca selected a wedge of Bleu Mont Dairy Bandaged Cheddar, an absolutely divine aged Cheddar with caramel sweetness and a hint of mossy-grass flavor near the rind. She set it on the cutting board and carved off small morsels, which she placed on a pretty china platter. She set the platter on the Madura gold granite counter. Daily we offered a tasting to our customers. It was one of the best ways to sell cheese. Most people couldn't resist buying a cheese if they bit into it and liked it.

"Are you excited about the big event?" Rebecca asked.

"The brain trust? Absolutely."

"All packed?"

"Yep."

"Rags, too?"

I nodded. He was going to stay with my cousin Matthew and family. Rags's canine buddy Rocket, a French Briard that Matthew's ex-wife had given her twin daughters when they lived at my house, would welcome Rags with open paws.

"Is Erin ready?" Rebecca asked.

"I'm sure she is."

Erin Emerald owned a spread at the north end of town called Emerald Pastures Farm, a local farmstead that had won awards for its goat cheese and now its Cheddar cheese. Erin and I had attended school together. I remembered the two of us, in fourth grade, spending a lot of time creating a history diorama on Ohio; it involved a lot of glue and sugar cubes and giggles. Starting tomorrow, Friday, with the help of an event coordinator, Erin was putting on what was called a *brain trust* for cheese makers. About twenty people, including a few cheese makers, distributors, journalists, and Jordan and I, had been invited to participate. Jordan, because he knows the art of *affinage*, which is the careful practice of ripening cheese, and I, because I understood the marketing side of cheese. The inn on the property could house half of us. We were checking in, in a few hours. The other attendees would stay at Lavender and Lace, the bed-and-breakfast next door to my . . . *our* . . . Victorian. During the two-day affair, Erin wanted us to immerse ourselves in the world of cheese. We would talk shop and compare techniques while we stirred, cut, drained, and milled curd.

"The better question is," I said, "are you ready?" I was turning the shop over to Rebecca to manage through Sunday. "It will get pretty busy in here."

Rebecca fluffed her hair. "Of course."

The brain trust idea had come to fruition because my grandmother, the town's mayor, had declared that the first days in May, starting this year, would feature our *annual* Cheese Festival Week. The festival would start tonight and run to next Wednesday. Never one to shy away from setting up too many activities, Grandmère had enticed a number of local restaurants to offer cooking classes or specialty dinners. She had encouraged the farmers to hold creamery tours or wine tastings. She had also dreamed up what she was calling the *Street Scene*.

For the *Street Scene*, a lane on each of the four main streets of Providence that girded the Village Green would be closed. A volunteer construction crew was putting the finishing touches on portable stages, upon which would appear singers, fiddlers, actors, and more. To cap it off, my grandmother named Fromagerie Bessette the sponsor for the artisan cheese competition. There would be two rounds of tastings, ten artisanal cheese farmers in each round. At the end of each round, we would pick a winner. The two would vie for the grand prize. Grandmère hadn't told me what the grand prize was yet. I was eager to find out.

The front door flew open. Grandmère, looking colorful in a yellow sweater and red slacks, hurried to the tasting counter and perched on a ladder-back stool. Her face, though weathered, glowed with energy. "Charlotte, *chérie*! You will be so excited to hear."

"Hear what?"

My grandfather followed her inside. "Our Charlotte has heard it all."

"Heard what?" I glanced from one to the other.

Though Pépère was flushed and harrumphing like a disgruntled elephant, there was a twinkle in his eye. And why shouldn't there be? He loved coming to the shop and sneaking pieces of cheese—*sneaking*, because Grandmère continually put him on a diet. Perhaps the latest regimen was working. His stomach did appear less paunchy, and his typically chubby cheeks looked almost lean.

"Heard what?" I repeated.

Pépère rounded the cheese counter, clutched me by the shoulders, and kissed me, *la bise*, on each cheek. Then he plucked a piece of cheese from the tasting platter.

My grandmother *tsk*ed. "Etienne."

"What is wrong?" He took another and plopped it into his mouth daring her to chastise him.

Grandmère frowned. What could she do? Pepérè was going to help out Rebecca for the next two days. She couldn't eagle eye him every minute. He would either have self-control or not. Most likely, *not*. Grandmère turned her attention to me. "She has come."

"She, who?" I asked, intrigued.

"That woman." Grandmère waved a hand. "The cheese author. The one who writes about all the farms and cheese shops in America."

"Lara Berry?"

"*Oui.*"

A thrill of excitement rushed through me. In my world, Lara Berry was a star. In addition to being an author, she was a consultant who advised cheese makers how to market their product. "Where is she?"

Grandmère said, "I saw her in La Chic Boutique buying a dress." The boutique was one of two women's dress shops in town. It offered classic styles at sky-high prices. "She is lean and tall, just like on the book cover."

"Why has she come?" I asked.

Grandmère squinted. "Is she not here to attend the brain trust?"

"She's not on the list of attendees. I've got to meet her."

"You have read all her works, *non*?" Grandmère mimed opening a book. "*Sont-ils de bons livres?*"

"Yes, they are very good books. *C'est fantastique.*" Occasionally my grandparents resorted to their native tongue. "She is very knowledgeable." Lara Berry was the go-to cheese maven for American cheeses. "I've seen her on talk shows, too. She has quite a sharp sense of humor."

"Do you like her?"

"Yes. Of course."

"*Bon.* Then it will not matter that she is bossy."

"Bossy?"

"*Oui.* Bossy. This is the correct word. She barks orders." This coming from my grandmother, who could bark with the best of them. Some called her *the little general.*

"Was Prudence being rude to her?" I asked. Prudence Hart, a woman with very strong opinions, was the owner of La Chic Boutique. She could rub people the wrong way.

"Perhaps." Grandmère chuckled. "Lara would not back down."

"Good for her." I appreciated a woman who could stand her ground.

The door to the shop flew open again. The chimes jangled. Matthew, my cousin, who reminded me of a Great Dane puppy mixed with a sheepdog, all arms and legs with a hank of hair invariably dangling down his forehead into his eyes, raced in. "Have you heard?"

I nodded. "That Lara Berry is in town? Yes." Lara not only knew her cheeses; she also knew wine. Her latest book, *Educate Your Palate: A Connoisseur's Guide to American Cheese and Wine*, was a must-read for people like Matthew and me. Thanks to Lara's research, I had discovered a wealth of new farms and creameries that put out excellent artisanal cheeses. Matthew had learned about a number of independent wineries, citing from Lara's book that at the turn of the century there had been about two thousand wineries in America; now there were over eight thousand. "Grandmère saw her—"

"No," Matthew cut me off. "That's not what I'm talking about. Have you heard about Meredith?" His wife and my best friend. "She's pregnant!"

"What? You're kidding." I did a happy jig. "How far along is she?"

"Three months."

I stopped dancing. "Three months and neither of you said a word to me?"

"She thought if she said something, she might jinx it. We've been trying. She lost one last year."

"She what?" I yelped. She hadn't confided in me? What kind of friend was she? What kind of friend was I not to have sensed her pain?

Matthew shrugged. "What can I say? Everyone's got a secret."